One of the world's leading science fiction writers,
Anne McCaffrey has won both the Hugo and Nebula
awards. Brought up in the US and now living in
Ireland, she is the creator and bestselling author of
the unique Dragon series.

Anne McCaffrey with Elizabeth Ann Scarborough

POWERS THAT BE

Anne McCaffrey

The Chronicles of Pern

First Fall

BANTAM PRESS

LONDON · NEW YORK · TORONTO · SYDNEY · AUCKLAND

TRANSWORLD PUBLISHERS LTD
61–63 Uxbridge Road, London W5 5SA

TRANSWORLD PUBLISHERS (AUSTRALIA) PTY LTD
15–25 Helles Avenue, Moorebank, NSW 2170

TRANSWORLD PUBLISHERS (NZ) LTD
3 William Pickering Drive, Albany, Auckland

Published 1994 by Bantam Press
a division of Transworld Publishers Ltd
Copyright © Anne McCaffrey 1993

A catalogue record for this book is available from the British Library

0593 035739

Printed in Great Britain by
Mackays of Chatham, plc, Chatham, Kent.

This book is respectfully
dedicated to
Jay A Katz
for many good reasons

TIMELINE

YEAR   **1**   Landing

  6   Torene Ostrovksy b.

  8.6   First Fall

  10   First Hatching

  Michael Connell b.

  Fort Hold established

  Evacuation of Landing – *The Dolphins' Bell*

  16   The Fever Year

  Emily Boll dies

  17   Pierre de Courcis starts Boll Hold

  19   Red Hanrahan's yarn – *The Ford of Red Hanrahan*

  22   Michael Impresses Brianth at 12

  Ongola moves his people to found hold

  25   Jim Tillek dies

  Torene Ostrovsky Impresses Alaranth

  26   Paul Benden dies

  27   Queens' battle – Porth, Evenath, Siglath

20 FF   **28**   Sean announces 3 new Weyrs – *The Second Weyr*

20 FF = Twenty Years: First Fall

Contents

The P.E.R.N. Survey   11
The Dolphins' Bell   25
The Ford of Red Hanrahan   77
The Second Weyr   121
Rescue Run   179

The P.E.R.N. Survey

'It's the third planet we want in this pernicious system,' Castor said in a totally jaundiced tone with his eyes fixed on the viewscreen. 'How's the hairpin calc going, Shavva?'

She looked up from her terminal, and screwed up her face for a moment before she spoke. 'I'm happy to report that it'll work out fine. Pity we can't have a look at the edge of the system,' she added. 'I'd love to have a look at those heavyweight planets and the Oort cloud but that can't be done when we've got to do an entry normal to the ecliptic. As it is, the slingshot will only give us ten days on the surface.' She cast him an expectant, wry look.

He groaned. 'We'll have to double up again.' When she gave him a long, half-stern, half-sardonic glare, he added, 'Fardles, Shavva, after so long together we all know enough of each other's specialties to do a fair report.'

'Fair?' Ben Turnien said, his quirky eyebrows raised in amazement. 'Fair, to whom?'

'Damn it, Ben, fair enough to know when a planet's habitable by humanoids: none of us needs a zoologist any more to tell us which beasties are apt to be predatory. And each of us has certainly seen enough strange life-forms and inimical atmospheres and surface conditions to know when to slap an interdict on a planet.'

There was a taut silence, a respectful one as the four remaining team members each vividly recalled the all-too-recent deaths; Sevvie Asturias, the palaeontologist-medic, and Flora Neveshan, the zoologist-botanist, both lost on the last planet the Exploration and Evaluation team had visited. Castor had inscribed in bold letters on the top of that report 'D.E.', for dead end. Terbo, the zoologist-chemist, had been felled in a landslide on the first planet of their present survey tour, but that had clearly supported some intelligent life so the initials I.L.F. ended that report. They'd lost Beldona, the second pilot and archaeologist, on the third in the same accident that had injured Castor: a planet initialled G.O.L.D.I. – good only for large diversified interests. And they'd orbited one that probes had given them all the information they needed to label it L.A. – lethal, avoid!

To a team that had been together for five missions the casualties were deeply felt. This system, with its primary Rukbat, was the fifth of the seven to be investigated on their latest swing through this sector of space.

'We can handle the geology, the biology and the chemistry,' Castor went on, frowning at the gelicast on his leg, which had not quite healed from the compound fractures incurred in the third system. 'Well, I can do the analysis when you've brought appropriate samples back. We might not be able to do the usual in-depth analysis of all the biota, but we can find the requisite five possible landing sites, regular or serious meteoric impacts, any gross geological changes, and if there's a dominant major life-form.'

'Hospitable planets are few enough, but Numero Tres does look very interesting,' Mi Tan Liu remarked in his gentle voice. 'I get good readings on atmosphere, gravity. I think probes are in order.'

'Send 'em,' Castor said. 'Probes we got to spare.' His lips began to twitch again at this further reminder of the recent disaster which had reduced an experienced team of eight to four.

'We're in a good trajectory to send off a homer, too,' Liu added. 'Federated Sentient Planets ought to know about the D.E. condition of Flora Asturias.' The bizarre and perhaps macabre practice in the Exploration and Evaluation Corps was to name planets after team personnel who had been unfortunate to lose their lives during surface surveys. 'We are obliged to report those and that L.A. immediately.'

'All right, all right,' Castor said, his tone irritable.

'Shall I do the report?' Shavva asked in an expressionless voice.

'I did it,' Castor replied in a tone that ended discussion. He called up the program and, when the copy was ready, he rolled it up into a tube to be inserted in the homing capsule. It would reach their mother ship some weeks before their projected return. 'They will want to know we've discovered another Oort cloud, too. Is it five or six?'

'Six, with this one. I still don't buy that space-virus theory,' Ben remarked, relieved to switch to a less depressing topic.

'Number Four System was dead,' Shavva said in an unequivocal tone.

'Can't prove the Oort cloud affected it in any way. Besides,' Ben went on dispassionately, 'the planet was bombarded by meteors and meteorites to judge by the craters and the craterites. Shattered the surface and boiled off a good deal of the major oceans. Just like Shaula III. That system had an Oort cloud, too.'

'But it had once supported life. We all saw the fossil remains in the cliff faces,' Castor said.

'Like a road sign: life was here, it has gone hence.' Shavva had been depressed by the landing. Ten days on a dead world had been nine and a half too many. The atmosphere was barely adequate and, to be on the safe side, they'd used support systems. A rough estimate suggested that the damage had been done close to a millennium ago. 'At the beginning of Earth's Dark Age, this planet had found the final one.'

'Pity, too. It must have once been a nice world. Great balance of land and water masses,' Castor said.

'I don't know what could have stripped it so completely,' said Ben.

'You never did like the Hoyle–Wickramansingh theory, did you?'

'Has anyone ever found those space-formed viruses? Even a trace in any Oort cloud?' Ben stuck his chin out with a touch of belligerence. 'I won't buy that space-virus theory, not when a planet is covered with city-sized craters. To have both would be overkill and the universe is conservative. One gets you just as dead as the other.'

'I searched the library for data on other stripped planets. Asturias matches up in every particular,' Liu said, his eyes on the screen. 'What particulars there can be, that is!' He rose, stretched and yawned broadly. 'What we really need is one in the process of being stripped.'

Shavva gave a bark of laughter. 'Fat chance of that.'

Liu shrugged. 'Something does it. Anyway I feel that the virus theory would be the rarest probability, while meteors are common, common, common. Look at what happened in our Earth's Cretaceous and Tertiary periods. We were just lucky! Probes away, Captain,' he said formally to Castor. 'Now, I'm for something to eat, then I'll pack the shuttle for the shot.'

'I'll give you a hand,' Shavva said. 'I want to be sure we get what we need this time,' she added in a low, angry voice, bitterly aware that Flora's negligence had cost her own life, and Asturias's. She was now the default leader of this under-staffed team and she was not going to repeat previous mistakes.

As a young biologist with latent qualities as a nexialist, she had joined the Exploration and Evaluation Corps for the diversity of duty, and the thrill of being the first human to walk on unexplored planets and catalogue new life-forms, but she hadn't counted on losing friends in the process. EEC teams developed very close bonds, having to rely on each other's strengths and weaknesses in dangerous, stimulating and testing circumstances no textbook, indeed often no other team reports, could imagine. This was her fourth tour of duty but the first one punctuated by disasters. Castor, still recovering from a serious leg injury sustained when he fell into a crevice on their third landing, was a competent pilot as well as a chemist and would remain on board as the exploratory vessel did its hairpin turn about the third planet. Shavva, Liu and Ben would do the fieldwork.

Shavva would have to double as botanist on this trip. She had fortunately been sufficiently acquainted with Flora's work to have gleaned considerable basic botanical com-petence. She could certainly determine enough about the ecology of the plant life, if there were sufficient pollinators, what sort of competition there was for the food crops as well as the nutritional possibilities of the native forms, and quite likely what disease agents and possible vectors existed within the ecology.

14

Ben was, fortunately, a geologist with enough knowledge of chemistry to cope with the planet's basic pulse – its air and land masses, magnetic fields, mass-cons, continental plate structure, tidal patterns, temperatures, the general topography and, especially, its seismic activity if any – and could evaluate the history of the planetary surface for at least the past million years. If the survey proceeded without unexpected glitches, he'd have a go at the longer term history, from magnetic reversals to sedimentary rocks, if present and usable, and if there'd been any regular large extinctions and date the last.

Liu, as nexialist, would investigate whatever remaining aspects of this planet they had time to consider. That is, if the probes brought back reports that would make a visit worthwhile. Numero Tres did look promising as they rushed towards it. Shavva had discovered that looks were very deceptive in this business. And not only looks.

The probes sent back reports that were sceptically regarded as being too good to be true. Castor muttered and clucked as they gathered around the screen, taking notes as the computer processed the information.

'Good balance of land and water masses,' Liu said, 'usual ice-caps, mountains, good plains areas. Parallels Earth in many respects. Initial P.E. for starters, Castor.'

'Atmosphere is breathable, slightly above normal in oxygen content: gravity slightly lower at 0.9 on the scale,' Ben contributed. 'Considerable vulcanism in that chain of islands extending from the southern hemisphere, nothing major at the moment. Rather a nice little planet, actually.'

'Plenty of green stuff down there,' Shavva said. 'What the hell?' she added in puzzlement as the computer began decoding topography. 'Have a gawk at these crazy circles!'

The probes were now on a low altitude vector, sending back more detailed sections of the terrain of the southern continent. Clearly visible were groups of circular patches . . . like ripples overlapping each other but held frozen on the planet's surface.

'Ever see anything like this before, Ben?' she asked, fervently regretting the missing Flora Neveshan, with her

15

years of experience as a xeno-botanist to analyse this phenomenon.

'Can't say as I have. Looks like some sort of local fungus on a huge scale. Seems to hit all vegetated areas, not just what appear to be grasslands.'

'Fairy rings?' Shavva suggested very brightly.

'Ha! What esoteric stuff you been reading recently?' Ben gave her a jaundiced stare.

'Whatever it is, be bloody careful, will you?' Castor demanded bitterly. 'We've got two more systems to work . . . and I'm running out of initials.'

'Thin red line of 'Erse?' Ben asked, trying to inject some lightness into Castor's mood. He knew that Castor would forever fault himself for the deaths of Asturias and Neveshan. He was the most experienced climber of the group and would very likely have prevented the disaster if he'd been down. The fact that no-one faulted Castor did not assuage his feelings of guilt.

Shavva set the shuttle down on the great plain of the eastern southern hemisphere, several hundred metres from a cluster of the rippling circles they had observed. She, Ben and Liu went through the routine landing procedures, confirming atmosphere, temperature and wind velocity before exiting, garbed in the cumbersome protective suits. At least they didn't need to resort to face masks and the back-wrenching burden of oxygen canisters. They all drew in deep lungfuls of the fresh air that a stiff breeze flung at them.

'Good stuff,' Shavva said with a pleased grin. 'No L.A., this one.' Suddenly, she felt an obsession for this planet to check out as habitable. From outer space it had had the look of the old Earth pictured in historical tapes. Such reassurance could be bloody, and bloodily, deceptive, she reminded herself but that didn't keep her from wishing!

The grassy plain on to which they stepped was springy underfoot and their heavy boots released sweet pungent odours from the bruised vegetation. Silently they walked over to the first of the ripples, Ben and Liu hunkering down, eyeballing it. Shavva took out a sampling probe and inserted it deftly into the soil, closing the lid as soon as she had retracted it. Liu poked a plas-gloved finger into the hole, fiddled with the dirt that adhered and dropped the grains carefully back into the hole.

'Funny. Feels like dirt. Common everyday dirt. Grainy. Rough, uneven.'

'The empirical test!' Ben chuckled.

'Let's get started, guys,' Shavva said. 'We've only got ten days to do eight people's work and clear a planet.'

'A snap!' Ben replied, grinning impudently. 'I'll start by switching on my geologist's brain.' He moved off to the next arc of the ripple and collected more samples of the discoloured ground. 'Hey, we've got ecological succession here,' he added suddenly, pointing to portions now speckled with new growth.

Shavva and Liu came to his side, seeing the promising green tufts.

'Great wind systems on this planet. They'd be strong enough to carry seed as well as dirt,' she remarked, facing into the stiff breeze. ''Nother few decades and this'll all be grass, or whatever, again. Well, we'll see what the samples say. Take some right by that new growth, will you, Ben? See what is aiding the regeneration, if anything.'

That first day they concentrated on dirt and vegetation samplings from that plain, moving on to other sites throughout the day, working from east to west to utilize as much daylight as possible. Ben added the odd rock or two but they were not, he remarked, all that unusual for this type of planet.

They took several deep cores in the rich soils of the southern plains and grasslands and, with more effort, drove rock-sampling cores. Asturias had been the team palaeontologist but they'd have his notes back on the ship to guide their report. Inland and south they went, to points which had shown possible ore sites, though the initial metallurgy probe readings did not suggest that the planet had any easily accessible ore or mineral wealth. They made their first nightfall on a vast headland poking north, on the sands of a great cove.

Marine life was diverse, with enough interesting variations of exo-skeletons and sea vegetation alone to give a marine biologist a lifetime employment. Liu scooped up samples of the red and green algae, and found some interesting fungi on the shoreline, some with visible movement. Larger marine forms were occasionally spotted in the deeper waters of the cove at dusk, a common feeding time. The explorers spent a pleasant evening taking samples and specimens along the seashore. Liu had found enough dead fronds and branches to build a fire on the sands. Shedding all but their protective footwear, they ate their evening rations around it – occasionally managing to capture various types of insectoids drawn to the bright flames.

'Possibly the pollinators we need,' Liu mused as he peered into the tube of captured insectoids. One had paused in its frantic flight so that its double wings were visible. 'Little buggers. I'd feel a lot better though if there were bigger things than these to contend with. The probe pictures should have shown us some sort of ruminants or grazers on these grasslands.'

'What about those large flying things we saw a while back?' Ben asked, and then snorted. 'They looked like airborne barges, squat and fat, and full.'

'Yeah, but what do they eat? And what eats them?' Liu asked morosely.

'Maybe we're between ice ages?' Shavva offered hopefully. She really didn't want to find fault with the planet – a totally unprofessional attitude to take. And dangerous as well. But she couldn't suppress the feeling of 'coming home' which was beginning to colour all her perceptions of this world.

Liu snorted, unconvinced. 'Ecology is right for 'em. They should be here.'

'If they are, we'll find 'em. If we don't . . .' and Shavva shrugged philosophically.

The next day they ventured as far as the ice-cap in the southern hemisphere, taking samples of the frozen crust and as far into the soil as the deep corer could plunge itself. Then they turned to the winter-held north. By then, Liu had become a bit paranoid about the lack of larger life forms. Reptiloids they had seen, scaled and basking.

'Quite large enough, thank you,' Shavva had remarked, narrowly escaping the attentions of a ten-centimetre thick, seven-metre-long example. They saw a great many more of Liu's flying barges.

'Wherries, that's what they were called,' he said suddenly that afternoon. 'Vessels that were used to ferry stuff between the English Isle and the European continent. Wherries, and call 'em the biggest life-form seen in the report. Maybe the term'll stick.' Liu rarely exercised that EEC team prerogative.

There were two identifiable types of the large avians, with raucous calls and the aggressive manners of predators, brilliantly plumed smaller, feathered fliers, a thousand types of what Shavva called 'creepy-crawlies', both inland and littoral. They had also discovered eggshells on southern beaches, shards littering what were apparently sand-buried nests. Of the egg-layers, or the previous occupants, nothing.

They did discover interesting fossil remains in an extensive tar pit, a good fifty thousand years dead and gone, but one specimen intact enough to expose the ground-down dental machinery for grazing: suggesting that they could be the ruminants Liu wished to see. While the short green spiky vegetation could be called 'grass', it wasn't, for it had no silicates, was visibly triangular in form and more blue than green.

'I want to see those grazers now, too,' Liu said firmly. But he was somewhat relieved to find the necessary variety of life-forms at a different epoch on the planet. It was not uncommon for life-forms to remain dormant over difficult seasons, sometimes for years, until conditions were appropriate for a resurgence to plague numbers in other years. Since the strange overlapping circles occurred on the grasslands and plains (also in the forests and even in the jungles, Ben reminded them), they could not connect them to the absence of expected life-forms though the conclusion was logical.

They also found a diamond pipe just below the surface in the major rift valley fault. Rough stones, one as large as

Shavva's fist, were prised out of the soil. They kept several as souvenirs, for the galaxy had produced many more exotic gemstones than these, though diamonds remained useful in technology for their durability and strength.

'I find it rather a relief not to have to be constantly on guard,' Ben said on their third night when Liu began again on the disappearance theme. 'Remember Closto, the L.A. in our last tour? I kept holding my breath, waiting for something else to latch on to me.'

Liu snorted. 'Absence is as ominous as presence in my tapes.'

'Could have been an axial tilt, you know, and what's now the ice-caps was their habitat,' Shavva suggested. 'They got caught in the blizzards and froze. We do have ice cores which could very well produce tissue and bone fragments.'

'Well, this P.E. has only a fifteen-degree axial tilt, the probes set the magnetic poles very near the ecliptic north and south, maybe fifteen degrees away from tilt.'

'We'll know when we get back to the ship and have a chance to study things. Are today's samples ready to go back to Castor?'

'Yeah, but I wish the fardles he'd sent us back HIS conclusions. He's had time,' Liu went on, scowling as he handed his latest containers to Ben to pack in the case to be launched back to the space craft.

'Maybe they all moved north,' Ben said in a spirit of helpfulness.

'To winter?'

'This continent's not in full summer yet.'

'Well, it'd never get hot enough to fry things, not with the prevailing winds this continent's got.' Liu refused to be mollified.

On their way north they paused on the largest of a group of islands; basaltic, riddled with caves, bearing the profusion and lush growth common to tropical climes. They noted several unusual reptilian forms, more properly large herpetoids of truly revolting appearance.

'I've seen uglier ones,' Ben remarked, examining at a safe distance one horny monster seven centimetres broad and five high, which waved tentacles and claws in an aggressive manner. They could discern neither mouth nor eyes. The olfactor gave a stench reading, apparently beloved of some insectoid forms for the creature's back was covered with trapped bodies.

'External digestive system?' Shavva suggested, peering at the thing. 'And . . . wow!'

The creature had sped forward suddenly, its nether end now covered with tiny barbs. While it emitted no sound, the olfactor reading went off the scale and a repellent stench filled the little clearing.

'Look, it backed into that spiny plant,' Ben said, pointing to the little bush. 'And got shot in the ass.'

Standing well back and using a long stick, Shavva nudged one of the remaining spines and was rewarded with a second launching.

'Well, a clever plant. Didn't just let loose in all directions. I wonder what would de-activate it?'

'Cold?' Liu suggested.

'There's a small one here,' and she sprayed it with the cryo, gave it an exploratory prod which elicited no response, and found an appropriate size specimen box from the supply sled in which to pack it.

That evening as they were readying the day's tube for Castor, Liu let out a whoop, holding up for the others to see a glowing specimen tube.

'That growth I found in the big cave. Some sort of luminous variety of mycelium.' He covered it with his hand. 'Indeed. Now you see it,' and he opened his hand to let the tube glow again, 'now you don't.' He closed his hand again, peering through thin cracks he permitted between two fingers. 'Does oxygen trigger the luminosity?'

'You are not going back into the cave tonight, Liu,' Shavva said sternly. 'We don't have the spelunking equipment necessary to keep you from breaking your damned fool neck.'

He shrugged. 'Luminous lichens or organisms are not my forte.' He carefully wrapped the tube in opaque plasfilm. 'Don't want it to wear itself out before Castor sees it.'

That evening they were all enticed from their camp by the

21

sound of cheeping and chittering. Parting the lush foliage that surrounded them, they peered out at an astonishing scene. Graceful creatures, totally different from the awkward avians seen in the southern hemisphere, were performing aerial acrobatics of astonishing complexity. The setting sun sparkled off green, blue, brown, bronze and golden backs, and translucent wings glistened like airborne jewels.

'The seaside egg-layers?' Shavva asked Liu in a whisper.

'Quite possibly,' Liu replied softly. 'Gorgeous. Look, they're playing a discernible game. Catch-me-if-you-can!'

For a long time, the three explorers watched the spectacle with delight until the creatures broke off their play as the swift tropical night darkened the skies.

'Sentient?' Shavva asked, wanting and not wanting those beautiful creatures to be a dominant sentient life of this planet.

'Marginally,' Liu murmured approvingly. 'If they're leaving eggs on a shoreline where storm waters could wash them away, they're not possessed of very great intelligence.'

'Just beauty,' Ben said. 'Perhaps we'll find large and related types of the same evolutionary ancestors for you, Liu.'

Liu shrugged diffidently as he turned back to their campfire. 'If we do, we do.'

They made notes of what they had witnessed and then turned in for the night. The next day had them examining the reef systems jutting out from the island, and its smaller companions. A trip to the more tropical eastern peninsula showed them a complicated system, similar to coral, with fossils of the same thing going right back, Ben estimated, some five hundred million years. At least this was a viable ecology, not a stalemated tropical rain-forest dense ecology, with the various elements, so to speak, taking in each other's washing. Such transitory ecologies did reinforce Ben's theory of a recent meteorite storm rather than an ice-age hiatus in evolution.

The bare circles were planet-wide, except at the caps and one small band of the southern hemisphere and, though the survey team had thoroughly investigated, they could not find the meteorites which might have been the cause. Nor, Ben fretted, were any of the circles either deep enough or overlapping in the pattern that a multiple meteorite impact would provide.

The northern hemisphere, though in part blanketed by thick snows, was duly cored for soil and rock samplings. Mud flats, emitting the usual dense sulphurous fumes all over the central plain's vast river delta, produced more regularities than differences, certainly a plethora of promising bacteria over which Shavva crowed. Further inland, up the broad navigable riverway, they found adequate lodes of iron, copper, nickel, tin, vanadium, bauxite and even some germanium but none of the generous quantities of metals and minerals that would interest a mining consortium. Those almost preferred asteroids and dead planets, avoiding attacks by the Green and Ecological protectors.

On the next to last morning of their survey, Ben found gold nuggets in a brash mountain stream.

'A real old-fashioned world,' he remarked, tossing and catching the heavy nuggets in his hand. 'Old Earth once had free gold in streams, too. Another parallel.'

Shavva leaned over and took one which was an almost perfect drop, holding it between thumb and forefinger.

'My loot,' she said, dropping it into her belt pouch.

She found one extremely interesting plant on the upper section of the eastern peninsula: a vigorous plant whose bark, when bruised, gave off a pungent smell. That evening, she made an infusion of the bark, sniffing appreciatively at its aroma. Empirical tests showed that it was not toxic and her judicious sip of the infusion made her sigh with pleasure.

'Try it, Liu, tastes great!'

Liu regarded the thin dark liquid with suspicion but he, too, found the odour stimulating to his salivary glands and wet his lips, smacking them to spread the taste. 'Hmmm, not bad. Bit watery. Infuse it a bit longer, or reduce the liquid. You might have something here.'

Ben joined in the sampling and, when Shavva experimented with grinding the bark and filtering hot water through it, he approved the result.

23

'A sort of combination of coffee and chocolate, I think, with a spicy aftertaste. Not bad.'

So Shavva harvested a quantity of the bark and they used it as a beverage for the remaining two days. She saved enough to take back to Castor as a treat.

Though none of the three made mention of the fact, they were all sorry to leave the planet and yet relieved that there had been no further accidents or untoward circumstances. Barring some unforeseen factor discovered in the analyses of soil, vegetation and biological samples, they were all three quite willing to let Castor initial it P.E.R.N. – parallel Earth, resources negligible. He added a C in the top corner of the report indicating the planet was suitable for colonization.

That is, if any colonial group wanted to settle on a pastoral planet, far off the established trade routes, and about as far from the centre of the Federated Sentient headquarters as one could go in the known galaxy.

The Dolphins' Bell

When Jim Tillek activated the red-alert recall sequence on the Big Bell at Monaco Bay, Teresa's pod, with Kibby and Amadeus leaping and diving right along with her, was there within minutes. Within the hour, the ones led by Aphro, China, and Captiva, arrived; a total of seventy, counting the three youngest calved only that year. Young males and solitaries surged in from all directions, squee-eee-ing, clicking, chuffing loudly and performing incredible aquabatics as they came. Few dolphins had ever heard that particular sequence on the Big Bell so they were eager to learn why it had been rung.

'Why ring the red?' Teresa demanded, bobbing her head up in front of Jim who stood, legs spread to balance his lean body on the rocking float anchored at the end of Monaco Wharf. Her nose bore the many scratches and scars of age as well as an aggressive personality. She tended to assume the role of Speaker for Dolphins.

The float was broad and wide, nearly the length of the end of the wharf and was traditionally where the dolphineers held conferences with pods or individuals. This was also where the dolphins came to report unusual occurrences to the Bay Watch or for rare instances when they required medical attention. The end timbers were smoother than the others due to the dolphins' habit of rubbing against them.

Above the float hung the Big Bell, its belfry sturdily attached to a massive six by six moulded plastic pylon well-footed on the seafloor below. The chain the dolphins yanked to summon humans now idly slapped against the pylon with the action of the light sea.

'We land folk have trouble and need dolphin help,' Jim said and pointed inland where the clouds of white and grey smoke curled ominously into the sky from two of the three previously extinct volcanoes. 'We must leave this place and take from here all that can be moved. Do the other pods come?'

'Big trouble?' Teresa asked, leisurely swimming beyond the bulk of the wharf to check the direction in which Jim had pointed. She raised herself high above the water, turning first one, then the other eye, to assess the situation. Her sides showed the rakings of many years' contact with amorous or angry males. 'Big smoke. Worse than Young Mountain.'

'Biggest ever,' Jim said, for a moment wishing that the eternal cheerful expression on dolphins' faces did not seem so out of place right now.

'Where you go?' Teresa reversed her direction and stopped in front of Jim, giving him her complete and seriously cheerful attention. 'Back to sick ocean world?'

'No,' and Jim shook his head vigorously. Since the dolphins had passed the fifteen-year journey on the colony ships in cold sleep, they had had no sense of the passage of time. From an installation in the Atlantic Ocean, they had entered their water-filled travel accommodations and had been awakened in the waters of Monaco Bay. 'We go north.'

Teresa ducked her bottlenose, flinging a spray of water at him as if agreeing. Then, dropping her head in the water she gave forth to the members of her pod a rapid series of word noises too fast for Jim to follow, even though, over the past eight years on Pern he'd learned a good deal of their vocabulary.

Kibby glided to one side of Teresa, and Captiva bobbed up on the other, all earnestly regarding Jim.

'Sandman, Oregon,' Captiva said distinctly, 'are in West Flow. They turn, return as fast as the flux allows.'

Then Aleta and Maximilian abruptly arrived, adroitly avoiding a collision with the others. Pha pushed neatly in too, as he was never one to be left out on the periphery.

'Echo from Cass. They speed back. New sun see them here,' Pha said and blew from his hole to emphasize the importance of his report.

'Yes, they do have the furthest to come,' Jim said, since

26

that pod was based in the waters around Young Mountain, helping Patrice de Broglie's seismic team. But dolphins could swim all night and Cass was one of the original and most reliable of the females.

The waters around the sea end of the Monaco Wharf facility were now so packed with dolphins that, when some of the dolphineers arrived, Theo Force remarked dryly to Helga Duff that they could probably have walked on dolphins across the wide mouth of Monaco Bay and never got their feet wet.

Some of the nine dolphineers and seven apprentices actually took longer to arrive than their marine friends since the humans had to sled in from their Stake Holds. Luckily, both Jim Tillek's forty-foot sloop, *Southern Cross*, and Per Pagnesjo's *Perseus* yawl were in port. Anders Sejby had radioed that the *Mayflower* was under full sail and would be there by dusk while Pete Veranera thought he'd have the *Maid* in on the late night tide. *The Pernese Venturer* and Captain Kaarvan had not yet reported in. She was the largest, a two-masted schooner with a deep draught, and slower than the other four.

Once all the humans reported in, Jim tersely explained that, with Mount Garben about to erupt, Landing had to be evacuated and everyone must help get as many supplies as possible to safety around Kahrain Head. The larger ships would be taking their loads as far as Paradise River Stake but that would be too far for the smaller craft, but everything that floated was to be used to shift material as far as Kahrain.

'We've got to transport all that?' Ben Byrne cried in an aggrieved tone as he flung an arm towards the wharfside where enormous piles of materiel were being deposited by sleds of all sizes. He was a small, compact man with crisp blond hair nearly white from sun bleach. His wife, Claire, who worked with him at Paradise River, stood at his side. 'There aren't that many ships of any decent size and, if you think the dolphins can . . .'

'We've only to get it to Kahrain, Ben,' Jim said, laying a steadying hand on the younger man's shoulder.

'Click! Click!' Teresa managed an ear-piercing shout for

27

attention. 'We do that, we do that!' Amadeus, Pha and Kibby agreed, nodding vigorously.

'Ye daft finnies, you'd burst yerselves,' Ben cried, incensed, wagging his arms at the dolphins facing him to be quiet.

'We can, we can, we can,' and half the dolphins crowding the end of the wharf heaved themselves up out of the water to tailwalk in their enthusiasm. Somehow they managed not to crash into the seething mass of podmates who ducked out of the way under water with split-second timing. Such antics were repeated by many, all across the waters of the bay.

'Look what you started, Cap'n!' cried Ben in an extravagant show of despair. 'Damned fool fin-faces! You wanna burst your guts?'

Sometimes, Jim Tillek thought, Ben was as uninhibited as any of the whimsically impetuous dolphins he was supposed to 'manage'. The difference between their enthusiasm and the reality of their assistance lay in the fact that all adult dolphins had spent a period training with human partners, learning to come to the aid of stranded swimmers and sailors, and occasionally damaged sailing craft. They were delighted to have a chance to practise on such a scale.

Harnesses from the training sessions were available – and more could be cobbled together – to 'hitch' dolphin teams to any of the smaller sailing craft. A big yoke already existed, contrapted for the ore barge which the dolphins had several times hauled from Drake's Lake. But never had the settlers had to call on *all* the dolphins.

'We've known something big was up,' Jan Regan said, her manner much calmer as befitted the senior dolphineer. She gave a snort that was half-laugh. 'They've been squeeing like nutters about underwater changes around here,' she added, flicking her hand at the crowded bay. 'But you know how some of them exaggerate!'

'Hah! With Picchu blowing smoke rings, of course they'd know something was going to happen,' Ben said, having recovered his equilibrium. 'Question is, how much time do we have before Picchu blows?'

'It isn't Picchu that's going to blow . . .' Jim began as gently

28

as possible and allowed the startled reaction to subside before he continued. 'It's Garben.'

'Knew we shouldn't have named a mountain after that old fart,' Ben muttered.

Jim continued. 'More important, Patrice can't give us a time frame.' That stunned even the solid and unflappable Bernard Shattuck. 'All he can do is warn us when the eruption is imminent.'

'Like *how* imminent?' Bernard asked soberly.

'An hour or two. The increasing sulphur-to-chlorine ratio means the magma is rising. We've two, maybe three days with just sulphur and ash . . .'

'The ash I don't mind. It's the sulphur that's so appalling,' and Helga Duff started coughing again.

'The real problem is,' Jim paused again, 'Monaco is also within range of pyroclastic missile danger.'

'Range of what?' Jan screwed up her face at the technical term. She knew as much as any human could about dolphins but ignored technical jargon.

'Range of what heavy stuff the volcano can throw out at us,' Jim said, almost apologetically.

'Worse than the ash and smoke already coming down?' Efram asked, for, though they hadn't been standing on the wharf that long, their wet suits were now grey with volcanic ash.

'The big stuff, boulders, all kinds of molten debris . . .'

'But we have Threadfall at Maori Lake this afternoon,' young Gunnar Schultz said, looking totally confused by the conflict of imperatives.

'We have to get all the materiel we can to Kahrain as soon as possible and *that* is the immediate priority, folks. Thread'll have to wait its turn,' Jim said with his usual wry humour. 'All available craft are to be used and the call's gone out to owners to either get here or appoint a surrogate. So all we have to do is explain to pod leaders what has to be done and the kind of co-operation we need from them.' He began passing out copies of the evacuation plans Emily Boll had given him forty minutes before. He glanced anxiously overhead as three heavy sleds seemed about to collide. 'Damn 'em. Look, read the overall plans while I go organize some air traffic control.'

The dolphineers dutifully read the evacuation plan, though Jan skimmed ahead to their responsibilities: the stuff building up on the beach. Loads were all colour-coded. Red and orange're priority, and red's fragile, for immediate transfer to Kahrain. Yellow should go in a hull of some kind; green and blue are waterproofed and can be towed.

Jim stuck his head out of the control-room window. 'Lilienkamp's sending us drums, wood, lines and whatever men he can spare to lash rafts together. At least the weather report's good. Decide which of the dolphins can be trusted to pull . . .'

'Any one of 'em you ask,' Ben said indignantly.

'And we'll need some sensible dolphs to swim escort on the smaller sail craft. Keeerist! What's that driver doing?' Leaning his long frame as far out of the window as he could, Jim began waving both long arms shoreward to prevent a heavy sled from colliding with two smaller ones, all of which were trying to slide into the tight landing spaces on the strand. 'Do the best you can!' he shouted at his team and pulled his head back in to restore some order to the traffic heading towards the bay.

'Jan, you, Ef and me explain,' Ben said. 'Bernard, start organizing those red and orange loads for the *Cross* and the *Perseus* already tied up. Let's get some of the larger small craft in to load. By then the pod leaders'll know what's expected and can make assignments of escorts. Gunnar, Helga, you others, start checking with the sailcraft, find out their load limits. Try to keep track of what went with whom . . .' He broke off, realizing the monumental task ahead of them. 'We'll need some hand recorders . . . You guys get started. I'll see if I can liberate us a few 'corders. There have to be some . . .' His voice trailed off as he climbed up the ladder to the wharf office.

'Right after we tell the fins *what* they're to do, we organize some sea police, huh?' Bernard said.

'Right, man! Right!' Efram said with heart-felt agreement. 'Now then, let's brief the pods . . .'

As they were all suited up, they moved along the length of

30

the float, spotting their own particular pod leaders. Then, gesturing to the dolphins to give them some space, they jumped in. It was the easiest way to impress on individual dolphins their particular tasks.

There was a sudden swirling of water around the dolphineers as the dolphins chose their favourite swimming partners. Despite the crush of mammalian life in the waters, Teresa emerged right by Jan Regan, Kibby by Efram: Ben got splashed by a well-aimed sweep of Amadeus's right flipper.

'Cut that out, Ammie. This is serious,' Ben said.

'No ruff stuff?' Amadeus asked and clicked in surprise.

'Not today,' Ben said, and gave Ammic an affcctionate scratch between the pectorals to take the sting out of the reprimand. Then he put his whistle in his mouth and blew three sharp notes.

Heads, human and dolphin, turned in his direction. Letting his legs dangle beside Amadeus and resting one hand lightly on his nose, Ben outlined the problem and what assistance was required of the dolphins.

'Kahrain near,' Teresa said, chuffing energetically from her blow hole.

'You have to make many trips,' Jan said and indicated the growing pile of crates, boxes, nets of every size and colour.

'So?' was Kibby's response. 'We start.'

Efram grabbed Kibby by the closest pcctoral. 'We need aisles,' and he demonstrated parallels with his arms, 'incoming, outgoing. We need escorts for the smaller ships. We need teams for the bigger rafts and bargcs.'

'Two, three teams to change to keep speed,' Dart said, nudging Theo Force. 'I know who thinks who is strongest. I go get them. You get harness.' With one of those incredible flips a dolphin body was capable of performing, Dart lived up to her name, arcing over several bodies and neatly re-entering the water. Her disappearing dorsal fin showed the speed she was travelling at.

'I get harness,' Theo echoed, making a foolish grimace at the others. 'I get harness,' she said again, as she swam with confident strokes to the nearest of the pier ladders. 'Why is she always one step ahead of me?'

' 'Cos she swims faster,' Toby Duff yelled.

'We, Kibby me, police lanes,' Oregon informed Toby. 'Use flag bobbers?'

Jan started to giggle. 'Why do we bother telling them anything?' she said.

'Flag buoys coming up,' Toby said, swimming for the ladder nearest the storage sheds where the racing buoys were kept. 'Green for incoming, red for outgoing.'

'There should be enough,' Efram said, following him, 'from the winter regattas.'

'These all the ships?' Teresa asked, swishing herself up high enough on her tail to look up and down the wharf.

'There should be a dozen or more luggers and sloops coming in from the coastal and downriver Stake Holds,' Jan told her. 'The bigger ones can sail right on down to Paradise River, but whatever we get around Kahrain Head'll be safe enough.'

'Busy, busy,' Teresa said and looked happier than usual. 'New thing to do. Good fun.'

Jan grabbed her left fin. 'Not fun, Tessa. Not fun!' And she shook her finger in front of Teresa's left eye. 'Dangerous. Hard. Long hours.'

If a dolphin could shrug diffidently, that's what Teresa did. 'My fun not your fun. This my fun. You keep afloat. Hear me?'

By the time Jim Tillek had managed to organize air traffic and get some beach wardens into position, the two lanes had been established with red and green buoys: three teams of the biggest males had been harnessed to the big barge which had been filled with fragile red loads and was already under way. The first flotilla of smaller sailcraft followed, dolphin-towed out of the congested harbour area to the point where they could safely hoist canvas on their way to Kahrain. Escort dolphins had been assigned.

'We're never going to keep track of this stuff,' Ben muttered to Claire. She had organized something to eat for the dolphineers while her friend, Tory, was busy with his team, hauling blue and green cargo out to dinghies and other less sea-worthy craft.

Even the big ceremonial canoe, smaller ones and kayaks were being pressed into service. These would have to be very closely watched as they were manned by relatively inexperienced sailors – many of them pre-teens – who had been assigned the unusual duty.

Jim Tillek had seen that they all had emergency jackets, gear and knew exactly how to call a dolphin to their aid. The supply of whistles ran out which worried some of the less competent kids but Theo Force had Dart demonstrate how fast she could come to their aid if they merely slapped the water hard with both hands. Fortunately the sea remained gently rippling.

'Those clodheaded landlubbers are more trouble than anyone else,' Jim said, striding landward on the wharf, raising his bull horn to chew out some Landing residents who were adding household goods to the stack of red priority cargo.

That was when his patience foundered, and striding to the nearest sled, he hauled the driver out, ordered him to put back what he had just unloaded. When that was done, Jim flew the sled to the 'space available' cargo at the far end of the strand. When the sled was once more unloaded, Jim took it up, despite its owner's voluble complaints, and used it for the rest of the day to make sure goods carted down from Landing went into the appropriate areas. Actually, even from a moderate altitude, he could keep an eye on what was happening everywhere in the Bay.

With a leeward breeze keeping most of the volcanic fumes wafting away from Monaco, Jim was sometimes startled to look inland and see how steadily the fumaroles on Garben and Picchu emitted clouds of white and grey, and probably noxious gases. He also felt a pang of near terror as he saw the mass of things to be removed from 'pyroclastic' activity. They'd need a ruddy armada . . . Why couldn't they send more stuff by air?

Yet he couldn't deny that a steady flow of sleds of all sizes was proof that immense quantities *were* being flown out. Even the young dragons had panniers of some kind strapped behind their riders.

Wiping his sooted brow with a kerchief nearly messier than his face, Jim watched the graceful creatures reach a high thermal and start the long glide down to the Kahrain cove. If they'd only more of them, more power-packs, more ships, more . . .

Someone tugged his arm: Toby Duff directed his attention to a raft that was foundering.

'Damn fool didn't balance the load . . .' he began, even as dolphins pushed against sagging barrels and pallets to keep them from floating off. 'I can't be everywhere,' he groaned.

'You're giving a good impression of it,' Toby remarked at his dryest. 'Look, under control.'

'But they aren't bringing it back in to be repacked,' Jim began.

'Use the binocs, Jim, Gunnar's there. Seems like he has it under control. What I need is your advice. Do you think we can cocoon in plastic some of the red and orange and entrust small loads to younger dolphins who can't help with the heavier stuff?'

Jim thought, glancing at the barely lowered stack of priority goods. 'Better give it a try. Better than having the stuff fried pyroclastically.'

Toby gave him an uncertain grin, a genuine laugh and trotted off to wharfside, jumping into the water to make the necessary assignments. Later, when Toby's expertise with dolphin communications was more acutely needed, Jim realized that he could have given that job to Amos Schultz since it only involved selecting an appropriate size crate or plastic cocooned pallet, netting it, and wading out to where the young dolphins waited in shoulder high waters to be harnessed.

Then, all too quickly, the swift tropical dusk descended and there was a scurry to determine how many of the ill-assorted carriers had made it safely to Kahrain, how many in transit would need lighting or other help, and what, if any, casualties or losses there had been.

To Jim's amazement, there were only minor human casualties – scrapes, bruises, cuts – and even after Ben continually excused his record taking, very little loss of common cargo – none of the red or orange priorities – and not too many scraped dolphins or wrenched muscles.

Each pod leader reported to Monaco Wharf that they were off to eat and would return at dawn. Not for the first time did Jim and the dolphineers envy the creatures who could put half their brains to sleep and still function perfectly.

Someone thoughtful had put a kettle of stew, loaves of bread and a pile of biscuits on the long table in the wharf office and, with little discussion, the hungry served themselves. Then, finding sufficient floor space, they curled up in blankets, old heavy-weather gear and whatever else sufficed to keep tired bodies warm. Such fire-lizards as looked to those sleepers arranged themselves on the pier, their eyes rivalling the emergency lights up and down the long installation.

The Big Bell roused all the sleepers and brought Jim and Efram stumbling out of the office to see what the problem was. Kibby and Dart were fighting over who was to pull the chain.

'Morning, morning, morning,' was the chant from several hundred dolphins, as fresh and eager as yesterday for the great new 'fun' their landfriends had discovered to please them.

Jim and Efram groaned, leaning into each other in sleepy incoherence. A seaward breeze made arduous the next day's work: sulphur-and-chlorine-tainted air caused eyes to water, and irritated throats and nasal passages. The dolphins seemed less affected, which was a blessing. Halfway through that day, most of the swimmers started using masks and oxygen tanks in the water and out.

There were more emergencies this day – with tired people, stiff-muscled from unaccustomed labours, valiantly trying to exceed the previous day's quota.

Skippering *The Southern Cross*, laden to the scuppers with a cargo of precious medical supplies, Jim spent more time on the comunit, issuing suggestions, orders, and trying to keep his temper over asinine errors that would never have been so dangerous at any other time. The sea path between Monaco and Kahrain was a mass, and a mess, of ill-assorted craft, struggling to transport beyond their capacities. Twice the *Cross* passed dinghies afloat only by virtue of the pairs of dolphins keeping them up on the surface of the water.

The third morning, Jim summarily ordered all small craft under seven metres out of the water at Kahrain. Most of their crews he left behind to help unload the larger ships and to off-load the dolphins whom he decided made better, and faster, transporters of small-to-medium-sized packets.

'Smart of you, Jim,' Theo Force said that evening when they gathered on board the *Cross* for the eastward leg. 'Kids got a big kick out of how often "their" dolphins made the trip. They even started snitching titbits for 'em as treats. Not that they could catch much fish with the waters so churned.'

'And my heart wasn't in my mouth so much,' Claire Byrne said, 'thinking of all that could go wrong with those cockle-shells.'

'Weather's disimproving,' Shattuck remarked.

'Too heavy for the seven-metre hulls?' Jim asked, perusing the lists of cargo still piled on the Monaco strand. Today's hard work had shown a definite lowering of the mass.

'Not with the more experienced crews,' Shattuck said after a thoughtful pause, 'but I'd feel happier if they had dolphin escorts. How're dolphs holding up?'

Jim snorted while Theo and Festa managed weary chuckles.

'Them?' Efram said with utter disgust. 'They're enjoying this game we thought up for their amusement!'

Ben was grinning as he leaned forward, elbows on his knees, hands cradling a hot drink. 'Didja hear that the pods seem to have some sort of competition going between them?'

'Based on what?'

'Weight hauled,' Ben said with a wry grin. 'You'll have noticed 'em humping the single packs about? Weighin' in.'

'No damage, I hope,' Jim said, trying to sound severe although the whole notion of anyone finding the situation one in which to start any kind of a competition tickled him. Leave it to the dolphins! Nature's born humorists. He wished there'd been otters still alive on Earth when the Pern colony

36

was being organized. They, too, were creatures who knew how to amuse themselves with the strangest objects! He sighed. 'We can't afford to lose anything we've been entrusted to get to Kahrain safely.'

'Once we get it all to Kahrain, what happens then, Captain?' Gunnar asked in a weary tone.

'Why then, my hearties, we have time to decide what has to be brought on the fleetest winds and vessels to the north.' There were sufficient groans to cause him to smile reassuringly. 'But with more leisure available to make choices.'

'It's a fair ol' haul to the place they've chosen in the north,' Anders Sejby said in a neutral tone. He was a big man, phlegmatic in temperament, but astonishingly agile physically. He had big hands, big feet, broad shoulders and solid legs that threatened to burst the seams of his water-proofed trousers. He tended to go barechested, and barefooted, but there wasn't a mariner on the planet that wouldn't sail anywhere with him: Jim Tillek included. 'Any sort of a pier there? Or do we have to lighter stuff in from the bigger ships?'

Jim gave him a blank stare. 'I dunno. I'll find out.'

'You mean,' asked Ben who fired up easily, 'we're busting our nuts doing all this and we've got to . . .'

Speaking into his comunit, Jim held up his hand to stem Ben's indignant protest. 'All will be prepared for us there.'

'Bet it wasn't until you mentioned it,' Ben said sourly.

'Be not of faint heart, Ben,' Jim said, laying his hand in benedictory fashion on the dolphineer's salt-encrusted curls. 'By the time we get there, we'll have wharf facilities. Paul Benden solemnly promised me.' Ben snorted, unrepentant. 'Now, let's sort out what we've got to move tomorrow.'

Garben moved first. The warning Patrice sent out gave them a scant two hours and the advice that everything that could leave Monaco should be gone well before that time limit. No-one had any coherent memories of that period. Neither of the bigger ships, the *Cross* or the *Perseus* were fully loaded when the alarm came. They were sailed far enough out of the projected danger area. If the wharf, and the cargo, were left

37

when the eruption was over, they would go back in and finish loading.

Everyone did have memories of Garben's spectacular eruption, seen at a safe enough distance to be clear of the pyroclastic debris. It was truly awe-inspiring, and immensely heartbreaking, to see the community that they had achieved in such a short time showered with ash, burning missiles, and disappearing behind dense grey clouds.

'Did everyone get out?' Theo called from waters on the starboard side of the *Cross*.

'So we were told,' Jim said. 'D'you want to come aboard?'

Theo raised her eyebrows at the already overcrowded sloop.

'Lord, no, Jim. I'm safer with Dart.' On cue the dolphin surfaced and pushed her fin against the hand Theo idly circled as she trod water. 'See what I mean . . .' And her voice dwindled as the sleek little dolphin propelled her further from the ship and Monaco Bay.

The few damaged loads and other debris were burned or buried before Jim Tillek allowed the *Cross*, as the last ship, to leave Monaco Bay.

'What about the bell?' Ben asked just as the gangplank was being pulled up.

Jim paused, squinting up at the bell. 'Leave it. The dolphins get such a kick out of ringing it.'

'Even with no-one to hear?'

Jim heaved a sigh. 'Frankly, Ben, I don't have the energy right now to dismantle it.' He looked around at decks crammed with lashed-down pallets. 'Hell, where'd we put a thing as big as that?' Then he shook his head. 'We can come back for it. Ezra'll be wanting to check the AIVAS interface once the volcanoes have settled.' Then he gave the orders to release the lines for'ard and aft. 'Yeah, we'll get it next trip.'

He did note the sadness on Ben's face as the bell, and the wharf, receded from sight. Not even the gay escort of two pods of dolphins seemed to cheer the man. Well, the disaster took people different ways. Paradise River was Ben's real home. And they'd have to abandon that. Perhaps it was the bell, as a symbol in itself. They'd left a lot more behind at

38

Landing than a bell. They sailed on, through the murky, reeking atmosphere that Garben and Picchu had made of the once clear air of Monaco Bay.

Kahrain was scarcely better organized than the Bay had been but there were hot baths and decent food available and a chance for tired bodies to sleep until they were rested. Not much ease, though, for Paul Benden, Emily Boll, Joel Lilienkamp, Desi Arthied, Ezra Keroon, the other captains, with Theo Force and Ben Byrne representing the dolphineers.

The evacuation had gone smoothly enough, thanks to Emily Boll's foresight. The only casualties had been, unfortunately, Marco Galliani and his bronze dragon, Duluth, who had collided with a sled. Or, as Emily put it in an expressionless voice, attempted to avoid a collision by going *between* as the fire-lizards did.

The young dragon's instinct had not been sufficient to bring them back from wherever *between* was and the other young dragonriders were suffering from trauma.

'I told them to take the day off,' she said, clearing her throat authoritatively; ignoring the fact that Sean had told her, in no uncertain terms, that he and his group would not be available for work until the next day. 'Pol and Bay have gone to give what consolation they could.'

'But the dragon actually went *between*?' Jim asked, amazed.

Emily nodded briskly, blinking against a sudden moisture in her eyes. 'I saw . . . Duluth do it. He and Marco were there, midair, one moment, the sled descending on top of them, and then . . . gone!' She cleared her throat noisily. 'So, if we have to find some good out of the tragedy, there it is. The dragons can do what the fire-lizards can. Now if their riders can now figure out how to do it on a . . . safe return basis, we may yet have our aerial force.'

'Right now, though, it's the naval forces we must organize,' Paul said, standing up and lighting the screen of his work terminal. 'Fortunately, there's a good warehouse at Paradise River where we can stash non-vital supplies for later runs.'

'So we do use the small craft again?' Per Pagnesjo asked.

Paul nodded. 'For one thing, those sailers are intrinsically valuable in themselves and not just for what we can load on them.' He turned to the dolphineers. 'How are your friends standing up to this?'

Theo gave a bark and Ben a snort. 'It's a nice new game we've figured out for them,' Theo answered.

'Glad someone's finding some enjoyment out of all this,' Paul said with a grim smile.

'Trust dolphins for that,' Theo said with a genuine grin which turned Paul's into one less strained. 'Well, we don't need to rush so much to get to Paradise, do we? That'll make it easier and safer.'

'We'll have to use personnel who are not slated for the next Threadfall, though,' Paul added, switching his terminal to another setting. 'We had to let Maori Lake take its chances but we've got to keep Thread burrows to a minimum.'

'Even if we're abandoning the southern continent?' Theo asked.

'We're not *abandoning* the continent, nor entirely removing everyone,' Paul said. 'Drake wants to continue, so do the Gallianis, the Logorides, the Seminole, Key Largo and Ierne Island groups. Tarvi's keeping the mines and the smelters going. Since they work underground or in the cement block sheds, they're reasonably safe from Thread, though food resources may have to be augmented from our supplies.'

'They may have to come north in the end if we can't supply them from our stores,' Emily said sadly.

'So . . .' and Paul briskly brought the meeting back to the matter at hand, 'Joel's got some imperative supplies that ought to be shifted north immediately. Kaarvan, your ship has the biggest capacity. Can you undertake that voyage while the other ships redistribute loads and follow when laden? Desi, can you give him a hand with the manifests?'

'If I get my crew to it now, we can shift and reload cargo and be ready to sail by the evening tide,' Kaarvan replied with a nod and left without further comment. He was not one who could endure long meetings but what he was asked to do he did with despatch and efficiency.

'Desi, I want manifests of every crate and carton you take, red and orange . . .' Joel Lilienkamp shouted after his assistant, and received a backhanded wave. 'How,' and Joel turned to the others, hands upraised in helpless resignation, 'are we going to keep track of what is where and . . . everything?'

For the first time since Jim Tillek had known the able Commissary Chief, he saw the energetic man at a loss, overwhelmed by the magnitude of the task. He felt a deep sympathy for Joel, too, for he had had everything so neatly catalogued and organized at Landing: could literally tell you on what shelf in what building the item you needed was stored. Even his legendary eidetic memory would be unable to cope with the present confusion.

'Joel,' Emily said firmly but somehow soothingly, 'no-one but you could have pulled off such a comprehensive evacuation of goods and people.'

Perhaps only Jim noticed the order of importance in her compliment and he decided to rub his face to hide an appreciative grin. In Joel's lexicon, people could take care of themselves, but goods had to be taken care of and their location should be known at any time of the day or night.

'We are in your debt on many counts, Joel,' Ezra said, pushing back his shock of hair with both hands. 'If you hadn't found those tiles so I could shield the AIVAS . . .'

Joel shrugged the gratitude away. 'It's what'll happen now that deeply concerns me. There're materials we have got to have immediate access to and, unless I have the records of all the loads that went out of Landing by sled as well as Monaco . . .'

At that point, Johnny Greene came in, looking jaded but also gloating. 'Don't anyone ever say "It can't be done" in my presence,' he announed to all. Joel perked up expectantly. 'Got generators up and running and ten terminals. Dieter's got 'em all programmed to take visual, audial or recorder inputs and then correlate. Will that do you for now, Joel?'

'It most certainly will,' and Joel bounced to his feet as if he hadn't just been in the depths of despondency. 'Where've you got them set up? Lead me.' He got as far as the shelter door before he turned back. 'I'll need personnel . . .'

'Whoever isn't doing something else I hereby authorize you to draft until those records are transferred,' Paul said with a chuckle. But his amusement died as he turned back to his own screens, pursing his lips with two fingers. 'We still have some pretty hairy problems. Ezra, can you also put back on your captain's hat? We'll have to take the smaller craft along the shoreline all the way to Key Largo before we make a final dash across to the northern continent. I can't see any other way of getting all the people and materiel there. One vast convoy, with dolphin support, keeping one of the bigger ships as guardian, while the others make straight journeys from Kahrain or Paradise to the Fort?'

'Let's also count on shifting the convoy guard ship now and again,' Jim said after exchanging a quick glance with Ezra. 'Even with decent weather, and that eruption's going to mess weather patterns past the predictable point, it's going to be some safari.'

'But can it be done?' Paul asked.

Jim twisted one shoulder. 'We got here. We'll get there. Sooner or later.'

'It's the later that worries me,' Paul added.

Jim hauled his recorder out of his pocket and tapped out a query. 'Well, let's just see what we can do, Paul.' He peered down at Benden quizzically. 'You and Em will go north to,' and he grinned in lazy irony, 'to prepare a place for us, so d'you want to be admiral of the Pernese Navy, Ez, or do I get the short straw this time?'

'Let's stick to being captains and working as a team as we usually do,' Ezra replied in his dry fashion but he clamped an affectionate hand as he peered over Jim Tillek's shoulder at the recorder's data.

'Not all the stuff's been lifted out of Landing yet,' Joel said, poking his head in through the door. 'I'm organizing all available sleds to bring up the last. Can I get the dra—'

Emily held up her hand. 'They'll be back on line tomorrow, Joel!'

Joel scrunched his eyes shut and grimaced. 'Sorry. Tomorrow'll be good enough.' And he was gone again.

*   *   *

'There was a fleet like this once before,' Jim said to Theo Force who was the duty dolphineer as the *Southern Cross* led the way out of Kahrain cove. The sloop slept eight comfortably so, with a captain and five regular crew, four dolphineers made use of the two extra bunks and the cockpit couches.

'Like that?' And Theo jerked her thumb over her shoulder at the strung-out line of ill-assorted vessels. Dressed in her body wet suit, breather flung over one shoulder to be ready for use instantly, she had stretched out her strong tanned legs on her side of the cockpit. Jim had an eye for a shapely leg, even one generally showing raking scars from many brushes with tough dolphin hide. He was also becoming accustomed to Theo's subtly attractive face. Not a pretty woman and well into her third decade, her rather plain features nevertheless indicated her strong character and purposefulness.

'Yup, something like the odd-bods fleet we have here,' Jim said, squinting at the way the mains'l was filling with a wind that was more capricious than he'd like for the beginning of this bizarre escort duty. 'Long time back now, but one of those bright moments in human history when people rise to an almost impossible challenge.'

'Oh?' Theo never found Jim Tillek boring, especially when he started yarning. She knew that he had sailed every sea on Old Earth and some on the newer colony planets as well in between his interstellar voyages as the captain of a drone freighter. Over the past few days she'd had a chance to admire the qualities of a man she'd barely chatted with before – mainly because a ship's captain and a dolphineer didn't come into contact that much, especially with Tillek taking the *Cross* on so many exploratory voyages. As Peri Cervantes, the apprentice seaman of his crew, was also dolphineer trained, Peri had done what contact was necessary with the pods Jim and the *Cross* had encountered on their journeys. But she liked listening to Jim Tillek and, though she kept as watchful an eye on their convoy as he did, she paid attention to his yarning.

'Half an army was pinned down on a beach, strafed by enemy aircraft, and likely all would have been killed there if the small craft skippers of that era hadn't saved 'em. Dunkirk, that was the name of the beach they were trapped on, with safety across a channel a mere thirty-four kilometres away.'

'Thirty-four klicks?' Theo said in surprise, the dark thick arcs of her eyebrows rising. 'Anyone could swim that.'

Jim grinned at her. 'Some *athletes* did, sort of a rite of passage trail for the helluvit, but not 300,000 troops in full battle gear. And,' he waggled his finger at her, 'no dolphins.'

'But dolphins have been around for yonks . . .'

'Not as we know them, Theo. Let's see, where was I?'

Theo scrunched down on the cockpit seat, grinning to be so subtly reprimanded. His face had a lot of sun wrinkles, which made him look older, but his body in the tank top and shorts was lean, fit and tanned. As usual on board, his feet were bare, his toes long and prehensile. Once or twice, she'd seen him hold a line tight with just his toes.

'Ah, yes, the Germanics had 300,000 British troops pinned down on the sands of Dunkirk which was on the European continent and, since the Brits had no wish to spend the rest of their lives in a prisoner of war camp, they needed to be evacuated across the channel to their homeland, England.'

'How'd they get across the channel in the first place?'

Jim shrugged. He had broad, bony shoulders, and only a sprinkling of hair on his chest – not a full pelt front and back which she didn't much like. 'Troopships convoyed 'em over when the hostilities broke out but those ports were already in the hands of the Germanics. One crucial problem with Dunkirk was that the beach was very shallow for a good distance before it shelved off into deep water. No proper docking or wharfs for the big draught ships to tie up at. Only a long wooden pier which the Germanics strafed with their war planes. Men were so desperate that they waded out, swimming the last part to climb up nets put down the sides of the ships to help 'em board. Then, someone had the bright idea of getting all available craft from the island, especially pleasure craft with low draughts so they could sail further in to the beach to pick up troops. Records have it that even sailing dinghies, no more than three metres long, made the passage successfully. And not just once but time and again until the crews succumbed to exhaustion. But the 300,000 men were all evacuated. Quite a feat of seamanship and courage.'

'It's no thirty-four klicks of a channel we have to navigate, Jim Tillek, but the coastline of half a world,' Theo said with some acerbity.

'Yes, but we don't have a war going on around us,' Jim said cheerfully.

'We don't?' Theo asked and gestured over her shoulder to the east, signifying the menace of Thread.

'You've got a point there,' Jim had to admit. 'Though it's not a people-shooting war. But I believe in starting every journey with a high heart and in good spirits and would you ever send Dart after that fool sloop with the spotted sail? Where do they think they're going? They're to tack right back into position.'

He finished his remarks to empty air for Theo had dived as neatly as her dolphin could over the safety rail and into the water to be joined by Dart who then towed her partner swiftly towards the miscreant.

It was amazing what heights the human spirit could rise to, Jim thought as he did a visual check through his binoculars. Theo and Dart reached their destination and he could almost hear the blistering reprimand she was issuing. She had her arms over the rim of the craft, gesticulating to leave no doubt in the young skipper's mind where he had erred. He watched as she trod water, one hand lightly on the dolphin's melon, while the little craft tacked back in line. When he saw her begin to swim back towards the *Cross*, Dart skipping along side her, he put the binoculars down.

Squinting to the fore of the flotilla, he could see the pennon on the mast of the five-metre yawl which had been put at Ezra Keroon's disposal as convoy leader. Ezra hadn't much actual sea experience but he was a superb navigator through any medium. Jim had himself done the sea charts on this coastline and knew the waters intimately. There were no reefs or unexpected dangers to cause problems for the inexperienced. As long as no ship ventured too far out so that the Great Eastern Current caught them, sea hazards were minimal. Once they got to Key Largo, there wouldn't be one of them who wouldn't be seasoned enough by then for the open water run across both of the Great Currents to the safety of Fort.

The coast beyond Sadrid to Boca was not that well known to him but he counted on the fishermen at Malay and Sadrid, and Ju Adjai Benden at Boca to know the local problems. The sailors at Key Largo Hold had also done a fair bit of charting in their coastal waters. He wished now that he'd done more of that, but he'd spent more time checking the eastern abysses and the island reef systems. Barring the weather, they should make it, no matter how slowly.

And the weather – he leaned forward to tap the barometer – could be an acute problem. Volcanic eruptions played havoc with weather conditions, messing up the upper reaches of the atmosphere. There'd already been some freak winds, squalls and higher than normal tides but Kahrain cove had sheltered them from the worst. They'd probably arrive in the north just in time for the ash fall-out that was already beginning to filter into the upper air currents to be pushed around the planet. He wondered if the volcanic fall-out would have any effect on Threadfall. If one had to find some good out of bad, that would be the option he'd pick – if he had one.

Two hours later he had to give the orders to land the small craft and for the bigger ships to hove to and anchor in a cove. Winds were picking up, erratic in direction, therefore dangerous to novice sailors, and so full of ash and grit as to make visibility poor.

If he and Ezra were disappointed by the progress they had made that first day out of Kahrain cove, they sloughed off queries with any number of logical explanations. No reason to deflate the good morale of the expedition. The early day did give them a chance to check all the cargoes and whatever size or shape hull contained them. Most of the forty pleasure boats were constructed of fibreglass with plastic masts and booms so decks and hulls were Threadproof. Canvas sails, some varieties of sheets and line were not.

However, they did have Andi Gomez and Ika Kashima, two of the colony's plastics experts among the passengers. Andi and Ika had spent their first day afloat designing rigid plastic sail covers that were Threadproof.

'I know the specs on that, Jim, like I know the lines on my

46

hands,' Andi had said, her long blond hair braided down her back. She was a tallish, well-built woman, the physical opposite of her work partner, the almost childlike and beautiful Eurasian. They still had to solve the problem of how to protect the people on the smaller craft which did not always have enclosed cabin space in which to take shelter. There were also not sufficient breathers for people to just dive under their hulls and remain there during Threadfall.

So this early evening, Ezra and Jim had more conferences on that problem while all around them, at campfires, the ill-assorted sailors of their convoy cooked the fish they had caught during the day. But it had been a very busy day and, by nightfall, there were very few who hadn't rolled up early in their sleeping bags.

An oily, ashy drizzle and light winds made the next day's sailing longer and certainly dirtier. But they did pull in to Paradise River's wide mouth to anchor before darkness fell.

Jim and Ezra called a meeting, having first discussed with Desi Arthied, the cargomaster of the expedition, the possi-bility of splitting the flotilla into several sections to make better progress. The larger ships were constantly having to reef canvas, even to drag sea anchors, so as not to outdistance the smaller ones. Of course, the cargoes that were destined to be stored here at Paradise River would be off-loaded and the remainder more evenly distributed. (The rafts were precari-ous vessels, at best, and were to be entirely abandoned, having served their purpose.) The dolphineers were grateful, for their teams had bravely tried to keep their assigned positions in the convoy and the strain was showing in galls and swollen flesh.

But the decision was made that, as soon as the unloading was done, Ezra would lead the larger craft forward at whatever speed they and two pods of escort dolphins could maintain while Jim followed with the slower, smaller vessels, and the large number of dolphin escorts. The smallest of the sailing dinghies would be dismantled or towed.

The bad weather persisted and the seas became too rough for all but the most experienced sailors, so the Paradise River continued to host them.

On the plus side, Andi Gomez and Ika Kashima used the layover to complete the manufacture of sail covers, and doors that could cover open cabin fronts. And Ika came up with an ethnic solution to the problem of protecting the nearly five hundred members of the flotilla from Threadfall. Plastic headgear, in a wide conical shape, made with wide weals and outward sloping sides – wide enough to cover most shoulders – with high crown, to fit on the head, tied under the chin. Once in the water, buoyed by the compulsory life-vests everyone wore, these cone 'coolie hats' would deflect Thread into the water where it was drowned or was consumed by fish which invariably arrived wherever Thread fell into the seas. The dolphins were known to partake of what they considered an unusual food.

The Paradise River contingent thought Ika's cone hat a definite improvement on the sheets of metal they'd use for protection if they were caught out in Fall. The slender Eurasian had been overcome by praise for a design which she said was by no means original to her.

'Well, it's a bloody good adaptation of a – what did you call it – coolie hat,' Andi said stoutly, 'and it'll work. Won't be too hard to turn out once we set the matrix for the design.' And she turned back to that task.

'We're lucky we have people of such differing back-grounds,' Jim told Ika kindly when she seemed to him uncomfortable with the success of her suggestion. 'You never can tell when something as simple as straw hats from rice paddies on Earth can turn out to be life-saving on Pern. Good thinking, Ika! Cheer up, child. You've just saved our lives!'

She managed to send him a shy smile before she retreated once again to the safety of Andi's company. But her husband, Ebon Kashima, strutted about the camp as if he had thought of the gear.

'The next problem will be getting our brave sailors to overcome fear of being *out* in Threadfall, and having it bang down on their heads,' Ezra said a little grimly, 'no matter how clever the hat they're wearing.'

'Look, Cap'n,' said Wade Lorenzo, who had fished off Sadrid, 'when push comes to shove and Thread starts falling on you and water's the only safe place, they'll jump in. I sure as hell did that time we got caught out in one of the first Falls. 'Sides, there're an awful lot of fire-lizards flitting about. Between them and the wild ones that congregate whenever there's Fall, I doubt much Thread'll hit any hat.'

'A little practical psychology,' Jim said, 'and us as good examples, and they'll take to it. They'll have little alternative.'

'There's that, too,' Ezra said bleakly.

'We'll start some proper chatter where it seems needed,' Ben said, nodding to the other dolphineers. They wandered off to start their brain-washing.

By the time coolie hats were extruded and ready to be passed around, most of the flotilla was willing to accept the measure.

'I'd rather be in a sled with a flame-thrower,' one of the barge mates confided to a friend within Jim's hearing.

'Yeah, but the barge has that slant fore and aft. All we gotta do is hide under that and we'll be safe enough.'

Jim and Ezra issued an order that anyone caught without life-vest and coolie would be subjected to severe discipline and demotion if they held any rank. They also ordered everyone to work a two-hour shift helping Andi, Ika and Ebon produce the protective gear.

As it happened, all the stores were housed, and accounted for by Desi and his helpers and nearly two thirds of the necessary Thread shields completed before the weather cleared, so both sections at least set off again together. But the bigger ships, with more sail, made the most of the following wind and soon outdistanced the slower craft.

'More like the boat people,' Jim remarked to Theo as he tacked back down the strung-out line of his charges.

'Boat people?'

'Hmmm, yes. War victims in the twentieth century. They tried to leave their country – Asians they were – in the most incredibly unseaworthy craft. Junks and sampans, they were called.' He shook his head. 'Totally unsuitable. Many died trying to escape. Many arrived at their destinations only to be turned back.'

'Turned back?' Theo was outraged.

'I don't remember the historical-political situation at the time. It was before Earth was really united by outward-bound goals. I don't think a single one of their craft was as good as the worst of these.'

Theo let out a sigh, pointed to starboard where one of the four-metre sloops was flying a distress flag, and dived overboard, surfacing to find Dart beside her. She was towed off to the crippled ship. Jim entered the matter in his recorder. Broken sheet, he thought, seeing the way the boom swung. Lordee, would they have enough line to see them through the constant breakages. He'd better hold another splicing lesson tonight.

'Ah, it was the Heyerdahl expeditions I was trying to remember,' he told himself, 'only he was doing it deliberately in primitive craft he'd built himself. Not the same thing as this at all.' He must remember to tell Theo. He grinned. He enjoyed yarning at her because she really listened. Occasionally, she responded with some stories of her days as a pilot. He rather thought she preferred being a dolphineer, or maybe she was just the sort of person who would make the most of what they had.

Too bad, he added, this feat will only be known to us Pernese. Our Second Crossing: in many ways far more remarkable than the journey here. On balance, though, he admitted candidly, thirty-four kilometres in open boats with enemies shooting at you was more impressive than this slow steady progress even if their journey was far longer.

They had two more emergencies that day – a slight brush with the following edge of Threadfall. Ezra spotted the now familiar greyness ahead. They'd made better time than expected and it became a choice of hoving to or giving their emergency gear a trial run. Jim and Ezra conferred with those ships that were on the flotilla comlink and it was unanimously decided to continue, and see just how effective the safety gear was. Better now, when they knew they'd only have to endure a half hour or more of Fall, rather than a longer period.

So the dolphins and dolphineers spread the command. Sails

50

were furled and shields put in place, fire-lizards sent off to collect enough wild ones to help, and the light sea suddenly blossomed with plastic cones.

Jim, his crew of five and the four dolphineers, though they could have weathered the Edge in the cabin, decided to provide a good example to the timorous. Donning their head protectors and grabbing plastic safety lines, they jumped into the water. That helped a few of the fearful to follow suit. The four dolphins would make rushes out to blow and squee-ee.

'Much good eating soon,' Dart informed them once.

'Don't overeat, you glutton,' Theo told her warningly. 'She likes 'em when they're bloated with water.'

Jim could not suppress a shudder which no-one could see since his coolie hat touched the water and obscured his face. Once he tipped the hat up so he could see but Theo tugged it back down.

'You'd lose your looks with a Threadscore across that prominent nose of yours,' she said, her words muffled under her own hat.

Jim felt his nose which he had never considered as particularly prominent.

'All there is to see is coolie hats and Thread.'

'How d'you know?'

'I've already had a look. Thread bores me on the ground. It was much more fun flying sleds through it.' Waves rippled out from her as if she had shrugged.

'Which do you prefer? I mean, profession – pilot or dolphineer?'

'I've done enough flying, though Threadfall was more exciting than the routine stuff I did,' she told him in a thoughtful voice as her body drifted towards his in the water. Their legs touched, his were much longer than hers, he noted absently in the clear water around them. They had drifted slightly away from the others, having let their safety lines play out to the full length. 'Dolphineering's something else again. Dart's super,' and Jim could hear the pride and the depth of her friendship for her sea partner. 'Sure beats the hell out of the one-sided arrangement you could have with domestic animals. Though I used to be right fond of an old moggie I

51

had once on ol' Earth. But teaming with Dart's totally superior to that sort of thing.'

'Did you try for a dragon?'

'No. You got asked to stand in that circle,' and Theo snorted. 'They wanted younger riders. Like I said, I've done enough flying.'

'You're not old . . .'

Theo's laugh was genuine amusement. 'Maybe not from where you swim, granddad,' she said but he took no offence from her teasing. He was after all in his sixth decade, twice her age, and should have been a grandfather . . . if he hadn't chosen a profession that would have denied him most of the pleasures of marriage and children. A month's home leave after sixteen or seventeen months in space wasn't enough time for a wife or kids. He'd never tried for any more than casual relationships.

As an emergency, Jim thought that Fall was rather a let-down but then he'd spent it safely in the water, and agreeably in Theo's company. Once or twice he had felt Thread plunk on the crown of his coolie hat and had inadvertently flinched but the stuff had slid off the slick plastic and hissed into the sea. He'd swung his legs out of danger as the Thread continued down into the water deep enough to be swallowed by Dart or Peri's Pha or some of the schools of fish who flitted about to feast on the manna. Hunger made them fearless and Jim felt the caress of scales now and then on his bare skin: startling the first time and producing a knowing laugh from Theo who was completely accustomed to such contact. The result was that he felt as protected by the sea as by the man-made artefacts. And the fire-lizards. Theo had told him to look up through the semi-transparency of the cone's flange to see the first of the fire-lizards flaming around and above them, deflecting Thread from the deck of the *Cross*. Since the deck was made of teak wood he had imported as part of his allowable weight as *Buenos Aires*'s captain, he was particularly happy to see it protected from Threadscore.

Then, almost too soon, the loud chuffings, squee-ee-ings and ecstatic breechings of dolphins told him the danger had passed.

52

'We'll do a quick tour,' Theo told him, holding out her hand in the water for Dart to supply a dorsal fin and the tow. 'Peri, you go to port, I'll go starboard.'

'Lemme know if there's been any scoring, especially any damage to the ships,' he called after them. So many of the smaller craft did not even have handsets but, with the dolphineers so swift to respond to emergency signals, that had not yet posed a problem.

Thinking on how well they had survived this recurrent menace, Jim hauled himself back on board, stowed his hat within easy reach, dried off and ordered the sail to be hoisted again.

'The enemy has been met and . . . consumed,' he muttered, grinning to himself at his paraphrases as he unlashed the helm that had been on a course diagonally away from the main Thread rain. But, oddly, he felt the better for that short brush and Theo's company. She was a sort of . . . comfortable person. He grinned again. That was not the sort of compliment a woman would appreciate.

The second emergency was more life-threatening – a burst plank below the water-line nearly sank a six-metre ketch, save for the quick action of the dolphins who all but swam it to shore on their own backs. As the cargo of the ketch was mainly irreplaceable orange-coded supplies, its timely rescue was a double blessing.

They anchored early that day so that they could not only find a replacement plank from those that Andi Gomez had extruded during the layover at Paradise River but also check sails and lines for Threadscore. No human had received injury and even those who had doubted the efficacy of 'coolies' against Thread had been reassured by the experience.

Though the ketch crew worked all night with the plastics experts, the flotilla did not make sail until noontime. A good wind helped make up lost time and certainly relieved Jim's frustrations. He missed Theo's company in the cockpit but she had this first watch off and was sleeping. It was a shame she was missing the best part of this fine day. Nothing, but nothing on any world, could be a more stimulating and satisfying occupation than sailing a good ship, in a brisk wind, down sparkling clear blue-green coastal waters. He wondered if Theo could appreciate that, too.

At Malay River Stake, they had to take time for major repairs to sail, sheet and hulls, rearrange cargoes again – to Desi's dismay. Crews put up with his fussing, and checked and double-checked the bar coding until all records were to his satisfaction.

The tropical storm, brewing up suddenly as they neared Boca, drove them back towards Sadrid.

Jim's nautical instinct had been warning him since early morning as they sailed westward on the gentle swells. Wade Lorenzo had reminded him only the night before of the suddenness of squalls on this stretch of coast. So he was watching for those little signs the experienced sailor knows: a smudge on the horizon that wasn't Thread, the sudden drop of the barometer, a change in the colour of the water, a sultry feeling of pressure in the air around him. He just had time to notice the alternation from blue-green to greyish green and the rippling change of the wave patterns.

'Theo,' he began as she was once more his cockpit companion, 'I think . . .'

The storm struck with a ferocity and suddenness he had rarely encountered on any previous seas. He had the impression of black suit and bare legs going over the side into the suddenly heavy sea as he tightened his hold on the helm. He didn't even have time to get the bow turned into the huge comber bearing down on them but the *Cross* had answered so that she wasn't hit broadside with four- and five-metre waves. His crew struggled to bring the sails down, reefing them even though they were all but washed off the deck – only the life-rails preventing their going overboard. As it was, young Steve Duff, struggling to tie down the boom, barely missed the lightning that flashed across the ship, slicing through the mast two thirds of the way up its length, snapping the mainstays into lethal lashes until they fell over the Monel life-rail. With the help of Peri Cervantes, Jim managed to keep the bow turned into the towering seas as once again the *Cross* thudded into a trough left by the latest monumental wave. What was happening to the more vulnerable small craft of his fleet drove terror into Jim's heart until the more immediate threat to the lives of himself and his crew banished all thought but survival.

Now and then, during the brief but thoroughly devastating squall, he caught sight of dolphins, hurtling through the air across a seething watery surface, purpose in every line of the sleek bodies. Sometimes their partners clung to the dorsal fins, other times the dolphins seemed to be acting independently, but certainly acting in accordance with their training.

Twice the *Cross*'s crew threw lines and hauled people rescued by the dolphins out of the water to the dubious safety of the plunging deck. Once they overran the upturned hull of a capsized ship, feeling the grind as their keel sliced across plastic hull.

As abruptly as it began, the storm vanished in the distance, a rolling dark vortex pierced by bolts of lightning.

Exhausted and somewhat amazed to be alive, Jim was suddenly aware that his right arm was broken and he was bleeding from a variety of cuts on both arms, chest and bare legs from wind-flung debris. None of his crew was totally unscathed. One rescued girl had a broken leg and a boy was concussed, his face badly contused and a long wound giving his hair a new parting. In the sea, still heavy from the agitation of the squall, survivors clung to spars, half-sunk hulks or pallets in an expanse of destruction that nearly reduced Jim to tears.

Ignoring his own wounds and his crew's urgings to attend to them, Jim scrabbled for the bull horn in the cockpit and released it from its brackets. He had Peri start up engines rarely used in order to conserve fuel. Ranging up and down wherever they saw flotsam, he shouted encouragements and orders, directing dolphineer rescues even as he wondered if all under his command could still be alive. And what cargo could be salvaged.

'It came up out of nowhere, Ongola,' Jim reported in an almost lifeless voice when Fort com answered his Mayday. By then they'd managed to get a lot of the shipwrecked to the sandy beach. The dolphin teams were still searching the wreckage but he needed help as soon as possible. He gazed with eyes that dared not focus too long on the human jetsam and the wreckage flung up on the long narrow strand that was the nearest landfall. His *Southern Cross*, five of the larger yawls and ketches and two small sloops had ridden out the storm. 'Wade warned me about the way squalls brew up in this area so I was on guard. Not that it did me any good. It hit out of nowhere. A change of the wave colour and pattern and then, bang! We'd no time to do anything except hope we'd survive. Some never had enough time to lower sail and steer into the wind. If it hadn't been for the dolphins, Zi, we'd've lost people, too.' That might not be Joel Lilienkamp's first concern but it certainly would be Paul Benden's as it was Jim Tillek's.

'Casualties?'

'Yeah, too many,' Jim said, absently smoothing the gelicast that bound his broken arm. He'd no recollection of breaking it. Only one of his cuts had needed stapling and Theo had done that, as well as apply the gelicast. Neither of them thought it was a compound fracture. Then he'd applied the sealant to the scratches on Theo's bare legs and arms, earned while she tried to squeeze into wrecked cabins to aid survivors. They'd separated, first aid kits in hand, to attend the needs of others to the best of their abilities.

Corazon Cervantes, who had accompanied this section as medic, diagnosed twelve with internal injuries and multiple fractures that the limited medical supplies she had couldn't handle. She had two coronary patients on the only life-support units that could be found in the *Cross*'s cargo. There were more but they couldn't find the right cargo without a lot of shifting which they didn't have the time to do.

'Can you send a sled for the worst injuries, Zi?'

'Of course. One's already being loaded with medics and supplies and will fly out to you in the next sixty seconds. Give me your approximate location again?'

'Somewhat east of Boca but west of Sadrid,' Jim said wearily. 'You can't miss us. The sea's filled with flotsam and overturned hulls. Has Kaarvan made port?'

'Yesterday.'

'The *Venturer* would be mighty useful to carry salvaged cargo back to Fort as well as the extra folk who no longer have a ship to sail.'

'What's Ezra's condition?'

'I haven't tried reaching him yet, Zi. He's a few days ahead of us and probably missed the storm or you'd've heard from him by now. There's really no point in sending him back: every one of his ships was loaded to the Plimsoll line. His group'll do better finishing their journey.'

Cyra Holstrom stopped beside him and handed him a mug of hot klah, which he put on the crate he was leaning against, and a twig-pierced fried fish from the tray she carried. She gave him a nod and moved on to the next person on the beach. Somehow she and her husband had managed to beach their seven-metre sloop, cargo intact, but mast and sail gone.

'And the *Cross*, Jim?' Ongola asked in genuine concern.

'Battered but afloat,' Jim said. The mast would have to be replaced, and the mainstays, but he still had all his canvas. Andi had already vowed that his new mast would be the first she'd make: she'd be making many if they were to sail any ships out of here. 'Which reminds me: we got some lightning burn cases, too. Three of the barges sunk completely but the dolphins are busy resurrecting cargo. Right now, the injured are my first priority.'

'As they should be. Ah, yes,' and Ongola broke off for a moment, 'Joel urgently needs to know if you can estimate how much and what cargo is irretrievable.' Jim caught an indefinable note of regret in Ongola's voice that indicated he felt such a question was importunate. It was, however, totally in character for Lilienkamp and Jim was too weary to summon much rancour.

'Hell, Zi, I haven't completed a head count! Desi Arthied's got broken ribs, had to be resuscitated, and Corrie says he probably had a coronary. But do reassure Joel that Desi's manifest recorder was tucked inside his life-vest next to his heart. That ought to cheer him up.' Jim couldn't keep the sarcasm out of his voice. 'I gotta go.'

'Help is on its way, Jim. My sympathics. I'll report immediately to Paul. Is there someone you can keep on the com?'

Bleary-eyed, Jim looked about him. The able-bodied were tending the injured but he spotted Eba Dar propped up against a fallen tree, his emergency splinted leg sticking out in front of him. He was chewing the last of the fish from its twig.

'Eba? You well enough to keep the line open to Fort?' Jim asked, peering into the man's lacerated face and eyes for signs of concussion. Eba's naturally sallow skin did not show pallor and the cuts on his shoulders and chest were already sealed.

'Sure. Nothing wrong with my mouth and my wits,' Eba said with a droll grin and, tossing the empty twig, reached for the unit. 'Who's on the other end?'

'At the moment, Zi Ongola. They're sending a big sled for the serious casualties and Kaarvan'll sail the *Venturer* down to pick up whatever cargo we can save.'

Eba looked out at a sea once again calm where oddments could be seen bobbing to the surface or floating in on the tide. Soon enough, Jim knew, the shallow beach would be littered and he'd better find enough people to haul the jetsam safely above the high-water mark. Shielding his eyes with his good hand, he peered seaward where dolphin fins cut from one upturned hull to another, their human partners hanging on to the dorsals, still searching for survivors.

'Damn her,' he said under his breath as he recognized Dart's smaller, distinctively marked body and Theo towed alongside. Small satisfaction that the sealant on those scrapes of hers should be stinging like hell. Was she mad, driving herself in that condition?

'Dolphins're doing great, aren't they?' Eba remarked. 'Wonder if we'd've all been safer *in* the water with them.'

'The dolphins were OK, but not all their partners,' Jim replied. 'Besides, you farmer types couldn't hold your breath long enough, the way dolphins can.' He gave Eba's shoulder a squeeze and limped off to see if, this time, he'd come up with a more accurate body count. Five people were still unaccounted for, three of them kids. He told himself that everyone had been wearing life-vests which had, indeed, saved lives.

Eba'd been not far from wrong about being safer with the dolphins. Equipped with breathers and able to dive with their

58

partners beneath the towering waves to escape the pummel-
ling, the dolphineers had been lucky – at least during the
squall. All of them, to one degree or another, had scrapes
from underwater hazards and being tumbled against the
sandy or rocky abrasiveness of the ocean floor. Now they
risked themselves time and again to rescue unconscious or
injured folk. Even before the storm ended, teams had
followed sinking ships down to save those trapped on board.
Many people owed their lives to the quick action of the
dolphin swimmers who had, in some instances, torn off their
breathers to give life-saving oxygen to the drowning.

It was also during those first few hectic hours after the
storm had passed that dolphineers received more serious
injuries, broken bones and wounds. Pha had gone so far as to
beach himself to get Gunnar medical attention for a deep
wound in his thigh, sustained when he'd pushed his way into a
cabin to free a trapped child. Efram, Ben and Bernard had to
be called in to haul Pha by the tail back into the sea, Pha
squee-eee-ing and complaining that they'd do him masculine
damage.

By the time the big sled from Fort arrived, Jim knew that,
by some incredible miracle, there had been no loss of life. The
five missing folk walked in from further down the beach
where their ketch had been stranded: one of the teenage girls
had a broken arm, the other a dislocated shoulder to which
the newly arrived medics instantly attended. They made the
walking wounded sit and sip at restorative 'cocktails' that had
been mixed and brought along.

Some injuries were still life-threatening – two heart attacks
and three strokes from exposure and exhaustion – but no-one,
Basil Tomlinson announced, who wouldn't respond to treat-
ment and therapy, even those who had had to be resuscitated.

Of the ships sunk, the dolphins had been able to locate all
of them and buoys now marked their positions. Most could be
raised, but the three small ships thrown up on the beach by
the heavy seas were too badly damaged to be worth repair.
The barges, unwieldy craft at best, had sunk so quickly that
they hadn't been battered by the high waves. Efram with
Kibby, Jan with Teresa, and Ben with Amadeus reported that

59

the cargoes were still lashed in place, though the barges had been full of low-priority freight, safe enough where it was for now.

As to cargo, no-one paid much attention to what they grabbed and hauled into piles well above the high-tide mark: it was enough to keep the jetsam on the beach, too much to identify what was what. Jim was calling for more people to help with the salvage when he noticed three of the medics walking towards him where he leaned wearily against a waterlogged and battered crate.

'Look, Paul, I'm damned sorry to add this to your problems,' Jim said wearily into the comunit.

'It's not one I expected, certainly,' Paul replied in the oddest voice. Jim heard the defeated tone and responded by couching his report in the most optimistic manner he could muster. He rubbed at his face, stiff from brine. 'Actually, Paul, the way the stuff is floating in on the tide, I wouldn't be at all surprised if we salvage most of it. Some's too waterlogged to estimate any damage but generally the packaging held. As to the ships, Andi's already figuring out repair lists . . .'

'No jury rigs, dammit, Jim. You've leagues to go yet to reach Key Largo, and Kaarvan told me it's no picnic crossing the two Currents.'

'I have no intention of setting sail again until all craft are seaworthy, shipshape and Bristol fashion as they used to say.' Jim spoke with all the conviction he could manage, adding that old seaman's tag to show he was in good spirits.

He was aware of shadows lengthening, covering the light from the westering sun. He turned slightly away from them, not wanting his conversation overheard. 'Hell, by that time, all the cargo will have dried out, too. Only a little of the cocooned stuff got torn open. Tomorrow we'll have dolphin teams start hauling up what was too heavy to surface on its own. You wouldn't believe what those critters can manage. I'll report in again later, Paul. Don't worry about us. Sled brought us all the help we needed.'

As he closed the comunit, someone cleared a throat and, surprised, Jim looked up to see Corazon Cervantes, Beth

Eagles and Basil Tomlinson regarding him with an odd sort of amusement.

'He's still on his feet,' Corazon remarked to the others.

Seeing how tired she looked made Jim aware of his own weariness.

'Only because he's leaning on that crate,' Beth said in her pragmatic way. She looked tired, too.

'Old sailors never die, they just fade away,' Basil said in a pontificating voice. 'No matter, Theo was right,' he added, pointing. 'He's ricked the gelicast around and split the staples. What's your opinion, doctors?'

'Repair, then bed rest,' Beth said and before Jim could protest, she pressed a hypo-spray against his arm. As his legs folded and his vision darkened, he heard her add, 'You know I don't think he realizes when it's time to take a break.'

The smell of roasting food roused him but his body was unwilling to respond to the initial commands he gave to leave the horizontal position. He was on his back, under a canopy of woven fronds, which was certainly rustically unusual. Under him, however, was an air mattress and a light cover kept the cool of the shade from chilling him. He made a slight error in judgement by rolling on to his right side, preparatory to rising. The sudden weight on a heavy and awkwardly covered right arm was painful enough to force a groan from his lips.

'Ah, you're awake, too, are you?' a voice said from his left.

He twisted about to see Theo lying beside him. She gave him a cocky grin.

'You sicced that unholy trio on me,' he accused, not appreciating that justice had similarly immobilized her.

'Dart informed on *me*,' she said with a shrug. 'So I figured I'd at least see I had decent company in my ward.' In gesturing to their surroundings, she displayed a right arm, marred by four heavily stapled and sealed spiral gashes that appeared to have been deep.

He reached over and took her hand, gently lowering her arm to her side. 'How'd you get those?'

She glanced in thoughtful surprise at her arm. 'I don't

61

rightly remember. I think we were checking out that five-metre ketch Bruce Olivine sailed. Dart was trying to poke her nose into the for'ard hatch when the whole ship shifted and something snagged me by the arm.'

'How're your legs?'

She kicked one free of the light cover. It, too, glistened with sealant. Dispassionately, she regarded the raw scratched flesh that ran from the top of her thigh to her ankle. The inside of her leg was only bruised. 'I used to be better *able* to squeeze through tight places. Should've been OK if I'd had on a full wet suit. It's only to regrow the skin I lost. But I gather we will spend some time here at our pleasant seaside resort.'

'Who's taking charge then?'

'The medics,' she said with a rude laugh. 'Hey, someone,' and she lifted her voice. 'We're hungry in here.'

'Coming,' a cheerful voice answered.

Jim groaned again as he levered himself up.

'Hey, they *are* coming,' Theo said in alarm. She even sat up as he headed towards the thick shrubbery behind their temporary accommodation. 'Oh! Always did think you guys had the best of the deal in circumstances like this.'

That short but critically necessary excursion proved to Jim Tillek that he had less strength than the fronds bowing to the light wind. It was going to take more time than he had to spare to recover from yesterday's excursions.

'Yesterday's?' Theo laughed lustily, making him aware that he had spoken outloud. 'Jim, m'lad, you've been out for the full thirty-six. Today's the day *after* yesterday.'

'My God, then who's . . . ?'

She grabbed his hand and gave one pull: sufficient to make his weak knees buckle. The air mattress cushioned his sudden descent but the jolt reminded him that he had other injuries as well as the broken arm. 'Paul sent another sled, with plenty of people to muscle the salvage and a team of Joel's apprentices to run bar codes through their recorders. Where there are bar code patches left, that is.'

Jim groaned just as the obscuring foliage was pushed aside and Betty Musgrave arrived with a laden tray which she set in the space between them.

'Hi, feel better, Jim? Theo?' she said with none of the forced cheerfulness that Jim would have found egregious.

'He's had a nice long sleep and a nice long . . .' Theo chuckled as Jim's half-growl cut off the rest of her sentence.

'Good, everyone'll be glad to hear that,' Betty said with genuine relief. 'And I won't have to ditch some of the urgent stuff Joel begged me to take to make room for him. Eat. You're lucky to get room service today.'

She settled back then on her heels and Jim got the impression that she wasn't going to move until they finished what she'd brought: klah, of course, and slices of fresh fruit, rolls that were still warm when he picked one up. That was enough to make him attack the meal ravenously and he mumbled gratitude.

'Yes, we've civilized your camp since you're likely to be here long enough to appreciate a few,' she paused, making a funny grimace, 'comforts.'

'What's happening at Fort?' Jim said, pinning Betty with a stern eye.

She raised her eyebrows and lifted her hands in a gesture that told him she didn't care to go into any great detail.

'There's good – we're safe in Fort. There's bad – we haven't enough power-packs left for sleds to mount any sort of defence against Fall.' She shrugged. 'So we'll sit tight. Safe enough in a cliff Thread can't penetrate.'

'Emily?'

Betty pulled mouth and head to one side and rocked a hand. No wonder Paul had sounded so defeated: he and Emily made a superb team, each supporting the other. Without her active participation, Paul Benden would have a great deal to cope with, even with Ongola's help.

'She's some better,' the pilot said, 'but it'll be a long convalescence. Pierre's taking real good care of her. Ongola's a rock as always and, if Joel would only stop yapping about losing so much cargo . . .'

'We haven't lost it . . .' Jim and Theo said in chorus.

Betty chuckled. 'If you two won't give up, I don't see that Paul should. And so I'll tell him.' She looked down at the wide digital on her arm and rose. 'I gotta go. Good to see you've got your appetites back.' And with a nod to each, she pushed back the foliage again.

'Leave it open, can you, Betty?' Jim asked because he'd caught a reassuring glimpse of the beach and the people moving about.

'I suppose so,' and she found a string that had been left for such a purpose and tied back the branch. 'Keep an eye on him, Theo.'

'Glad to,' Theo said with a deep chuckle.

'Oh, one last bit of news, Jim,' Betty said, 'Kaarvan sailed the *Venturer* out of Fort last night on the tide. He'll come straight down. Be here in a couple of days.'

Not long after, they both heard the swish of a powered sled rising and craned their necks out of their impromptu door to see the rear of the big airborne sledge as it flew north-west towards Fort. Jim was just gathering himself to rise when Beth Eagles appeared.

'You both should have been on that sled,' she said without preamble, staring down at them with an expressionless face. 'Unfortunately, Dart refuses to work with Anna Schultz,' she said to Theo who almost looked happy about such non-compliance, 'and Paul said that you'd probably crucify anyone else who tried to sail your precious *Cross* so we'd better get you well enough to captain her. Kaarvan's bringing more supplies and enough technicians so you can get this ridiculous fleet floating again.'

'It isn't ridiculous,' Jim said, leaning back and sighing with intense relief. He had had a very nasty moment when Betty Musgrave had brought his breakfast. She never shirked hard duty and he'd been sure she'd meant to include him in her passenger list.

'However,' and Beth knelt to run an instrument over his body, 'I think the sooner you're out on that boat . . .'

'Ship,' Jim corrected automatically.

'Ship, then, the more likely you are to rest.'

'But I have to . . .' And he waved at the activity he could plainly see.

'You have to rest, same as Theo here, or you won't be any good to any of us and Paul doesn't need anything else to worry him . . . like the recuperation of Captain James Tillek!' She turned her back on him to check Theo. 'And you're going out to the *Cross* with him so that little mammal of yours can see you. But Teresa, Kibby, Max and Pha have been told to make sure she won't let you in the water until you've got skin again. Hear me, Theo Force?'

'How could I avoid it?' There was a ripple of laughter – and something else which Jim couldn't identify, in the dolphineer's husky voice.

That evening they were carefully escorted – they refused to be carried though Theo walked stiff-legged and had turned very white under her tanned skin – to a dinghy, and were towed by Dart and Pha out to the *Southern Cross*. Efram and Cor te Poel caught each under the arms and lifted them aboard. Jim managed a dignified descent to his own cabin which he noticed had been set to rights after the storm had thrown his few possessions around. Theo had to be carried to her bunk, unable to bend her abraded knees to get down the short companionway.

'We're sleeping aboard,' Efram said, handing Jim a hand-unit, 'but if you've any problems, just give a shout.'

'Or call that Dart,' said Anna Schultz, poking her head around the door. She made a grimace but it wasn't ill-natured. 'She's on patrol around the ship. I just hope she doesn't keep Theo awake, banging her nose into the hull by her bunk.'

Both dolphineers had scrapes and bruises where their body suits hadn't adequately protected them but they didn't seem as worse for wear as Theo.

'I'm cook,' Anna went on, 'but I've orders not to wake you for breakfast so it'll be laid out in the wardroom whenever you do get up.'

When the *Venturer* arrived, she dropped anchor near the *Southern Cross* and Kaarvan rowed over to pay his respects to Jim Tillek who was trying to schedule repairs and set the next day's duty roster. Kaarvan stood in the doorway for a long look, ducked his head and, in one short step for such a big man, grunted as he saw what Jim was doing.

65

'As I heard it, you're supposed to be convalescing. You don't look even that fit.'

Jim laughed. 'Old sailors never die . . .'

'But they fade away, my friend,' and deftly, without offence, Kaarvan removed the notepad from the desk. 'This is my job for now.'

Since even the minor decisions he'd had to make to get halfway through the schedule had tired him, Jim threw up his hands and grinned cheerfully up at the swarthy skipper. It was only sensible to let Kaarvan take over. But each evening, the unsmiling Kaarvan came on board the *Cross* to report the day's achievements, how much the dolphin teams had retrieved from the seabed and discuss the next day's schedule of repair. Jim appreciated that in Kaarvan: he felt less a supernumerary and somewhat involved in the restoration of his 'command'.

During the day, he went topside to watch through his binoculars the temporary shipyard and, without any aids, the antics of the working dolphins. Since Theo said the sun and fresh sea air promoted healing, she somehow got herself on deck and stretched out on the cockpit, trailing a hand over the side for Dart to nudge from time to time. Theo had talked her into 'co-operating temporarily' with Anna.

The dolphins were tireless, finding netted materiel and pallets that had been rolled considerable distances away on the ocean floor by the tide; coming back to ask for harnesses to haul their finds back to the beach.

'They're wearing us out,' Efram told Jim one evening, so tired that raising his fork to his mouth was an effort.

'You all need some time off,' Anna said severely. 'Give us apprentices a chance to see how the dolphins do underwater salvage. They know. We should.'

Jim raised that point with Kaarvan that evening and he immediately gave all the regular dolphineers three days' shore leave. Not being affected by that order since she was a substitute swimmer, Anna continued to berth on the *Cross* when the others went ashore, but Jim took over the cooking and prided himself on being able to make a decent meal out of their limited supplies.

'How come you know how to cook so well?' Theo asked, having complimented him once again on the stuffed fish roll-ups he had served her. 'You were married?'

'Me? No, that's why I know how to cook.' He grinned at her.

He enjoyed those days, fishing for their dinner to supplement the provisions and fresh fruit which Dart brought them in her net. He also enjoyed Theo's undemanding company, especially after she asked him for the loan of his reader and the historical tape that mentioned the Dunkirk evacuation.

'I think we've sort of turned it all around, the flotilla being rescued by men and dolphins,' she said, 'but those troops must have experienced the same sense of amazed wonder that they survived!'

Jim grinned down at her, knowing exactly what she meant. In fact, he was beginning to half-wish their convalescence would last a long time. But he was getting stronger, able to do several laps around the *Cross* even though the gelicast arm was awkward. Beth remarked that he was putting a little flesh on his old bones and the break was knitting nicely. At Theo's insistence, she reinforced the sealants on her wounds and let her join Jim in their laps, Dart now squee-eee-ing joyfully to accompany her partner.

'Dart's better than the *Cross*,' Theo remarked one day after she had carefully and slowly climbed the rope-ladder. The rake wounds made her movements stiff on land: in the sea she regained some of her usual grace.

'How so?' Jim replied, surprised.

'Dart talks back,' Theo said with a grin as she gingerly arranged herself on the cockpit cushion.

'And you think my ship doesn't communicate with me?'

'Does she?'

'In her own fashion. Like right now,' he said, feeling the alteration of the waves under her. He leaned across and tapped the barometer. Just then the comunit buzzed.

'Squall's on its way, Jim,' Kaarvan said. 'Estimate it'll arrive in an hour, give or take five minutes. Need any help?'

Suddenly Dart breached the water, walking on her tail and

67

talking so agitatedly that Jim didn't understand her. Theo did.

'She *said*,' and Theo grinned, 'sea is changing and will get rough. Storm coming.'

'Now we know it's true,' and Jim grinned back. 'I'll just close the for'ard hatches. We are anchored properly to ride out a squall so that doesn't need to be altered.'

'Need any help?'

'No, you get below before we get any choppy water.'

Theo grimaced but swung her legs around and pushed herself up.

As he battened down the hatches and checked the other gear on deck, Jim saw that the beach dwellers were also taking precautions. Dolphin fins zipped about the area, landing partners. An unaccompanied group – and Jim thought it was Kibby leaping at the head of the pod – headed towards the storm to bring a report back to Kaarvan.

'I'd feel safer out there with Dart,' Theo said, scowling at him when he joined her in the wardroom. She had fixed some klah and laid out some food.

'You know, Eba Dar remarked on that.' Jim slid in to his usual seat at the end of the table.

'We were safer because we could just go deeper, to calmer water. I'd plenty of oxygen in my breather,' Theo said, sipping her klah. Her right arm was regaining flexibility but she still couldn't raise it all the way to her mouth. 'I knew you lot were having a helluva time topside but we kept watch below.'

Jim covered her right hand, soothing fingers that twitched impatiently. 'I know you did. The reason we'd no loss of life was you dolphineers!'

'That's our job,' she said with a cocky grin and a jerk of her head. She let her fingers lie still in his grasp.

Under them, the *Cross* responded to the sea's agitation. The comunit buzzed.

'Kaarvan here. Dolphins report it'll be short and sweet but a bit heavy. You ready for it?'

'As we'll ever be.' He switched off and turned to Theo, absently catching his cup of klah as it slid towards the raised edge of the table. 'Would you be more comfortable in a bunk? It might be rough on that healing skin of yours.'

She gave him an odd look and an odder smile. 'It might at that.'

She eased her way across the cushions to the end of the table. He joined her, slipping one hand under her elbow as the ship gave a convulsive rock. They could now hear the wind rising, the slap of lines against the mast and feel waves slamming into the starboard side of the *Cross*.

Her good hand balancing her against the increased pitching, Theo made her way to the forward cabin where the double bunk in the space under the bow allowed her just that much more space than the narrower singles. Jim followed, anxious that she didn't get thrown against the walls, banging arm or legs. He had his own right arm tucked against his body, his left held up in case he needed to balance himself.

Just as she reached the cabin, the *Cross* pitched again and she fell against him. Instinctively he grabbed and held her close, a life-time of experience helping him to balance them both against the erratic movement. She wrapped her left arm about his waist, hugging herself to him. He could feel her trembling and the smoothness of her skin against his; no-one wore more than basic clothing anyway. He tightened his arm, surprised by a number of conflicting and long-forgotten emotions.

'It won't be as bad a blow as the other one,' he said, thinking to reassure her. Though why Theo would need reassurance . . .

'I'm not scared, you iggerant old fool,' she said in a taut voice. Switching her left arm to around his neck, she hauled his head down to hers and kissed him so thoroughly that he lost his balance and they both tumbled into the cabin as the *Cross* took a part in this matter and pitched them forward. Nor would Theo let go of him even after they had fallen across one of the smaller bunks.

'Your legs? Your arm,' Jim began without lessening the pressure his right arm exerted in keeping them together. 'I'll hurt you . . .'

'There are ways, dammit, Jim Tillek, there are ways!'

Despite the rolling and pitching of the *Cross*, which

69

sometimes worked to their advantage, he discovered that indeed there were ways and very little hurting. In fact, Jim decided that the next hour could be termed therapeutic – among other adjectives which he had had no occasion to employ for too long a time.

'We're neither of us young,' Theo said when the *Southern Cross* lay calmly at anchor again, 'but you're definitely not beyond it, my friend.'

'No,' Jim said in a drawl, allowing surprise and pride to colour his reply, 'and glad to prove it. Especially with you!' And he kissed her tenderly.

The comunit began to buzz and, with a sigh of resignation, Jim rose to answer it.

'Dart approves of you, you know,' Theo called after him.

He let a chuckle answer that sally but he felt a little taller all the same. Dolphins were extraordinarily good readers of human characters and defects.

Beth Eagles gave Jim the go-ahead to undertake 'light' employment. 'And I mean "light", Jim Tillek, though you do look rested.'

'I am,' he said with no inflection and sought Kaarvan to see how he could lightly employ himself to advantage.

He knew enough of ship design and chandlery so that Kaarvan shared with him the supervision of the repairs. The squall had done little damage to the makeshift boatyard and released only a few more errant bundles which the dolphins brought close enough to be collected by Joel's apprentices.

Theo also complained that inactivity was driving her nuts so Beth allowed her to come ashore every day and help decipher waterlogged bar codes on the pile of 'mystery' cargo.

If Jim and Theo preferred to row back out to the *Cross* for their evenings, no-one seemed to regard that as odd, especially when Dart followed.

'Do they think Dart plays the duenna?' Jim asked slyly. When Theo looked puzzled, he explained the term and she laughed.

'Not her. You'll notice she doesn't swim between us,' she said with a sly grin.

Jim laughed because he hadn't. 'That's good because it'd be awful if she came between us,' he said, masking the apprehension he felt at even such a subtle mention of their relationship. He wanted the association to continue but wasn't sure how to broach the subject.

'You got the *Southern Cross*, I got Dart.'

'We also have each other?' Jim made the sentence not quite a query, certainly not a statement. He was suddenly rather more anxious than a man his age should be, or maybe that was why, to hear her reply.

'So we do,' she said in the most equable of tones, calmly gazing at the *Southern Cross* as they neared her.

Grinning with relief, Jim put his back into the last few pulls on his oars.

A happy event – the birthing of Carolina's calf – helped raise the morale of the fleet survivors, tediously repairing storm damage. Malawi and Italia had been her midwives and the three of them brought the new female close enough in to shore to be admired. The dolphin nurses and mother were shouting a name between their chuffs and other excited noises. Theo had to stay on the shore but Carolina's swimmer got far enough out to be able to identify what the dolphins were trying to communicate.

'Atlanta! Atlanta!' Bethann called, between strokes back to the shore. 'People don't believe me when I tell them my dolphin knows as much as they do about Old Earth.'

Everyone on the beach then began waving at the dolphins and chanting the name to show their approval.

'Most appropriate. I'm sort of surprised we haven't had one named that before,' Jim said as a grinning Bethann joined him and Theo. 'Did you help Carolina pick the name?'

The girl grinned, wringing out her long hair which she usually kept braided. 'Sort of. Carrie wanted to name her calf after something big and wet.' Jim let out a guffaw. 'Well, it's close enough to "Atlantic". I tried to tempt her with "a" ending states and countries and stuff because I couldn't think of any big lakes with "a" endings. Even the colonies don't have feminine lakes or oceans.'

71

'You made a good compromise,' Jim said with warm approval.

The next day, Ebon, Efram and Toby, assisted by Kibby, Oregon, and Dart swam the new mast out to the *Cross*. With much ceremony and a lot of hard work, it was properly stepped, new mainstays in place, the boom rehung and the patched canvas threaded on to the sheet and dutifully raised to flap in the light breeze.

In Jim's experience, *events* had a habit of occurring in 'threes'. The third one came from Paul Benden and his almost incoherent account of the reappearance of the seventeen dragons and their riders. Jim took the call at his makeshift beach office where he was figuring out how and what to load on the ships that would soon be ready to continue their westward journey.

'They just appeared in the skies above Fort, Jim,' Paul said, the astonishment and elation in his voice such a tonic that Jim changed the setting to wide range so that everyone near by heard his account. Soon everyone was alerted and crowded about to hear the news. 'The dragons were spouting flame, charring Thread, diving into tangles, disappearing, and reappearing. The riders of the queens were carrying flame-throwers they'd talked out of Peter Chernoff at Seminole. The males chewed firestone and belched flame until they ran out of stone – just about the time Thread got up into the Range where it can't hurt rock much.

'And then,' Paul went on with a ring in his voice, 'those devious young rogues landed and demanded numbweed and medical supplies for their dragons before they paid any attention to my orders to report to me on the double.'

Jim grinned as did many of those listening. The seaman thought of his ship first, his own safety second: the dolphineer of his mammalian partner, the rider his dragon. He exchanged a significant glance at Theo.

'That done, damned if young Sean Connell didn't march 'em smartly right up the entrance to the Hold. *Then* he had the impudence to introduce me to what he called "the dragonriders of Pern"!'

Jim laughed as he leaned towards the speaker unit. 'Well, that's what they are, aren't they, Paul?'

'Indeed! Now I'm sure we'll make it, Jim. I'm sure!'

'So are we all,' and Jim circled his hand to raise three cheers from the audience. 'Give them our compliments, too. Such news gives us new heart as well.'

He was surprised to see Theo wiping tears from her eyes and, later, when they lay beside each other in the double bunk, asked her why.

'Look, swimming with Dart is the best thing – well, almost the best thing,' and she grinned at him, 'that ever happened to me. But I think flying a fighting dragon would be a notch . . . well, maybe several notches above that, given the fact they're our equivalent of the battle of Dunkirk. So few against so much.'

All the work seemed to finish up at the same time, which Kaarvan said was the result of good planning and Jim was equally certain was due to the boost in morale. So they loaded the *Pernese Venturer* with the last of the more important items and distributed the remainder, unreadable bar codes notwithstanding, among the ships that were to sail west again.

At Key Largo, Jim conferred with Paul who had sent all four of the large ships, *Pernese Venturer, Mayflower, Maid* and *Perseus* to await their arrival at the jump-off point. It had become a matter of honour to the now well-seasoned skippers of the small craft in his flotilla to bring their ships into the new port. But few of them were capable of sailing across the two Great Currents without some assistance. And for that, the four ships with more powerful auxiliary engines would escort them. Jim had thought long and hard how to manoeuvre the flotilla past this hazard and was pleased when Kaarvan, Sejby, Veranera and even the overcautious Per Pagnesjo agreed with him. The plan was to sail in the quieter coastal water from Key Largo, beyond the point where the Eastern Current was at its closest to the Western one, then turn bravely into the Eastern Current and let it carry the vessels a good day's sail away from their final destination, slip across the current into the calm dividing waters. Then, using outboard engines and the big ships towing the ones that didn't have the speed or bulk to cross the Western Current, manoeuvre that hazard till they reached the safe waters at the end of the Boll peninsula. The coastal sail up to the Fort Harbour ought then to be routine.

They sent dolphins ahead for two days' sail-worth to check on incoming weather. Then, once assured of fair weather and decent wind, they experienced no heart-stopping moments on the Crossing and made the quieter northern coastal waters. Some powered ships even had a little fuel left. Dolphin teams had swum in constant escort in case of engine failure. Then it was plain sailing. Almost anti-climactic, Jim thought, as the *Southern Cross* slid majestically into the darker northern waters bound for her last port of call.

Not quite her last, Jim amended. While stopping at Key Largo, he and the other skippers had had a long talk about how to protect their ships during Threadfall.

'They built us a sort of boatshed under the wharf,' Kaarvan said, sketching the facility as he spoke. 'Masts have to be unstepped of course but that's neither here nor there. *Venturer* just fits with two other big ships or four of the smaller ones.'

'Those'd be enough to supply Fort with fresh fish when there're clear days,' Sejby said, scrubbing at the bristle on his chin and gazing thoughtfully at Jim.

Jim caught the unspoken words. Lifting his gelicast arm, he managed a grin. 'Well, this'll keep me out of action for a while.'

'There's good news, too, Jim,' Veranera said quickly. 'Ozzie mentioned a big sea cavern on the eastern end of the Big Island, the one Avril mined in. He said it was large enough to sail into. Deep water even at low tide, and the roof tall enough so the masts needn't be unstepped. We sort of figured we could take it turn and turn about. Keep at least one or two of the big ships on duty and store the others in the cavern.'

Jim hauled the chart of that area to him. The site of the cavern had been marked.

74

'You're sure it's deep enough? There's no depth marked . . .'

'Ozzie was sure and if he's sure, you can be,' Sejby said.

'I've no objections. In fact, for me and the *Southern Cross*, it makes a lot of sense. Be a nice easy sail.'

'After what you just did, it would indeed,' Per Pagnesjo remarked with unusual levity for him. 'I take some shore time or the missus get annoyed with me.'

They decided then that the *Cross*, the *Maid* and the *Venturer* would come, too, to bring the other crews back. Kaarvan wanted to establish whether or not the cavern was big enough to accommodate his ship which was the largest. If it was, he'd rest her the following year.

'Then we can keep more seamen working because the wharf will shield the smaller ships,' Kaarvan said. 'That keeps more people happy.'

Jim knew it would but it was odd that Kaarvan should voice such an opinion.

'You're putting the *Southern Cross* in . . . what did they used to call it?' Theo asked when he told her the plan.

'Mothballs.'

'What're they?'

'Basically cocoons. Moths came from cocoons. Flying insects that were attracted by flames.' Jim wasn't really paying much attention to what he was saying since they were in the night-time quiet of his cabin.

'You'll miss sailing, Jim.'

He knew he would but they both knew that his decision was sensible. He tired so easily these days, even doing what he loved most.

'I will but I'll enjoy it even more when we get back to it.'

'We?'

'Well, Dart has no problem with becoming official escort to the *Cross*, does she?'

'Noooo,' and Theo smoothed his hair back from his ears. 'You need a haircut.'

'Possibly.' She could make totally irrelevant observations but they only endeared her more to him. 'Two, with Dart, can handle the *Cross* on the way to Big Island . . .' he went on, still resisting in his inner heart the necessity of mothballing his beloved ship.

'A honeymoon?' And Theo giggled.

He gave her a quick hug. 'Then next year . . .'

'There'll be three of us, Jim . . .'

He roused up to look down at her. 'You don't mean . . .'

She laughed in great delight at his astonishment. 'Told you you weren't beyond it, man. Thought I might be but Corazon said I got in under the wire.'

At that point, he forgot what other plans he had intended to discuss with her and knew that his decision to harbour the *Cross* was for the best possible reason.

It was a cloudy day, mist whisking in and out of the little bays to port as the *Southern Cross* made her way towards the wharf Kaarvan had just announced on the comunit was not far ahead now. The jibsail was barely full of wind but a gentle current was helping the forward motion.

Suddenly the peeling of a bell sounded through the mist. Abruptly every dolphin of the escort broke the surface in ecstatic leaps of unusual height: a couple walking on their tails in their joy. Even Jim could distinctly hear them shouting 'bell, bell, bell!'

Theo looked at Jim in perplexed astonishment. 'But you didn't take the Monaco Bell . . . How . . . ?'

'The *Buenos Aires* carried more than one bell in her hold,' Jim said, putting an arm around her shoulders.

'Damn,' Theo said, sniffing, and he saw tears sliding down her cheeks. 'That was damned thoughtful of someone. Look how glad they are that there's a bell for them here, too. Just listen to the noise they're making.'

Jim was beginning to know when the dolphins were 'singing'. He knew, too, that, somehow, they had come across the seas of Pern to . . . home! Especially when there was a dolphin bell to guide the seafarers home!

The Ford of Red Hanrahan

'Look, I *know* that, Paul,' Red Hanrahan said, almost irritably brushing his shaggy mop of silver-shot red hair back from his forehead. 'We waste less keeping it all central. And my having supplies doesn't mean I won't share 'em whenever necessary.'

It occurred to Paul Benden that most of the male residents of the vast Fort Hold were in need of hair cuts: except, of course, the young dragonriders, now over five hundred strong in their Weyr. They cropped theirs to a stubble – easier to wear under the hide helmets they'd adopted. But there couldn't be that much of a shortage of scissors, could there?

Then he jerked his attention back to what Red was saying: he didn't like this tendency of his mind to go wandering off on tangents.

'But the fact remains that most of the horses are infected with thrush from having to stand on soggy wet bedding that we don't have the resources to change and they are acutely in need of *regular* exercise which they can't get here. The cave structure at the place I've found is sandy floored, much easier to keep clean, and big enough so I can have an indoor exercise area for those days when Thread keeps us immured.'

'And . . .' Paul began again for he hadn't been able to complete a sentence since Red had desperately launched into his rationale for moving out of Fort Hold.

'I've checked with Sean. We won't be a burden on him and the Weyr. Thread has never, yet,' and Red gave a rueful smile which made him look slightly less haggard, 'come right over the place I've found. And,' Red waggled a finger at Paul as he opened his mouth, 'Cobber and Ozzie have thoroughly explored the tunnel system shown on the echo survey with Wind Blossom's little photo-sensitive uglies and ensured that the dangerous ones are blocked off. We've got a small hydro-electric system using one of the nearby streams and Boris Pahlevi has plotted out the most efficient way to use the rock cutters and the borers. Cecilia Rado's given us plans to enlarge and improve the main chamber to give us a lot of apartments in the façade. We'll use the cut stone for housing along the base of the cliff, just as you've done here so we'll have workshops as well as separate quarters,' and Red emphasized that aspect by enunciating each syllable, 'to accommodate the families coming with us. That's the biggest incentive in moving out, Paul.' He gave a convulsive shudder. 'I know we've all had to cram in together for mutual support and safety. But enough is enough. Especially in my profession. I'm losing the best breeding years of my mares' lives. And, now that we've got the dried seaweed to add protein and fibre, we can get by with just the one feed-maker.'

Paul held up both hands. 'Let me get a word in edgewise, will you, Red?' He grinned. 'I have no objections to you moving out.'

'You don't?' Red was genuinely surprised. 'But I thought . . .'

Paul Benden indulged in a rare laugh. That made the big vet realize how much Paul had altered in the past nine years. Unsurprising when one thought how many burdens he had assumed since Emily Boll's death from the plague. Paul rose and went to the wall in his office that was covered with survey maps taken by the probes as the colony ships were moving into their parking orbit. The areas which had been explored by various teams showed the symbols of metals and minerals found in various locations: red marked the cave sites with rough sketches of the tunnel systems made from the probe echo system. Three enlargements depicted the sprawling immense Fort Hold, the old crater, Fort Weyr, which the dragonriders inhabited, and the newest human habitation at Boll, initiated the summer before.

'I *won't* let anyone make an ill-advised move, Red, just to get away from here. Decentralization is essential . . .' And Red knew that Benden feared another of the lightning swift fevers which had decimated the Hold three years before. 'We must begin to establish autonomous and self-sufficient units.

That's part of the Charter I'm determined we must implement. On the other hand, with Threadfall a constant menace, I must limit new settlements to those that won't overtax the dragons during a Fall. We can't even consider expanding unless they can give aerial protection. I won't risk any more precious lives – not after the most recent plague.' Paul's expression turned grim. 'I know that's one reason you want to move out and I can't blame you, but Basil warns that moving out might mean you're also spreading the disease, since we still don't know what caused it.'

There were few family groups in Fort Hold that had not suffered losses in the debilitating fever that had hit the already distressed colonists. The old, the very young, and the pregnant women had been the most vulnerable and, before the frantic medical team could develop a vaccine, the disease had run its course, leaving nearly four thousand dead. Nevertheless, the living had been immunized against a resurgence. Though all possible vectors – food, ventilation, allergies, inadvertent toxic substances from the hydroponics unit – had been examined, the trigger for its onset remained a mystery.

The fever had caused another problem: a large number of orphaned children between eight and twelve years. These had to be fostered, and although there had been no shortage of volunteers a certain amount of reshuffling had occurred to find psychologically suitable matches of adult and child.

'But those who leave here *must* go to properly surveyed and explored . . .' Paul gave a mirthless laugh, 'Premises.' Red grinned wryly back at him: 'premises' was an odd noun to apply to cave-dwellings. 'Pierre and his crowd were lucky to find such a network at . . .' Paul dropped his eyelids briefly, still finding it hard to make casual mention of his long-time colleague, 'Boll.'

'We're lucky Tarvi and Sallah explored so much of this region when they did,' Red added ingenuously, giving Paul time to recover from the tension that suddenly contracted the muscles in his face. 'You also don't need to lose too many of the valuable skills from a central facility. Fort should remain the primary teaching headquarters.' In Red's mind

79

was the warren of caves adjacent to the main Fort where the medics had originally set up isolation wards for the fever victims. Three years on, and the wards had become class-rooms, workshops and dormitories, somewhat relieving the crowding in the Hold.

'So,' Paul said with more vigour, 'who's going with you? Those grandchildren of yours?' And he managed a small smile because Red and Mairi had more of their second generation underfoot than their first. Sorka seemed to have a baby almost every year, despite arduous riding in the queens' wing. Red and Mairi fostered the five of them, leaving the dragon-riders with less to worry about while coping with the insidious Fall and training the young dragons. Michael, the eldest at nine, spent every moment he could up at the Weyr, often illegally borrowing a mount from his grandfather's remuda to make the uphill trip. His red hair matched his temperament and tenacity.

'No,' Red replied, slightly rueful but more relieved. Mairi had enough on her hands supervising their own fosterlings as well as looking after their son Brian's four to allow his wife, Jair, to continue mechanical engineer training under Fulmar Stone. 'Not when our going to the new place meant Michael would have too far to go to visit whenever he can sneak away.' Red chuckled. The boy was dragon mad and his father wouldn't let him stand as a candidate until he had reached his twelfth birthday. 'There's supervision for them now at the Weyr if Sorka's busy. And schooling.'

The Weyr, now housing five hundred and twenty dragons after nine years of enthusiastic breeding by the eleven queens of the first two hatchings and more lately Faranth's first daughter, had asked for additional personnel to help with the domestic tasks the riders had little time to manage. Some of the older fosterlings had moved up the mountain, and enough families and single adults to perform necessary tasks and skills.

Though it was not common knowledge, the Weyr supplied its needs by judicious hunting in the southern continent. Sorka had often sent Michael back to Fort with a sack of fresh fruit and a haunch or two of beef tied to the back of his saddle.

'We've singles, fosterlings, and enough mature couples

with full training,' and Red handed over his list. He'd care-fully screened those picked to accompany him and Mairi for compatibility as well as useful skills. 'I'd like your permission to draft more of the trainees when they've passed their tests. I would, of course, in the future be willing to take in any who show a knack for animal husbandry or agriculture . . .'

'You and Mairi have been splendid in sharing the caring.' Indeed, Mairi would have taken in as many fosterlings as she could but common sense dictated a limit to the time she could spare for each grieving pre-adolescent. 'So you are taking the entire regiment?'

Red grinned, knowing the nickname his expanded family had been given. 'Mairi's always had a touch with young folk and she'd feel she was abandoning them just when they've got over their bereavement. I can certainly use them all.'

Paul ran one finger down the list, written on a thin width of grey paper that had already been recycled several times. The precious remaining plassheets were now used only for special documents. Some personal computers were still in use, thanks to Egend Raghir's production of generators from the junked shuttles and other spares, but people had got out of the habit of using them as short-term record processors.

Red's list included four veterinary students but there were more than enough experienced practitioners and apprentices in the Hold so four caused no real depletion of staff at Fort. Red would complete their training and qualify them. Mar Dook's second son, Kes, had been well trained in agronomy by his father, and he was bringing his young family: Tim Andriadus's son, Akis, had just qualified as a general prac-titioner and his wife, Kolya Logorides, had studied gynaecology and midwifery with Suc O'Hara, so that gave the new Hold the medical support it would need: not that Mairi couldn't manage most minor medical emergencies. Max and Emily Schultz were two of the oldest fostered, plus two Wangs and two Brennans: in the fosterings, siblings had been kept together so there were also three very young Coatls and two Cervantes. Red had listed the training of the other fosterlings and wondered if Red was trying to get at least one represen-tative from every ethnic group: there was even a Langsam, whose family tended to gravitate towards teaching. Ilsa had just qualified as a primary teacher and would have more than enough pupils. But Red and Mairi had covered the general skills that would be needed in their choices: metal-working, engineering, teaching, as well as agronomy and medical.

'Hundred and forty-one all totalled, huh?' Paul said, 'And a good cross section. What are you springing loose from Joel, since you've the foresight to bring one of his kids?'

'Turn the sheet over,' Red said, amused, since the 'foresight' of attaching young Buck was not moving his father an inch in terms of what he'd allocated to a new settlement.

'Stingy, ain't he?' Paul said with a snort.

'Cautious with community property and ever aware of the charge of "nepotism".'

'An airlock door? What're you going to use that for?' Paul demanded in surprise.

'Well, it isn't being used for anything else and it'll make an impressive entrance: also impregnable,' Red said. 'I took the dimensions last time I was down in the storage cellars. Ivan and Peter Chernoff dissected the frame panel, too, which fits in the opening as if meant to be there. Seated it in some of that hull-patching compound Joel couldn't find another use for. Peter even rescued the floor- and ceiling-bar holders. A spin of the airlock wheel and we can drive home the lock bars top and bottom so that nothing can get past that door once it's closed. Cos Melvinah called it a neat bit of psychological reinforcement.'

Paul nodded his head in appreciation of the intrinsic idea. 'Good job of recycling materials, too. I will miss you, Red . . .' And he paused.

'But you won't miss having to arbitrate the disputes in the beast hold,' Red finished for him with a grin.

There were constant quarrels over who had what space in the low caverns that housed the colonists' animals, and who got what fodder. Red had been waging a clever and diplomatic war with the Gallianis and the Logorides, the other major breeders. During the frequent breakdowns of the overworked grass incubators, the Hanrahan family had fed their animals their own bread rations and searched the shoreline – some distance from the safety of the Hold – for the seaweed which could be dried and shredded into a fodder the horses would eat.

'They can't complain when your exodus leaves them with a lot more space.'

'No, but they'll agitate to try and bring up more of the stock they had to leave behind,' Red said with some acerbity.

Paul shook his head. 'No transport. There's no-one will get Jim Tillek to bring his precious *Cross* out of that watery cavern he's stored it in. And, with Per and Kaarvan gone fishing most weeks . . .' Paul shrugged. 'I see you're requisitioning the use of five sled-wagons? How long will you need them?'

With almost no power-packs left to run more than five airsleds, many had been stripped to hulls and fitted with wheels as ground vehicles. The smaller ones were useful enough to haul stone from excavations within the Hold. The bigger ones were too wide for roads other than the well-travelled route down to the sea. But they were capacious and had even survived – better than the goods they'd carried – unexpected long drops down mountainsides.

'Who else is moving out, Paul?' Red asked. Rumours were rampant but, so far, his party was the only one asking for a final clearance.

'Zi Ongola'd like to try that western peninsula.' Paul went to the map and tapped the marker on the tip of the landmass.

'Good on him. No wonder I couldn't get any more of the Duffs to come with me. We'll bring the wagons back as soon as we've finished using them. And I'll loan out the oxen teams I've trained if that'll help Zi.'

'It certainly would, and I know he'll thank you when I pass the information on.'

'He's got the longer haul.'

'He's also got to find a passable way through the High Ranges,' Paul said with a sigh. 'The cave system's satisfactory where he wishes to settle. The way there is not. We might be able to bore a tunnel if necessary. Plenty of hydro-electric sites.'

Red knew that Paul would miss Zi Ongola who had been

his second officer and close friend since the two had served together in the Cygni campaign. Red was a little surprised that Zi would leave but he'd be a good leader and pressures in the Fort had to be reduced. Many dissident voices were silenced only because the admiral was universally admired and the justice of his regime respected as fair and equable.

Most of the problems afflicting the Hold were due to the cramped conditions. There was actually more 'space' in Fort Hold than there had been on any of the colony ships (since much of their mass had been taken up by support machinery) but that argument was dismissed. The 'good' years when the colony was starting up had allowed people freedom and scope which they treasured all the more now that it had been denied them by the terrible fall of Thread. During the first few years when Fort Hold had protected them, they had been too grateful for the haven to hate its deficiencies – like inadequate privacy, especially when the birth rate soared and the stony corridors had resounded with the cries of fretful babies. In the wry words of Basil Tomlinson, 'there hadn't been that much else to do in the long nights' – crowding and cramping figured as the reason for many other, less easily solved problems.

The establishment of South Boll was the first major attempt to relieve the congestion, and was successful for those who had resettled at the new holding under Pierre de Courcis's leadership. Exploring appropriate 'premises' was time-consuming, with Thread falling so that any outbound journeys had to be carefully timed and safe lay-over shelters built along the way. Some caves were either waterless or weren't large enough to shelter enough people to be worth development.

'Yes, Zi's got a big job ahead of him yet we must make the attempt if this colony is to succeed. Threadfall won't last for ever!' Paul brought one hand down with a hard slap on his armrest. 'By all that's holy, Hanrahan, we'll still make Pern *ours*, with everyone owning his or her own place, no matter what rains down on us!'

'Of course we will, Paul. And we Hanrahans will hold our place! And multiply. You can be sure of that!' Red said, grinning smugly since Mairi had just weaned their latest and, he hoped, 'last' child. Gestation was taking too much out of her to achieve the dozen offspring she'd told Red she wanted to have.

'For Mairi's sake, I hope you have too much to do for any more of that,' and there was a twinkle in Paul's eye as he regarded the veterinarian. 'How many have you fathered now?'

Red waved his hand, his grin broader. 'Nine's enough to ensure our genes will continue. Ryan's the last I'll permit her. And made sure of no more to come,' he added soberly for Ryan was born two and a half years after they'd lost their youngest to the fever.

Benden gave a snort. 'Especially when your sons and daughters are like to pass you out in production figures in a year or two.'

'Well, Mairi's good with children. She genuinely likes them in all stages of their development. More than I do,' Red added with some acerbity.

'Got a name for this Hold of yours?'

Red made a disclaiming sound. 'Hell, Paul, I've been so busy with plans, lists and contingencies, naming's a detail I haven't given much thought to. We'll think of something appropriate, Mairi and the rest of us.'

Paul Benden rose then, made an effort to straighten the slump of his shoulders and held out his hand.

'Good luck, Red. We'll miss you here . . .'

'Ha! You'll be glad to see the backsides of us. And so will the Logorides and the Gallianis.'

Benden gave a genuine laugh at that barb.

Despite the fact that breeding had had to be kept to an absolute minimum, the Logorides and Gallianis had felt themselves constantly deprived by the restrictions. Pierre de Courcis had taken nine of the scions of those of the two large families, and a substantial number of their cattle, when he went south to settle Boll but the two senior men continued to grieve for the 'marvellous fine bloodlines and stock' they'd had to leave behind at their southern Stake Holds.

'They'd enjoyed freedom far longer than most of us. It was harder to give it all up,' Benden said in oblique apology.

Red cocked his head briefly to one side. 'Who hasn't given up a lot? To stay alive!'

Paul added his other hand over Red's and gave it one final hard shake. 'When do you plan to go?'

'Sean says we've got three full clear days come Tuesday. We'll be organized and ready by then.'

'So soon?' Benden's tone was almost wistful.

'On a good horse, Admiral,' and Red couldn't resist teasing the former naval man, 'you could ride the distance in two days. Be good for you to get away now and again.'

'I've never even got as far south as Boll and that's nearer . . .'

'T'isn't with those hills to climb,' Red protested. 'I'll send you a special hand-engraved invitation, Paul Benden, and you'll come for the good of your sanity! I'll sic Sean and Sorka on you. A-dragonback's the shortest way to come,' he added as he paused at the door.

Benden laughed. 'You talk Sean into letting someone else ride his precious Carenath and I'll come!'

'Good!' Red gave a brief sharp nod of his head and grinned. 'Then we'll show you what we've done with the new Hold when we've done it!'

Nearly a third of the Hold's population managed to be on hand when the Hanrahan expedition moved off, every ridden animal laden as well with some bundle or other going to the new Hold. The sleds were carefully packed and the largest, with the Hold door, was drawn by six teams of oxen, beasts Red had carefully picked for their docility and trained for such work. He'd bred them himself from a genetic pattern Kitti Ping had produced for him: slightly adjusting weight, bone, thickening hide, enlarging both heart and lungs to encourage a disease- and fatigue-resistant hardy animal: much stronger and more adaptable than the Terran beasts that had been brought *in vitro*.

Safely stored in an insulated crate were the special fertilized eggs with which Red Hanrahan hoped to develop varieties of equines more suitable to Pern's needs: a heavyweight animal of Percheron proportions for the plough; a swift, lean racing type, a good doer, who could carry messengers long distances on little fodder; and a comfortable riding animal, a pacer like the ancient Paso Fino which had been a mountain breed of

86

great agility, endurance and, more importantly, possessing the easiest possible long-distance riding gait.

He would make his Hold the place where all others would come to buy their burden beasts and racers. His most private dream was of founding a race-horse line to rival what Earth had once possessed. There was no reason, once Thread had passed, that they couldn't revive the sport of kings. The practical could co-exist with the exotic. Let Caesar Galliani develop meat animals if that was his passion but he'd go for horses.

Red's thoughts on the importance of the step he was making, separating himself, family and followers from the main Hold, had to make way for his present duties. Riding his bay stallion, King, the best of the fine animals he had bred from the fertilized ova he had brought with him, he ranged up and down the line, encouraging, and rectifying small errors in the order.

He had positioned one of the heavy sleds, but not the biggest which carried the shuttle door, to break trail with teams of his strongest young folk to widen the way whenever necessary. The way north through the main Fort valley was easy enough but soon they would come to the less travelled ground. Not that he didn't know the track like the back of his hand, he'd been up and down it so often, but a lot of it wasn't geared for wide traffic.

There were people waiting for them, too, at the new 'premises': the four fostered youngsters who were old enough to help Egend Raghir and David Jacobsen, who were supervising the mechanical apparatus in the Hold. Madeleine Messurier, in charge of the domestic arrangements, had the others well organized. Maurice de Broglie was still checking the rock formations and tunnels with Ozzie and Cobber on loan from the specialists' work pool. Soon those would move on to investigate other possible sites for holdings.

As soon as the wagon train was around the bend and Fort was out of sight, Red sent his fire-lizard, Snapper, to Maddie to announce that they were on their way. Useful creatures, the fire-lizards, though there were fewer of them about these days.

Sorka said it was because they went back to their native sands to lay their eggs. Being more responsible, the little golden queens remained to see them safely hatched before coming back to their humans. The golds, bronzes and browns were generally more faithful. The green females laid their eggs and then forgot about the matter and, being shatter-witted, probably forgot that they had once had human friends. Duke remained faithful as did Sean's two browns and Snapper, another brown. Slowly though, there were fewer and fewer of the winsome creatures in and out of Fort Hold.

'They may mind the cold and dreary winters more than we do,' Sorka suggested. 'We could go back to Landing and see if there're any clutches about to hatch.'

Red had caught Sean's frown. The lad . . . Red corrected himself with a private grin because 'lad' no longer applied to this confident adult. Sean, rider of bronze Carenath, was known as the Weyrleader. And, if he had certain traits of the martinet, they were needed to shape his growing dragonrider contingent. Whatever, his orders were strictly obeyed and, to Red's thinking, were sensibly formulated. There would be little spare time for the dragonriders to go looking for fire-lizard nests. Except that one return journey.

When Ezra Keroon had been fretful with the fever that wracked him, Sean had very willingly gone back to Landing on Carenath. Sean had returned – Sorka remarked – almost as soon as he'd left, to reassure the old captain that the AIVAS building, which Ezra had so carefully shielded with shuttle tiles against Garben's eruption, remained intact and unscathed. Later, Sean had reported more fully to Paul that the old settlement was just so many mounds under a thick carpet of grey volcanic ash. However, the knowledge that the interface with the *Yokohama* was still intact had soothed the querulous Ezra and he'd gratefully subsided into a sleep from which he didn't wake: another victim of the undiagnosed fever.

Red could quite easily name his new place after Ezra Keroon. Certainly the man had been one of the heroes of the Evacu-ation – in fact, the last man to leave Landing, bar the admiral and Joel Lilienkamp. He'd been heroic enough in the Nathi

War, too. Yes, it wouldn't be a bad thing to name his Hold 'Keroon'. Or 'Kerry'. That was a good way to keep long-lost but well-loved places, or people, alive.

A request for his presence at the head of the caravan was called down the line to him so Red cantered King to see what the problem was.

They made camp the first night where he had often done so, in a rocky clearing by one of the streams that fed into the bigger Fort River. Water was never much of a problem in the north whereas, in the south, some of the inland Stakes had had to drill wells. All the stock was hungry enough to munch happily enough on the dried shredded seaweed which some of the fussier eaters tended to refuse.

A campfire is a cheerful affair, even when made of dried animal dung. Someone – possibly Pei Pei Ling who proved imaginatively inventive – had contrived a solution in which to immerse the dung that replaced any lingering unpleasant odours with that of apple wood. The dinner stew was known to be nutritious and was even seasoned appealingly so that, if you didn't think how it had been processed, you could relish the meal. Red was too hungry to be the least bit finicky and let the hard travel bread soften in the leftover juices.

Snapper returned with a note from Maddie attached to his leg.

> *The welkin will ring when we sight you. River's high with last week's rain. Don't let the sleds bog down.   M.*

Mairi had made their bed under one of the sleds. She had insisted that her bones required a certain amount of padding. Red wouldn't admit that his own did, too, and was grateful to lie down with only her and Snapper near him. He was thinking of the absolute wealth of three good-sized rooms at . . . Keroon Hold – naw, that didn't sound right – just for Mairi and himself.

The morning brought an unexpected delay. Some of the beasts had to be treated for harness galls: mainly those

89

hauling sleds. The harness had been new but Red had thought it had been softened enough not to rub. Mairi dug about in their household belongings and brought out cotton which she had saved from the last crop at Landing and some well-cured sheep fleeces. Red first applied the numbweed salve that was now in everyone's first aid kit, then padded the abraded spots to prevent further friction sores. But the delay cost them several hours. They also redistributed the lighter items from the sleds of the galled teams to ease their burden. Red himself made certain that all harnesses were flexible enough and fitted perfectly. One thing sure, Red announced, he'd personally inspect every strap of harness this evening after it had been cleaned.

However, they finally moved out in good heart, with smiles on faces that hadn't been there before. Almost as if the sheer joy of being *out* on their own, away from the burden of so much imprivacy – was that a word? Red wondered, but it fitted what he meant – outweighed any minor snag. Red was relieved and glad for many reasons to see this attitude adjustment. The new place still needed considerable hard work to complete it and make it liveable, never mind comfortable. For a while, there'd be other inconveniences and makeshifts. While they carved out their new habitation from the basic cavern system, everything would be covered with stone dust. He had brought as many masks as Joel would allow him but there weren't enough for more than the people right at the work face. And rock dust had an insidious habit of permeating and clinging to objects well away from the actual excavation sites. Mairi had complained about the state of his clothing after his first long stay at the Hold cave.

He hoped that Max Schultz had managed to get his gang to finish the stud fencing. Red'd paid almost his last credits to have the plastic extruded for enough posts and rails to provide paddocks. He wanted barn-sour animals to spend as much time as possible out-of-doors, even if it would be a while before any grass could get started. There wouldn't be that much time to exercise horses at first but they did have stables and byres inside the immense low cavern that would hold all the beasts. Turn-out paddocks were essential. He'd get

Deccie Foley, who had a knack for teaching animals, to train the dogs with a certain call or whistle to round up the animals so that just one person'd be needed to help the dogs get them all in under cover when Thread fell.

Towards afternoon a drizzle began: proper rain, not Thread; though, for a moment, the greyness of the sky over the western range did cause the heart to stop when cloud blotted out the sun. But Thread always moved from east to west. Red had prudently built into the eastern face of his precipice so every window gave a view of the direction that danger came from.

To make up for lost time, they ate a quick lunch while they watered the animals at one of the many streams they had to cross. Maybe he should put something about streams in the name of the place. His land had almost as many as Fort did, since this eastern side of the High Ranges drained well into the sea.

A wet night-time camp meant cold food again, though Mairi contrived enough of a fire under the high sled to boil water for hot drinks all round. And enough warm water to soap and soften the harnesses which Red personally checked. Red also inspected every one of the burden beasts, with Jess Patrick dancing behind him and peering over his shoulder, afraid he might not have spotted a possible rub. Betsy Sopers was vetting the horses, ridden and pack, just in case.

Despite the wet chill damp of the early spring rain, Red was asleep beside Mairi almost as soon as he got himself comfortable. The way Snapper coiled between their warm bodies, Red wondered how much longer the little fella would remain faithful in this inclement land.

The rain was heavier the next day. Mairi insisted they have a hot porridge in their bellies to keep out the chill. Licia Dook, Mila Larr and the children made quantities of hot klah for the thermoses. The availability of the warming beverage did make the difference during that very long cold day.

The trace, for it certainly couldn't be called a trail, was more mud than dirt now and further slowed them down. Despite that, by the time light was fading from the sky, Red knew they were not that far from the river that he had chosen as the border for his Stake: the river about which Maddie had warned him had risen. The ford they were to cross was a wide basin where the river spread out over a shale rocky bottom.

He ordered lanterns lit for such light as they gave. The mycelium luminescence with which Ju Adjai Benden had been experimenting cast sufficient light in an enclosed space but suitable shielding to make it useful outside hadn't yet been developed.

'We've reached the river, Dad,' Brian yowled from the darkness ahead. 'And it's in spate.'

Red groaned. He'd wanted to get across as much because, across the river, was *his* as because the further bank was a better site for an overnight camp. He considered waiting for daylight but made a decision when he saw that the flatter land on this side of the river was already under an inch or so of water. If the river was this high now, come morning, the water would be too high for the wheels of the smaller sleds. They might float away downstream if they got loose. And this was the best ford within klicks. That is, if he could find it in the murky darkness.

Now, so close to his own private place, he was loath to let high water bar his way.

He borrowed a lantern from one of the smaller carts and trotted through the mud to the front of the caravan. Reining King in beside Brian, he looked glumly at the swiftly moving surface of the swollen river. Rising up in his stirrups, and holding the lantern high over his head, he peered to his left, trying to find the cairn of stones he had placed to mark the upper edge of the ford.

'Under water, too, dammit,' he muttered to himself.

'Would we have to worry about an undercurrent here, Dad?' Brian asked, pointing to a large branch floating serenely, and quickly, past them.

'If it gets too high, that's a possibility. By tomorrow, it will definitely be high enough to cause us problems with those lower loadbed sleds. Damn it, we've got to try tonight or we might spend days here, just in sight of our destination!'

'Let's give it a go then, Dad,' Brian said firmly. 'I'll try to

92

the right. After all, I *have* been across this ford a couple of times. And Cloudy's a good swimmer.'

He kneed his grey into the water but the animal, head down, snorting at the rushing flow, was not as eager to go forward as his rider had boasted.

'Don't push him, Bri,' Red shouted. 'Horse's got sense. I'll look to the left. If I could see the rocks . . . Ah!' His high-held lantern showed the bulge of water surging over an obstacle just below the surface and he kneed King forward. A brave horse under any circumstances, the stallion stepped in and moved smartly out, Red legging him to the left as the ford took a diagonal slant across the river. The bank on the far side was too dark to make out and, since the water was high on this side, the incline there might be submerged as well.

As King waded confidently forward, the water not up to his knees yet, Red pondered the wisdom of crossing now, tonight, in the dark. Yet, if they found the ford, they could make a safe passage. And be on their own land! But floating sleds might haul the burden beasts off their feet. Rope the sleds, then, and have riders alongside to keep the sleds within the ford. King walked on and, through his horse's body, Red knew that the stallion had walked on the rocky shale base of the ford.

'Thataboy, King, that's a good lad!' Red encouraged his mount, trying to peer ahead in what feeble light the lantern shed. Oh, for a power torch! The ones allotted to his operation were naturally all up at the cliff premises, their clear beams penetrating the stygian darkness of the tunnel complex.

'BRIAN! Follow me!' Red called, swinging his arm in a wide circle so that the light colour of his waterproof would be visible in the darkness. In moments, Cloudy's light head and body came out of the night, splashing as he cantered forward. 'We need the power beams that are up at the Hold to get us across tonight. As soon as we reach the other side, I want you to go hell fer leather and bring 'em back. Bring anyone still awake, too. We'll need all the help we can get. And ropes, and those great horses Kes has been using to break ground.'

'Whoa, Dad. I get the drift.' Brian's laughing voice followed him.

The water was over King's knees suddenly and he tossed his head in surprise. Red looked over his shoulder, trying to gauge their angle from the bank but they were about halfway across and neither bank was clearly visible now.

'I'll put a lantern where we entered,' Red told himself, 'and another where we emerge. The beams will give a broad enough swathe to light the ford itself adequately. At least we'll see where we should be going.' King pulled to the right and Red corrected him and was instantly in water to his own knees. King gave two plunges leftward and, snorting mightily, was back on the shale footing. The horse gave an offended blow as if criticizing his rider's directions. 'All right, boy, you know which way to go, so go! I didn't do so well, did I?' Affectionately he slapped the stallion's muscled crest, letting the reins slip through his fingers. God, that river was cold! Ice melt as well as the rain.

Behind him, Brian avoided a similar mishap. One more time, just where the shale bank ended, the water surged up to caress Red's stirruped feet but he was glad when they were obviously ascending the slope out of the river, splashing through fetlock-high water.

Standing in his stirrups, Red swung the lantern, kiyi-ing their success as Brian added his yodels of triumph.

'D'you know the way to the Hold from here, son?' he asked, slightly anxious because Brian had not made the going all that often and in the dark, any landmarks would be obscured. 'Here, better take my lantern.' He leaned over towards Brian.

'Look, Dad, you'll need that as a beacon . . .'

'I'd rather *you* had it and got safely to the Hold. Off with you, and trust Cloudy.'

'Don't I always!' Brian said, angling Cloudy beside the stallion to take the lantern. 'Whoops! Got it!' And with that, trotted off left up the gentle incline.

Red watched him for a long moment before he set King back into the water, heading directly for the lanterns on the other side. That made his transit easier. They divided up the available lanterns. Mairi again had foreseen the need for small fires, more cheerful than effective as light sources but

94

certainly beacons in the dismal night. Red had Jess and Buck pound a steel pole into the water's edge by his marker cairn. Then they securely fastened one lantern at its top, a second one hooked at man height and they tied a heavy rope at waist height for those on foot to grab. There'd need to be people helping to guide the burden beasts and keeping them to the path of the ford's shallows.

That preparation completed, Red fastened the other end of the rope around the saddle horn and coiled it carefully to play out across the river. He took up three more lanterns and two more poles, and led other riders with lanterns to follow him and King back into the river. He positioned the riders at intervals, holding lanterns to guide and to be available to give assistance as required. When he reached the far bank, he hammered in another pole, hooked on the lantern and tied the end of the rope in one of those clever hitches Jim Tillek had once shown him.

Then he walked King to where he thought the right-hand edge of the ford should be, and kneed him into the water: right up to his waist. King lurched mightily out of that hole and back on to the shale, shaking himself as if annoyed at his immersion. Red clamped his teeth against the cold of that dunking. Fortunately he'd managed to keep the lantern from being doused. He walked King back up the shale footing to the bank where he stabbed the last pole into the ground and settled the final lantern. That would give them beacons enough . . . if no-one panicked. There was just enough width of the fordable part to accommodate the largest sled. Just enough! Even one of the team putting a foot wrong could result in disaster.

He cantered King back across the ford, more an act of bravado than common sense for he knew King was tiring but this crossing had to be completed with the minimum of delay.

Mairi was right there as he emerged from the water.

'Not another step do you go, Red Peter Hanrahan, until you've something warm in your stomach to take away the chill of that water! I heard you splashing about.' She handed him up a cup and he was glad enough of it as the klah spread through him and down into his belly. He managed to suppress a shudder as the cool rain-laden breeze blew across his sodden breeches.

He handed her back the cup with thanks and then, rising in his stirrups, addressed the group waiting to hear his decision.

'Listen up, folks. We'd best make the crossing tonight. The river's rising fast with what I bloody well know is ice melt as well as today's rain. Right now the ford's no higher than King's knees if you keep to it and head on the left diagonal to the far shore and the left-hand lantern. The ford itself is shale, so the minute you feel your mount moving into something softer, get back on the hard stuff. Now let's get moving. Those of you leading pack horses move out first. Tie them on the far bank and then bring your mounts to form a very careful line on the right-hand side of the ford. Watch that hole I fell into. It's a cold one!'

He trotted King down the line to various carts and gave them their travel orders, leaving the heavy sleds till last, for they'd need the most help.

Shouts from the river told him there were minor troubles but each time he turned King to go and investigate, he heard reassurances that the crisis was over.

The led horses, the other pack animals and four of the carts had got safely across and there were sufficient riders marking the ford's boundaries so that he sent the loose animals across, though the dogs nearly caused a commotion and several had to be roped to safety when they were in danger of being caught by the current. The goats were the worst. They seemed to want to go for a long swim. So Red asked everyone with fire-lizards to keep the goats in line. Snapper dived at the bell nanny, clipping her on her right ear to turn her to the left. That got her back in line and the others followed, urged on by attend-ant fire-lizards. Then, without any warning, and before the goats had started climbing out on the far side, Snapper and the other fire-lizards let out a dreadful sound and disappeared.

'What the hell?' Red said, totally surprised and vastly irritated by the abrupt abandonment. Snapper'd always been reliable . . . He pushed King forward to deflect the lead nanny from yet another wayward plunge and was relieved to get the little herd safely out of the river.

By then, help had arrived from the Hold and he was distracted from the fire-lizards' desertion by the need to organize the final stages of the crossing. Madeleine Messurier had sent along hot soup and some sort of hot bread filled with one of her spice concoctions. It didn't take much persuasion from Brian and the Hold reinforcements for him to pause long enough to eat. Especially, as once the powerful beacons were in place they shone the clear path across the now perceptibly higher water, foaming in its hurry to reach the sea, many long klicks to the east. Red knew that he'd miss the sight and sound of sea near him but feasible 'premises' had not presented themselves nearer along this coast. He'd always lived in sight of an ocean but that was a small price to pay for what he'd *have* here.

He was cheered, too, by the sight of several campfires on the far side. A shiver ran up his spine for, despite warm food in his guts, he was wet through and through now and he could feel the stallion's tiredness in his occasional stumble and slide in the mire. He counted on the great heart of the horse and his own determination to last until they got all his people past this ford.

The first yoke of the three pairs harnessed to the largest sled baulked at being asked to enter dark waters, though the beams lit their way as clearly as the sun. The drivers energetically cracked their whips overhead; two men used prods; Maurice and Peter, who were no small men, as well as Ozzie, Cobber and Brian hauled at the nose rings of the stubborn oxen. Aggravated by the stupidity and aware that the river deepened every minute, Red ordered the animals blindfolded but that old trick wasn't having any effect with the water swirling about their knees and reinforcing their sense of 'danger'. He was trying to think what else might motivate them, damning Snapper's disappearance when he might have repeated his successful motivation of the goats, when there was a commotion on the far bank, horses whinnying and bucking about while their startled riders tried to calm them. The cattle lowed in such panic that there could be only one cause of such widespread reaction.

Peering above, into the drizzling night sky while King

97

cavorted wildly, Red just barely made out the shape of a dragon overhead, bronze hide momentarily illuminated by the dying campfires.

'SEAN!' he bellowed at the top of his lungs, reining King into as small a circle as he could to keep even this well-trained animal from bolting away from the source of alarm.

'*Sorry, Red,*' Sean's voice replied from somewhere overhead.

Still circling King, though it took a lot of strength to hold the frightened stallion with one hand, Red made a megaphone of the other.

'Don't be sorry. Be useful! Get behind this stubborn team and get them *moving* across the ford. We haven't got all night and the river's rising.'

'Get out of my way, then,' Sean's voice drifted down to him. 'At the count of ten . . .' The instruction dwindled away into the night.

'OK, fellows,' Red yelled to the men in front of the team. 'Sean's going to dragonize them. Be prepared for a rough ride. And *somehow* keep 'em left. At all costs, keep 'em left!'

He eased the pressure on King's bit but still kept a tight hold on the reins and kneed him towards the cairn, facing the horse towards the river, away from the sight of an incoming dragon. He was just in time, for out of the darkness of the drizzle came a huge shape, flying low and heading right for the reluctant team.

The smell of dragon was almost sufficient in itself, for the yoke bawled in fright and plunged forward, away from the sky-borne terror.

Sean must have the eyes of a cat, Red thought, for he'd sent Carenath over at just the angle that made the oxen head straight across the angled ford. Despite the load the beasts hauled, they didn't stop when they reached the other side, stampeding through those on the far bank until Red wondered if this had been such a clever manoeuvre after all.

'We'll land upwind of you, Red, so I can talk,' Sean's voice said faintly out of the murk and King began to buck and rear, but not as earnestly as before.

Maybe it was the distance, the murkiness of the night, but Sean's tone sounded odd. Red dismissed the thought as he concentrated on finishing the work at hand. Maybe he was a grandfather . . . again.

Now only the smaller of the two big sleds was left to cross but the animals were still keyed up by the recent appearance of a dragon overhead and were eager to get as far away from it as possible. Once they got in the water, what Red had feared occurred. The river level was now above the wheels and the sled, for all the weight in it, began to float. The yoked beasts were pulled off balance and only the quickness of the left-hand guide-liners kept the sled from drifting downriver. As it was, the ropes had to be kept taut all the long way across the ford until the wheels once more took the weight and the sled was hauled above the river's current.

Red sent a tired, reluctant King back across the ford to meet with Sean and to help Mairi put out the fires. Sean was already giving her a hand. Mairi's piebald mare, tied to a rock, stood as placid as always, unconcerned by the proximity of a dragon.

'Thanks, Sean,' Red said, holding out his hand to his son-in-law. A sandy hand gripped his and Sean's face was briefly visible before he scuffed wet sand over the fire. 'Had about run out of options to get those stupid damn fool oxen across.'

'Well, fear's a mighty mover.' Sean's voice did sound odd, choked, but with no more light to see his face, Red had no inklings and just then, Mairi joined them.

'How come you arrived so fortuitously?' she asked. 'There's nothing wrong with Sorka, is there?'

Although Sorka, queen Faranth's rider, was pregnant again, she generally had no more trouble with parturition than her mother.

'Oh, no no,' Sean said quickly, raising his hand to dispel her anxiety. 'We came to welcome you to the new Hold but you hadn't arrived yet. Maddie said you'd sent for help at the ford. I sort of figured Carenath might be some help.'

Red laughed wearily, blotting his wet face on an already soaking kerchief. 'Where'd you stash him? A dragon's hard to hide even on a rainy night.'

'Carenath?' Sean called, just that vague hint of amusement which only partially reassured Red. 'Show Red and Mairi where you are.' Barely fifty metres away a sudden blue-green light appeared in the darkness, glistening and slightly whirling – the faceted eyes of a dragon. Red tightened his hand on King's reins but the tired horse's head hung down too low for him to see the gleaming eyes. 'Thanks, Car!' And the jewel-clear light disappeared.

'Is he standing there with his eyes closed?' Mairi asked.

'No, he's raised a wing to shield,' Sean said, again using that almost lifeless tone. 'You should be just able to make 'em out behind the wing membrane.'

'Oh, yes, so I can,' Mairi said, sounding delighted at the concealment.

'Look, Red, one of the reasons I came was to be sure you had got there safely. We expect Threadfall over this area tomorrow morning fairly early and I didn't want you caught out in it.'

Red sighed. With all the problems of fording the river, he had just been considering staying here the rest of the night and starting fresher in the morning.

'You're not that far,' Sean said encouragingly.

'I know, son, I know.' Red paused, to give Sean a chance to speak whatever was clearly on his mind and bothering him. He had a very good relationship with his son-in-law and he wanted nothing to jeopardize it. It couldn't be that he and Mairi had sent his children up to the Weyr for that had been Sean's idea long before he knew of the projected move.

'Is your Snapper back yet?' Sean asked.

'What's happened at the Weyr?' Mairi said, immediately clasping Sean's arm and peering up into his face. 'Don't lie to me . . .'

Sean ducked his head, lifting his free arm to rub his face. Rain wouldn't have bothered him.

'No reason to lie,' he said and now both could hear the roughness.

Mairi embraced the bronze rider. 'Tell us, Sean,' she said in her gentlest voice, lifting an edge of her kerchief to dry his cheeks.

Red altered his stance, moving nearer the Weyrleader.

'Alianne died in childbirth,' he said, tears now making

runnels down his cheeks. 'We couldn't stop the bleeding. I went for Basil.'

'Ooooh,' Mairi said in the soft expression of true empathy.

'That's not all of it,' and Sean sniffed, rubbing his nose and eyes, giving way to the misery he had bottled up. 'Chereth . . . went . . . *between*. Like Duluth and Marco.'

'Oh, Sean love,' and Mairi brought his head down to her shoulder. Red put his arm across the rider's bowed shoulders.

There had been many injuries, some serious enough to end the fighting abilities of six dragons, but only four deaths. Actually an astounding record of which Sean as Weyrleader had every right to be proud. The loss of a queen magnified the tragedy. No wonder Snapper and the others had disappeared. They had gone to the Weyr to mourn.

Red and Mairi were quietly comforting, allowing Sean to express a grief he had probably suppressed until now.

'I'll come if I can be of any help,' Mairi said with a quick query at Red who nodded approval.

Sean raised his head, sniffed and then blew his nose on a handkerchief he hauled out of a jacket pocket. He blew it in such a way that Red knew he had vented the worst of his sorrow.

'Thanks, Mairi, but we'll come through. It was just such a shock. It's one thing to lose a fighting dragon but . . .' His voice trailed off.

'We understand, dear.'

'So nothing would do Sorka but that I checked to be sure you were all right, too. I admit to getting a fright when I didn't see you at the Hold . . .' And Sean managed a wry smile.

Red put a hand on Sean's shoulder and gave it an affectionate squeeze which he hoped expressed both his sympathy and appreciation. 'And you've Thread to fly tomorrow,' he said with deep regret. People needed time to mourn.

'Best thing that could happen, actually,' Sean said, mopping his eyes once more before he put away the handkerchief.

'Yes, I suspect you're right about that,' Mairi said slowly.

'Off with you now, son,' Red said, giving Sean a gentle shove towards Carenath. 'You were more than good to check up on us and give those oxen the inducement they needed. Soon's Mairi and I get across, we'll push on. We'll be under cover tomorrow so don't worry about us.' Then another thought struck Red. 'You've enough ground crew for Fall tomorrow?'

Sean gave his father-in-law a wry smile. 'As I understand it, Red, this river marks the boundary between Fort Hold and your place. You're not obliged to ground-crew . . . If any of you were up to it. Just push on and get undercover tonight. That's the best way to help Sorka, and me!'

'We'll do just that,' Mairi said, handing over the well-wrapped sleeping Ryan to Sean while she mounted Pie.

'So this is my son's youngest uncle,' he said, pushing back the blanket to peer at the little face.

'Definitely his youngest,' Red said. 'Hand him up to me,' he added as he swung up on the stallion. 'King's that bit higher above the water, Mair. You'll get a soaking as it is.'

Mairi gave a little laugh. 'Not if I hike my knees up,' she said. 'Give my dearest love to Sorka, will you, Sean? And our deepest sympathy to all at the Weyr.'

'I will indeed, Mairi. And . . . my thanks!'

The Weyrleader stepped aside then as she kicked her mare forward. The piebald was one of those rare placid beasts and stepped from land to cold water with neither hesitation nor so much as a twitch of her well-shaped ears when water swirled around her fetlocks and then up to her knees.

'We all grieve with the Weyr, Sean,' Red said, raising his hand in farewell. Looking over his shoulder, he saw Carenath uncover his brilliant eyes as Sean returned to him, sorrow displayed by the droop in his broad shoulders. Red sighed.

Then he couldn't help but notice how closely King was following the mare, needing no urging at all to wade into the river once more. King stretched his neck out to sniff at her tail which she clamped tightly to her rump and picked up her legs into a splashing trot. Red grinned as he felt the sprightly lift in the tired stallion's step, pursuing a mare who was apparently about to come into season. And this year, Red thought, he could breed every mare he had!

As the swifter current of the still-rising river tugged avidly at the stallion's legs, he held his son more tightly in the crook of his arm. He could see that Mairi had brought her knees up, nearly to her chin as the water rose up the smaller mare's side but Pie kept her footing as she trotted sturdily forward. Red heaved a sigh of relief in unison with King when they climbed the far bank for the last time.

'Let's leave Sean's news until tomorrow, Mairi,' he said before they reached the others.

'Yes, of course. Hearts are weary enough without being sorrowful, too. And I don't want anything to spoil our arrival.' Then, after a brief pause, 'Is that selfish of me, Peter?'

She only used his Christian name when she was uncertain.

'No, kind. We've had sadness in full measure. We can wait to add this one.'

With those from the Hold to share the tasks of the weary travellers, Red let himself be persuaded to sit on one of the carts and lead King from the back of it. In the darkness, he even permitted himself to lay back. But the cart seemed full of crates and parcels of hard edges and pointed corners, and non-yielding surfaces. He twisted and pushed and finally formed a backrest that wouldn't dislocate a rib or poke his kidneys too hard. He regretted that he hadn't paused long enough to find some dry clothes but he wrapped himself in the blanket Mairi had thrust at him and that kept the chill off. Snapper reappeared and burrowed into his shoulder, wrapping his tail around Red's neck and Red stroked the little beast, sensing his sorrow and need to be comforted. But soon enough, Red hadn't the energy for more caresses and, instead, propped his head against the lithe warm body a substitute pillow so soothing that, despite every good intention, Red Hanrahan was fast asleep when the cart pulled into the brightly lit circle in front of his Hold.

'Mairi was all for leaving you asleep in the cart,' Brian told him when the wail of a tired child roused him, 'but it's only got two wheels and we'd nothing to prop it with.'

Futilely Red roared at everyone for depriving him the sight of a triumphal entry and he resisted every effort to get him inside and to his bed until he had seen all his livestock safely ensconced in 'a proper-style barn'.

'Sean said there's Thread across the river tomorrow morning early,' he told those who tried to get him to go to bed, 'and he's usually right about where it'll fall but I want everything under cover. Just in case for once he'd be wrong!' And he stormed down to the animal hold.

Half of the beasts were already down on the sandy flooring, fast asleep while others dozed as they stood. Red made straight for King's stallion box at one end of the equine stabling. The horse, dark eyes glittering in the soft light, whuffled slightly and then closed his eyes.

'Even the *horse* has more sense . . .' Mairi began in as close to a scolding tone as she had ever used on him.

'I had to see 'em, Mair,' Red muttered wearily. 'I had to see 'em safe where I've seen them in my mind ever since I knew this place was right for us.'

'And righter for them,' she said, steering him out of the cavern and towards the hold proper.

She half-pulled him up the ramp to the as yet wide-open entrance – but only after he had made sure that the big sled-wagon carrying the door had been parked near by – and into their Hold.

'And if you think you're going to prowl about and see if we've made any progress during your absence,' Maddie said, fists planted on her belt, 'you've another think coming. Furthermore, Ozzie has offered his rubber mallet to knock you out if you don't get straight to your quarters and sleep!'

His quarters, for now, were currently the office to the left of the main entrance and he reeled slightly in that direction. Candlelight showed him that the room had been altered – and he grabbed at the doorframe to steady himself, his tired mind trying to cope with the difference.

'Well, a bed big enough for both you and Mairi wouldn't fit in here with all your clutter,' Maddie said, 'so we moved that next door. Now that there is a next door.' She gave him a push and Mairi, still holding his hand, got him into the room.

The door was closed firmly and Mairi was opening jacket and shirt, deftly pulling the sleeves off him before she pushed him backwards on to the bed. Out of a marriage-long habit, he lifted one leg so she could remove first one, then the other boot as he managed with fumbling fingers to undo his belt and trousers.

A long time later, he woke.

He roared at first, annoyed that he had been deceived and cosseted when there was so much to be done but Brian pretended to take umbrage that his own father wouldn't trust him to see to the care of his precious stock. Mairi set before him a steaming mug of klah and fresh bread with – his eyes gleamed to see it – a knob of butter he wouldn't have to share with anyone. So he forgave the conspiracy and demanded to know if people were settling in: if they weren't, he'd have their complaints that very evening.

A communal kitchen, with everyone taking turns at food preparation for the main meal, had been established and the main Hall, bare though it was, was large enough to seat five times the numbers that sat at the trestle tables that night.

Before the meat was served, Red Hanrahan rose from his seat at the T-junction of the two long tables.

'Many of you may already know from your fire-lizards that Alianne, gold Chereth's rider, died in childbirth and her dragon soon after.' He paused to let those who hadn't known absorb the shock of such a loss. 'We will all stand and have a moment's silence in tribute to them.'

While the announcement put a damper on the beginning of what would have been a more convivial evening, by the time the splendid cakes Madeleine had made for the occasion were brought in, most people had recovered.

'You don't think of the dragons as being *that* attached to their riders,' Kes Dook remarked just down the table from Red. 'I mean, I know the Impression is life-long . . . but the queen was so young. Surely someone else could have taken over?'

'Not as we understand it,' Red said, toying with his mug of quikal. He did miss a decent drop of wine and wondered if Rene Mallibeau would ever find his south-facing slopes to grow the precious vines still tended in the hydroponics shed. 'Once Impression is made, that's it and the dragon is unable to function without that special human partner.'

'But the Weyr keeps looking for likely candidates. Surely one of them could have filled in,' Kes continued.

'Perhaps it all happened too fast,' Betty Sopers suggested, her eyes red for she'd known Alianne very well. 'So few women die in childbirth . . .' And she looked hopefully down the table to the two medics.

Kolya looked properly sympathetic while Akis Andriadus nodded his head encouragingly.

'I haven't heard what went wrong with Alianne,' Kolya said. 'She's . . . she had two children but I'll certainly ask for a report.'

'And I've had nine,' Mairi said in a no-nonsense tone, 'so don't you be fretting, Betty Sopers.'

'Especially if you aren't even preggers,' Jess Patrick said, with a slightly hopeful leer, for he was quite friendly with his fellow student.

'Of course, I'm not,' she replied firmly, although a blush coloured her face under her tan. Then her expression clouded. 'But she was so young and dragons are so . . . strong.'

'I'm delighted to hear that opinion expressed in this Hold,' Red said firmly. 'Without the dragons and those who ride them, we wouldn't be here today.'

'How *did* Sean get those bullocks to move?' Kes asked. 'It was too bloody dark to see anything by then.'

Red laughed, glad to be able to turn the evening's conversation to a lighter vein. 'The oxen may be stubborn but stupid they're not. They made tracks as fast as they could from the dragon behind them!'

'How did Sean get them to go in the right direction then?' Peter Chernoff asked. 'I could barely keep up with them, much less keep them left or right.'

'As I said, Sean was behind them, but slightly to their right so of course they stampeded left,' Red replied. 'And we are here, safe and sound. Pat, son, run get my fiddle and your mother's bodhran. D'you know where your flute is, Akis? I know your dad taught you.'

'I've got a good jug,' Ozzie said and rose from the table as Pat, getting explicit directions from his mother on where to find the instruments, ran from the Hall, Akis following.

It took no time at all to clear and dismantle the tables and set the chairs and benches along the walls and provide a happy ending to the first official day in Red Hanrahan's Hold.

The next morning was different. Red was up at first light, rousing Betty, Jess, Fyodor and Deccie to feed the animals. By the time they returned to the kitchen, Licia Dook, Emily Schultz and Sal Wang were starting breakfast under the watchful eye of Madeleine.

With breakfast eaten and a fresh mug of klah, Red called a meeting of the various supervisors and discussed the day's priorities. That set the pattern for the spring weeks to come, while they were establishing pastures, crops and garden, but still making the most use of the heavy equipment that would improve and enlarge the cave system. Hanrahan had never shirked hard work and did as much time on the stone-cutters or the borer – the hardest of the machines to use – as he did in the fields or the breeding-yard. He could and did leave a lot of the general management of his precious stock to Brian, Jess and Betty with whichever fosterlings could be spared from building. But he was sensible that reasonable rest and relaxation were as vital as a good day's work.

Even that he used somewhat to his own advantage since he made outings to map the Holding a special treat: certainly a change from the unremitting labour of turning a cliff into a human habitation or the sheer drudgery of ploughing, sowing and weeding. First he had to be assured by the Weyr that there were a few safe days in hand, then he set directions and goals for his teams. The extent of his legitimate Stake, combined with the acreage of those who had joined him in the enterprise, added up to a considerable hunk of real estate, as Brian put it. Now what had been delineated on probe cartographic surveys had to be thoroughly explored, posted, and potentials assessed.

In form, the Hold land was slightly pie-shaped, the most northern point the thinnest part of the wedge, and the high and very cold mountain tarn lake the blunt end. The holding widened out from the lake, bordered on both sides by rivers: on the southern side the river they had so perilously

107

crossed; on the north-east the next large one, two days' steady ride from the first riverine boundary. Red needed to know how many more possible cave sites were available when his present population multiplied itself out of these facilities.

With material excised from the interior, stone cottages were to be erected along the foot of the ramp all the way to the animal accommodations. In his master plan, those ultimately would be workshops for the various crafts needed in a large and prospering community.

He was fond of Brian, got along well with him, hoped to do the same with the younger ones, but his sons would need land of their own, where the da wasn't sitting over every decision. And the Stake was large enough to support many separate establishments. There should be room for future generations to expand, too. When this Fall was past, even though Red might not live to see that glorious time, his kin could spread out, all over the Hold. In his mind's eye, Red saw that even more clearly now, as magnificent a dream as he had ever envisioned since he and Mairi had decided to join the Pern colony.

So, whenever possible, he sent scouts out to find what other riches – accommodation being the main one – the Stake could provide. Sometimes he went himself to check on possible ore sites, for they'd need more coal to run the hypocaust system that Egend had devised for warming the living quarters of caves than the one seam they'd found near by provided.

Egend was an ingenious engineer. He'd been successful at Fort Weyr in drilling into the old, still-hot magma chamber that provided delightful quantities of heat, especially for the hardening of dragon eggs on the sandy floor of the Hatching Ground. It had taken the dragons weeks of hard work hauling in the appropriate sands from the beaches near Boll but the Weyr now had an approximation of the conditions Kitti Ping felt the dragons required. Not that there hadn't been clutches successfully hatched on makeshift warm beds but the sand flooring appealed to the queens. Like the babies appearing so continuously at Fort, dragon eggs seemed to be continually in one stage of maturation or other at the Weyr.

Whenever his duties had permitted him, Red had attended

the happy occasions of Hatchings but Mairi managed to get to them all, and was quite an expert on what colour dragon would emerge from what shell.

Egend had seen no problem in heating Red's Hold by hypocaust and such hearths as could safely be extended up to the heights. Egend had unearthed some solar panelling among Joel's supplies which would do for heating water. There was nothing like a good bath to soothe a body after a hard day's work. And, after having to put up with other people's dirt and grime for so long, having a bath, more so clean clothes when you wanted them, was a real luxury in the new Hold, made possible by the use of the solar panels.

Of his fostered youngsters, young Ali Arthied had studied enough engineering under his father that he could set up and monitor that system with Jonti Greene's assistance. They were very clever in adapting and contriving mechanicals, that pair. He planned to send both back to sit their exams with Fulmar Stone who had been monitoring their studies.

Educating the young had become a race between the jobs that *had* to be done to survive and the studies that *had* to be done to keep skills from dying out.

Well, maybe, Red thought as he rose the morning they were finally going to hang the airlock door, when that chore was done, they could stop moving at such a hectic pace. Success in their first year here was crucial for many reasons: not the least of which was proving it could be done expeditiously. Grass *was* up in three of the seeded paddocks; the first shoots of alfalfa (the last of his seed allowance) were pushing through the assiduously fertilized earth, for night soil was among the many resources recycled. The fruit trees, puny as they were, had been planted in the walled orchard which could be covered against Threadfall by translucent plastic sheets which Sal Khalil had coaxed out of the old machine Carlos Minzentes had used. The vegetable garden, also walled, was coming on with few failures and the rows could be quickly covered with plastic shields.

It was a bright sunny spring morning, too, Red was happy to notice: auspicious, especially since he had coaxed Paul Benden and a few other special guests from the Fort to

109

gather for this momentous occasion – the Dooring of . . .

'Scorch it,' Red swore under his breath as he jammed his feet into his steel-capped work boots. He still didn't have the *right*-sounding name for the place.

Mairi hadn't been at all in favour of naming the place Keroon or even Kerry which he had thought she'd go for.

'Oh, it should be something of *us*, or *ours*,' she'd said, her face screwed up as she tried to express what she meant.

'Hanrahan Hold?' he'd asked, almost facetiously.

'Good heavens, no. That smacks of lord of the manor.' Then she'd given him one of her sly sideways grins. 'Though you are, you know. Lord of all this,' and she'd gestured broadly through the deep-set window of their upstairs bedroom.

The day they had moved their bed from his old office – which immediately became his office again – to the three-roomed suite that had been carved out of the cliff face – that had been *her* day. He was not likely to forget the joy on her face as she had directed Brian and Simon just where her heir-loom chest – once more glued together since its dismember-ment for the Second Crossing – should be placed. When she'd seen it settled exactly where she wanted it, she'd given such a happy, contented sigh. Then she shooed everyone out so she could polish it to a soft gleam.

She was so long at that task that Maureen ended up feeding her baby brother.

'That's not like Ma,' she'd told her father as she cuddled Ryan in the crook of her arm.

'It is today, Maureen,' Red replied, swilling the last of the klah around in his cup before he drained it. 'Settling that chest means this place is definitely your mother's home now.'

'First thing Ma asked for when we landed here was glue to put the chest together,' Brian told his much younger sister and winked at his father.

'Apart from the stones we stand on, that's the oldest object in this hold,' Red remarked in a sentimental tone. 'Cherished for generations in your mother's family . . .'

'And doubtless for generations here,' Brian added with an understanding grin. 'So, when are we getting the front door in place, Dad?'

'The invitations have been accepted,' his father said, 'so let's get the hoists in place.'

Since its arrival, the heavy steel door and its fittings had remained in the sled by the ramp to the Hold entrance, a reminder that switched from a source of irritation, because it wasn't in place, to anticipation as the 'day' drew nearer.

Today! Red told himself. He'd new trousers hiding the work boots and a fine new shirt over which Mairi insisted he wear one of the leather jerkins that had become useful work apparel.

'At least until that thing is in place. We've ever so much spare hide,' she'd said, 'but no time to set up Maddie's big looms yet, so spare the cloth and wear the jerkin.'

Today, too, Sean and Sorka, with their newest son, would join the celebrations. A dragon or two might come in useful bringing in guests, though not in a million years would Red *ask* that a dragon be employed in any task but the one they had been bred to do.

He knew how bitter Sean had been when 'all' the dragons could do was carry things from one place to another. Of course, that was before they had learned to fly *between* and chew the firestone that made Thread-charring flame. Sean might be a tad arrogant over his present high position but Red would not fault him. He, and the other young dragonriders, risked hideous death and many injuries to keep Thread from ravaging this one area of Pern that humans could survive in. And more power to the lad – no, man that Sean had become – he was a true leader of his riders and a fine manager of the new species. The night that Alianne and Chereth had died had been the only time Sean had given any show of the burden of responsibility he had undertaken. In one sense, Sean's emotion had been a sign of real maturity in Red's eyes: a man had the right to tears of grief, no blame attached. Red genuinely admired Sean for that. But then, he had always admired Sean, even when he'd been a wild, young and unknown quantity as the proud possessor of two brown fire-lizards.

Now, tantalizing odours of the beef and sheep roasting over the glowing coals in the barbecue pits wafted across the rough road that led past the fields to the front of the Hold. Red could hear the fuss from the open kitchen doors and windows as Mairi, Maureen, and most of the fosterlings were pressed into service to prepare the feast for those who would gather here to set the door in the portal.

The mechanicals to perform that setting were set in place, awaiting the arrival of the guests; the hoist, securely supported, jutted from the window directly above, and the chains were already attached to the door to lift it out of the sled-wagon. The durasteel had been well rubbed with fine steel wool, removing the minor scrapes acquired during its first occupation. Red wondered briefly which shuttle it had been taken from. He hadn't asked Joel Lilienkamp, too relieved to get the door released to him to irritate the old man with a minor detail. He'd say it was from the *Eusijan*, the shuttle in which Sallah Telgar and Barr Hamil had piloted the Hanrahans down to the surface of their new planetary home. Who could argue with him? The shuttles had all been the same in design.

Suddenly a bronze fire-lizard came streaking in through the opening, chittering wildly at him. Snapper appeared and the two conferred. The bronze then approached Red who held out his arm for the creature to land. Snapper popped to his shoulder, overseeing any attentions from a stranger. Chittering again, the bronze held up one foot on which a message capsule was tied.

Red carefully untied it, thanking the fire-lizard.

'"Where the hell's this ford you told us to take? PB,"' he read aloud.

Red laughed, sensing the frustration in the bold writing of the terse note. He poked his head out the window. 'Someone saddle King for me. Paul can't find my ford.'

By the time he got downstairs, not only King was saddled and waiting, but ten other riders.

'Should we bring a boat to make him feel at home?' Brian asked, grinning as he swayed easily with Cloudy's excited cavortings.

'No, let's just make tracks and get him here or the day'll be done with no door in place,' Red said, swinging up into his saddle.

'And no feast tonight either if my front door's not in place,

112

Peter Hanrahan,' Mairi yelled from the kitchen door.

'Let's go then, lads, or we go hungry!' The moment Red eased the reins, King took off and the others were showered by the pebbles the eager stallion kicked up behind him.

Depending on speed, the ford was an hour's distance on a fast horse; four hours' travel by wagon or cart. As he rode, Red hoped that his guests' horses were still fresh enough to make the return journey at a decent speed. Maybe Paul had been practising riding. Gorghe Logoridcs had bred a beast similar to a walking horse but though the animals were easy to sit, they were plainsbred. His Paso Fino types would be more useful here in the hilly north.

They paused only once to give the horses a breather and surprised the party on the other side of the ford by their sudden appearance.

'Ahoy, there, Admiral Benden, be ye bogged down by a mere river?' Red shouted through cupped hands. Beneath him, King blew vigorously through his nostrils but he was in such good condition that he was only slightly sweaty from the run and his breath rate quickly returned to normal.

'Ahoy yourself,' Paul bellowed back, getting to his feet. 'How're we expected to get across *that*?' and he pointed disgustedly at the swirling current of muddy water that separated them.

'I told you to look for the cairn and line up the poles,' Red shouted back, pointing to the right and then indicating the – to him – plainly visible steel pole on his side of the bank. 'Spare me from spacemen who need a bloody computer to navigate and a blinking beacon to guide them. Hi, there, Ju, Zi!' he added, noticing Paul's wife and the big dark man among the nine or ten others who now joined the admiral where he stood just short of swirling water.

Paul directed some of his party to find this alleged cairn and pole of Hanrahan's, speaking loud enough for his voice to carry across the ford.

The river was high from the rains the previous week but not quite as high as it had been the night Red had got his party across.

113

'River's a bit high, isn't it, Dad?' Brian said, a little anxiously. 'Could the cairn have come down?'

'I hope not. You did cement it, didn't you, when you returned the sleds?'

'Sure did, and put my initials on it but there's growth now along the bank on that side. Maybe it's hidden.' Brian started to urge Cloudy forward as the search seemed futile.

'Well, we're just wasting time,' Red said, and kneed King forward, pressuring him just slightly to get him to yield left to the exact centre of where Red knew the ford was. 'Guess we'll just have to lead the blind into the kingdom of the sighted.'

As he entered the water, he heard Brian's chuckle and a surreptitious glance over his shoulder, showed that his escort had fanned out in a phalanx as wide as the ford. The water was not quite to King's knees as the big horse pranced across, all too eager to make a show of his stallion self.

'I found it!' one of Paul's party cried, planting his foot on the top of the cairn.

'Hiding your precious landmarks, are you?' Paul roared. 'The arrogance of you, walking on the water like that!' He stood, hands on his hips, grinning with sardonic good humour as the welcoming party splashed up to him.

Leaning down, Red extended his hand to Paul and gripped it firmly.

'Well, the river's running muddier'n usual or you'd have seen the shale that makes fording possible right here,' Red said. He motioned for Brian to go check the cairn and the pole.

'You could at least have painted it,' Paul suggested as his mount, one of Caesar Galliani's lean, legged, ribby walking horses, was led forward by one of Caesar's girls. She was giving King the once over, too, and grinned up at Red.

'I'll add it to my list of chores,' Red said, grinning, 'and maybe build the cairn higher so no-one can miss it.'

The Galliani girl, whose name escaped Red, gave Paul a leg up, checking the girth and deftly slipping the stirrup on the admiral's foot when she was finished.

'You got here so fast, you can't be far away?' Paul's remark had a tinge of hope in it.

'Not at the rate I usually ride,' Red said with a slightly malicious grin, 'but even at a steady pace, we're not more than an hour and a bit away. Had a comfortable ride?'

Paul was not really riding *into* his saddle as one accustomed to the exercise. As the bay gelding stepped out into the very smooth flowing pace that was his natural stride, the admiral winced slightly and eased his butt. Riding would never be more than a necessary evil for Benden. Still, he had come, so Red made no disparaging remarks. Zi Ongola looked more comfortable on horseback and so did Ju Adjai Benden. In fact, she looked downright pleased, glancing about her, taking in the lay of the land.

Cecilia Rado had come along to see how Red had translated her architectural drawings. Balding and slightly tubby Arkady Sturt and the lean and grizzled Francesco Vasseloe were also in the party and Red decided he knew who was joining Zi Ongola in settling the western peninsula. Three of the numerous Duff offspring and two more young Schultzes made up the rest of the expedition.

Even at a gentler return pace, the imposing façade of the Hold was soon in sight, its stone blending from an orange to an orangey red. Indeed, Red had planned the sweep of the road with just that view in mind and listened with real pride to the complimentary remarks from all sides about the distinctive orangey red of the cliff face.

Then the Galliani girl drew up beside him, sitting well on a rather fractious little chestnut mare.

'Dad sent me along as a spy,' She said. 'I'm Terry, in case you need to know.'

'You're welcome, Terry, and spy all you like,' he said, grinning amiably down at her.

'That stallion's one of Sean's Cricket's produce, isn't he?' she said, her eyes feasting on the superb conformation and easy forward movement that came effortlessly from King's shoulder.

'He is.'

'*This* weed is all Dad would let me have,' she said with disgust. 'He's such a pain sometimes.'

'He's your father,' Red said a little severely though he

sympathized with the girl, noting the mare's jarring trot.

'That is all too true,' she said, unrebuked, 'but, if a person's got a few ideas of her own to try, isn't this planet big enough for differences?' Her tone was plaintive.

'Going with Zi Ongola?'

She nodded. 'I'd like to. He'll need a tougher horse than we breed.' Once again she admired King and the others that had been ridden out from the Hold. 'You may well have a customer in Zi.' She gave him another grin and circled around to fall back beside Cecilia.

'Baths can wait, Mairi,' Paul Benden repeated firmly when Mairi again tried to insist that he ease his sore muscles immediately. 'I'd rather do the lot after we've seen that damned door in place. The klah'll do me till then.' So he sipped from his mug and was even persuaded to eat some of the freshly baked sweets which the fosterlings were passing around while others, including Terry Galliani, were taking the horses to be unsaddled and groomed.

Tables had already been set up outside with a variety of snack and finger foods and klah, chilled and hot. The roasting meats were a good advertisement for the feasting to come.

'Mairi, now we've all got travel dust out of our mouths,' Cecilia said, 'why don't you give me and Ju the five-credit tour while the muscles do their mite?'

'We'll give a shout before we shut you in,' Red said jovially as he was showing Paul, Zi and Fran Vasseloe the preparations that had been made and how cleverly Peter Chernoff had set the lock frame into the stone of the portal. Once he glanced towards the position of the sun and Paul sent him a querying look. 'Sorka and Sean said they'd be here to watch the dooring and join us in the feast. And . . .' Red paused, looking from Ongola to Benden. 'Once we get producing, I plan to send the Weyr a tithe of all we grow and make. They've enough to do without having to forage for food as well.'

'Ah, yes,' and Paul rubbed the back of his neck, not meeting anyone's glance. 'As it is now, they often bring *us* fresh meat and fruit when they've had to go south to feed the dragons. I don't know how much longer Ierne Islanders can hold out, but,' Paul grinned wryly, 'as you all know, it's meant the difference.'

'Tell me, Paul,' and Red leaned over conspiratorially, his eyes twinkling, 'is it Ierne Island produce they get or some of the stock the Logorides and Gallianis had to let loose?'

'Well, now, you know, I've never asked,' Paul replied, regarding Red with a very bland expression.

'Still and all, they shouldn't have to scrounge for provisions,' Red said. 'The Hold should supply the Weyr that protects it.'

'I shall tithe from my Holding as well,' Ongola said, his deep voice making his words a solemn vow.

'Alianne's death has certainly made all in Fort aware that we're asking a great deal from these young men and women,' Paul went on, 'and they've met the challenge magnificently. I had a chance to discuss support personnel with Sean and he's suggested that we send him some of the older fosterlings to take over maintenance and domestic chores. They'd be available, too, as candidates for the new eggs. I got Joel to spring loose enough supplies so additional personnel won't be a burden on the Weyr's resources. They've got space, we've got too many warm bodies . . .' He gave a wry smile. 'Alianne's mother is staying on, to help rear the grandchildren. She's widowed and says the place needs a firm hand in its domestic management. The queen riders really don't have enough time especially if they've a broody queen.'

'Seems to me one queen or another's broody all the time,' Red said with a chuckle.

'Which also means the dragon population is growing large enough to protect four Holds,' Paul said, with justifiable pride. 'Maybe more, if the "premises" are feasible. Telgar says he'd like to be closer to the ore lodes in the eastern mountain range. He's done as much as he can to improve the warrens of the Fort.' He kept his voice level and added a smile at his use of the word 'warrens'.

Red wondered if his leaving, and Ongola's projected Hold, was causing more, or less, dissension in Fort.

'I think you and Ongola have given hope and inspiration. Despite Joel's concern over dwindling supplies, a lot of his inventory are items that will not be in demand again,' Paul said with a wry grin. 'We're stepping down to a lower level of technology, based on what is available to us here, not what we once had. That was, after all, the purpose of this colony. You've made it, so did Pierre, on a minimum of basics and look what you've achieved.' Paul gestured to the imposing façade behind him. 'No, it's definitely time to stop huddling in Fort and move out. I'd like to see more evidence of courage in our people after the trauma of Threadfall and the dreadful loss of lives in the Fever Year.'

'I think there're more than just Sean and Sorka coming,' Ongola said, shielding his eyes with one big hand as he looked upward.

Everyone had to crane their necks to see dragons, gold, bronze, brown, blue and green, settling themselves on the top of the Hold cliff. Careful, Red hoped, to avoid the solar panel installation.

'The more the merrier,' Red said, laughing. 'They make a brave sight there, don't they?'

'But they've no riders,' Zi remarked.

'Didn't want to scare your beasts again, Red,' said Sean, emerging from the Hold, Sorka beside him, one arm crooked about her latest son. Behind him sauntered more riders. 'We wanted to do you honour and half a wing seemed an appropriate escort.'

Mairi and those she had taken inside the Hold were the last to emerge.

'They took the stairs down,' she said in a distracted fashion, for she was determined to wrest her grandson from his mother's arm, 'so now I know why you insisted on carving steps all that way up, Red. It wasn't just to service the solar panels.' She turned to Cecilia. 'But we'd just got the storeys cleaned up when he cut those steps and dust sifted all over again. Oh, isn't he a love, Sorka? What have you named him?'

'Ezremil,' Sean said, slightly accenting the first vowel. It took a moment for people to register the fact that he had joined the names of two of the colony's heroes.

Tears came to Mairi's eyes. 'Oh, what a splendid notion!'

'Oh, yes, indeed,' and Ju Benden choked on a sob before

she managed a laugh. 'Much better than encumbering the poor lad with Ezra or Keroon or even Emile. We ought to use more such truly Pernese-style names.'

Paul put an arm about his wife's shoulders, smiling fondly down at her.

'We could really dispense with surnames altogether. Ezremil of Fort Weyr! Ryan of . . .' Paul turned on Red. 'What *are* you naming this place?'

With none of his suggestions, and he'd had a lot of ideas since the initial 'Keroon' and 'Kerry', Red shrugged. 'It'll come to us. The right name will come to us. Now, can we get this door into position?'

With the dragons safely out of the sight of any animals, Red sent Brian to get the bullocks whose mighty thews would haul the airlock door up to the opening. That was the signal for everyone to gather in front of the Hold. Red could see Mairi keeping an eye on the young toddlers, one of Brian's being the sort that got into everything *first* and, when scolded, would reply that 'No-one had said he couldn't'.

Authoritative cracks of the bull-whips started four yokes of oxen moving forward, with men at each wide head, to steady them up. Slowly, the heavy metal door rose from the sled. When it hung free, the men whom Peter Chernoff had chosen to help turned it sideways so that the hinges could be aligned. They were with a very audible clunk to indicate contact.

'HOLD!' Peter Chernoff said, raising both hands and the oxen were halted in their tracks. The open clamps of the hinges were then shut, each with its own separate metallic clink. 'EASE UP!'

The oxen were backed, first one step, then another, taking the weight slowly off the hoist chains.

A loud hurray burst from the breathless onlookers.

'Hold that, too,' Peter shouted. 'We gotta be sure it,' and, as he spoke, he leaned against the great door, 'closes.' Obediently the former airlock swung in with such ease that one man had to jump out of its way. Simultaneously, Peter grabbed the bevelled edge with a restraining hand and was dragged forward one step. Bracing himself, he stopped it from closing completely.

119

A second cheer went up and Peter, wiping sweat from his forehead, turned with an engaging grin and a sweeping bow to Red.

'My lord of the Hold, will you complete the ceremonial closing?'

Grabbing Mairi by the hand, and waiting only until she had time to pass Ezremil back to his mother, Red strode up the ramp to the imposing metal door. Then they both inspected Peter's handiwork. He had done well, adapting the thick air-lock door to domestic purposes. Keeping Thread out was now as important a function as keeping atmosphere in had once been. Red nodded to Mairi who put her hand over his on the interior wheel and they both pulled the door to. With a power-ful spin, Red turned the wheel and heard the bars thud home in their floor and ceiling sockets. The Hold was now closed!

'Wouldn't they be surprised if we didn't open it?' Red asked, embracing Mairi's still-slender form against him.

'Yes, and I'd be furious because I wouldn't get any of that succulent meat we've been roasting since midnight!' Mairi stood on tiptoe and kissed her husband.

'A very good point . . .' He gave an equally powerful reverse swing on the locking wheel and the bars slid free. Red gave the door a push. 'Well, at least that devil of a grandson won't be able to open this door.' He gave a heftier shove and the door swung silently open.

He and Mairi strode forward to applause. He was briefly startled when the dragons on the heights added their deep voices to human cheers.

'Admiral, Commander, Weyrleaders, one and all, be welcome to . . .' He stopped short, a grin suddenly broaden-ing across his face as inspiration seized him. 'Be welcome to the Hold of Red's Ford. In the old language, Rua Atha.'

'Ruatha!' Mairi called out in her clear voice, her eyes looking up to his, for his approval of that elision. 'Oh, that's a splendid name, Rua Hanrahan!'

'To Ruatha Hold!' he shouted.

'TO RUATHA HOLD!' was the roar of acceptance. And, for the first time on the heights of Ruatha Hold, the dragons of Pern lifted their heads and bugled in rejoicing!

The Second Weyr

'You were over there again, weren't you?' Sorka said to Torenc in an amused undertone as the young queen rider sauntered past the Weyrwoman on her way to the day hearth. The lower cavern was deserted at this hour, well past midday and not yet time to prepare the evening meal.

Torene grinned over her shoulder at Sorka as she continued to the hearth. She served herself some soup from the big pot, broke off a wedge of bread and came back to the table where Sorka was also having a late lunch. She swung one of her elegantly leatherclad long legs over the low chair back and sat down, neatly putting her meal in front of her, all in one graceful movement.

'How'd you guess?'

Sorka had to grin at the girl's insouciance. Torene hovered on the edge of impudence but never quite offended. Of course that would have given both Sorka and Sean reasons to reprimand her but she seemed instinctively to know the limits. Sorka would have been particularly loath to bring her up sharp because she, who had been a reserved child in the restricted society she had been born into on Earth, admired Torene's candid charismatic manner and her irrepressible gaiety. Sean found them less easy to deal with but then, the responsibilities of the Weyr and the nurture and care of the dragons obsessed him and he had never been very light-hearted.

Sean generally knew everything that went on in the Weyr, sooner or later. He certainly knew that there was great interest in the east-coast crater that was touted as the next official base for dragonriders. But he probably wasn't aware of how often hopeful riders went to survey these likely premises.

Establishing another Weyr was no longer an idle notion but an urgent need. Fort's accommodations were terribly over-crowded, even when they sent wings to live temporarily in the less than comfortable cavern systems at Telgar or on nearly tropical Big Island where they had had to send mating and clutching queens to reduce the stress and the possibility of more accidents. Sorka gave a little shudder, remembering last year's disaster, and how close they had come to losing three queens in an aerial battle that left all three wounded. The bronzes and browns who had finally separated them had not come away unscathed either.

The entire Weyr had learned a terrible lesson: one queen in heat could precipitate the condition in those also near their season. No queen would share bronze and brown followers with another. Tarrie Chernoff still woke up with nightmares in which Porth was going *between* and she couldn't follow. Evenath, the first queen that Faranth had produced in her third clutch, had lost an eye as well as the use of one wing and Catherine's Siglath had so much wing fabric destroyed that neither could fly in the queens' wing again. All three queens had horrific scars on their bodies from talons and fangs during that battle. There were still queens enough to do the low flying with flame-throwers, joined as they usually were by any green rider in the first or third trimesters of pregnancy when constant dropping into the cold of *between* might cause miscarriage. But Jays, there were more than enough dragons and riders to form three Weyrs and give everyone decent space. They needn't all cram in like holders.

Sean delayed, Sorka felt, because he could not yet bring himself to delegate final authority to anyone else. His was the responsibility, his would be any blame. He was intensely proud and immensely caring of the fighting force he commanded: the force that indeed he had *created*.

No-one denied that. Every rider knew that dragon welfare came first with Sean and he constantly strove to maximize their effectiveness, at the same time reducing personal injury. Initially, when the dragons and riders moved up to Fort Weyr, he had spent endless hours with those who had had pilot experience during the Nathi Wars and with the admiral and both captains. He had found what he could of military history and strategy tapes to figure out the most successful way to combat Threadfall: he had come up with a combination of cavalry and dog-fighting techniques. Then he had refined formations to apply them to the different ways Thread would fall.

As the numbers of available fighting dragons increased, he had decided on the appropriate and handiest number for small units – wings of thirty-three dragons, with a wingleader and two wingseconds so that, even if the wingleader and his dragon had to drop out because of injuries, there would be a secondary rider responsible and trained to take charge. This was especially necessary, he felt, when the numbers of the smaller dragons, the blues and greens, increased. The wingleader should know each dragon in his wing well enough to see signs of strain and send the pair back to the Weyr to rest. Some blue and green riders, determined to prove that their partners were every bit as good as the larger ones, took risks and rode their lighter, less sturdy beasts beyond their endurance.

'Even a dragon has limits,' Sean repeated and repeated during weyrling training. 'Respect them! And yours! We don't need heroes in every Fall. We need *dragonriders* every Fall.'

The fortunately rare deaths, of either rider or dragon or both, had a sobering effect on even the most audacious. Injuries – so often due to carelessness – always dropped off after a death or a bad accident. Those that happened during weyrling training were the ones that Sorka hated the most – because they would haunt Sean through his dreams and turn him into an implacable martinet during his waking hours. Sorka would, however, take him to task when Sean became too autocratic. She made herself always approachable by any rider and never assumed a judgemental attitude.

'You upset morale throughout the Weyr,' she'd tell him firmly.

'I'm trying to improve *discipline* throughout the Weyr,' he'd shout back at her, 'so we won't *have* more deaths. I can't stand the deaths! Especially the dragons! They are so special and we need every one of them.'

That was true enough, especially now that more people were moving out of Fort Hold and setting up on their own wherever they could find appropriate cave systems. Boll and Ruatha Holds were thriving. Tarvi Telgar had moved his mining and engineering group into an immense system in the mountains above lodes he was currently working. Naturally he called his Hold Telgar. After five years of searching for the 'right' name, Zi Ongola had finally called his Tillek, in memory of the man who had brought a gaggle of pleasure yachts along the entire coastline of the Southern Continent and, despite storm and other difficulties, led them north to Fort's docks. As the newly dubbed Tillek was on shores full of fine fishing, the name was all the more appropriate.

'How'd I *guess*?' Sorka now repeated to Torene. 'Not a guess. You have that indefinable look of someone very pleased with herself. And, if you listen a moment, you'll probably hear all the dragons talking about it. I know Faranth is asking questions.'

Torene did listen a moment, her eyes going briefly out of focus before she made a grimace of resignation. 'There's a distinct disadvantage about being able to hear all the dragons, especially if you want to be discreet.' Then, eyes widening in concern, she glanced anxiously about the low-ceilinged room.

'Sean's not here,' Sorka said with a chuckle. 'He and two wings went south to hunt early this morning.' She sighed. 'I really look forward to having that tithe system they keep talking about in full operation.' She went on more briskly. 'By the time they're due back, there will be other things for dragons to talk about. Or the ones here'll all be asleep. It's a nice sunny day.'

'Sorka,' Torene cocked her head as she leaned towards Sorka, the expression in her large dark eyes anxiously earnest, 'can't *you* persuade Sean that we desperately need a second *permanent* Weyr? It's not just for the space it'll give us to spread out. It's needed to . . .' And Torene closed her lips on whatever point she'd been about to make.

Sorka gave a little laugh and finished for her. 'It's needed to give someone else a chance to run a full Weyr.' Seeing

Torene's stricken face, she patted her arm. 'I know my weyrmate, dear. His faults . . .'

'But that's it, Sorka, he doesn't *have* any. He's always *right*.' She said that without any malice but with some despair. 'He is the best possible Weyrleader we could ever have but . . .'

'There are other very capable riders who would also make good Weyrleaders.'

'Yes, and that isn't all.' She leaned ever closer. 'I heard that the Ierne Island bunch are going to come north, too. They want to settle on the east coast. I mean, we've boasted so often that distance is nothing to a dragon,' and now Torene's grin was amusement, 'that they say we can protect them on the east coast just as easily as here in the west.'

Sorka gave a genuine burst of laughter. 'Hoist on our own petards, as my father used to say.'

'What does that mean?' Torene blinked in bewilderment.

It was slightly unfair, Sorka thought, for a girl to have such long eyelashes as well as a beautiful face, an elegant (Sean said 'sexy') figure with personality and brains as well. Even her short hair, close cropped to be more comfortable under the skull-fitting helmets they wore, formed exquisite curls that framed her high-cheeked and distinctive countenance.

'It means getting caught in one's own trap, actually, but in this case the "trap" is the boasts we dragonriders keep making.'

'Oh!' Then the girl giggled. 'Well, we have, but if we don't move in right *smart,* those Ierne Islanders will take the better cave system and we'll be left with second best,' she added indignantly.

'You're a true dragonrider, girl,' Sorka said. 'Nothing but the best for us.'

'Oh, I don't mean it that way, Sorka, and you know it. But the old crater is perfect for a second proper Weyr,' said Torene, leaning forward again in her enthusiasm, ignoring her cooling soup. 'Even better than this one in some ways, because it's a double crater system, one nearly circular, the other oblong, with a deep lake, enough space to keep herdbeasts, instead of having to go south to catch dinner

125

when our provisions run short. Best of all, there's one immense vaulted cavern that would be big enough for a half dozen queens to clutch in . . .'

'One at a time is quite enough.'

The enthusiasm in Torene's eyes dimmed slightly in memory before she rushed on, 'And we wouldn't have to do much to it at all since it's got some sand in it, and a hypocaust system could be installed in one of the side niches. Furthermore, my mother says that the stone-cutters have about had it. If we don't get to use them soon, we might have to chisel out individual weyrs with our bare hands.' Torene gave a sharp nod of her head at that unwelcome option.

'Those cutters've done more than they were designed to do,' Sorka said, remembering what her father had said when he'd used them nine years ago at Ruatha Hold.

'Well, I want to design our Weyr with them . . .'

'Our Weyr . . . ?' Sorka raised a quizzical eyebrow at the young rider.

Torene closed her eyes and made a rattling sound of dismay with her tongue, covering her face with her hands at having made such a gaffe. She uncovered her face and grinned impishly at Sorka. 'You can't blame me for dreaming. Someone's going to be Weyrwoman and you told me yourself that Alaranth's the biggest gold yet.'

'And have you planned who's to be Weyrleader?' Sorka asked gently.

Despite that kindliness, Torene blushed furiously. She had the uncomfortable feeling sometimes that it was wrong of Alaranth to be a full hand taller in the shoulder than her dam, Faranth, although Sorka had always appeared delighted by the improvement. The young queen was nearly mature enough to make her first mating flight. Though Torene discounted her physical attractiveness whenever someone complimented her, she played no favourites among the male riders who were constantly in her company. Being candid by nature, she was unable to play the flirt as some of the woman riders did. So she treated the young men all the same as they vied for her attention, trying to fix her interest. The only exception was Michael, the bronze rider son of Sorka and Sean.

Mihall – to use the pronunciation of his name that he preferred – was as dedicated a dragonrider as his father. Sometimes more so, his mother ruefully thought. Since coming to maturity three years ago, Mihall's bronze Brianth had sired sufficient clutches that Sean had grounded the randy bronze in queen-mating flights. One of Sorka's duties was to keep very precise records of which clutch was sired by which bronze or brown so that any queens resulting from that pairing would not be rematched with their sires. Mihall had shrugged and remarked that that was fine by him; there were plenty of greens who liked Brianth enough to twine necks with him any time.

Torene replied quite seriously to Sorka's question about the choice of Weyrleader. 'No, I wouldn't plan that far, Sorka, because Sean would make such an important appointment, wouldn't he?'

'Probably,' Sorka replied discreetly because Sean had a notion on the best way to decide that.

'Surely you've some preference as to which dragon mates with Alaranth?' Sorka asked with gentle inquisitiveness.

Torene flushed but answered quickly enough. 'That depends on who's fast enough to catch Alaranth, doesn't it?' She grinned back, avoiding Sorka's subtle probing. Torene wasn't being arrogant in suggesting that the bigger males were going to have to fly very well indeed to mate with her Alaranth. That young queen would lead them a long and very dizzy chase. Torene added a giggle to her grin. 'I only hope I'm strong enough to last. Don't try to figure out who I really fancy. You might be surprised.' Her mobile face turned solemn. 'Seriously, though, Sorka, dragonriders have got to move quickly to secure that twin-cratered place as our own.'

'I agree with you, Torene, except that there's no way in except to fly, and that could prove awkward for a number of reasons.'

'Ah,' and Torene held up one finger in triumph, 'I know where to put an access tunnel.' From a thigh pocket, she extracted a limp, well-used plasfilm, an echo survey of the double crater, with top, side- and ground-level elevations: probably from one of the original probes. Sorka didn't realize that there were other copies. But then, Torene's parents, the Ostrovskys, were mining engineers and would have had personal copies of all the preliminary surveys.

Torene spread the sheet out carefully, her touch almost caressing as she smoothed it down on the table and put salt and pepper mills to hold down the curling edges. 'Now, there's a natural opening quite far in. See the shadow here? Two thirds of the way to the lake. OK, the ceiling in the central cavity is only about two or three metres high but you wouldn't have to dig a very long tunnel to hook to it from either direction. There's your ground access.'

'You do seem to have studied the entire site well,' Sorka admitted.

'Not just me,' Torene replied quickly. 'A bunch of us go.' She hitched her chair closer and whispered across the space to Sorka. 'Couldn't you act as mediator for us?'

'Which bunch of you?'

Torene's dark eyes sparkled. 'Nyassa . . .'

'Really?'

'Well, Milath's due to clutch soon and Nya doesn't like the Big Island ground, hates the cold at that place above Telgar and doesn't *want* to clutch here when she has to share the sands again with Tenneth, Amalath, and Chamuth.'

'I take her point.'

'D'vid and Wieth, N'klas and Petrath . . .'

'Hold it, Torene. D'VEED and N'KLAS?' Sorka didn't believe her ears.

'Oh, hadn't you heard them?' Torene was surprised and then added quite casually, 'No, I guess you wouldn't have. I hear them all the time during Fall because it's what the dragons call other riders when they're warning *their* dragons to be careful. They're speaking so fast they sort of . . . well, compress names. So Day-vid has become D'vid, Nicholas Gomez is N'klas, and Fulmar is F'mar.'

'Are you T'rene?' asked Sorka, diverted.

The girl thought a moment. 'No, but Sevya'll be Sev and Jenette, Jen. They're sort of fast names anyway. I mentioned it one day after Fall and . . .' She gave a helpless shrug. '. . . everyone wanted to know their dragonish name.'

128

'Do they shorten their own, or others?'

'No,' and now Torene shook her head vigorously and flashed Sorka a dazzling smile. 'Dragons always know who's being spoken to.'

'I see,' and Sorka tried to appear that she comprehended the distinction.

'We think it's kind of nice to have a dragon nickname. It means they care about each other's rider, too.'

'I guess it would. Tell me, how do they shorten Sean?'

Torene shook her head, bouncing her curls. 'They don't. He's always "Leader" and I'd say they capitalize the "l", too.' She shot Sorka a sly grin.

'Oh, g'wan with you, now.'

'No, honest, Sorka, they're always respectful of Sean. And you're always a full "Sorka".'

'Are you buttering me up, young woman?'

'Now, why would I do a thing like that?' Torene made her eyes rounder. 'Just because I've asked you to be softly persuasive . . .'

Sorka laughed again. There was no other young woman in the Weyr quite like Torene; so refreshingly herself, without guile and yet exceedingly clever in her directness. 'Now who else is in your select bunch that's dropping over to the site all the time?'

'Sevya and Butoth, R'bert and Jenoth, P'ter and Siwith, Uloa and Elliath . . .'

'That makes three queens . . .'

'The new Weyr could accommodate four at least,' Torene said, 'and we've got interest from six more bronze riders, one a wingleader and two wingseconds; fifteen brown riders, three wingseconds among *them*; and ten blue and eight more green riders.'

'How long has this been going on?' A faint unease about the activities of the younger riders replaced amusement. Torene was far too candid in her dealings to be plotting a subtle mutiny of sorts. Sorka did a quick figuring – but forty-seven riders? Who were eager to start fresh in a new location? That was unsettling. She was certainly going to speak to Sean if this was the scale.

129

'Oh, nothing's been going *on*, Sorka,' Torene said, genuinely alarmed and, making immediate eye contact, laid a reassuring hand on Sorka's arm. 'We'd just – basically – like to have more space. Except for Nyassa and Uloa, we're all younger riders, stuck upstairs or downstairs or wherever we can be fitted in. Sevya says her mother has a bigger cupboard in Tillek than she and her dragon have here.' A tinge of dissatisfaction did colour the girl's voice and she bit down on her lip, flushing at having spoken criticizingly.

What she said was fair enough, Sorka knew. Sevya and Butoth, just graduated from the weyrling barracks, were in embarrassingly tight quarters. Though Torene had not mentioned herself, Alaranth did not even have proper headroom in the weyr she and her rider shared. In fact, they did not have two parts to their quarters as most partnerships did and Alaranth had to go to the Rim to sunbathe, a daily activity of all dragons. Soon enough Alaranth would be fully mature and by then there was no question that she could not continue in such a cramped accommodation.

'We haven't wanted to rock the boat, Sorka, but really, we can't *afford* to lose the chance of this place,' and Torene tapped the diagram. 'See here? Just above ground level where there are three natural caverns, one after the other? Made-to-order Weyrwoman's quarters . . . and with a little bit of alteration, these – here, here and here – would be spacious for the other queens. And over here, opposite what would be great domestic areas, is a series of caves just right for weyrlings, instead of having to cram them side by each. Why, the place would be wasted on holders,' and she laid a slightly disparaging stress on that noun.

'It would and it won't be,' a voice said, startling both women.

Torene turned a dull red under her tan as Sean appeared from behind them and sat down at their table, a cup of klah in his hand. He had obviously just returned, for just the top of his flight jacket was undone; hat and gauntlets were still clutched in his free hand. A quick glance at the Weyrwoman assured Torene that Sorka was just as surprised to see him. Well, they had been absorbed in a discussion which Torene knew had startled the older woman even though Sorka also saw the merit of tagging the double-crater for dragonriders.

Sean placed riding gear on the table beside his cup as he shrugged out of his heavy fleece-lined riding jacket. He finger-combed sweaty silvering red hair back from his forehead and craned his neck so he could see the plasfilm. Then had a slight smile for the anxious look which Torene couldn't dissemble.

'Glad there's more than one copy . . .'

'Mother . . .' Torene began in explanation and then couldn't go on.

Sean's grin broadened. 'Mothers have their uses.'

Torene gulped and, seizing this amazing opportunity, plunged right in. '"It would and it won't be", you said. We'll get the place? Ierne Islanders won't grab it?'

Sean snorted. 'They had notions but I persuaded them that the other cliff site was far more viable and only slightly less scenic. There's a valley with good soil for cultivation, a river for access to the coast, and south-facing slopes that are just what Rene Mallibeau's been screaming for, complete with the shale he insists he needs. I've been hoping to get back and go over this place,' and he tapped the plasfilm with his forefinger, 'with Ozzie, if Telgar could spare him.'

'Mother made me take him with us when she gave me this,' Torene said, sending a quick glance at Sorka who was, as usual, all eyes for her husband. Torene was scarcely the only female in the Weyr who envied them their double bonding.

'Starting your own splinter group with Alaranth, are you?' Sean asked, his expression carefully bland. But his cheek muscle didn't twitch the way it did when he was about to chew out an erring weyrling or rider.

Torene chose quickly between the options that bland question gave her and smiled brightly at Sean – not over-brightly because that would annoy him – but brightly enough to make him believe that she wasn't that much of a fool. Good thing the table concealed the shaking of her knees.

'Well, you know how big Alaranth's getting and honest, Sean, we just don't fit where we are any more and it isn't as if there's anywhere here we could switch to. I've just been

131

daydreaming, really.' She let her voice dwindle down to an apologetic whisper.

As she spoke, Sean sipped klah, looking neither at her nor Sorka.

Yes, she's telling you truly, Torene heard Carenath tell his rider. *She is very excited about the place and has been over every inch several times. So Alaranth says.*

Torene did not let her expression change but she saw Sorka peer at her with a slight frown drawing her brows together.

'Sean, have you forgotten that I can hear Carenath?' she spoke almost plaintively, as she felt she should remind him since it amounted to inadvertent eavesdropping. 'He's got a strong thought to him, you know.'

Sean gave her one of his quietly thoughtful regards, neither accusing nor accepting. 'Yes, even though it proves to your advantage.'

Torene let herself grin now with less anxiety. 'Either way I'd've heard him.'

'I think that can prove to be an asset, young Torene,' he said, surprising her almost as much as hearing total approval from Carenath. Was the bronze dragon merely echoing his rider's thoughts or was that his sentiment, too?

His and Sean's, Alaranth said in that very quiet way she had of speaking only at her rider. *But he's not thinking at Carenath right now.*

Sean was indeed thoughtful as he ran fingers along the shadowed 'open' areas within the crater walls shown on the plasfilm, finally laying his hand on the lake-site. He nodded once, finishing the klah in his cup and rose.

'Have you finished, love?' he asked Sorka with a brief apologetic nod to Torene.

'Yes, actually, I have.'

'Keep the diagram handy, would you please, Torene?' Sean added and then, one hand under the elbow of his weyrmate, walked away with her.

Torene let out a whooshing of relief and, dipping a piece of bread in her soup, began to eat, more as a release of taut nerves than from hunger. The appearance of Sean Connell had taken away her appetite. The sop of bread was cold but she ate it. You didn't waste food and, even cold, the soup tasted good.

'She's brought matters to a head, Sean,' Sorka said when they had arrived at their apartment, a series of five adjoining cavern bubbles which had needed only minor alteration and addition to be a comfortable, and private, living space. 'There's a group of forty-seven young people who dream of occupying that place.'

'Probably more,' he said, hanging his riding gear on the pegs near the entrance.

'You knew?'

He shrugged, once again smoothing back his hair, dry now. 'It's honest speculation, according to Dave Caterel, Paul and Otto. It would come sooner or later – a need to split into separate groups to cover the ground that's going to be cultivated and keep it Thread free. Red had a go at me last time Thread fell on Ruatha lands.' He shrugged again and, taking a seat, held up his right leg. Sorka straddled the leg, braced herself for his push and hauled the boot off: automatically repeating the process for the left boot while they talked. 'Torene would have done better getting Dad to intercede for them.'

'Now, Sean . . .' Sorka began, ready to defend Torene.

'Don't "now, Sean" me, woman,' he said. She glanced quickly over her shoulder to test his mood. 'She's right for all I think she's a tad young to be so . . . so beforehand.'

'There isn't an ounce of malice in Torene Ostrovsky,' Sorka said staunchly.

'I haven't suggested there was, lovey,' he said and, scattering his boots, pulled her by the waist on to his lap. 'But it's obvious we'll have to move quickly on this, now that the ball's rolling.'

He laid his head between her shoulder-blades as he often did, not amorously, but because he was better using gestures than words and had many ways of expressing his love for her.

'Have you decided who will lead the new Weyr?' she asked, covering his hands on her waist with hers and leaning into the close embrace.

133

'Weyrs,' he said, giving her a final hug before he gently put her back on her feet.

'Weyrs?'

'Yes. Plural,' he rose and, stripping off his shirt as he walked towards their bathing room, gestured with his head for her to follow.

'We've more than enough dragons, with three clutches hardening, to populate three, maybe four Weyrs . . .

'Torene's dream site, Big Island, that crater in Telgar's Holding, and where else?'

He paused on his way through their bedroom long enough to step out of his pants and heavy socks, and ball them up to throw into the laundry basket.

'We've got two other choices, one down on that mid-eastern peninsula and another up in the high ranges, the crater with all those spiky peaks. But, to make the necessary improvements even in the east-coast place, we'll need to monopolize the remaining functional stone-cutters . . .'

'Is there enough fuel?'

'Fulmar Stone's got all of 'em rigged to run off generators,' and Sean grinned at Sorka as he stepped into the steaming bath. Having a copious supply of thermally heated water was one of the luxuries he enjoyed. The excess water ran off down the pipes that helped keep the Weyr warm. Far underground, the water went through a filtering system and returned, cleansed, to the reservoirs, to be pumped up again. Other pipes brought drinking water from the cisterns that were kept topped up by mountain streams.

'But the actual cutting surfaces are wearing out.'

'True, but Telgar's trying to make replacement abrasives that'll slice rock. There're enough industrial diamonds near Big Island to give us a fair approximation of the cutting surface. T'any rate, I dealt with the Ierne group. They get the second east-coast cave system and give us a work force to make our own adaptations.' He grinned both with pleasure as he sank into the warm water up to his chin and with an understandable pride in the success of his machinations. 'With them there, and in a fertile area, they'll have enough to tithe the new Weyr.'

'You thought all this up?'

He opened his eyes and grinned at her, suddenly boyish. 'Hell no, your old man gave me the wink and the nod, and stood by me while I fought it all out with Lilienkamp.' After Paul Benden's death last winter, Joel Lilienkamp had been voted into the management of Fort Hold. He was, in some ways, much harder to listen to in the further disbursement of people – whom he regarded as renewable resources – and of irreplaceable materiel which the colony had to conserve.

'You mean, you weren't hunting south with the others?'

He nodded once and then also shook his head and began vigorously soaping himself. 'Nope. Carenath made do nicely with an injured bullock that had fallen into a crevasse that your father said we could have. I didn't want any more rumours to circulate than necessary.' He grimaced. 'There seem to be enough.'

She had to wait until he had ducked his head to clear the soap suds from his hair before she asked the next question.

'Who're to be Weyrleaders?'

He gave her an enigmatic smile and she knew why he was going for three new Weyrs: that way he'd avoid any complaint of nepotism. The young people who had been born on Pern, especially those orphaned by the Fever eight years ago, were quick to make that charge when the children of still-living fathers and mothers were promoted more often than any from their numbers. Mihall *expected* to become a Weyrleader. Sorka knew that and she knew that Sean was aware of those aspirations even though their eldest son never made any allusions to his hope. Indeed, he pointedly did not, scrupulously serving as wingleader, helping to train weyrlings as part of the duties of his rank and, except when Brianth lifted in a mating flight, never stepping out of line on any matter, despite his relationship to them. 'Because of it,' Sean had once said to Mihall's mother.

So Mihall, if Brianth flew a senior queen designate, would reach the objective he had set himself from the moment he had stood on the Hatching Ground at twelve, the youngest ever to Impress a bronze. There had been mutterings about that among older candidates but Sean's answer had been firm.

'The dragon chooses. Mihall could have been left standing.'

There'd been a few private words between the new bronze rider and his father, the Weyrleader, but Mihall had never once taken advantage of the relationship. In his group of weyrlings, he had almost been shunned because he always did more than was necessary, 'showing up' the others.

If Sean had been self-contained and private as a boy, Mihall was doubly so. Her own first born and she didn't really know or understand him, Sorka thought, and yet she did.

The boy had been mad about dragons as soon as he was old enough to understand what his parents did and, despite being mainly raised by his grandparents and with his own siblings, he spent as many waking hours as he could up at the Weyr, making the long hike by himself if there was no-one to escort him.

'We've got twenty mating queens . . . discounting you – because no-one flies Faranth but Carenath,' and he cocked a stern finger at her, provoking her to grin smugly, 'and . . . the three injured . . .'

'Porth can fly . . .' Sorka objected on Tarrie's behalf.

'But she doesn't fly long enough to have a good clutch . . .'

'Tarrie's got experience managing Weyr problems,' Sorka said staunchly, knowing how often she'd relied on her friend during her pregnancies or when the children were too ill for her to cope with all that went to running a Weyr.

'All perfectly true, but I mean to start the new Weyrs with young leaders who'll see their group through the rest of the Fall: who can pass on what we had to learn the hard way.'

'So how will you determine these young leaders?'

'Figure it out, love,' he said and slipped once more under the surface of the hot bath water.

'You would!' she said to the ripples which floated soap down the outtake pipe.

Three Weyrs? My word, she thought, with relief and a certain amount of awe for Sean's ambitious plan. Jays, when he let go, he let go with a vengeance. Young leaders! That made excellent sense and there were enough. Any one of those who were currently wingleaders could manage a Weyr: they'd been thoroughly indoctrinated by Sean, with emphasis on safety and tactics. Even the wingseconds would make good leaders. Too bad the blues simply hadn't the stamina to keep up with a queen. At that, there were only two blue wingseconds. And she didn't see either Frank Bonneau or Ashok Kung as Weyrleaders. Nice enough young men but better as subordinates than leaders.

But that meant, and she found herself clutching the bath sheet under her breasts in relief, that Mihall would most certainly be one of the new Weyrleaders: one of three so no-one would be able to cry 'nepotism' on them. Besides, as everyone had been told repeatedly, the preferences of the queen and her rider had to be reckoned with. Sorka allowed herself a small smug smile. There wasn't a girl in the Weyr who wouldn't be proud to have her queen flown by Brianth and to be able to *stay* in Mihall's company as his Weyrwoman. Ah, but would her handsome red-headed son, who had shown himself as willing to bed a holder as a rider, be willing to settle to *one*. The Weyrleadership had to be stable or the Weyr would be disrupted. What behaviour Sean would condone in his son in his current capacity would alter once Mihall became a Weyrleader. It was time for the boy to settle any way, she thought firmly, and on the end of that, decided she would *not* interfere with a word to the wise to him. Mihall was man enough now to recognize a need for fidelity.

'Well, don't stand there, woman!' Sean's voice brought her back and, with an apologetic murmur, she handed her dripping husband his towel.

'You're also a very clever man,' she said, then added to keep him from being too smug, 'Did you know that dragons elide riders' names?'

'Sometimes, during Fall if it's especially heavy, I've heard Carenath slur a name or two,' Sean said, vigorously rubbing himself with the towel. 'Why?'

'It seems to have caught on, at least with some of the younger riders.'

'No harm in that!'

'I do have it on very good authority that neither your name nor mine, however, is ever slurred.'

'I should hope not!'

137

*　*　*

By the time the southern hunting party made it back that evening – replete dragons did not go *between* – Torene had had a chance to calm down from the excitement of knowing the double-cratered place was going to be a Weyr. She also decided not to mention her conversation with the Weyr-leaders to any of the 'bunch'. They were high enough as it was from their eastern hop: the boys planning which Weyr they'd make their own, Sevya and Nya figuring out just how much sand would be needed to give a good deep bedding for hardening eggs. Siglath was hopeful in a wistful way, or so Nyassa told the youngsters. The 'bunch' tended not to mouth their enthusiasms near the more conservative older riders and Alaranth would keep her counsel. Torene grinned. Her queen took her cue from her rider. And sometimes that worked the other way round, too.

So Torene applied herself to checking her riding gear. Sean might just call a snap inspection – they had Fall the day after tomorrow. Out of several years' habit now, Torene rechecked the flame-thrower tanks she used, the nozzles, the carrying straps. Even though a good bit of the weight of them was carried by Alaranth, the long wand was hefty enough. Then she checked her safety harness, the heavy plastic-coated gloves for any sign that the fingers might have spillage of the HNO_3 on them. Eventually the plastic wore through and had to be recoated. Her hands sweated from the non-porous material but it was better than acid burns. She made sure her goggles were clear, too. Sometimes a fine spray was blown back before the HNO_3 ignited and she needed clear, not clouded, plasglas.

She was just about finished when F'mar or Fulmar Stone Junior, bronze Tallith's rider, swung into the queens' ready room, helmet and gloves in hand, riding jacket open.

'Hey, gal, we're back!' F'mar was grinning from ear to ear. 'And boy, did we bring home the bacon!'

'Real bacon? Is Longwood curing pig so early?'

'You can be so literal sometimes, 'Rene.'

She hadn't told Sorka that was how *her* name had been compressed since it was humans who had shortened it.

138

Slapping his gloves on his leg with some irritation, F'mar went on, 'No, actually, we brought back steaks and a lot of stew meat. They're culling herds for the winter down there. Or don't you remember how seasons switch?'

'I remember that much,' she replied evenly. Fulmar Stone had been five when he and his family had Landed so he was eight years older and had Impressed a bronze of a Weyrleader's clutch at nineteen. Half-trained to follow in his father's mechanical engineering specialty, F'mar had salved his father's shock at taking up an entirely different life's work by taking charge of all the Weyr's mechanicals. These were, however, so well designed or redesigned that they rarely needed more than a drop of oil – or so F'mar insisted.

'You should've come.' Then F'mar, as tall as Torene but rangier in frame and bony shoulders, leaned towards her with a friendly leer. 'It was more fun than climbing about rock faces and peering in holes.'

Torene grinned placidly at him. 'But I like cliff climbing and Alaranth hunted yesterday with the other queens. I'd better go help with dinner if there're steaks.'

'I have to, too,' F'mar said, grimacing because he didn't enjoy that segment of the additional duties that the riders assumed inside the Weyr. 'In fact, Tarrie sent me to find you.'

'For steak, I'm findable,' she said. 'Just let me wash my hands first.'

'Can I help?' he asked with a second amicable leer.

Torene laughed at him, evading his half-serious interference with a direct path to the sinks.

F'mar was nothing if not persistent in his efforts to attach her. He pushed his luck whenever he had the chance, like now, trying to persuade her that *he* was her best possible weyrmate as his Tallith would be the perfect bronze to twine necks with her queen. F'mar was looking for any opportunity to prove his worth – in advance. He was also a wingleader which he thought gave him an advantage over others of their 'bunch'.

For her part, she treated them all alike and no-one knew if she'd any experience at all. She'd got rather skilful in evading answers and importunities. Sometimes, to tease, she'd mention one or another of the apprentices at Telgar Hold whenever she'd been to visit her parents and sibs.

Actually, she liked F'mar best of them all, with his good humour and pleasant good looks, though she'd never give him any encouragement. He might just try joining her in her tight squeeze of a weyr. As well she was in such an uncomfortable weyr. Everyone knew she slept right beside her queen. Warmer that way, anyhow. Two human bodies wouldn't have fit and she wasn't about to be seen leaving a male rider's weyr. Or hiding if she chose to be *in* one.

When they reached the kitchen cavern, Tarrie and Yashma Zulieta were supervising the carving up of the carcasses. It was much too late in the day to have spit-roasted the whole sides which was the usual way of preparing meat in quantity. Torene knew they'd have several meals from all this mess. Good big meaty animals. Well, the grass at Longwood had produced many a fine meal for the Weyr when Fort's supplies ran short.

It was indeed a fine meal. While comestibles like flour, dried beans and legumes, and dairy produce were provided by Fort now, the dragonriders could add to the bare necessities by going *between* to the southern continent, returning with fruits, fresh vegetables and herd animals. Slowly but surely, the task of provisioning the Weyr was being handled by the Holds so, one way or another, the dragonriders often ate far better than holders. That, and the glamour of being a dragonrider, were reasons why so many young people were ready to take their chances on the Hatching Ground even though their parents might have had other careers in mind for their children. At one stage in the early days, Sean and Sorka had had to become rather autocratic in demanding enough boys and girls to stand on the Hatching Ground – especially older boys who would be mature enough to fly in Fall as soon as their dragons were old enough. Gradually, however, to have a son or daughter become a dragonrider was a mark of prestige for a family. Although birth rates were high the first six years at the Hold, there were only so many available to stand as candidates now. Lately they'd had to include pre-adolescents to be able to present enough of a choice to the hatchlings.

With eggs hardening on the Ground and Hatching quite near, the Weyr was presently hosting candidates. They were, Torene noted, the ones that came back for seconds and thirds of the juicy steaks. Not that she blamed them. She remembered her stomach rumbling far too often in the days when she lived 'at home'. There were not that many days when food was scarce – for a dragonrider.

And, if one happened to find a fire-lizard's clutch in the southern sands, a rider could barter eggs for anything he or she desired. That was one bad aspect of living north: there were fewer and fewer of the lovely creatures looking to humans. They didn't like the cold and, with so few belonging to riders, the hundreds that used to augment dragon fire during Threadfall had dwindled to a couple of fairs.

That was how Ierne Island had managed to hold out so long against coming north. The shores of Longwood, Lockahatchee, Uppsala and Orkney, were fire-lizard havens and every man, woman and child had dozens of fire-lizards to help protect them during Fall. At least the proposed site for Longwood and Orkney personnel would be warmer than the double-crater. They'd keep their fire-lizard friends that much longer.

When Torene's kitchen duties finally allowed her to sit with her 'bunch', they talked more about the fine eating than their afternoon activities. Torene didn't mention her encounter with Sean. But Torene did notice the Weyrleader glancing over in her direction from time to time. The second time she observed his casual glance, she spoke to Alaranth. So she concentrated that little bit harder but Carenath was fast asleep.

He didn't ask him anything all night, volunteered Alaranth, also sleepily.

Probably because he remembers that I can hear.

No, Sean asked Carenath his opinion of some of the candidates. It would be good for Dagmath's rider to have some of his own persuasion.

Torene considered that. The blue rider preferred boys to

girls. Sean would prefer to have fewer of the speedy little green dragons out of action because their riders were taking maternity leave.

Are there any prospects in that line? Torene asked. Even among the colonists there were some traditionalists who had trouble coping with such orientation.

Three.

Torene grinned. Now that was certain to please the Weyrleader.

'Who's the grin for?' F'mar asked. He was sitting beside her and now leaned heavily against her shoulder.

'For me to know and you to guess,' she said, chanting the old tease.

'You're not giving anything away, are you?' He sounded irked. 'You did go to the craters today, didn't you?'

'Sure, but that conversation had been gnawed to the bone by the time I got here,' she replied. 'It would really make such a splendid Weyr,' and she gave a wistful sigh.

'I think,' and now F'mar whispered in her ear, his breath tickling, 'that Sean's about to *do* something about establishing a new one.'

'You do?' She pulled back to look at him with an eager surprise which was genuine enough.

F'mar bent close again. 'Sean wasn't hunting all the time he was gone.'

'He wasn't?' Torene used that as an excuse to widen the distance between them.

'I think,' and F'mar put one hand to the side of his face, lowering his voice so that only she could hear, 'that he's busy making some deal with the Langsams and the Mercers at Ierne.'

'Oh, so they'd be happy with the lower site and leave the higher one for us?' He nodded. 'You could be right,' she replied, imbuing her tone with hope. 'Oh, good, music! The perfect end for such a meal!'

She used that opportunity to slip away from F'mar completely, hauling the penny whistle from a thigh pocket as she joined the other players.

*   *   *

Torene always woke early on a Fall day – even if Fall wasn't until afternoon as it was today over Fort and parts of Boll.

Rumours had been flying yesterday. The dragons were as bad as the Weyr's residents, repeating their riders' stories, supported by this and that odd statement by Sean or Sorka, or even what one of the bronzes who had gone south had to say about suspected meetings with Longwood and Orkney Stakeholders. Torene listened and wondered if she ought to report some of the more implausible theories to the Weyrleaders. And then decided against it. There was no need to tell tales out of turn. The prospect of a new Weyr, however, did raise spirits often full of jitters before any Fall, especially one over occupied lands.

As was his custom, Sean sent riders ahead to watch for the Leading Edge and check the composition of today's Fall. It would begin halfway across Big Bay, coming in over the port area – where the dolphins would swarm for the good eating and to provide what help they could. Then the Fall would sweep south-westerly across Fort and Boll lands and down the other side of the mountain range. Over the last year, the Weyr had extended their protection to that area, too, at Pierre's request, for Boll folk were spreading out, making small Holds under the jurisdiction of the larger.

Torene always managed to eat breakfast but, like many other riders, she skipped any noontime meal, settling for a cup of klah before she changed into riding gear, and asked Alaranth to come down to be tacked up. The other queens began to assemble, joined by the seven green riders whose condition required them to fight with flame-throwers. There were nine more green riders unavailable in early and late stages of pregnancy so the greens would have to ride longer shifts to keep the wings at proper strength. Sean did not like drafting in spare riders from the wings temporarily stationed at Big Island and Telgar. Wingleaders found that a gap in the rank was better than a diffident replacement who wasn't sure of wingmates. She listened carefully as Sorka gave the greens their positions in the low-flying wing of queens. Most of them were seasoned riders though there was one newcomer – Amy

143

Mott who was pregnant by Paul Logorides as a result of her green's first mating flight.

It was almost a relief to hear Carenath's bellow and look up to see the massed wings ranged along the Weyr Rim, awaiting the signal to chew firestone. Torene mounted the kneeling Alaranth and helped those who were lifting the heavy tanks to their positions on either side of the queen's withers. The tanks tethered, Torene attached the wand to the right-hand one and gave a good turn of her wrench to be sure the connection was firm. Thanking her helpers, she then peered up to the Rim to wait for Sean's signal to Sorka and Faranth as leaders of the queens' wing.

Follow me, Carenath said, loud and clear in Torene's ears. Faranth heard it and responded. Torene had always waited for Sorka's signal since her first flight with the queens' wing when she had moved off ahead of Faranth. That was the day she admitted, shamefacedly and feeling she was guilty of a terrible sin against Weyrleaders and the Weyr, that she could hear other dragons' speech. As she made her stammered confession to the Weyrleaders only, she had obeyed their injunction that she keep her ability to herself and be discreet at all times in exercising this unique talent.

Faranth made the all-important first leap off the ground, springing with tremendous power from her hindlegs and Torene, riding right point to Faranth, gave Alaranth the go-ahead.

As often as she had fought Thread, Torene felt the excitement knot in her belly, felt the surge of adrenalin in her blood as her queen's wings described mighty strokes. With three, they were above the Weyr walls, gliding into their in-flight position under the massed wings of Fort dragons.

She took from both Carenath and Faranth their destination, felt that awful sinking into the cold blackness that was the medium through which the dragons passed on their telekinetic way from one place to another, and came out over the sea, just beginning to darken as Thread slanted down across it. She was close enough at a roughly thousand-foot altitude to notice the churning of the water beneath where schools of every fish that thrived in Pern's seas had gathered to feast on drowning Thread.

The aerial defenders of Pern waited, high above, at about eight thousand feet, Torene estimated, for the Leading Edge to get closer to the port facility. No sense wasting dragon flame on what would drown.

Then the nearer wings went into action and flame sprouted red-orange, caught and Thread burned into blackness. It was clumping today, Torene noticed, and turned the regulator on her wand to a widespread setting.

She also tuned her hearing to listen to the dragons already engaged and wondered if Sorka was asking Faranth about the nicknames.

She is, Alaranth promptly replied, as an overlay of messages briefly confused Torene, *Watch your left, F'mar! That's coming in at two o'clock, B'ref! Big mother clump descending right over you, D'vid. Firth, watch right!* That last came directly from the Weyrleader dragon to Shih Lao's.

Torene giggled. There was nothing dragons could do with *that name*!

S'lao, was Alaranth's prompt reply. *Stuff getting through. Veer right!*

Sorka and Faranth had already begun to swing and Torene and Alaranth followed. Habit kept Torene listening in with half an ear, as the queens' wing began to mop up: mostly single Threads which the upper level of fighters ignored in order to concentrate on the clumps and tangles. Faranth directed some of the quicker green riders to spread out to catch the outer edges of these and, then, in an aside, ordered Alaranth to supervise.

Sometimes Torene's neck ached with craning her head upwards. Occasionally Alaranth eased her forequarters upwards so that the strain was reduced but such an awkward manoeuvre was also hard for the queen to sustain.

A dragon screamed and instantly Alaranth identified the beast – Siwith, P'ter's blue.

Wing damage, Alaranth said. *We go.*

We're assisting, Elliath, Uloa's queen said and the pair went *between* the brief distance to the falling blue for Siwith's right wing had been shredded. He couldn't sustain flight, managing no more than a downward spiral.

Spouting flame, two greens appeared, clearing Thread from the path of the two queens as they arrived to arrest the blue's descent.

Alaranth and Elliath had done this manoeuvre so often in the past two years that it was nearly routine now. As Torene laid herself flat against her queen's neck, Alaranth, being the larger beast, slipped up under the falling blue, matching his downward speed and then coming up under his smaller body, holding it along her spine. Torene could feel Siwith's hot and pungent breath on her back and hoped she wasn't going to lose another suit of riding gear from scorching. Elliath hovered above them both, her forelegs poised to grab Siwith by the wing shoulders if he slipped.

Nice catch, Carenath told Alaranth.

Siwith's whistles of pain were muted as the little fellow valiantly tried to stifle the agony of a wing injury.

We have him, Alaranth told her rider who could feel the strain through her queen's body.

Siwith, Torene said, *relax now while we take you* between. *We've got you safe. Elliath, we go . . . now!*

The transfer to Fort Weyr was accomplished. Sometimes the wounded panicked when they weren't in control of a movement *between*, another reason for the second queen ready to grab wing-shoulder joints.

Alaranth arrived at the Weyr with her casualty still in place. The extra weight had her skimming the surface though she landed smoothly just where medics waited.

'Are you OK, P'ter?' Torene shouted over her shoulder. That gave her a whiff of scorched leather.

'Yeah. Thanks, 'Rene! Just missed *me*. Ah, Siwith, you'll be all right. You'll be all *right*!' P'ter's voice was ragged with concern and shared pain.

'Hang on while we transfer you.'

Alaranth tucked her left wing as well as she could under the limp wounded blue's pinion, Elliath caught Siwith by his uninjured joints and, as Alaranth eased out from under Siwith, Elliath supported his body and gently eased it to the

146

ground. Hoses had already sprayed numbweed on the underside of the mangled wing membrane, now the medics could reach the upper surface. The blue's rider unbuckled his fighting straps and started slathering the upper back. Siwith's whistlings of pain were reduced to murmurs of relief.

'D'you need new tanks, Uloa?' Torene asked as their rescue was successfully finished.

'No, I'm fine for another hour.'

'Me, too.'

Torene looked skyward, giving Alaranth the signal to be ready. Both queens sprang from the ground at the same instant and, sufficient altitude gained, winked *between* back to the Fall.

The evening meal was served at a late hour. While ground crews said that little had got through the wings, there had been sufficient injuries that all the riders knew Sean would have words with the Weyr in general before they were dismissed.

'He's sure to say today's flight injuries are due to careless riding, bad concentration and stupidity,' N'klas muttered as he followed Torene into the lower cavern.

'And he'd be right,' Torene said, grinning back over her shoulder at the morose N'klas to take the sting out of her agreement. 'But clumps are the hardest to fly, and he's sure to admit that before he starts lambasting us.'

'Nice catch on Siwith, by the way. P'ter says he'll be out months growing back wing membrane.'

'Thought so from what I could see when we brought him in.'

'At least he got the best ambulance team.'

When she and Uloa had got back to the queens' wing, Faranth and Greteth were in the process of catching another wing injury.

Sorka says your timing is excellent. You have command of the wing, Faranth said directly to Torene. *We have him, Greteth. Easy now, Shelmith. We have you. Relax, will you?*

I still fall, Torene heard Shelmith say, frightened.

Of course, you do but I fall right under you. You are caught. Feel my back under your belly.

I do! I do!

'What about Shelmith?' she asked N'klas. She hadn't had time to check on the injured yet. The queens' wing always made contact with ground-crew leaders before returning to the Weyr.

'He's only got holes in one wing but body scores and some bad tracks down the right hindquarter,' N'klas said, wrinkling his nose at the extent of the injuries. 'We need rear-view mirrors.'

Torene laughed. 'Where on earth would we attach them?'

'Oh, shoulder, peripheral vision reflex mirror, maybe.'

'Lord, we'll have to take front seats tonight,' she said, noting that they were the only ones not occupied at the dining tables perpendicular to the slightly raised Weyrleader and wingleaders' table.

'You did great,' N'klas said. 'You've got no cause to feel guilty. Too bad you aren't bigger,' he added with a grin, for he was heavy through the shoulders and chest. 'I could hide behind you.'

'You've nothing to worry about. You brought Petrath in with no scores, didn't you?'

N'klas paused before he answered, his remorseful expression verging on the comical. 'Not exactly, though,' he hastened to add, 'he won't be out of action more than a week, I'd say.'

'I'm sorry, I didn't know.' She glanced up at him with a rueful smile.

N'klas shrugged his wide shoulders. 'Nothing a bucket of numbweed didn't soothe. Dragon hide grows back quickly, thanks be!'

The kitchen crew were quick to serve riders as soon as they seated themselves. The top table was not occupied as yet – Torene knew that Sean would be having a few words with wingleaders over poor performance but clump Falls were always the trickiest and, while she knew a lot of dragons had not finished the Fall due to minor wounds, there were more minor than major ones. Every wing had missing members so the Weyr was flying a bit short to allow some wings to have a vacation. Queens only got time off for clutching so Torene had been on duty for over two years without a break.

We fly well as a team. We do excellent rescues, Alaranth said.

Oh, beloved heart, Torene said, immediately chagrined that she'd been thinking so negatively. *We do, we do. But I am tired. Like most of the riders. Everyone needs some time off, not just a visit home or to the east coast.* Well, she added to herself, maybe Sean would announce that some of those recuperating at Big Island would be reporting back for duty and that would take the burden off the short-manned wings.

The meal was good – one of Yashma's special casseroles, more of the beef, plus legumes and tubers, served with fresh hot bread and slabs of butter. Torene grinned as she slathered her bread with it before passing on to the impatient rider next to her. Butter in this quantity obviously had come in from Ierne Island. Would they be able to have dairy products when Longwood settled on the east coast? She'd miss them. In the Hold, milk products were reserved for babies and growing kids. What was being tired to the many advantages of being a rider, not the least of which was having Alaranth?

You like me better than butter?

Of course, I do, but there's absolutely no doubt that you couldn't be spread on hot bread!

Bread is all right. Alaranth was unenthusiastic. From time to time, because Alaranth was curious, Torene had given her queen samples of what she ate.

But not for a carnivore like you, darling. You aren't hungry again, are you?

No, but you were!

Alaranth also found it hard to understand why her rider had to eat several times a day when once or twice a week sufficed the much bigger dragon.

Before the casseroles were passed around the tables for the second time, the Weyrleaders and wingleaders took their places. Torene thought they all looked relaxed and were pleasantly conversing with each other. That did not jibe with her notions of the Weyr getting a lecture on recklessness and inefficiency.

A spicy nut-filled bar provided a sweet and then ale was served along with refills for any wanting just klah.

149

'He must really be going to take slices from our hides,' N'klas muttered in her ear.

'Then why is F'mar grinning from ear to ear?' Torene wanted to know because the young wingleader was looking excessively smug. Of course, reviewing the injuries, there hadn't been any in his wing so he could afford to be at his ease. But F'mar kept trying to catch her eye.

Torene 'listened' for Tallith but the bronze was asleep. *Alaranth, did I miss something?*

What?

I don't know and F'mar's grinning like a fool at me.

He does that all the time.

Torene caught a certain almost impatient and irritable note to her queen's remark.

Don't you like F'mar? Or is it Tallith you don't fancy?

Torene often asked her queen which bronze she preferred. As she had no particular favourite among the riders, maybe her queen had one among the bronzes. Torene did have to think in terms of her queen's mating flight, an event which could happen soon now. Sorka had no difficulty in telling her queen riders exactly what to expect – and Torene hoped it would be for her as thrilling as reputed. Sorka never exaggerated.

Bronze dragons are much the same in a mating flight. But I will be hard to catch!

'What's so funny?' N'klas asked her when she burst out laughing at her dragon's boast.

'Alaranth,' Torene said and shrugged, indicating a private joke.

She nodded at him to pour some ale in her glass after he'd filled his own. She was getting to like the stuff which was just becoming readily available. She preferred it to the jarring taste of quikal. Tonight, she had the feeling that she'd need the loosening beer provided.

Suddenly noise in the dining area subsided and Torene saw that Sean had risen.

'Oh, oh,' N'klas said, scrunching himself small beside her.

'Oh, don't be an idiot,' she said rather sharply because N'klas tended to dramatize.

This time he was right. Unexpectedly Sean held his glass in one hand.

'You all know that the wings did not perform very well today, but I take the nature of today's Fall into consideration. We all know that clumps and tangles are the worst types to combat and that the very nature of such a Fall can cause injuries to even the most alert rider and clever dragon. I don't excuse you and I shall have words with some of you who were caught unawares, and to those of you who managed to escape when you bloody well deserved to be scored.' Sean's expression was harsh as he looked over the crowded tables. 'Injuries could have been worse.'

When he paused again and let his gaze sweep the riders, Torene had the feeling that something momentous was going to happen. She was positive she knew what that had to be and inhaled, sitting straighter. She felt N'klas shift beside her as if he, too, felt impending news.

'The holders all agree that new Weyrs . . .' And he stopped as dramatically as N'klas might, to let the plurality be absorbed. '. . . must be formed.'

He would have gone on but wild cheering and stamping ensued and made him smile as he held up his arms for silence.

'Some of you,' and Torene caught him looking at her, 'may think that the double-cratered site on the east coast is an ideal site for one. And you'd be right.' More cheering punctuated that statement. Torene had her ribs dug by N'klas and she saw that F'mar was also watching her, a broad happy and very smug grin on his face.

Well, she thought, he had the makings of a good Weyr-leader and his wingseconds swore by his competence.

'We'll start that one first,' Sean went on, 'and there will be two more adapted as soon as possible. I project that we'll need two more at the rate our queens are laying so we should prepare now for our needs while holder enthusiasm for our profession continues strong.' He gave a wry smile which brought a ripple of appreciative laughter. 'Big Island is also a firm choice, to give us a warmer climate not only where our injured can convalesce but also where our disabled can still be of assistance. Telgar needs one to protect the miners,' and there was a ripple of mild dissent because Telgar was mountain-cold. 'There is a crater in the sandy peninsula to the east and another in the far north-west. But we already have contingents at Big Island and Telgar so those will be completed first.'

He waited until that wave of whistles and cheering died and then, with a slight grin on his face, continued.

'Ierne Islanders are coming north and Longwood wants the secondary site on the east coast. They will also help us prepare that Weyr in appreciation of our willingness to protect them.' Sean grinned more broadly now.

'So that's how he's done it,' N'klas said, his eyes shining with respectful awe.

'Done what?' Torene asked in a low voice.

'Made *them* think we're doing *them* the favour when it's the other way round,' N'klas replied. 'Oh, he's clever, is Carenath's rider.'

'Lockahatchee and Uppsala fancy Big Island and they will help us enlarge the existing facility there,' Sean went on. 'Telgar's promised as many miners as he can spare for some of the excavation work on all sites so I think we will be able to provide protection in four locations even as the Weyrs are being adapted to the needs of our dragons.'

Four Weyrs! – including the one she had yearned for. Torene couldn't believe it! One would have occasioned great joy. But four Weyrs? Well, and she did a quick count, Sean could put twenty wings in the air for any given Fall even if all were not accommodated at Fort. Three new Weyrs also meant three new Weyrleaders and Weyrwomen. Who had Sean and Sorka chosen to promote? Probably from the senior riders and she couldn't but be happy for Uloa's and Arna's sakes, or David Caterel and Peter Semling. They were logical choices but who else?

'We have twenty mature queens,' Sean was saying, 'and well over a hundred bronzes and ten or twelve browns who would make admirable leaders. This being the case, I feel that we'll let chance play a part in what is too difficult a choice for us,' and he indicated Sorka, 'to make. So you're going to draw which Weyr you'll go to. We're splitting up the queen dragons, with the exception of Faranth who stays here, with me,' and Sean scowled fiercely, receiving the widespread laugh that was expected at the notion of any other dragon but Carenath flying Faranth. 'Nora will pass the bag among the gold riders. Tarrie has a bag for wingleaders, as I think it's best if the wings go forward as a unit to whichever Weyr the wingleader draws. Does that seem a fair way to distribute riders?'

Despite an almost universal surprise, approval was not slow to come that this was the fairest way to make the assignments. Looking around at the faces she could see from her position, Torene saw many expectantly hopeful expressions but she put her hands to her ears in a vain attempt to shut out the tumultuous responses from dragons to their riders' anxious and hopeful reactions. She shook her head and then felt Alaranth's mind helping her shut off the 'noise'. Usually she could filter unwanted messages but not tonight. Not that she could blame either party.

'Of course, we've three clutches of eggs ready for Hatching and we'll divvy them up as soon's we know what they are,' Sean added with a grin.

Torene looked around for Tarrie and Nora and saw them rising from a table on the far end of the cavern. She'd be one of the last to choose and the agony of such a wait, short though it would be, was exquisitely painful. Dare she dream of drawing the east-coast Weyr? Or would she stay on here at Fort since she was the youngest queen rider and had so much to learn? She ought to wish she'd be stationed at Telgar for then she'd be nearer her parents, especially now her brothers and sisters were away on their apprenticeships. Not that with Alaranth she was ever more than a couple of deep breaths away from there wherever she happened to be. But she had developed a special feeling for the double-crater and had so brashly planned how to use its many natural caverns: just as if she had the right to!

Brown and bronze riders began to shout out their new assignments, leaping from their seats or just waving their arms about in delight. Surprised, Torene heard as much pleasure at being assigned to Telgar as east coast or Big

153

Island. Everything was happening so quickly on the far side that she really didn't see who had got the east-coast assignment. She was surprised when she saw Tarrie go to the head table and pass the bag to the wingleaders sitting there. Why had F'mar been grinning so much then? She saw him reach his hand in and was so eager to know where he was going that she was surprised to have someone touch her arm and see Nora standing beside her.

'You're the last queen rider present to pick,' Nora said with an encouraging expression. 'Hope it's the one you want. Then Sorka will draw for the absentees.'

Holding her breath, Torene dutifully slipped her hand into the bag and felt several slivers. Squeezing her eyes tight, she let her fingers close on one, drawing it out.

'Do exhale, 'Rene,' Nora said with amusement.

She did so, grinning nervously at the queen rider before she had the nerve to look at what she held. She read it, then read it again.

You keep saying 'east coast', she heard the patient tone of Alaranth remark. *Are we to go to the place we want?*

'Yes, oh, yes, yes,' Torene breathed, clutching the all important message to her breasts.

'"Yes, oh yes, yes", where'd you get?' N'klas asked, showing her his slip and he'd pulled 'east coast' as well.

She hugged him in a most uncharacteristic gush of joy. He was too surprised to take full advantage of it before she, as abruptly, released him.

'East coast!' Oh, she was so happy, and she squeezed the message in hands suddenly moist. Radiantly she smiled up the head table, caught Sorka's smile and Sean's nod of approval. As her eyes slid away, she saw F'mar's face and he wasn't smiling quite so broadly now. She raised her eyebrows queryingly at him and he mouthed 'Telgar' at her.

She made a moue of disappointment but actually she wasn't at all.

Tarrie and Nora had brought the bags up to the main table and Sorka drew for the absent queens, Sean for the six absent wingleaders.

'So you now all know which Weyr you'll be stationed at –

for now – since we'll have to make other divisions if we decide to expand to six full Weyrs. All of you wingleaders are experienced and know as much about managing a fighting Weyr as I do. I've seen to that!' His face was touched with a slightly smug smile and he received appropriate responses to that remark, whistlings and jocular remarks. 'There's really only one fair way to decide who becomes Weyrleader.' He used another of his pauses to increase suspense. Torene had never seen her Weyrleader in such teasing good spirits. He really enjoyed stringing all this out. 'We leave it up to the queens,' and Sean surprised them all by making a gracious bow to Sorka. 'And we'll leave which queen up to chance, as well. Chance plays a greater part in our affairs than you may be aware, but I feel the Weyr has profited by random choice and we will continue this. Therefore, the first queen in each new Weyr to rise to mate will decide which rider will be Weyrleader!'

That announcement met with a stunned moment of silence which was broken by quiet murmuring. Torene was even more surprised than most. She didn't know which other queens had been assigned along with her but she was suddenly very sure that somehow the draw had been arranged so that she, and Alaranth, would go east. For Alaranth, of all the twenty fertile queens, would undoubtedly be the next queen to rise to mate: wherever she had gone, save Fort. Was that what Sean had meant when he said Torene's ability to hear all dragons was an asset? How long had he been planning to form new Weyrs?

She shot a quick glance at the Weyrleaders but they were not looking in her direction.

Am I right, Faranth? Torene broke her self-imposed rule never to initiate a conversation with another's dragon.

You can hear all of us, Faranth said. *It would be wise to have you over there. You will be a very good Weyrwoman. Sorka thinks so and so does Carenath and Sean. Be easy!*

As if she possibly could at a moment like this! Chance, indeed! Torene stared fiercely at Sorka, wanting to catch the Weyrwoman's eye but Sorka was leaning across the table to talk to Tarrie and Nora.

'So, those of you who have to remain here with Sorka and myself can be excused. I think the new Weyrfolk ought to have a bit of a gather and find out who goes where. Big Islanders, assemble at the far right tables, Telgar these in the middle, and east coast on my left.'

As Sean pointed, his eyes at last met Torene's. His expression did not change – except for the slight tilt of one eyebrow. So she could read more into this public exhibition of 'random choice'? But how could he have arranged it? The odds against were four to one.

She was startled out of her reverie when F'mar leaned down, lips to her ear.

'I would have liked to have you as my Weyrwoman, 'Rene,' he murmured. Before she could remark on the arrogance of him, being so sure that *he* would end up Telgar's Weyrleader, he had moved to the centre tables.

'Sour grapes?' N'klas asked, jerking his thumb at F'mar's retreating back.

'No, no sour grapes,' she said, with a not too saccharine smile. 'He's got as good a chance as anyone to make Weyrleader at Telgar. See—' And she pointed at Arna, Nya, and Sigurd already seated at the head of one of the Telgar tables.

She welcomed Uloa with a happy cry, and then Jean, Greteth's rider, only to be overcome with chagrin. Uloa and Jean would know that Alaranth would be the first queen assigned there to rise to mate. So did Julie, for her queen had just clutched and wouldn't rise for months. Torene's thoughts must have been transparent, for Uloa leaned close to her.

'And why not Alaranth?' Uloa murmured. 'Better you than me. You're young enough to cope.'

'My sentiments entirely,' Jean added quietly, then raised her voice. 'N'klas, pass the beer pitcher, will you? Who else have we got for wingleaders?' And she looked about as riders shifted to the appropriate tables. 'Besides you, N'klas. Hello, there, Jess. You're one of us? Great.'

Torene glanced shyly at the older bronze wingleader. She hadn't had the chance to get to know him but she'd never heard unfavourable reports. She saw David Caterel making his way to them. He and Polenth were of the original seventeen dragonriders. He had always been pleasant to her but the look he gave her now made her blush. *He* knew. Young Boris Pahlevi who had risen quickly to the rank of wingleader on Gesilith was also on his way over. And behind him . . . Torene blinked but the lithe redheaded figure was still that of Mihall, Brianth's rider, and the Weyrleaders' oldest son.

Well, she thought, an odd numbing sensation running over her, he was one of the best wingleaders, why should she resent him being in *her* Weyr? Silly! It's not *your* Weyr, yet, m'girl. He gave her a sharp nod as he stopped a little behind N'klas, reversed a chair and sat, leaning his arms on the back of it. He took the mug of beer passed to him but only sipped politely.

Wingseconds and some of the other wingriders ranged casually near their leaders, chatting among themselves.

'Well, well and well,' said Uloa, grinning about her, her black eyes snapping with wry amusement. 'David, your Polenth is the oldest dragon, do you wish to take charge of this first meeting of us new weyrmates?'

'Why should I, when you're doing so well, Uloa,' he replied good humouredly and endured a bit of teasing from his wingmates. 'Anyway, you've seen more of our new Weyr than I have.'

'Shouldn't all of us go there now, to see what needs doing?' asked Jess Kaiden whose bronze, Hallath, came from the same Hatching as Uloa's queen.

'Not now,' Uloa said, amused, 'as it's past midnight there and we couldn't see much.'

'We go when it's daylight then,' Jess said with a shrug.

'All of us?' asked one of the blue riders, seated near David. Torene didn't know his name. That was one detail she'd have to remedy.

Martin who rides Dagmath, Alaranth said.

'Yes, all of us,' David replied, 'since all of us will share the making of this Weyr.'

'Does it have to stay known as the east-coast Weyr?' Boris asked in some disgust. 'What a mouthful!'

157

'See it first, name it later,' Jean said. 'I've only been there once myself.'

'Just how much help will we get from the settlers?' N'klas asked, shooting Torene a quick look because they were aware of how much work would be required to make the place liveable.

'I think we'll have to ask Sean that,' David replied.

''Rene, you got that film on you?' N'klas asked, turning to her.

Torene knew she flushed up. She ducked her head on the pretext of opening the thigh pocket where she kept the plas-film and recovered her composure somewhat by the time she could spread it out on the table in front of her. Everyone began to press in to have a look. David, who was tallest of those nearby, took it and held it up high enough for more to see.

'Shaded areas show the echo spaces inside. Some only need to be broken out. And Torene spotted where we can put a ground level access tunnel.' N'klas craned his head and, stretching out one arm, pointed out the various features. 'Hatching Ground, bigger'n' Fort's – plenty of ground level caverns for support staff, kitchens, weyrling barracks, queens' quarters and there're tunnels underground. One to a cavern big enough for us to put hydroponics . . .'

'If we do our job properly, we'll get supplied by the holders we protect,' David Caterel said. N'klas was not the only one whose mouth dropped open in surprise. 'That's the plan which has just now been accepted by all holders.' David grinned at the effect of his words. 'That's what allows us to decentralize the fighting force. The Holds we protect will tithe to support the local Weyr. That way Fort won't be overburdened. We won't always by able to sneak south for food, especially after Ierne is abandoned. Their fire-lizards have done a great job to help the wings we've sent there. But they'll be leaving, too. We've got to let the grubs dig in and spread. A good start's been made at Key Largo, Seminole and Ierne but it's a long-term process.'

Although everyone knew of the two-part programme to distribute the anti-Thread organism that Ted Tubberman had bio-engineered, they also knew that it would take several hundred years for grubs to spread across the southern continent to make ordinary vegetation less vulnerable. The second part of the programme was to introduce the grub to the northern continent. But first the life-form had to be well enough established in the south before the colonies of it could be transferred north.

'So that's what all this coming and going's been about,' Uloa said, propping her fists on her hips and glaring at David. 'And you never gave us so much as a hint.'

David recoiled slightly. 'I never had so much as a hint myself until this evening. You know how close-mouthed Sean can be.'

'That's true enough,' said Jean with a wry laugh.

'What he dislikes is that the dragons'll have to do a lot of hauling.'

Jean made a real grimace this time and sighed deeply. 'Then it's only fair that the holders help us dig!'

'That was Sean's point.'

Jean couldn't see the diagram so she pulled it down. 'So this is how we'll be spending our free time?'

'What free time?' half a dozen voices chorused around her.

'The free time tomorrow when we'll all go over and formally take possession of our Weyr,' David said firmly. He glanced around, looking for acknowledgement. 'Go easy on the beer. We'll make a daylight start.'

'Ours, of course!' said an anonymous voice from the back.

'He's got more sense than to interfere with your beering tonight,' Jean said tartly.

From the middle of the room a roar went up, 'Telgar! Telgar Weyr!'

'As if they had any choice,' she said at her drollest, 'though I'd like to suggest a name now and let you think about it.'

'What name?'

'Benden!' she said in a proud quiet tone, lifting her chin. There was a long moment of respectful silence.

'What's to think about?' asked a firm baritone voice from the rear.

'Could there be any other name that would be more fitting?' David Caterel asked and Torene could see that his eyes had filled.

The murmur grew quickly, almost gladly, as the name was repeated throughout their small gathering. Jean touched her glass to David's and suddenly everyone got to their feet, raising theirs.

'To Benden Weyr!' David Caterel said though 'weyr' came out raggedly.

'To Benden Weyr,' and mugs, cups and glasses were raised high and then drained.

Torene had to sniff and dash the tears from her eyes but she felt uplifted by that little ceremony. Hers had been the last Hatching the ailing admiral had attended. She remembered that he had sought her out and wished her and her new queen the very best. Though he still walked with an erect back, his step was short and jerky. Mihall, she remembered, and one of his sons had escorted him.

Many riders began to circulate then, some to get more beer, some to drift off, but Torene was more or less hemmed in by the other queen riders and wingriders.

'You got this copy from your mother?' David asked, spreading it carefully out on the table now. And, when she nodded, he went on, 'Any chance we can get more? And at least one set of enlargements for each elevation?' Torene nodded again. Her parents would be extremely proud of her assignment and willing to co-operate any way they could. 'And you've been there recently?' His manner was kindly as if she were much younger than she actually was and needed to be led. She didn't resent that from David as much as she would have from one of her peers, but she was twenty-two.

'A whole bunch of us went the day you and Sean went down to Ierne to eat,' Uloa said, with a 'put-you-in-your-place' tone.

Grinning back at her, David said, 'If I'd known Sean was going to pull it off, I'd've come with you. What I need to establish is how recent your visit was.'

'Very.'

'And where is this access tunnel you found, Torene?'

160

N'klas was closer and jammed his index finger down on the spot. 'Here.'

David kept looking at Torene for his answer.

She nodded and explained. 'This echo reads as two metres high, ground to ceiling,' and she indicated. 'Here and here Ozzie says there're tunnels that can be enlarged, with an entrance into the . . . into Benden Weyr—' She was interrupted by comments like 'Sounds good,' 'Paul'd be pleased,' 'Perfect name!' 'Has a ring to it, doesn't it?' '—and an exit on high ground above the river, here.'

'That would be the priority project, so we can get materials and people in and out easily.'

'We still have to shift by dragon-back. Couldn't send a land expedition when we don't know the overnighting places.'

'Kaarvan wouldn't mind a good long sail. He's bored with fishing the Bay.'

'Iernans can bring in a lot of their own gear on their ships.'

Other riders, eager to contribute, began to crowd in, and Torene, courteously letting people past her, suddenly found herself excluded.

'It's my map,' she said under her breath, trying to suppress a surge of bitterness as she took a further step back.

'It'll be your Weyr, 'Rene,' said a soft, amused tenor voice at her elbow. She looked down into Mihall Connell's slightly mocking grey-blue eyes. She'd never been close enough to see their colour before. 'Come the time Alaranth flies. She'll fly soon, but you know that, don't you?'

There was no mockery in his tone and he'd made more of a statement than a question.

'Well, if you intend to be Weyrleader, why aren't you in there, mapping your space?' The moment the words were out of her mouth, she regretted them and bit her lip. 'I'm sorry, Mihall.'

'Why?' His very regular eyebrows quirked briefly and his grey-blue eyes, not a trace of mockery in them, met hers once more, his head tilted up at her. 'I should *like* to be Weyrleader. I *intend* to be Weyrleader. Everyone *knows* that,' and now the mockery was back. 'The question is, how does Alaranth feel about Brianth?'

161

'Isn't it more how I feel about you?' She shook her head and stamped her foot because those words, too, came out when that wasn't what she intended to say.

Mihall rose slowly until he was looking down at her, an intense look in his startling eyes. 'No, it's ultimately the dragons who decide: the one who decides how to fly this queen and the one who decides who she'll let catch her.'

Torene knew now why she hadn't been in his company much. He wasn't at all like the other bronze and brown riders in her 'bunch'. And, knowing the reputation he and Brianth had in 'catching' queens, she had, acting out of some instinct, deliberately – though she only now realized it – avoided being in his company. She also knew the opinion the other queen riders had of him and that only confused her more. 'Polite?' 'Quick?' 'Deft and considerate?' 'Too controlled?' None of those comments fitted what she sensed of him.

He knows he is the son of his parents, Alaranth said.

'Yes, he would know that,' she said almost sadly for that couldn't be easy on him. When Mihall politely raised his eyebrows in query, she realized she had spoken aloud. 'Brianth,' she added and gave Mihall what she hoped was an understanding smile. From his stunned expression, she found she had only compounded her blunder and he had assumed the logical interpretation. 'Oh, lord, both feet are in my mouth tonight. Do you want a copy of your own when I ask mother for them tomorrow?' She tried to keep her voice even and pleasant but to herself she sounded irritated.

Mihall inclined towards her. 'I'd appreciate it,' he said but all the warmth she had seen – so briefly – in his eyes was gone and they were coldly grey. He stood clear of the chair and before she could walk away from her embarrassment, he left her.

I could just scream, she told Alaranth. *It all came out so wrong, Allie. How could I possibly have said the things I did to him? And the way I said them! Oh, how could I?*

There was a long pause when she thought that her dragon was too sleepy, to answer.

Don't worry. The voice was not Alaranth's.

Brianth?

He's right. Too late now, was Alaranth's not too reassuring reply.

'Where did Torene go?' David's voice rose above other conversations.

'I'm here,' she said and allowed the alacrity with which the riders parted to let her back in soothe her frustration and self-accusation.

She asked the watchdragon to wake her at daybreak Telgar time. She wanted to get there before their workday started or she'd have to drag her parents back from a mine-face. Tarvi Telgar drove his people as much as he drove himself.

'To forget Sallah,' her mother had once told her daughter, her face drawn down in mournful lines.

'Everyone knows that,' Torene replied, but she'd been little more than nine or ten when she asked why Telgar worked such long hours, especially when that deprived her of her parents' company.

'Ah, but dushka,' her father had said in his deep way-down bass voice, '*not* as he knows it and lives with it. Eh, Sonja?' Volodya Ostrovsky would cast a knowing glance at his wife and fellow mining engineer.

'To us the tragedy is that it is *after* that he realized that she was the jewel she was,' Sonja replied, her voice doleful. Her mother's expressive face and voice had always fascinated Torene: she ran such a gamut of emotions throughout a day.

That morning Torene and Alaranth arrived at her parents' cavern just as Sonja was pouring klah and, to her daughter's astonishment, she was pouring it into three cups. There was also a third bowl of steaming porridge set at the table.

'How did you know I was coming?'

'How could we not know?' Sonja said, clasping her daughter to her ample bust and joyfully, proudly, embracing her with arms well muscled from a lifetime of mining. 'Telgar announces to us there will be four Weyrs, and one of them here.'

'Up there,' Volodya corrected his wife, pointing north-east, but he rose from his seat and kissed his daughter, hugging her nearly as enthusiastically as his wife had but with some consideration for Torene's ribs. 'And you are named to be at the east-coast one.'

'At Benden Weyr,' she said, hoping that at least the name would be a surprise.

'Ah!' Her mother's face lit up and she embraced her daughter again before she mopped a tear from each eye.

'As it should be. As it should be,' Volodya said, sitting down at the table and beginning to spoon his porridge into his mouth, stoking his tall heavy frame for another day's exacting work. 'Sit! Eat! You will need it.'

'So, how many copies do you come for me to make for you?' Sonja asked slyly, giving Torene a little push towards the spare place.

'Oh, Mother!'

'And why shouldn't you, dushka?' Sonja was unperturbed. 'Always you are putting yourself behind. And where else is there a replicating machine that works? You will want enlargements, too, of each elevation? How many in all?'

'Mother . . .' Torene began in protest and then burst out laughing.

'Sit! Eat!' her father repeated and gestured her firmly to take her seat. 'Copies we can talk of later. Now you will have breakfast with us and tell us news we don't get to hear at Telgar.'

She left, stuffed with two bowls of porridge and more klah than she liked to have swirling in her belly going *between*. She also had a plastic tube full of copies, enlargements and more of each than she would have had the nerve to request. Sonja blithely replicated four copies each and every possible angle of the original and secondary surveys of Benden Weyr. Torene reckoned that one reason they were so willing to go over the top was because they were so pleased with that naming.

'No, is for you, dushka,' Sonja said, kissing her daughter a hard kiss on her cheek in farewell. 'We are proud to have a queen rider daughter. Keep her safe, Alaranth!'

With her many-faceted eyes gleaming in the shadows cast by Telgar's high mountain peaks, Alaranth turned her head

164

and lowered her forequarters to the ground, as much to aid her rider to mount as to acknowledge the parting.

Who else is to keep you safe? Alaranth said as she turned and dropped off the ledge into the valley below.

Torene laughed at her phrasing, the speed of their descent snatching the sounds away. *You sound just like my mother!* Alaranth had a habit of mimicking some speech patterns.

We go now to Benden Weyr?

Torene squeezed her eyes, filled slightly with tears of pride at the grand sound of the name, and then concentrated on the scene of the double-cratered bowl. The bowl of Benden Weyr.

Yes!

She was certain all that klah and porridge would turn to ice in her belly but then they were out in the warm spring sunlight, gliding down the Weyr towards the lake.

Good morning to you, and Torene recognized Brianth's voice though she didn't see him below, nor any sign of Mihall.

He's on the rim behind us, sunning, Alaranth told her, well pleased with them both that they had started their own errand earlier than this pair.

Torene's mouth felt dry as Alaranth swung back to the upper crater and lost altitude. She had a view of Brianth, sunning himself on the heights. Backwinging, Alaranth landed neatly on the surface, the breeze from her pinions making the gravel rattle. A man's head peered out from the nearby opening to what Torene thought would be the Hatching Ground. Mihall still wore his flying gear so he couldn't have been here long, Torene thought.

He didn't rush, but his stride covered the distance between them so that he was at her side when she reached the ground.

'You've been busy this morning, I see,' he said and nodded pleasantly at the tube.

Keeping a stern grip on her tongue, she smiled pleasantly. 'Their daybreak, not ours,' she said, opening the tube.

He looked into the tube's contents and whistled, grinning down at her with approval. That was the first time she had seen him smile so openly and she wondered why he didn't more often. It would have improved his reputation.

165

Then she could see his fingers twitching, eager to see every sheet she had brought. Was that why he had got here so early? How could he have been certain she'd do her errand so promptly?

Brianth told him we'd left.

This time she was careful to keep her immediate response to herself. Had Brianth slept with one eye open?

The watchdragon will speak to anyone who asks politely. This came from Brianth and, although she knew dragons couldn't laugh, there was amusement of that quality in the bronze's tone.

'Here,' Torene said, diverted and irritated now by both rider and dragon, as she tapped the tube so the roll would fall out.

Mihall was that much quicker and had the films in his hands before she could catch them.

'It's less windy inside here,' he said, impatient to unroll the sheets but not willing to risk their damage.

When she got inside the vaulted chamber, she saw that he had been here long enough to make a small fire, set far enough in the shelter of the front wall to be protected from the wind, and secure in a neat circle of stones. A klah pot balanced close enough to keep its contents hot. A bulging sack was propped up against the wall, along with an opaque sheet of plastic wrapped around a number of finished plastic shafts.

'Yes,' he said, noticing her surprise, 'the klah's ready if you'd like a cup,' and he nodded to the sack. 'If not, help me put the table together. It's easier with two.'

Torene shook her head at the first offer and started to untie the bundle. When assembled, the table was exactly the same size as the largest of the replicated elevations. Mihall produced pushpins and a narrow strip of plastic. He worked deftly and, before she knew it, one full set of drawings was secured to the table with the plastic strip holding down the top edges so that the diagrams could be flipped over without being torn.

'You are handy,' she said, pleased and somewhat amused by his preparations.

166

'I know the largest size that replicator can print,' he said, shrugging off her implied compliment. 'Ah, this is the one I wanted to see,' and he turned to the side elevations of the upper crater.

There are more coming now! Brianth and Alaranth spoke almost in unison.

'About time,' Torene and Mihall said, also in chorus and, catching each other's eyes, laughed. Blue dominated the grey in the bronze rider's eyes.

For Torene, that marked the beginning of the most intense period of activity she had ever experienced, even when she was first learning how to care for Alaranth.

David Caterel had borrowed Ozzie from Telgar, although the old prospector insisted that everything he and Cobber had discovered in these craters was written up or symbolized on the plasfilm they had in their possession.

'We used some of those first uglies Wind Blossom bred to check out the tunnels,' he said, tapping a joint-disfigured finger on the drawings. '"X" marks spots you don't go. 'S'all here. Took her,' and he pointed at Torene, 'and her,' at Uloa, 'him,' N'klas, 'him,' D'vid, 'through every one of 'em, up and down, and the ones in between. The between you get to when you walk,' he added, favouring David Caterel with a droll eye.

'Had you anything better to do today?' David asked, grinning. 'You can sit here, drink all the klah . . .'

'You didn't think to bring any beer, didja? Prefer beer.'

'In fact, I did, knowing your preference,' David said, and began to haul large bottles from each of his thigh and jacket pockets.

'Good man,' and Ozzie took one, broke the seal, took a long pull before he wiped his mouth with the back of his sun-riddled hand and sighed with deep appreciation before he looked up at David again. 'I'll tell ya if ya do anythin' wrong,' he assured them. 'That one,' and he pointed to Torene again, 'knows most of 'em anyway so she can lead you. I'll just stay here in case ya go wrong. Then I'll findja.'

Smiles were carefully concealed from the wiry old man as David turned purposefully now to Torene.

'So, what do you want to see first?' she asked, holding her hands out in compliance.

'Everything,' David said. 'Starting with here and where can we put the hypocaust to keep the sands warm.'

'This way, lords and ladies,' Torene said impishly, remembering the phrases from the stories her father had told her as a child. There were always lords and ladies in Volodya Ostrovsky's bedtime tellings.

By noontime, they had climbed about, or been flown to by obliging dragons, every cave, niche, nook and cranny in the eastern side of the upper crater. They paused to eat, review their notes and the diagrams, and then, with only slightly diminished zeal, explored the western side, including and most intensively where Torene had thought ground access was possible. The plasfilm that had been pristine that morning showed all kinds of marks and new legends in the margins. Lists of materials urgently needed were stuck in under the top rail.

By the time darkness fell, not only was everyone tired, scratched and bruised from clambering over, under and past unforgiving stone, but also full of intimate knowledge of their proposed home.

The next day queen riders, wingleaders and seconds held conferences with Ierne's representatives to see what materials would be needed to start work on the access tunnel.

Though they were not asked, the dragons insisted on helping dig once the stone-cutters had excised the cliff face of the proposed access tunnel. David Caterel tried to stop them.

'You're fighting dragons, not digging dragons,' he said, scowling at his own Polenth. 'Torene, Uloa, Jean, speak to your queens.'

'Sternly?' Jean asked, grinning back and smearing the mud on her face as she mopped sweat, a shovel handle leaning against her.

This will be our home, too, Alaranth and Greteth said and the bronzes bugled agreement.

'Think you got outvoted,' Uloa said. 'It's only because

168

you're one of the first and Sean fussed so about doing carrier duty.'

'This is different,' Jean said, replacing gloves preparatory to attacking the rubble again. 'This is for *us*!'

The dragons gave another bugle and David, shaking his head, surrendered. There was no question that dragon assistance lightened the task. Ozzie was on hand, too, 'to make sure the echoes were accurate', he said. But he sat in the sun on a convenient boulder and pulled away at his beer, making 'supervisory remarks'. Hard work but better done with cheerful company.

Torene was not the only rider who brought her sleeping furs, spare clothes and what food she could wangle from Tarrie's kitchen. She had dumped her things in one of the smaller caves that she could climb to if Alaranth was asleep. It was three times the size of her accommodation at Fort; palatial in comparison. Alaranth thoroughly approved of the ledge in front which got the morning sun.

By pooling their food, the group who stayed on overnight managed quite a satisfactory meal. Despite being tired, some of the bronze and brown riders excused themselves after-wards.

'Wonder where they're going?' Uloa asked.

'Not where, not even why,' Jean said, groaning, 'but *how* do they have the energy to go at all! Fresh fruit would go nice for breakfast.'

'Did any of them check for Threadfall in the south?' Torene asked.

'Mihall did,' R'bert said, offering round the klah pot.

Jean rolled her eyes and Uloa sighed, stretching warily.

'D'you think he'll bring back a hot bath?' she asked.

'That would be heaven,' Jean said. 'What did Ozzie say about the possibility of tapping into some thermals here?'

'He said that it was possible if there was enough pipeline left from doing Tillek,' Torene said, thinking longingly of a hot bath herself.

We could go back to Fort? Alaranth suggested.

I don't think I have muscles enough to climb up to your back, Torene replied.

She was half-asleep when the riders returned. They brought not only fresh fruit and several braces of chickens but each dragon had also brought a fat bullock or cow struggling in his claws. These were deposited down by the lake where they bawled out their terror for hours before finally settling.

'Where'd you find the chickens?' Jean asked, eyes wide with delighted surprise.

'They take shelter in the old caves, the Catherine caves I think they were called,' Mihall said.

'Yes, they were,' Jean said as she watched him untie their legs. Squawking, each released fowl ran off into the bowl. 'We've nothing to feed them with.'

'I think I threw some crusts and heels on to the compost heap,' Torene said and got up.

Mihall caught her by the shoulder. 'If it's there, they'll find it on their own. What's the matter?' he added as he saw her wince.

'My shoulder's stiff.'

'Whose isn't?' Uloa said, groaning and rubbing her right one.

'Didn't one of you think to bring some numbweed?' Mihall asked with a grin.

A widespread groan answered the question of so obvious an immediate remedy. Jean rose stiffly to her feet. 'My pack's nearest.'

'Where? Let me get it,' Mihall said, moving nimbly to stop her.

'Oh, would you? I'm in the third cave on the left on the first level. It's an easy climb.'

They took turns rubbing the salve into abused muscles. Somehow – and she couldn't reject the courtesy without sounding uncivil – Mihall managed to be available to work on Torene's shoulders. Then she was much too grateful for the sure firm touch of his massaging fingers as he worked the salve in.

'Thanks, Mihall,' she said, rotating shoulder blades that no longer ached.

'Just take it easy tomorrow or you'll be back to me again,'

170

he said and turned to Genteelly who was waiting for similar ministrations.

She slept easier that night – once she tuned out the bawling of the cattle – because of the massage. The next day, at an appropriate hour, she asked Polenth to have David bring along a big jar of the numbweed when they returned to Benden.

In effect, they now worked two shifts: those staying at Benden did the first one and took a rest break when the Fort-based contingent arrived, fresh. The first week saw them complete the penetration of the tunnel, though the interior work slowed since the tunnel was not dragon sized, nor meant to be.

The four Benden wings were excused from Threadfall at Fort, though they began to catch the eastern Falls to see how they could protect the Benden Hold property. Ierne Island had acclaimed the choice of name for the Weyr and promptly adopted it for the Hold. A nearby source of phosphine-bearing rock was indicated on the survey maps and David sent a work group of blue and brown riders to begin to stockpile the all-important firestone.

A team arrived from Tarvi Telgar to set up the hypocaust system in the Hatching Ground so the campers moved their belongings across the bowl to what would be the living quarters. The first hearth and its chimney were built against an outside wall. Ozzie and Svenda Bonneau plumbed for and found a thermal vent and Fulmar Stone supplied the pump and instructed his apprentices in setting the pipes that would supply the individual weyrs as well as the main living accommodations.

More cattle, and other types of herdbeasts which had managed to survive Threadfall in the south, were added to the herd that occupied the lake end of the craters. The chickens laid eggs and it became an early morning exercise to find where, in the sands, they had been secreted. Some were left to the broody hens but others supplied the cooks. Julie, the fourth queen rider for Benden Weyr, arrived from Big Island on her Rementh who had now recovered from wing scoring. Julie had broken her leg, trying to dismount in a hurry to tend

171

to her queen. She wasn't yet out of the gelicast so she announced that she'd act as domestic manager.

Then Captain Kaarvan and the *Pernese Wanderer* dropped anchor at the mouth of Benden River and the promised assistance from Ierne broke trail to be the first to make use of the access tunnel. The workers they supplied included masons and carpenters and soon individual caves became proper weyrs, with partitions between dragon and rider accommodations, and bathrooms were installed.

Work was also done on what would be the quarters of the two Weyrleaders, the large room that would be used for private conferences, and one below that which could be an office.

No-one minded the hard work and the long hours because they were building for their own comfort as well as that of generations to come. So they built well and carefully.

When Benden Weyrfolk decided that sufficient provision for them had been made, they and their dragons flew down to the Hold, which was progressing slowly, and used the skills they had learned to help the holders settle in their new accommodation.

The only break the Benden riders took was for the Hatching at Fort. That was always a glad occasion for dragonriders and could not be missed, especially when some of the hatchlings would be assigned to Benden Weyr. Sean allotted most of the sixteen of Amalath's hatchlings to Benden. That provoked a complaint from F'mar, in the name of Telgar Weyr, although no work had yet been started on that facility.

'The next clutch will go to you, F'mar, especially as you've no place to put them yet but here at Fort,' Sean said, almost dismissing F'mar's protest out of hand.

'Young Fulmar better stop hassling Sean,' Jean murmured to the other Benden queen riders. 'Especially if he keeps on acting like he's already Weyrleader. That's a long way from being decided.'

'But someone has to be in charge, sort of, don't they?' Torene asked. 'I mean, David . . .'

'David Caterel has the right,' Jean said firmly. 'You've no

complaints, have you?' she eyed Torene speculatively.

'Me? No. He listens to any objections anyway,' she said, once again made conscious of the fact that no-one *said* anything to the point of her being Benden's Weyrwoman, but the knowledge hovered and her specific decisions were often sought.

Granted, working shoulder to shoulder, day after day, had given Torene insights into all of the bronze and brown riders. She liked most of them so she supposed Alaranth would have the final say. Of the younger riders, N'klas, L'ren, T'mas, D'vid, kept as much in her company as possible. David Caterel was always courteous to her, but he treated all the women riders the same way, even Julie whom Polenth had last flown. The Weyrleaders' quarters remained unoccupied.

It was Mihall who cried 'Get the queens away!' while people were finishing their midday meal. He came pounding in to the lower cavern, straight up to Torene. He caught her hand and, pulling her to her feet, urged her to action. 'Get your queens out of here, Jean, Uloa. Where's Julie gone?'

Licking the fingers of her right hand sticky from peeling red fruit, Torene did not resist Mihall's urgent tugging.

'How could she go into heat without me noticing?' she cried, almost on a wailing note because she had been keeping a close watch on Alaranth.

'Today, because she's been lounging in the sun,' Mihall said, and turned her by the hand he held so that she was facing the right way. He pointed. 'She's more than just gold right now.'

Torene inhaled sharply because Alaranth, stretching legs and wings in a manner that Torene instantly identified as sensual, was gleaming a bright gold that had nothing to do with clean skin and sunlight. Mihall jerked round as Jean, Uloa and Julie came pelting out of the lower cavern, in flying jackets too large for them and helmets that were as obviously borrowed. No time to get their own riding gear. Each rider threw anxious glances over their shoulders at the luminous Alaranth and scrambled aboard their own dragons.

'Look,' and Mihall swivelled her about again so that she could see the male dragons beginning to gather on the Rim, their eyes taking on the avid orange of arousal. Their riders were converging on Mihall and Torene and suddenly she was the focus of their awakened sensuality. Despite herself, she recoiled, tearing her hand free of Mihall's grip. His eyes had turned an intense blue. 'Remember,' Mihall said then, 'don't let her . . .'

'I know, I know, I KNOW!' she cried, resenting each and every one of them for the way they looked at her. No-one had told her about *this* part of a queen's mating. Especially this flight when the reward of Weyrleadership went to the winner. She backed up until she was against the stone of the Weyr, mouth gone dry, even as sweat began to ooze from her pores, and a strange sensation enveloped her guts.

At her final shout, Alaranth woke completely and Torene made the mental linkage. The rock wall supported her. Not even the calm explicit recital Sorka had given her covered the depth or intensity of the emotions the dragon was feeling, much less Torene's reluctant but inexorable response to the lust. A blood lust, first, with Alaranth aware of an insatiable hunger.

Glittering in the summer sunshine, Alaranth extended her wings and bellowed a challenge. She knew the male dragons were watching and she turned to display her proud strong body, throwing back her long neck and stretching it. She retracted in the blink of an eye, arching herself and, with a graceful, powerful motion, leaped into the air. Taking three long sweeps of her gleaming wings, she then glided down to the lake, scattering the beasts – her prey – with the suddenness of her appearance and the hungry cries she was uttering.

Blood it, Alaranth. Blood it! Don't eat! The instructions Torene had been drilled in jumped to mind as Alaranth landed on the bullock. *Blood it only!* Torene kept her voice firm, stern, putting every ounce of authority into her tone.

Alaranth snarled back at the distant tense circle of humans before she tore the throat and sucked greedily at the blood that pumped down her own throat.

Blood it! Hear me now! Alaranth! Torene could not give her any leeway in this. Blooding gave the mating queen the quick energy she needed: flesh would only weigh her down and she would not achieve the height required in a truly successful mating flight. Height, and safety, was essential, for dragons locked in conjugation could plummet to the ground before finishing if sufficient altitude had not been attained.

Blood only, Alaranth! Torene repeated as her queen leaped on a second large bullock. *You must fly the highest you can. You must not eat to do that! Blood it only!*

Though they were the length of the Weyr apart, Torene felt as if she was also there, beside her ravenous queen, felt as if the hot blood was running down her throat and wondering why the sensation wasn't choking her. With another part of her consciousness, she felt hands touching her, realized that she was surrounded by many sweaty male bodies but her immediate concern was not herself, but Alaranth. The queen seemed to pulse goldenly even from this distance.

The terrified herdbeasts were stampeding about but they had nowhere to go and, as their circling took them too close to the blooding queen again, she casually made a little hop and landed on one of the smaller creatures.

Blood it! Don't you dare take the flesh, Alaranth, Don't you dare!

Even though she was in her queen's mind with an immediacy she had never experienced since Impression was made, Torene gasped as Alaranth suddenly flung aside the last kill and, with a gigantic push from her hind legs, surged aloft. The male dragons on the Rim were equally surprised by the sudden move. They sprang up though two or three dropped off the Rim and were somehow airborne and rising faster than their rivals. For Torene it was just a blur of wings behind her for she was Alaranth more than she was Torene, increasing the distance between herself and the males with every beat of her broader, longer wings.

The peaks were also falling fast below and the air cooled a body heated by blooding, by sexual drive at its most potent point. Alaranth revelled in her speed, in the height she was gaining so effortlessly. She caught a thermal and soared on it, attaining more altitude. This was higher than she had ever ventured and she felt strong, felt the powerful lift of air under

175

her wings, caressing her body, stoking the fires already consuming her.

Far below her sparkled the sea, blues shading to green and aqua. She felt, rather than saw, the shadow: sensed the proximity of another. Craning her head around, she saw the cluster of males below and some distance behind her. They would not catch *her* so easily. They hadn't her wings, her strength, her . . .

Strong talons gripped her shoulder joints, a powerful neck twined with hers, and wrenching herself about to meet her attacker, only too late did Alaranth realize she had done exactly as the bronze had hoped and she was well and truly caught. As he made sure of his conquest of her, wing to wing, necks twined, talons locked, Alaranth realized that only one had ever been in contention for her and she abandoned all restraint.

'Now! Torene, now!'

Torene was no longer aloft with Alaranth in the throes of the dragons' mating passion, she was naked in the arms of his rider: naked and her body demanding the same glorious orgasm that her dragon had just experienced.

'Damn it, Torene,' that rider was saying as he attempted to penetrate her body, 'did you have to wait until *now*?' His cry was more criticism than surprise.

She gripped him to her, her nails digging into the muscular flesh of his back. The hurt was a mere moment's discomfort, immediately forgotten in the powerful surging of lust that rose from some unexpected, limitless depth within her.

'TOREEEEEEEENE!'

The cry of her name produced mild astonishment in her for the tone held more than triumph, more than surprise, more than intense pleasure. So she opened her eyes to see whose dragon had flown hers so skilfully, which rider had taken her.

His face was still buried in her neck, his body limp with repletion alongside hers. He smelled of sweat, as she did. Even his hair was damp. They were both dripping, but, as she wrapped slippery arms about his slippery back, she knew him,

176

knew him more intimately now than she had known any other man.

'Polite?' 'Considerate?' her errant mind went through the comments of the other queen riders about this man. 'Deft?' Well, he had certainly been that, both with his bronze's tactics and with herself. 'Controlled?' Oh no, not a bit controlled. Not polite and more angry with her virginity than considerate. But then, had she been all that wise, leaving her first experience until her queen's first flight? Well, it had been her option and she was glad she had. That way she was sure that it was her dragon who would choose, not some silly preference of hers.

'Mihall?' She spoke his name softly. His breathing had slowed now and she didn't know if he slept where he lay on her. He wasn't that heavy and she'd better get accustomed to it anyway, since he was now indisputably the Weyrleader and her weyrmate.

He gathered himself to move and she held him fast. She liked his body. Indeed, she liked it very much for the way it had made her feel, completed her.

'You made for the thermal current right off?' she asked, having figured out just how he had managed to achieve his goal.

'Hmmm,' and he moved his head to emphasize the agreement.

Vividly blue eyes regarded her with solemn appraisal. His short hair was dark red with sweat but it curled as much as hers did. She expected that they'd have curly, redheaded children and smiled to be thinking that far ahead right now.

'Only way,' he murmured. Then, almost as if he expected her to resist, he ran a wondering finger down her cheek.

'Alaranth hadn't a chance against that technique.'

'I didn't intend that she should, 'Rene,' he said with a slow smile and stroked her cheek again. It was the warm smile she liked so much. 'I couldn't let any other rider have *you*.'

She looked up at him quizzically at his unexpected phrasing and emphasis. Not 'dragon', but 'rider' and '*you*'. He meant her, not just what she brought to this union, her dragon and the Weyrleadership.

'Rider?'

He raised himself on his elbows, looking down at her face as if he had to memorize every detail. 'You are exceptionally beautiful, you know, and those eyelashes are totally unfair!' That marvellous smile of his again curved his firm mouth.

'But you said you were going to be Weyrleader.'

'Oh, I'd've been that one way or another, sooner or later,' he said in a blithe tone. He gave her very tender kisses on the edges of her lips.

'Polite?' 'Restrained?' She couldn't help smiling up at him, thinking of how very wrong the other women had been and how very glad she was they were.

'It was always *you* I ached to have,' he said, still memorizing the planes of her face, kissing her cheekbones. 'From the moment I saw you Impress Alaranth. But my father had warned me off the queen riders. I had to shadow Admiral Benden in order to get anywhere near you then without having my backside flayed.'

'*That* long ago?' Who had been avoiding whom since? She raised her eyelashes then, swept them teasingly across his forehead. His arms tightened and there was nothing polite or considerate about his response: a response that had nothing to do with his dragon.

We both have what we wanted, said a dragon in a sleepy, satisfied tone.

Try though she would in all the years she and M'hall were the Weyrleaders of Benden, Torene was never sure which dragon had spoken. Or to whom.

Rescue Run

'Ma'am?' Ross Vaclav Benden said in a surprised tone, 'there's an orange flag on the Rukbat system.' He swivelled from his position towards the *Amherst*'s command chair and the battle cruiser's captain, Anise Fargoe.

The *Amherst* had been assigned to conduct a determined search through the Sagittarian sector of space for any evidence of new incursions by the Nasties. The punitive war of six decades ago proved insufficient to dissuade those intruders from annexing remote elements of the Federation. There had already been incidents in the Rigel sector despite a powerful Federated force. A massive seek-and-destroy operation was now five years in progress with, mercifully, only a few infiltrations discovered. And those, outposts and two space stations, had been obliterated. Not until all adjoining space and every peripheral system had been investigated and warning devices strategically strewn would the Federation enjoy any sense of security. A second prolonged Nasties campaign would ruin the already depleted Federation. Quick sharp thrusts now, the Combined Joint Staffs had wisely decided, should suffice.

As the *Amherst* had so far had a very boring swing through their sector, Lieutenant Benden's unexpected comment roused everyone on the bridge.

'Orange? This far out?' Captain Fargoe asked, her eyes widening in a flare of excitement. 'Didn't know we had colonies in this sector.'

'Orange' signified that an investigation should be initiated by any vessel close enough to the flagged system to do so.

'I'm accessing files, ma'am,' and Benden, suddenly remembering family history, breathlessly awaited the entry. He tapped his thumbs restlessly on the edge of the keyboard and

179

got a quick repressive glance from old Rezmar Dooley Zane, the duty navigator. 'Oh,' he added, deflated as the file header informed him that a distress message had been received from the colony on Pern, Rukbat's only inhabitable planet.

'Well, let's see the message,' Captain Fargoe said. Anything to relieve the tedium of the fruitless search through this deserted – almost deserted – sphere of space. 'Screen it.'

Benden transferred the message to the main screen.

Mayday! Pern colony in desperate condition following repeated attacks of an uncontacted enemy invasion force employing unknown organism . . .

'Nasties don't *need* germ warfare,' muttered brash Ensign Cahill Bralin Nev. Someone else snickered.

. . .which consumes all organic matter. Must have technical and naval support or colony faces total annihilation. There is wealth here. Save our souls. Theodore Tubberman, Colony Botanist.

There was an almost embarrassed silence for the tone of the message.

'Hardly the Nasties then,' the captain said dryly. 'Probably some old weapons system has been triggered. Perhaps one of the Sifty units we ran into in the Red Sector. I thought only survivor types were chosen to be colonists. Mr Benden, what does Library say about this Pern expedition?'

Ross didn't need to search for the official documentation on the Expedition. He knew most of the tale by heart, but he keyed up the file.

'Captain, a low-tech, agrarian colony was chartered for the third planet of the Rukbat system, under the joint leadership of Admiral Paul Benden and . . .'

'Your uncle, I believe.'

'Yes, Captain,' Ross replied, keeping his tone level. Proud though his entire family was of Paul Benden's most honourable service record, he had taken a lot of gibing during his first cadet year when his uncle's victory at Cygnus was telecast

180

as a documentary and in third year when Admiral Benden's strategy was discussed in Tactics.

'A most able strategist and a fine commander.' Fargoe's voice registered approval but her sideways glance warned Benden not to presume on his uncle's sterling record. 'Continue, Mr.'

'Governor Emily Boll of Altair was the other leader. Six thousand plus colonists, chartered and contracted, were transported in three ships, *Yokohama*, *Buenos Aires* and *Bahrain*. The only other communication was the regulation report of a successful landing. No further contact was expected.'

'Humph. Idealists, were they? Isolating themselves and then screaming for help at the slightest sign of trouble.'

Ross Benden gritted his teeth, searching for some polite way to assert that Admiral Benden would not have 'screamed for help' and he bloody well hadn't sent that craven message.

Fortunately, after a moment's thought, the captain went on, 'Not Admiral Benden's style to send a distress message of any kind. So, who's this Theodore Tubberman, Botanist, who affixed his name to the plea? A Mayday should have been authorized by the colony leaders.'

'It wasn't a *standard* capsule,' Benden replied, having noted that emendation. 'But expertly contrapted. It was also sent to Federation headquarters.'

'Federation headquarters?' Fargoe sat forward, frowning. 'Why HQ? Why not the Colonial Authority? Or the Fleet? No, if it wasn't signed by Admiral Benden, the Fleet would have shifted it to the CA.' Then she sat, chin on one hand, studying the report, scrolling it forward from her armrest key pad. 'A non-standard homing device sent to Federation HQ indicating that the colony was under attack . . .hmm. And nine years after a successful landing, forty-nine years ago.

'How far are we from the Rukbat system, Mr Benden?'

'Point 045 from the heliopause, ma'am. Science officer Ni Morgana wanted a closer look at that Oort cloud. She's interested in cometary reservoirs. That's when I noticed the orange flag on the system.'

181

'They wanted squadrons then?' The captain gave a short bark of laughter. 'Nearly fifty years ago? Hmmm. No Nastie activity was noticed that soon after the War. This Tubberman fellow doesn't specify. Maybe that's what he intended. Big unknown alien life-form attack might have stirred Federation.' She gave a dubious sniff. 'What sort of resources does this Pern have, Mr Benden?'

Benden had anticipated that request and inserted a smaller window on the main screen with the initial survey report. 'Pern evidently only had minimal resources, enough to supply the needs of a low-tech colony.'

'No, that sort of ore and mineral potential wouldn't have interested any of the Syndicates,' the captain mused. 'Too costly to use an orbiting refinery or to transport the ores to the nearest facility. Nine years after touchdown? Long enough for those agrarian types to settle in and accumulate reserves. And the EEC doesn't list any predators.' She paused in her review of the data and made a slight grimace. 'Have Lieutenant Ni Morgana report to the bridge,' she said over her shoulder to the communications officer.

The captain tapped her fingers on her armrest, which caused the crew to exchange glances. The captain was thinking again!

'Doesn't compute that Paul Benden would send any distress message,' she went on. 'So where was he when this Tubberman sent off his contraption? Had the menace from outer space done for everyone in authority?'

'Internal conflict?' Benden suggested, not able to believe his resourceful uncle would have been destroyed by a mere organism after surviving all the Nastie fleet had thrown at him. That would be ironic. And the admiral had certainly researched the colonial scheme from every aspect, but he might have relied on Rukbat's isolated position in Federated space to diminish any hostile attacks. The EEC report listed no hostile organism on the planet. Of course, no-one could rule out such a bizarre possibility as an attack by a remnant weapons system. Sections of the galaxy were strewn with the unexploded minefields from ancient wars. Not necessarily of Nastie origin.

The grav shaft whooshed open and Lieutenant Ni Morgana entered, stood to attention and snapped off a salute. 'Captain?' And she tilted her head awaiting her orders.

'Ah, Lieutenant, there is not only an Oort cloud surrounding the Rukbat system but it appears to be orange tagged, distress message,' the captain said gesturing for Ni Morgana to read the data which now occupied several windows on the big screen.

'Coming on a bit thick, weren't they? Alien invasion!' Ni Morgana gave a snort of disgust after a quick perusal. 'Although,' and she paused, pursing her mouth, 'it's just possible that the "unknown organism" has been seeded into the cometary cloud to camouflage it.'

'What are the chances of it containing some engineered organism that attacked the planet fifty years ago?' Captain Fargoe was clearly sceptical.

'I am hoping that we can obtain samples of the cloud as we pass it, ma'am,' Ni Morgana replied. 'It is unusually close in to the system for an Oort cloud.'

'Have Oort clouds ever been found to harbour natural viruses or organisms that could threaten a planet?'

'I know of several cases where it's always been assumed that inimical mechanisms have been launched from one solar system to another – "berserkers" they were called.'

'Could the organism this Tubberman mentions be a Nastie softening agent? Destroying all organic matter seems like a weapon of some kind, doesn't it?'

'We've learned not to underestimate the Nasties, Captain. Though their methods, so far, have been much more direct.' Ni Morgana's smile was tight, understandable when you knew that the science officer was the only survivor of her family, solely because she was at the Academy when the enemy had attacked her home world. 'However, since the Nasties have been trying to establish bases far from well-travelled space, it becomes a possibility out here.'

'Yes, it does, doesn't it,' the captain said thoughtfully and then grimaced. It was the ambition of every member of Fleet and EEC from the lowliest long-distance single scout to the commander of the heaviest battle cruiser to discover the

Nasties' home world, and Captain Fargoe was scarcely an exception.

'Whatever the attack on Pern was, they would not have sent for help unless their situation was desperate,' Ni Morgana added. 'You are aware that the Colonial Authority exacts punitive payments for such assistance?'

A complex series of expressions rippled across the captain's face. 'Far too high for the service they give, and the time it takes them to respond. The colonists would be mortgaged, body, blood and breath, unto the fourth generation to repay such a debt. Also the message was not sent by Admiral Paul Benden. That's one man I'd like to pipe aboard the *Amherst*.'

'He'd scarcely be alive now,' Benden heard himself saying. 'He was in his seventh decade when he started.'

'A good colonial life can add decades to a man's span, Benden,' the captain said. 'So, I think we can entertain a rescue run to Pern. Lieutenant Zane, plot a course that will take us through the system close enough to this Pern to launch the shuttle. We can give the other planets and satellites a good probe on the swing past. Mr Benden, you'll command the landing party: a junior officer and, say, four marines. I'll want your crew recommendations, and calculations on projected journey to rendezvous with the *Amherst* on her turn back through the system. Allowing, say . . . How long did the EEC survey team take? Ah, yes, five days and a bit . . . Allowing five days on the surface to make contact with the colonists and establish their current situation.'

'Aye, aye, Captain,' Benden replied, trying hard to keep elation out of his voice. Lieutenant Zane on the navigation board shot him a malevolent glance, which he ignored, as he did Ensign Nev to his right who was all but tugging his sleeve to remind Ross that he'd had xeno training.

'I suggest you talk with Lieutenant Ni Morgana, Mr Benden, when she has completed her survey of the Oort cloud matter. There might just be some connection and these ancient weapons can produce some awkward surprises.' She awarded Ross Benden a quick nod. 'You have the con, Lieutenant Zane.' With that, the captain slid from the command seat and left the bridge.

As Saraidh Ni Morgana took her seat at the science terminal, she winked at Ross Benden which he interpreted as a sign of her support in his assignment.

On the 3-D globe on the *Amherst*'s bridge, the ship seemed only centimetres from the edge of the nebulosity that was the Oort cloud. As she approached at an angle to sample a core through the thickest part of the cloud, a great net was fired from a forward missile tube on the port side. The net would both collect debris and clear the ship's path. No ship would barrel through such a cloud where particles were as close as tens of metres. The biggest particles were about a kilometre apart. The problem was to avoid collision of the net with anything above a tonne, which would tear it and bring the ship's meteorite defence into play.

During the next two weeks, while the *Amherst* passed beyond the cloud, heading in to the Rukbat system, the science officer carefully examined the material. First she asked permission to rig an empty cargo pod with remote waldo controls and monitors. A workparty towed the pod out to a point at which there was no risk to the *Amherst* and yet close enough to make frequent trips to the net feasible.

Then, with a workparty she jetted out to the net and selected fragments which might be worth examining. The cargo pod was already divided into sections. At first these were all kept in vacuum status at –270° Celsius or 3° absolute. Once back in the *Amherst*, Ni Morgana activated the monitors and began one of her legendary forty-hour days.

'I've got a lot of dirty ice,' was her initial comment four days later after she'd had some sleep and a second review of her data. 'Most of the stuff has identifiable intrusions, particles of rock and metal, but there are also—' There was a long pause, '—some very unusual particles that I have never encountered before. Before anyone gets an idea I don't want to give, there is no evidence of any artefact.'

As the science officer held five degrees in different disciplines and had landed on three or four dozen alien surfaces, that was an intriguing admission. The next morning she suited up again and jetted around the netted debris, looking for her special interest, 'space worms'.

Captain Fargoe had approved Lieutenant Benden's preliminary flight data and Ross continued his study of the EEC survey reports and the two cryptic messages that were the only communications from the colony world.

'If there is a life-form,' Ni Morgana said at her most tentative in the officers' meeting that week, 'its response time is far too slow for us to discern. There have been some anomalies, both in superconductivity and in cryochemistry that I want to follow up. I shall begin a series of tests, slowly warming some representative samples and see what occurs.'

The next week she reported: 'At -200° Celsius, some of the larger particles are showing relative movement but whether this is driven by anomalous internal structure, or reaction to the warmer temperature I cannot as yet ascertain.'

'Keep in mind at all times, Lieutenant,' the captain said at her sternest, 'what happened to the *Roma*!'

'Ma'am, I always do!' The 'melting' of the *Roma* when the science officer brought aboard a metal-hungry organism was the cautionary example drummed into every science officer.

The following week Ni Morgana was almost jubilant. 'Captain, there is a real life-form in some of the larger chunks from the cloud. Ovoid shapes, with an exceedingly hard crust of material, they have some liquid, perhaps helium, inside. They're very strange but I'm sure they're not artefacts. I'm bringing one sample up above 0°C this week.'

The captain held up an admonishing finger at her science officer. 'At all times, keep the *Roma* in mind.'

'Ma'am, even the situation on the *Roma* didn't happen in a day.'

In the process of leaving the conference room, the captain stopped and stared quizzically at Ni Morgana. 'Are you deliberately misquoting something, Lieutenant?'

'Mr Benden!' The peremptory summons of the science officer over the comunit by his ear jolted Ross Vaclav Benden out of his bunk and to his feet.

'Ma'am?'

'Get down to the lab on the double, Mr!'

Benden struggled into his shipsuit as he ran down the companionway, stabbing feet into soft shipshoes. It was o-dark-hundred of the dog watch for no-one was even in Five Deck's lounge area as he raced across it and to the appropriate grav shaft down to the lab. He skidded to a halt at the door, skinning his forearms on the frame as he braked and fell into the facility. He almost knocked over Lieutenant Ni Morgana. She pointed to the observation chamber.

'Funkit, what in the name of the holies is that?' he wanted to know as his eyes fell on the writhing, greyish-pink and puke-yellow mass that oozed and roiled on the monitor screen. He could understand why everyone was standing well back even if the mass was, in reality, ten kilometres from the *Amherst*.

'If that is what fell on Pern,' Ni Morgana said, 'I don't blame 'em for shrieking for help!'

'Let me through,' and the captain, clad in a terry-cloth caftan, had to exert some strength to push past the mesmerized group watching the phenomenon. 'Gods above! What have you unleashed, Mr?'

'We're taping the show, ma'am,' Ni Morgana said as well as prominently waving the hand she held over the 'destruct' button that would activate laser fire. Benden could see her eyes glittering with clinical fascination. 'According to the readings I'm getting, this complex organism exhibits some similarity to Terran mycorrhizoids in its linear structure. But it's enormous! Damn!'

The organism suddenly collapsed in on itself and became a thick viscous inanimate puddle. The science officer tapped out some commands on the waldo keyboard and a unit extruded towards the mass, scooped up a sample in a self-sealing beaker and retreated. Lights glittered on the remote testing apparatus that analysed the sample.

'What happened to it?' Captain Fargoe demanded and Benden admired how firm her voice was. He was very much aware that he had the shakes.

'I should be able to tell you when the analysis is finished on that sample of the residue but I'd hazard the guess that, with such rapid expansion, if it found no sustenance in the chamber – and there was none apart from a very thin atmosphere – that it died of starvation. That's only a guess.'

'But,' Benden heard himself saying, 'if this is the Pernese organism . . .'

'That's only a possibility at this point,' Ni Morgana said quickly. 'We must first discover how it managed to get from the cloud to Pern's surface.'

'Good point,' the captain murmured and Benden was almost angry at her amused tone. There was nothing remotely funny about what they had just witnessed.

'But if it did, and it's what attacked Pern, I can't blame 'em for wanting help,' said Ensign Nev whose complexion was still slightly green.

The captain gave him a long look that caused him to flush from neck to a scalp that was visible under his latest space trim.

'Captain,' Ni Morgana said as she pressed the destruct button, destroying it by laser fire, 'I request permission to join the Pern landing party to pursue my investigation of this phenomenon.'

'Granted!' The captain paused, stepping over the lintel of the lab, with a wicked grin. 'I always prefer volunteers for landing parties.'

Whoever might have envied Lieutenant Benden the assignment had different feelings once the details of the 'organism' became scuttlebutt. A concise report from Lieutenant Ni Morgana was published to quell the more rampant speculations and her lab team became welcome as experts at any mess.

Ross Vaclav Benden had nightmares about his uncle: the admiral, unexpectedly garbed in dress whites, great purple sash of the Hero of the Cygnus Campaign, and a full assortment of other prestigious and rare decorations on his chest, struggled against engulfment by the monstrosity of the lab chamber. Determined to do his best by his uncle, Ross studied, to the point of perfect recall, the EEC valuation of

Pern. The terse all-safe message by Admiral Benden and Governor Boll and Tubberman's Mayday were easy to memorize, the latter tantalizingly ambiguous. Why had the colony botanist sent the message? Why not Paul Benden or Emily Boll, or one of the senior section heads?

Although this was not Benden's first landing party command, he believed in checking and double-checking every aspect of the assignment. Since there might be hostile conditions, including omnivorous organisms and other enigmas to be solved or avoided on Pern's surface, Ross Benden judiciously plotted an alternative holding orbit until the escape window opened up for their rendezvous with the *Amherst*. The landing party had five days, three hours, fourteen minutes on the surface to conduct its investigations. To his chagrin, Ni Morgana asked for Ensign Nev as the junior officer.

'He needs some experience, Ross,' Ni Morgana said, blandly ignoring Benden's disgruntlement, 'and he's had *some* xeno training. He's strong and he obeys orders even as he's turning green. He's got to learn sometime. Captain Fargoe thinks this could give him valuable experience.'

Benden had no option but to accept the inevitable but he asked for Sergeant Greene to command his marines. That tough burly man knew more about the hazards that could embroil landing parties than Benden ever would. Having seen the organism which Saraidh had unleashed, Ross wanted solid experience to offset Nev's ingenuousness. If that was the proper word for the boy.

'Just what were you like as an ensign, Lieutenant?' Ni Morgana asked, giving him a sly sideways glance.

'I was never that gauche,' he replied tartly, which was true enough since he'd been reared in a Service family and had absorbed proper behaviour with normal nutrients. Then he relented, grinning wryly back at her as he remembered a few incidents that he hoped she had no access to. 'This sounds like a fairly routine mission: find and evaluate.'

'Let's hope so,' Saraidh replied earnestly.

Ross Benden was, in another sense, delighted to be teamed up with the elegant science officer. She was his senior in years but not in Fleet, for she had done her scientific training before applying to the Service. She was also the only woman who kept her hair long, though it was generally dressed in intricate arrangements of braids. The effect was somehow regal and very feminine: an effect at variance with her expertise in the various forms of contact sport that were enjoyed in the *Amherst*'s gym complex. If she had made any liaisons on board, they were not general knowledge though he'd over-heard speculation about her tastes. He had always found her agreeable company and a competent officer, though they hadn't shared more than a watch or two until now.

'Did you see the tape of that thing?' Ross Benden heard the nasal voice of Lieutenant Zane saying later as he passed the wardroom. 'There'll be no-one left alive down there. Ni Morgana has proved the Oort cloud generated that life-form so it wasn't Nastie manufacture. There's no rationale for taking a chance and landing on that planet if any of those *things* are alive down there! And they could be with an entire planet to eat up.'

Benden paused to listen, knowing perfectly well that, despite the dangers involved, Zane would have given a kidney to be in the landing party. Nev was at least an improvement on the sour and supercilious Zane. And when the navigation officer added some invidious remarks that Benden was only chosen because of his relationship to one of the leaders of the colony, Benden passed quickly down the corridor before his temper got the better of his discretion.

As the *Amherst*'s majestic passage through the system approached the point where the shuttle could be launched, Benden called for a final briefing session.

'We'll spiral down to the planetary surface in a corkscrew orbit which will allow us to examine the northern hemisphere on our way to the site of record on the southern continent at longitude 30°,' he said, calling up the flight-path on the big screen in the conference room. 'We've landmarks from the original survey of three volcanic cones that ought to be visible from some distance as we make our final approach. Survey report said the soil there would be viable for hardy Earth and

Altairian hybrids so it is reasonable to assume that they started their agrarian venture there. The Tubberman Mayday came in some nine years after landing so they should have been well entrenched.'

'Not enough to avoid that organism,' Nev said flatly.

'Your theory would hold water, Ensign,' Saraidh said at her mildest, 'if I could figure out how the organism transported itself from the Oort cloud to Pern's surface.'

'Nasties sowed it in Pern's atmosphere,' Nev responded with no hesitation.

'Nasties are more direct in their tactics,' the science officer replied with a diffident shrug and turned to Benden with a question.

'We taught 'em to be cautious, Lieutenant,' Nev went on. 'And devious. And . . .'

'Nev!' Benden called the ensign to order.

Benden kept his expression neutral but he wondered if Ni Morgana was regretting her choice of the irrepressible Nev and his wild theories. If the science officer hadn't found a transport vector for the organism, the Nasties were unlikely to have discovered it. Their *forte* was metallurgical, not biological. Nev subsided and the briefing continued.

'Once we have made landfall, we may also have answers to that question and others. It is obvious our search must begin at the site of record. We will also have made a good sweep of the entire planetary surface and can deviate if we find traces of human settlements elsewhere. We board the *Erica* at 0230 tomorrow morning. Any questions?'

'What do we do if the place is swarming with those *things*?' asked Nev, swallowing hard.

'What would you do, Nev?' Benden asked.

'Leave!'

'Tut tut, Mr,' Ni Morgana said. 'How will you ever increase your understanding of xenobiological forms unless you examine closely whatever samples come your way?'

Ensign Nev's eyes bugged out. 'Begging your pardon, Lieutenant, but *you're* the science officer.'

'Indeed I am,' and Ni Morgana rose, the scrape of her chair covering a mutter of gratitude from the end of the table occupied by the four marines assigned to the landing party.

Launched from the *Amherst*, the gig proceeded at a smart
inner system speed towards the blue pebble in the sky that
was Rukbat's third planet. It began to dominate the forward
screen, serene and clear, beautiful and innocuous. Benden
had plotted the gig's course to intercept the geosynchronous
orbit of the three colony ships to see if the colonists had left a
message to be retrieved. But when he opened communications, the only response was the standard identification
response, stating the name and designation of the *Yokohama*.

'That might not mean anything,' Saraidh remarked as
Benden looked disappointed. 'If the colony's up and running,
they won't have much use for these hulks. Though I find that
sight rather sad,' she added as Rukbat suddenly illuminated
the deserted vessels.

'Why?' Nev asked, surprised by her observation.

Saraidh gave a shrug of her slender, elegant shoulders.
'Look up their battle records and you might appreciate their
present desuetude more.'

'Their what?' Nev looked blank.

'Look up that word, too,' she said and, in an almost cloying
tone, spelled it for him.

'Old sailors never die, they just fade away,' Benden murmured, eyes on the three hulks, feeling a constriction in his
throat and a slight wetness in his eyes as the gig drifted away
from them, leaving them to continue on their ordained path.

'Soldiers, not sailors,' Saraidh said, 'but the quotation is
apt.' Then she frowned at a reading on her board. 'We've got
two beacons registering. One at the site of record and another
much further south. Enlarge the southern hemisphere for me,
will you, Ross? Along 70° longitude and nearly twelve
hundred klicks from the stronger one.' Ross and Saraidh
exchanged looks. 'Maybe there are survivors! Pretty far south
though, over mountain ranges of respectable height. I read
altitudes of 2,400 rising to more than 9,000 metres above sea
level. We'll land at the site of record first.'

As the gig slanted in over the northern pole, it was obvious that this hemisphere was enduring a stormy and bitterly cold winter: most of the landmass was covered by snow and ice. Instruments detected no source of power or light, and very little heat radiation in areas where humans usually settled; the river valleys, the plains, the shoreline. There was one hiccup of a blip over the large island, just off the coast of the northern hemisphere. The reading was too faint to suggest any significant congregation of settlers. If they had followed the usual multiplication so characteristic of colonies, the population should now be close to the 500,000 mark, even allowing for natural disasters and those mortality patterns normal for a primitive economy.

'We'll do another low-level pass if we've time later. The settlers were determined to be agrarian but they might be using fossil fuels,' Saraidh said as they plunged towards the equator, leaving the snow-clad continent behind them and slanting down across the tropical sea. 'Lots of marine life. Some big ones,' she added. 'Bigger than the survey team reported.'

'They took Terran dolphins with them,' Nev said. 'Mentasynth-enhanced dolphins,' he added, as if that altered the fact.

'I don't think rescuing dolphins is what Captain Fargoe has in mind, even if we had the facility to do so,' Saraidh said. 'Have either of you any training in other species' communications? I don't. So, let's table that notion for now.'

'There's another consideration: how long do dolphins live?' Ross asked. 'Remember, this trouble started when the colony was down eight to nine years. In your report, Lieutenant, you did mention that further tests with the organism proved that water drowned it and organic fire consumed it. Mentasynth-enhanced creatures have good memories, sure. But how many generations of dolphins have there been? Would they even be aware of what happened on land? Much less remember?'

'Would they want to, is more the case,' Saraidh said. 'They're independent and very intelligent. Clearly they have survived and multiplied from the complement that came with the colony. They'd cut their losses and survive on their own. I would, if I were a dolphin.'

Then Saraidh started the recorders on the gig's delta wing to take a record of the plunging antics of the large marine life as the *Erica* swooped over the ocean on their final descent towards the site of record.

'Records state that the *Bahrain* brought fifteen female dolphins and nine males,' Nev said suddenly. 'Dolphins produce – what? Once a year. There could be nearly eight hundred of 'em in the seas right now. That's a lot of terrestrial life-forms we'd be abandoning.'

'Abandoning? Hell, Cahill, they're in their element. Look at them, they're doing their damnedest to keep pace with us.'

'Maybe they have a message for us,' Nev went on earnestly.

'We look for humans first, Ensign,' the science officer said firmly. 'Then we'll check the dolphins! Ross, I'm not getting anything from the ship-to-ground interface that's recorded for the site. It's inoperative, too.'

'Now hear this! Buckle up for landing,' Ross said, opening a channel to the marines' quarters.

'Muhlah!' was Saraidh's awed comment as they saw the two ruined volcanic craters and the smoking cone of the third.

Ross could say nothing, appalled by the extent of the eruption. He'd expected nothing so catastrophic as this. Or had this devastation occurred after the organism had begun to fall? While he had more or less resigned himself that he was unlikely to encounter his uncle, he had hoped to chat with the admiral's descendants. He certainly hadn't anticipated this level of devastation. They flew over the landing field tower, its beacon now blinking, activated by the proximity of the gig.

'See those mounds, just coming up on portside?' Saraidh pointed. 'They've got the outlines of shuttles. How many did the colonists have?'

'Records say six,' Nev replied. '*Bahrian* had one, *Buenos Aires* two and the *Yoko* three. Plus a captain's gig.'

'Only three parked there now. Wonder where the others went.'

'Maybe they were used to get out of this place when the volcano blew?'

'But where to? There were no signs of human habitation on

194

the nothern continent,' Benden said, sternly repressing his dismay.

Saraidh let out a thin high whistle. 'And those other regular mounds are – were – the settlement. Neatly, if not aesthetically, laid out. Must have built well, for nothing seems to have collapsed from the weight of ash and dirt. Lava's cooled. Ross, got a reading of how deep that ash is over the ground?'

'We do indeed, Saraidh,' Ross replied with relief. 'A metallic grid is present a half metre below the surface. No problem landing – it'll be nice and soft.'

Which it was. While waiting for the disturbed ash to settle, both officers and marines suited up, checking masks, breathing tanks, and strapping on lift-belts. These would convey them safely above the ash to the settlement.

'What're those?' one of the ratings asked as the landing party assembled to hover a metre above the ash-coated ground outside the *Erica*. He pointed to a series of long semicircular mounds, bulging up out of the ash. 'Tunnels?'

'Unlikely. Not big enough and don't seem to go anywhere,' Ni Morgana said, deftly manipulating her attitude and forward jets. She hovered to one side of the nearest mound and pushed with her foot. It collapsed with a dusty implosion and a stench that the filters of their masks worked hard to neutralize. 'Faugh! Dead organism. Now, why didn't that puddle?' She took out a specimen tube and carefully gathered some of the residue, sealing it and putting that tube in a second padded container.

'It fed on ash or grass or something?' asked Ensign Nev.

'We'll check that out later. Let's look at the buildings. Scag, stay by the gig,' Benden ordered one of the marines. And then gestured for the others to follow him up to the empty settlement.

'Not empty,' Ross said an hour later, increasingly more pessimistic about finding any survivors. Contact with a cousin or two would be something to write home about. So he clutched at a vain hope. 'Emptied. They didn't leave a thing they could use. Nasties would have obliterated any trace of humans.'

'That's true enough,' Saraidh said. 'And there's no evidence of Nasties at all. Merely an evacuated settlement.

There is that second beacon to the south-west. There's certainly nothing here to give us any explanations. Your point about everything being emptied is well taken, Benden. They closed shop here but that doesn't mean they didn't open it up elsewhere.'

'Using the three missing shuttles,' Nev added brightly.

Airborne again in the *Erica*, heading directly towards the beacon, they overpassed the rest of the settlement, taping the one smoking volcano crater and the melted structures below it. No sooner were they over the river than the landscape showed another form of devastation. The prevailing winds had minimized the dispersal of volcanic dust but, oddly enough, there were only occasional stands of vegetation and large circles of parched soil.

'Like something had sprinkled the land with whopping great acid drops,' Cahill Nev said, awed at the extent of the markings.

'Not acid. No way,' Benden replied. He keyed the relevant section of the report he knew so well. 'The EEC survey team found similar circular patches and they also reported that botanical succession had started.'

'It has to be the Oort organism,' Nev said enthusiastically. 'On the cruiser it died of starvation. It had plenty to eat here.'

'The organism has to get here first, Mr,' Ni Morgana said bitingly. 'And we haven't established how it could cross some 600 million miles of space to drop on Pern.' Ross, glancing at her set expression, thought she was rapidly considering improbable transport media. 'Terrain's flat enough here, Mr Benden, try a low-level pass and give us a closer look at that . . . that diseased ground.'

Benden obliged, noting once again how responsive the *Erica* was to the helm, smoothly skimming the often uneven terrain. Not that he expected something to pop up out of those polka dots, but you never knew on alien worlds. Even ones thoroughly surveyed by Exploration and Evaluation teams. They might not have found any predators but something dangerous had put in an appearance nine years after the settlers took hold. And the Tubberman appeal hadn't mentioned a volcanic eruption.

196

Klick after klick they passed over circles and overlapping circles and triple circles. Ni Morgana remarked that some succession was visible on their peripheries. She asked Benden to land so she could take more samples, including clods of the regenerating vegetation. Across a broad river there were swaths of totally unharmed trees and acres of broad-leafed and unscathed vegetation. Over one wide pasture they caught sight of a cloud of dust, but whatever stirred it disappeared under the broad leaves of a thick forest. They spotted no trace of human habitation. Not even a dirt-covered mound that might be the remains of a building or a wall.

The second beacon signal became stronger as they neared the foothills of a great barrier of mountains, snow clad even in what must be high summer in this hemisphere. Gradually the pips altered from rhythmic bleeps to a sustained note as they homed in on the beacon.

'There's nothing here but a sheer cliff,' Ross said, disgusted as he let the gig hover over the destination, the single note exacerbating his nerves.

'That may well be, Ross,' Saraidh said, 'but I'm getting body-heat readings.'

Nev pointed excitedly. 'That plateau below us is too level to be natural. And there are terraces below it. See? And what about that path down into the valley. And hey, this cliff has windows!'

'And is definitely inhabited!' exclaimed Saraidh, pointing to starboard where a doorway appeared in the cliff face. 'Put her down, Ross!'

By the time the *Erica* had settled to the smoothed surface, a file of people came running down the plateau towards it, their cries, audible from the exterior speakers, were of hysterical welcome. They ranged in age from early twenties to late forties. Except for the white-haired man, his mane trimmed to shoulder length, whose lined face and slow movements suggested a person well into his eighth or ninth decade. His emergence halted the demonstrations and the others stood aside to allow him a clear passage to the gig's portal where he halted.

'The patriarch,' Saraidh murmured, straightening her tunic and settling her peaked cap straight on top of her braids.

'Patriarch?' Nev asked.

'Look it up later – if the term is not self-explanatory,' Benden shot at him over his shoulder, operating the airlock release. He glanced warningly at the marines who replaced their drawn hand weapons.

As soon as the airlock swung open and the ramp extruded, the small crowd was silent. All eyes turned to the old man who pulled himself even more erect, a patronizing smile on his weathered face.

'You finally got here!'

'A message was received at Federated headquarters,' Ross Benden began, 'signed by a Theodore Tubberman. Are you he?'

The man gave a snort of disgust. 'I'm Stev Kimmer,' and he flicked one hand to his brow in a jaunty parody of a proper Fleet salute. 'Tubberman's long dead. I designed that capsule, by the way.'

'You did well,' Benden replied. Inexplicably, Benden suddenly did not care to identify himself. So he introduced Saraidh Ni Morgana and Ensign Nev. 'But why did you send that capsule to Federation Headquarters, Kimmer?'

'That wasn't my idea. Ted Tubberman insisted.' Kimmer shrugged. 'He paid me for my work, not my advice. As it is, you've taken nearly too damned long to get here.' He scowled with irritation.

'The *Amherst* is the first vessel to enter the Sagittarian sector since the message was received.' Saraidh Ni Morgana said, unruffled by his criticism. She had noted that Ross had not given his name. She hoped that Ensign Nev had also noted the omission. 'We've just come from the site on record.'

'No-one came back to Landing, then?' Kimmer demanded. Benden thought his habit of interrupting Fleet officers could become irritating. 'With Thread gone, that'd be the place they'd return to. The ground-to-ship interface's there.'

'The interface is inoperative,' Benden said, carefully neutral as the old man's arrogance grated on him.

'Then the others are dead,' Kimmer stated flatly. 'Thread got 'em all!'

'Thread?'

'Yes, Thread.' Kimmer's palpable anger was tinged with deep primal emotions, not the least of which was a healthy fear. 'That's what they named the organism that attacked the planet. Because it fell from the skies like a rain of deadly thread, consuming all it touched, animal, man, and vegetable. We burned it out of the skies, on the ground, day after fucking day. And still it came. We're all that's left. Eleven of us and we only survived because we have a mountain above us and we hoarded our supplies, waiting for help to come.'

'Are you positive that you're the sole survivors?' Ni Morgana asked. 'Surely in the eight or nine years you had before this menace attacked you—'

'Before Thread fell, the population was close to 20,000 but we're all that's left,' Kimmer said, now defiant. 'And you cut it mighty fine getting here. I couldn't risk another generation with such a small gene pool.' Then one of the women, who bore a strong resemblance to Kimmer, tugged at his arm. And he made a grimace that could be taken for a smile. 'My daughter reminds me that this is a poor welcome for our long-awaited rescuers. Come this way. I've something laid by in the hope of this day.'

Lieutenant Benden gestured for the two marines to remain on board before he followed Ni Morgana down the ramp, Nev treading on his heels in his eagerness.

The silence which had held Kimmer's small group while he had addressed the spacemen relaxed now into gestures and smiles of welcome. But Benden took note of the tenseness of the oldest three men. They stood just that much apart from the women and youngsters to suggest they distanced themselves deliberately. They had a distinctly Asian cast of countenance, jet black hair trimmed neatly to their earlobes: they were lean and looked physically fit. The oldest woman, who bore a strong resemblance to the three men, walked just a step behind Kimmer in a manner that suggested subservience – an attitude which Benden found distasteful as he and his party followed them to the entrance.

The three younger women were ethnic mixes in feature, though one had brown hair. All were slender and graceful as they tried to contain their excitement. They whispered to each other, casting glances back at Greene and the other marine. At a brusque order from Kimmer, they ran on ahead, into the cliff. The three youngest, two boys and a girl, showed the mixing of ethnic groups more than their elders. Benden wondered just how close the blood bonding was. Kimmer would not have been fool enough to sire children on his own daughters?

Exclamations of surprise were forced from each of the three officers as they entered a spacious room with a high, vaulting ceiling; a room nearly as big as the gig's on-ship hangar. Nev gawked like any off-world stupe while Ni Morgana's expression was of delighted appreciation. This was clearly the main living space of the cliff dwelling for it had been broken up into distinct areas for work, study, dining, and handcrafts. The furnishings were made of a variety of materials, including extruded plastic in bright hard colours. The walls were well hung with curious animal furs and hand-loomed rugs of unusual design. Above those, and all along the upper wall space, a vivid panorama had been drawn: first of stylized figures standing or sitting before what were clearly monitors and keyboards. Other panels showed figures who ploughed and planted fields or tended animals of all sorts; panels which led around to the innermost wall that was decorated by scenes Benden knew too well, the cities of Earth and Altair and three spaceships with unfamiliar constellations behind them. At the apex of the ceiling vault was the Rukbat system, and one planet that was shown to have a highly elliptical and possibly erratic orbit from slightly beyond the Oort cloud to an aphelion below Pern's.

Ni Morgana nudged Benden in the ribs and said in a barely audible whisper, 'Unlikely as it seems, I've just figured out one way the Oort organisms might have reached Pern. I'll be damned sure of my theory before I mention it.'

'The murals,' Kimmer was saying in a loud and proprietorial voice, 'were to remind us of our origins.'

'Did you have stone-cutters?' Nev asked abruptly, running his hand over the glassy smooth walls.

One of the older black-haired men stepped forward. 'My parents, Kenjo and Ito Fusaiyuki, designed and carved all the principal rooms. I am Shensu. These are my brothers, Jiro and Kimo: our sister, Chio.' He gestured to the woman who was reverently withdrawing a bottle from a shelf in a long dresser.

With a searing glance at Shensu, Kimmer hastily took the initiative again. 'These are my daughters, Faith and Hope. Charity is setting out the glasses.' Then with a flick of his fingers, he indicated Shensu. 'You may introduce my grandchildren.'

'Pompous old goat,' muttered Ni Morgana to Benden but she smiled as the grandchildren were introduced as Meishun, Alun and Pat, the two boys being in their mid-teens.

'This Stake could have supported many more families if only those who had said they'd join us had kept their promises,' Kimmer went on bitterly. Then with an imperious gesture, he waved the guests to come to the table and be served of the wine he was pouring; a rich fruity red.

'Well come, men and women of the *Amherst!*' was Kimmer's toast and he touched glasses with each of them.

Benden noticed, as Ni Morgana did, that the others were served a paler red by Meishun. Watered, Benden thought. They could at least be equal to us, today of all days! Shensu hid his resentment better than his two brothers did. The women seemed not to notice for they passed dishes of cheese bits and tasty small crackers to everyone. Then Kimmer gestured for the guests to be seated. Benden gave a discreet hand signal to the two marines who took the end seat at the long table and remained watchful, taking only small sips of the celebratory wine.

'Where to start?' Kimmer began, setting his wine glass down deliberately.

'The beginning,' Ross Benden said wryly, hoping that he might learn what had happened to his uncle before disclosing his identity. There was something about Kimmer – not his anger nor his autocratic manner – that Benden instinctively distrusted. But perhaps a man who had managed to survive in a hostile environment had the right to a few peculiarities.

'Of the end?' And Kimmer's spiteful expression served to increase Benden's dislike.

'If that is when you and the botanist Tubberman sent that homing device,' Benden replied, encouragingly.

'It was and our position was then hopeless, though few were realists enough to admit it, especially Benden and Boll.'

'Could you have got back up to the colony ships then?' Ni Morgana asked, nudging Ross Benden when she felt him stir angrily.

'No way,' and Kimmer snorted with disgust. 'They used what fuel the gig had left to send Fusaiyuki up to reconnoitre. They thought they might be able to divert whatever it was that brought the Thread. That was before they realized that the wanderer planet had dragged in a tail that would shower this wretched planet with Thread for fifty frigging years. And if that wasn't bad enough, they let Avril steal the gig and that was the end of any chance we had of sending someone competent for help.' The recital of that forty-year-old memory agitated Kimmer, and his face became suffused with red.

'It was definitely established that the organism had been carried from the Oort cloud?' Ni Morgana asked, her usually calm voice edged with excitement.

Kimmer gave her a quelling glance. 'In the end that was all they discovered despite their waste of fuel and manpower.'

'There were only three shuttles left at the landing site. D'you suppose some people managed to escape in them?' said Ni Morgana in a deliberately soothing tone. Benden could see the glitter of her eyes as she sipped calmly at her wine.

Kimmer glared at her with contempt. 'Where could they escape to? There was no fuel left! And power-packs for sleds and skimmers were in short supply.'

'Barring the lack of fuel, were the shuttles still operational?'

'I said, there was no fuel. No fuel,' and he banged his fist on the table.

Benden, looking away from the man's deep bitterness, noted the faint look of amusement on Shensu's face.

'There was no fuel,' Kimmer repeated with less vehemence. 'The shuttles were so much scrap without fuel. So I haven't any idea why there'd be only three shuttles at Landing. I left the settlement shortly after the bitch blew the gig up.' He glared impartially at the *Amherst* officers. 'I had every right to leave then, to establish a Stake and do what I could to preserve my own skin. Anyone with any sense, charterer or contractor, should have done the same. Maybe they did. Holed up to wait out the fifty years. Or, maybe they sailed away into the rising sun. They had ships, you know. Yes, that's it. Old Jim Tillek sailed them out of Monaco Bay into the rising sun.' He gave a bark of harsh laughter.

'They went west?' Benden asked.

Kimmer favoured him with a contemptuous glance and made a wild gesture with one arm. 'How the hell would I know? I wasn't anywhere near the place.'

'And you settled here,' Ni Morgana asked blandly, 'in the dwelling built by Kenjo and Ito Fusaiyuki?'

Her phrasing was, Benden thought, a little unfortunate for the question angered Kimmer even more. The veins in his temples stood out and his face contorted.

'Yes, I settled here when Ito begged me to stay. Kenjo was dead. Avril killed him to get the gig. Ito'd had a difficult birth with Chio and his kids were too young to be useful then. So Ito asked me to take over.' Someone's breath hissed on intake and Kimmer glared at the three sons, unable to spot the culprit. 'You'd all have died without me!' he said in a flat but somehow cautionary tone.

'Most assuredly,' Shensu said, his surface courtesy not quite masking a deep resentment.

'You have survived, haven't you? And my beacon brought us help, didn't it?' Kimmer banged on the table with both fists and sprang to his feet. 'Admit it! My homer and my beacon have brought us rescue.'

'They did indeed lead us to you, Mr Kimmer,' Benden said in a tone he barefacedly borrowed from Captain Fargoe when she was dressing down an insubordinate rating. 'However, my orders are to search and discover any and *all* survivors on this planet. You may not be the only ones.'

203

'Oh yes, we are. By all the gods, we're the only ones,' Kimmer said, with an edge of panic in his voice. 'And you can't leave us here!' His eyes turned a bit wild.

'What the lieutenant means, Mr Kimmer,' Ni Morgana put in soothingly, 'is that our orders are to search for any other survivors.'

'No-one else survives,' Kimmer said in a flat, toneless voice. 'I can assure you of that.' He splashed wine into his glass and drank half of it, wiping his mouth with a trembling hand.

Because Ross Benden was not looking at the old man just then but at the three brothers seated across the table, he caught the glitter in the eyes of Shensu and Jiro. He waited for them to speak up but they remained silent and inscrutable. Palpably they had knowledge that they would not communicate to their rescuers in front of Stev Kimmer. Well, Benden would see them privately later. Meanwhile, Kimmer was coming across as a somewhat unreliable opportunist. He might assert that he had the right to set off and establish a Stake when the colony was obviously in terrible straits but, to Benden, it sounded more as if Kimmer had fled in a craven fashion. Was it just luck that he had known where to find Ito, and this Kenjo's Stake?

'My sled had a powerful comunit,' Kimmer went on, revived by the wine, 'and once I'd erected the beacon on the plateau here, I listened in to what was broadcast. Not that there was anything important beyond where the next Fall was. How many power-packs had been recharged. If they had enough sleds able to cover the next Fall. A lot of the Stake-holders had come back to Landing by then, centralizing resources. Then, after the volcanoes blew, I heard their messages as they scurried away from Landing. There was a lot of static interference and transmissions got so fragmented that I couldn't hear most of what was said. They were frantic, I can tell you, by the time they abandoned Landing. Then the signals got too weak for me to pick up. I never did find out where they planned to go. It might have been west. It might have been east.

'Oh,' and he waved one hand helplessly, 'I tried when the

last signal died. I only had one full power-pack left by then. I couldn't waste that in futile searches, now could I? I'd Ito and four small kids. Then Ito got so ill, I went back to Landing to see if they'd left any medicines behind. But Landing was covered in ash and lava, great rivers of it, hot and glowing. Damned near singed the plastic off the hull.

'I checked all the stations on the lower Jordan. Paradise River, Malay, even Boca where Benden lived. No-one. Fierce waste of materiel, though, piled as storm-wrack along the coast at one point. Looked to me as if they'd lost the cargo ships in a storm. We got bad ones blowing in from the sea – or maybe the aftermath of a tsunami. We had one of those after some sea volcano blew up to the east somewhere. Missed us though on Bitkim Island.

'Last message I ever heard, and only parts of it at that, was Benden telling everyone to conserve power, stay inside, and just let that frigging Thread fall. I guess it got him, too.'

Ni Morgana's thigh deliberately pressed against Benden's and he took it as sympathy. Though the old man's rambling had been confused and sometimes he contradicted himself, his statement had the ring of truth as he sat silently contemplating his wine glass. Then he roused, raising a finger to bring Chio to his side. She refilled his glass. Then, with an apologetic smile, she offered wine to the other guests whose glasses were barely touched. Down the table from Kimmer, the three brothers sat very close together, saying little but looking, with a thinly veiled hatred of Kimmer.

'We had eight good years on Pern before disaster struck,' Kimmer was saying now, casting further back in his memory. 'I heard that Benden and Boll swore blind that they could lick Thread. Except for Ted Tubberman and a few others, they had half the colony behind them, too entranced by the great reputations of the admiral and the governor,' and the titles were pronounced disparagingly, 'to believe they could fail. Tubberman wanted to send for help then. The colony voted the motion down.

'Where we were on Bitkim Island, we didn't get much Thread but I heard what it did: wiped out whole Stakes down to the metal they'd been wearing. Ate anything, Thread did, gorged until it blew up too fast to live: but it could burrow down and the next generation would begin. Fire stopped it, and metal. It drowned in water. The fish, even the dolphins, thrived on it or so the dolphineers said. Humph. Damned stuff only let up a couple a years back. Otherwise, we've had this frigging menace raining down on us every ten days or so for fifty fucking years.'

'You did well to survive, Mr Kimmer,' Saraidh said in a flattering purr as she leaned forward to elicit more confidences, 'for fifty long years. But how? It must have taken tremendous effort.'

'Kenjo'd started 'ponics. Had some sense, that man, even with this fanatic thing he had about flying and being in the air. Space crazy he was. But I was better at contrapting the things you need to live. I taught this whole bunch everything I knew – not that they're grateful to me,' and his spiteful eyes rested on the three Fusaiyukis. 'We saved horses, sheep, cattle, chickens before Thread could ooze all over 'em. I'd salvaged one of the old grass-makers they used the first year, before they'd planted Earth grass and that Altair hybrid got started.' He paused, narrowing his eyes. 'Tubberman had another type of grass growing before they shunned him. I'd none of that seed but enough to keep us going until we could plant out again. As long as I had power-packs, I foraged and saved every scrap I could find. So we survived, and survived real good.'

'Then others could have, too?' Saraidh asked mildly.

'NO!' thundered Kimmer, banging the table to emphasize that denial. 'No-one survived but us. You don't believe me? Tell her, Shensu.'

As if making up his mind to obey, Shensu regarded first Kimmer and then the three officers. Then he shrugged.

'After Thread had stopped for three months, Kimmer sent us out to see if anyone lived. We went from the Jordan River west to the Great Desert. We did see long overgrown ruins where Stakes had been started. We saw many domestic animals. I was surprised to see how many animals had managed to survive, for we saw much devastation of fertile land. We travelled for eight months. We saw no-one human nor any evidence of human endeavour. We returned to our Hold.' He shot a single challenging look at Kimmer before his expression settled into its mask.

Benden had a stray thought – Kimmer had sent them out, not to search for survivors, but hoping they wouldn't return.

'We're miners, too,' Shensu continued unexpectedly. Kimmer sat up, too enraged at the bland disclosure to form words. Shensu smiled at that reaction. 'We have mined, ores and gemstones, as soon as we were strong enough to wield pick and shovel. All of us, my half sisters, and our children, too. Kimmer taught us how to cut gems. He insisted that we be rich enough to pay our way back to civilized worlds.'

'You fools! You utter fools! You shouldn't have told them. They'll kill us and take it all. All of it.'

'They are Fleet officers, Kimmer,' Shensu said, bowing politely to Benden, Ni Morgana, and the astonished Nev. 'Like Admiral Benden,' and his eyes slid and held Ross Benden's briefly. 'They would not be so basely motivated as to steal our fortunes and abandon us. Their orders are to rescue any survivors.'

'You will rescue us, won't you?' Kimmer cried, suddenly a terrified old man. 'You *must* take us with you. You must!' And now he embarrassed Benden by beginning to blubber. 'You must, you must,' he kept on insisting, pulling himself towards Benden to grab his tunic.

'Stev, you will make yourself ill again,' Chio said, coming to disentangle the grasping hands from Benden's clothing. Her eyes showed her abject apologies for an old man's weakness and her plea for reassurance. The other women fastened apprehensive eyes on the Fleet party.

'Our orders are to establish contact with the survivors—' Benden began, taking refuge in that protocol.

'Lieutenant,' Nev intervened, his face contorted with anxiety, 'we'd have a weight problem, taking eleven more aboard the *Erica*.'

Kimmer moaned.

'We'll discuss this later, Ensign,' Benden said sharply. Trust Nev to be loose-jawed. 'It is time to change the watch.' He gave Nev a quelling look and gestured for Greene to accompany him. Greene looked disgusted as he fell in behind the chastened ensign who was flushed as he realized how badly he had erred.

As Kimmer kept on sobbing 'you must take me, you must take me,' Benden turned to Shensu and his brothers.

'We do have orders to follow, but I assure you that if we find no other survivors to make your continued residence viable, you will either come with us on the *Erica* or another means will be found to rescue you.'

'I appreciate your constraints and your devotion to duty,' Shensu said, his composure in marked contrast to Kimmer's collapse. He made a slight bow from the hips. 'However,' and his face lightened with the slightest of smiles, 'my brothers and I have already searched all the old Stakes without success. Will you not accept our investigations as conclusive?' His dignified entreaty was far harder to ignore than Kimmer's blubbering.

Benden tried to assume a non-committal pose. 'I will certainly take that into consideration, Shensu.' He was also trying to calculate just how to accommodate eleven extra bodies on the *Erica*. He'd three-quarters of a tank: if they stripped unessential equipment, would that still give him enough fuel to lift and a reserve if last minute adjustments were needed in the slingshot manoeuvre? Damn Nev. His orders were for search only, not rescue. One thing was certain, he trusted Shensu far more than he did Kimmer.

'This mission has another goal, Mr Fusaiyuki,' Ni Morgana said, 'if, under these trying circumstances, you could find your way clear to assist us?'

'Certainly. If I can,' and Shensu executed a second dignified bow to her.

'Would you have any documentation that Thread comes from the stray planet as Mr Kimmer intimated?' she asked, pointing to the ceiling and the system diagram. 'Or was that only a theory?'

'A theory which my father proved to his satisfaction at least, for he flew up into the stratosphere and observed the debris which the stray planet had dislodged from the Oort cloud and drawn into this part of the system. He had noticed the cloud on their way through the system. I remember him telling me that he would have paid far closer attention had he any idea of the threat it would pose.' Shensu's well-formed lips curled in a wry smile. 'The EEC report evidently gave the erratic planet only a mention. I have my father's notes.'

'I'd like to see them,' Saraidh said, her voice edged with excitement. 'Bizarre as it is,' she said to Benden, 'it is plausible and unique. Of course, this erratic planet could be a large asteroid, even a comet. Its orbit is certainly cometary.'

'No,' Benden replied, shaking his head, 'the EEC report definitely identifies it as a planet, though probably a wanderer drawn into Rukbat's family only recently. It orbits across the ecliptic.'

'Our father was too experienced an airman to make a mistake.' Jiro spoke for the first time, his voice as impassioned as Shensu's was cold. 'He was a trained pilot and observed critically and objectively on those missions. We have notes of thanks from Admiral Benden, Governor Boll, and Captain Keroon, all expressing gratitude for his investigation and his selfless dedication to duty.' Jiro shot a contemptuous look at Kimmer who was still sobbing, his face pillowed in his arms while Chio tried to comfort and reassure him. 'Our father died to discover such truths.'

Saraidh murmured something appropriate. 'If you would co-operate, further information about this phenomenon would be invaluable.'

'Why?' Shensu asked bluntly. 'There can't be other worlds that are infested with this menace, can there?'

'Not that we know of, Mr Fusaiyuki, but all information is valuable to someone. My orders were to find out more about this organism.'

Shensu shrugged. 'You're too late by several years to do the most valuable observations,' he said with a wry note in his voice.

'We saw some,' Saraidh fumbled for an exact description of the 'tunnels' they had seen at Landing, 'remnants, dead shells of these Thread. Would there be any near you that I could examine?'

Shensu shrugged again. 'Some on the plains below us.'

'How far in terms of time?' Saraidh asked.

'A day's journey.'

'Will you guide me?'

'You?' Shensu was surprised.

'Lieutenant Ni Morgana is the science officer of the *Amherst*,' Benden put in firmly. 'You will want to assist her in this investigation, Mr Fusaiyuki.'

Shensu made a small gesture of obedience with his hands.

'Jiro, Kimo,' Chio spoke up. Kimmer seemed to have subsided into sleep. 'Help me carry him to his room.'

The two men rose, their faces blank of expression and picked him up, much as they would a sack, and carried him towards a curtained arch through which they disappeared, Chio following anxiously.

'I'll check on Nev,' Benden said, rising, 'while you arrange tomorrow's expedition with Shensu, Lieutenant.'

'A good idea, Lieutenant.'

Benden motioned for the two marines to remain as he made his way out of the superb room, his eyes on the gorgeous murals and their story of Mankind's triumph over tremendous odds.

'I could wish, Ensign Nev, that you would learn to think before you speak,' Benden said sternly to the chagrined junior when he returned to the *Erica*.

'I'm real sorry, Lieutenant,' and Nev's face was twisted with anxiety, 'but we can't just leave them, can we? Not if we can actually rescue them?'

'You've made such calculations?'

'Aye, sir, I did, as soon as I got back on board,' and eagerly Nev brought his figures up on the monitor. 'Of course, I could only estimate their weight but they can't weigh *that* much and the inward journey only took a quarter of our fuel.'

'We've a planet to search, Mr,' Benden said sharply as he bent to study the figures. This was going to be a command decision on his part: to abandon the search on the basis of the opinion of a few local witnesses or to carry out his original orders scrupulously.

'We weren't expected to *find* survivors, were we?' Nev asked in a tentative voice.

210

Benden frowned at him. 'What exactly do you mean by that, Mr?'

'Well, Lieutenant, if Captain Fargoe had expected there'd be survivors, wouldn't she have ordered a troop shuttle? They'd carry a couple of hundred people.'

Benden regarded Nev with exasperation. 'You know our orders as well as I do: to discover the survivors and their present circumstances. Nothing was intimated that we wouldn't find survivors. Or that we wouldn't find them able to continue their colonial effort.'

'But this lot couldn't, could they? There aren't enough of them. I don't trust the old man but that Shensu's OK.'

'When I need your opinion, Mr, I'll ask for it,' Benden said curtly. Nev subsided into glum silence while Benden continued to peer at the numbers on the screen, half-wishing they would cabalistically rearrange themselves into a solution for his dilemma.

'Establish how much we'd need to jettison, Mr, without seriously affecting safety during slingshot. Ascertain just where we can put eleven passengers and take into your weight consideration the extra padding and harness we'd need to secure them during lift-off.'

'Aye, aye, sir.' Nev's enthusiasm and the admiring look he gave Benden were almost harder to endure than his chastened funk.

Benden strode to the airlock and out of the ship, taking the crisp air into his lungs as if that would aid his thinking. In a sense Nev was right: the captain hadn't expected that they would find survivors in need of rescue. She had assumed that either the settlers had overcome the disaster or that all had succumbed to it. However, these eleven could not, in the name of humanity, be left behind on the planet.

The *Erica*'s remaining fuel would barely accomplish that rescue. It certainly wouldn't allow the Pernese to bring anything, like metal ores, back with them to start again elsewhere. Possibly some of those gemstones Shensu had mentioned could be permitted. With no more than the usual shipwreck allowance, these people would be seriously handicapped in the high tech societies on most of the Federation

211

planets and financially unable to establish themselves in an agrarian economy. They had to have *something*.

If Kimmer could be believed, and possibly with the estranged brothers corroborating his statement, it was true that these eleven constituted all that remained of the original colonial complement, then a further search would be fruitless as well as a waste of fuel that could, really, be put to better use. Did the brothers have any reason to lie? Not, Benden thought, when they hated Kimmer so much. Ah, but they'd want to leave this place, wouldn't they? Even if it meant perjuring themselves!

Unusual noises attracted his attention and he walked to the edge of the plateau to check. Some twenty metres below him he saw four people, Jiro and the three youngest, mounted on Earth-type horses, herding a variety of four-legged domestic beasts through a huge aperture in the cliff. He heard an odd call and saw a brown, winged shape hurtling after them. As he watched, a heavy metal door swung on well-oiled hinges to close off the opening. The evening breeze, for the light was beginning to fail now on their first day of their five on this planet, wafted some curious smells up to him. He sneezed as he made his way across the plateau to the door to this unusual residence. They'd have to turn those animals loose. Bloody sure, there was no room on board the *Erica* for that mob.

When Benden re-entered the big room, he spotted Ni Morgana and Shensu poring over maps on a smaller table to the left of the main entrance. There were cases of tapes and other paraphernalia along that section of the smooth carved wall.

'Lieutenant, we've got both the original survey maps here and those that the colonists filled in with detailed explorations,' Saraidh called to him. 'A crying shame this endeavour was so brutally short-lived. They'd a lovely situation here. See,' and her scripto touched first one, then another of the shaded areas on the map of the southern continent, 'fertile farms producing everything they needed before disaster struck, a viable fishing industry, mines with on-site smelting and manufacture. And then—' She gave an eloquent shrug.

212

'Admiral Benden rose to the challenge magnificently,' Shensu said, the glow in his eyes altering his whole appearance, making him a far more likeable person. 'He called for centralization of all materials and skills. My father commanded the aerial defence. He had flame-throwers mounted on sleds, two forward and one aft, and developed flight patterns that would cover the largest area and destroy quantities of airborne Thread. Ground crews were organized with portable flamers to incinerate what did get through to the ground, before it could burrow and reproduce itself. It was the most valiant effort!'

There was an excitement and a ring in Shensu's voice that made Benden's pulse quicken – he could see that Saraidh was also affected. Shensu's whole attitude was suffused with reverence and awe.

'We were just young boys but our father came as often as he could and told us what was happening. He was always in touch with our mother. He even spoke to her just before . . . before that final mission.' All the animation left Shensu and his expression assumed its habitual taciturnity. 'He was brutally murdered just when he might have made the discovery which would have ended Threadfall and preserved the whole colony.'

'By this Avril person?' Saraidh asked gently.

Shensu nodded once, his features set. 'Then *he* came!'

'And now we have come,' Saraidh said, pausing a moment before continuing on a brisker note, 'and we must somehow gather as much evidence after the fact as possible. There have been many theories about Oort clouds and what they contain. This is the first opportunity to examine such a space-evolved creature, and the disaster it causes on an uninhabited planet. You said the organism burrowed into the ground and reproduced itself? I'd like to see the later stage of the organism's life cycle. Can you show me where?' she asked, looking exceedingly attractive, Benden thought, in her eagerness.

Shensu looked disgusted. 'You wouldn't want to see any stage of its life cycle. My mother said that there was only the hunger of it. Which no-one should encounter.'

213

'Any sort of residue would aid the research, Shensu,' she said, reaching out to touch his arm. 'We need your help, Shensu.'

'We needed yours a long time ago,' he said in a voice so bitter that Saraidh withdrew her hand, flushing.

'This expedition was mounted as soon as your message came up on the records, Shensu. The delay is not ours,' Benden replied crisply. 'But we are here now and we'd like your co-operation.'

Shensu gave a cynical snort. 'Does my co-operation guarantee escaping from this place?'

Benden looked him squarely in the eye. 'I could not, in conscience, leave you here,' he said, having in that moment made his decision, 'especially in view of the fact that I also cannot assure you that you would be relieved by another vessel in the near future. I shall however need to have the exact body weights of everyone and frankly we'll have to strip the *Erica* to accommodate you.'

Shensu kept eye contact, his own reaction to Benden's decision unreadable. Benden was aware of Ni Morgana's discreet approval. 'Your ship is low on fuel?'

'If we are to successfully lift additional passengers, yes.'

'If you did not have to strip the *Erica* to compensate for our weight?' Shensu seemed amused as he watched Benden's reaction. 'If you had, say, a full tank, could you allow us to bring enough valuables to assist us to resettle somewhere? Rescue to a pauper's existence would be no rescue at all.'

Benden nodded in acknowledgement of that fact even as he spoke. 'Kimmer said there was no more fuel. He was emphatic about it.'

Shensu leaned his body across the table and spoke in a scarcely audible whisper, his black eyes glittering with what Benden read as quiet satisfaction. 'Kimmer doesn't know everything, Lieutenant.' And now Shensu chuckled. 'He thinks he does.'

'What do you know that Kimmer doesn't?' Benden asked, lowering his own voice.

'Spaceship fuel has not changed in the past six decades, has it?' Shensu asked in his whisper.

'Not for ships of the *Amherst*'s and the *Yoko*'s class,' Saraidh replied, quietly eager.

'Since you're so interested,' Shensu said in a conversational voice level as he rose from the table, 'I'd be happy to show you the rest of the Hold. We have a place for everything. I think my esteemed father had visions of founding a dynasty. My mother said that had Thread not come, there were others of our ethnic type who would have joined them here in Honshu.' Shensu led them towards a hanging which he pushed aside, gesturing them to proceed through the archway. 'They accomplished much before Thread fell.'

He let the hanging fall and joined Saraidh and Benden on the small square landing where stone-cut steps spiralled in both directions. Shensu gestured that they were to ascend.

Saraidh started up. 'Wow! This is some staircase,' she said, as she made the first turn.

'I must warn you that the living room has peculiarities – one of which is an echo effect,' Shensu said. 'Conversations can be overheard in the passages outside. I don't believe *he* has yet recovered from his – disability – but Chio, or one of his daughters, is always eavesdropping for him. So, I take no chances. No, continue up. I know the steps become uneven. Balance yourself against the wall.'

The steps were uneven, unfinished and several had no more than toe space.

'This was deliberate?' asked Saraidh, beginning to show the effort of the climbing. 'Oh, for a grav shaft!'

Benden was in agreement as he felt the muscles in his calves and thighs tightening. And he had thought that he'd spent adequate time in PT to keep himself fit for any exertion.

'Now where?' Saraidh asked as she came to a very narrow landing. The thin slit of a tiny aperture did nothing to illuminate the blank walls all around them.

Shensu apologized as he squeezed past the two officers, the half smile still on his face and, to their chagrin, he was showing no signs of effort. He put his hand, palm down, on a rough, apparently natural, declivity in the wall and suddenly a whole section of the wall pivoted inwards. Light came on to illuminate a low deep cave. Benden whistled in surprise

215

because the space was full of sacks, each tagged with some sort of coded label. Sacks of fuel, row upon row of them.

'There's more here than we need,' Saraidh said, having made some rough calculations. 'More than enough. But,' and now she turned to Shensu, her expression stern, 'I could understand your keeping this from Kimmer but surely this was fuel those shuttles could have used? Or did they?' For she had also noticed that some of the closer ranks were thinner where sacks had obviously been removed.

Shensu held up his hand. 'My father was an honourable man. And when the need arose, he took what was needed from this cavern and gave it, willingly, to Admiral Benden, doing all within his power to help overcome the menace that dropped from the skies. If he had not been murdered—' Shensu broke off the sentence, his jaw muscles tensing, his expression bleak. 'I do not know where the three shuttles went, but they could only have lifted from Landing on the fuel my father gave Admiral Benden. Now I give the rest of the fuel to a man also named Benden.' Shensu looked pointedly at the lieutenant.

'Paul Benden was my uncle,' he admitted, finding himself chagrined at this unexpected inheritance. 'The *Erica* is also economical with fuel. With a full tank, we can lift you and even make some allowance for personal effects. But why is the fuel *here*?'

'My father did not steal it,' Shensu said, indignantly.

'And I didn't imply that he had, Shensu,' Benden replied soothingly.

'My father accumulated this fuel during the transfer from the colony ships to the surface of the planet. He was the most accomplished shuttle pilot of them all. And he was the most economical. He only took what his careful flying saved on each flight and no-one took harm from his economy. He told me how much was wasted by the other pilots, carelessly wasted. He was a charterer and had the right to take what was available. He merely ensured that fuel was available.'

'But—' Benden began, wishing to reassure Shensu.

'He saved it to fly. He had to fly,' and Shensu's eyes became slightly unfocused as his impassioned explanation

216

continued. 'It was his life. With space denied him, he designed a little atmosphere plane. I can show it to you. He flew it here, in Honshu, where no-one but us could see him. But he took each of us up in that plane.' Shensu's face softened with those memories. 'That was the prize we all worked for. And I could understand his fascination with flight.' Shensu took in a deep breath and regarded the two Fleet officers in his usual inscrutable fashion.

'I'm not sure I could live happily stuck landside for ever,' Benden said earnestly. 'And we're grateful to be taken into your confidence, Shensu.'

'My father would be pleased that his saving ways permit a Benden to save his kinsmen,' Shensu said in a wry tone and with a sly glance at the lieutenant. 'But we will wait until late tonight, when there are few to notice our activity. Those marines of yours look strong. But do not bring that ensign. He talks too much. I do not want Kimmer to know of our transaction. It is enough that he will be rescued from Pern.'

'Have you checked these sacks recently, Shensu?' Saraidh asked and, when he shook his head, she had to crouch to enter the low cave and inspect the nearest. 'Your father did well, Shensu,' she said over her shoulder, peering at the sack she had tilted upside down. 'I was afraid there might be some contamination from the plastic after fifty-odd years but the fuel all seems to be clear, no sediment, well saved.'

'What gemstones would be worth bringing with us?' Shensu asked casually.

'Industrial technology requires quantities of sapphire, pure quartz, diamonds,' Saraidh told him as she left the cave, arching her back to relieve the strain of crouching. 'But the major use of natural gemstones is once again decorative – for pets, high-status women, courtly men.'

'Black diamonds?' Shensu asked, his lips parting in anticipation.

'Black diamonds!' Saraidh was astonished.

'Come, I will show you,' Shensu said, allowing his lips to part in a pleased smile. 'First we will close the cave and then descend to our workshops. Then I will show you the rest of the Hold as I said I would do,' and he grinned back at them.

Benden was not sure whether going down was worse than climbing. He felt not only dizzy from the short arc of the stairs but had the sensation that he would fall forward down this interminable spiral. He considered himself competent in free fall or in space walking but this was a subtly different activity. He was only marginally relieved that Shensu was in front of him but, if Saraidh fell into him, was Shensu sturdy enough to keep all three from pitching down?

They passed several landings which Shensu ignored, and seemed to descend a very long way before they emerged into another large room which must be under the main living chamber. It was not as high-ceilinged or as well finished but it was clearly furnished for a variety of activities. He identified a large kiln, a forge hearth and three looms. Work tables were placed near racks of carefully stored tools. Hand tools, not a power tool among them.

Shensu led them to a plastic cabinet a metre high and wide with many small drawers. He pulled out two, evidently at random, and scattered their contents on the nearby table, the facets of the cut stones sparkling in the overhead light. Saraidh exclaimed in surprise, scooping up a handful of carelessly thrown stones of all sizes. Benden picked a large one out of her hand, holding it up to the light. He'd never seen anything like it, dark but glittering with light.

'Black diamond. There's a whole beach full of them below a dead volcano,' Shensu said, leaning back against the table, arms folded across his chest. His smile was amused. 'We have drawers of them, and emeralds, sapphires, rubies. We're all good lapidaries though Faith is cleverest in cutting. We don't bother much with what Kimmer terms semi-precious though he has some fine turquoise which he says is extremely valuable.'

'Probably,' Saraidh murmured, still absorbed in running a shower of the diamonds through her hands. She was absorbed but not, Benden noted, covetous.

'The blacks are why I know you won't find any survivors in the north,' Shensu went on, his eyes on Benden who was less involved in the gemstones.

'Oh, why?'

218

'Before the sled power-packs died, Kimmer made two trips to Bitkim Island where he and Avril Bitra had mined both the black diamonds and emeralds. He brought me and Jiro with him both times to help gather the rough diamonds. I saw him leave our camp late one night and I followed him. He went into a big water cavern before he disappeared from sight. He had the light. I didn't dare go further. But in the cavern lagoon three ships were moored, masts lashed to the decks. They were plastic hulled and their decks were badly scored by Thread. It couldn't pierce plastic but it could melt grooves on it. I went down into one of the ships and everything was neatly stowed aboard, even in the galley where there were supplies in tight containers. Everything left in readiness for the ships to be sailed out of the cavern again.' Shensu paused dramatically. Shensu had a feeling for the dramatic, Benden realized. But that was not a fault. 'Three years later, we came back for a last load. And no-one had been near the ships. There was a thick coat of dust on everything. Nothing had been touched. Except there was a lot more algae on the hulls and wind-blown debris on the decks. Three years! I say there was no-one left to sail them.'

Saraidh had let the diamonds drip through her fingers to the table and now she sighed. 'You said there was a volcanic island? Was it active when you were there? That could account for that heat source we noticed,' she added to Benden.

'Kimmer would stretch the truth every which way,' Shensu said, 'to make himself look good. But he desperately wanted to have a larger gene pool – for his own pleasure if not ours.' The last was said with an understandable malice. 'If only a few more had survivied, there'd be that much more future for all of us.'

That gave both Ross Benden and Saraidh Ni Morgana a lot to mull over as Shensu showed them round the additional facilities: the animal barns, the well-supplied storage areas. He paused at a locked door to a lower level.

'Kimmer keeps the key to the hangar so I can't show you my father's plane,' Shensu said. Then he gestured for them to ascend the stairs to the upper floors. Benden was relieved that these steps were wide and straight.

When they returned to the main level of Honshu Hold, they found the women busily preparing a feast: certainly a feast for those who had been five years on a mission. Not that the *Amherst* did not cater well but nothing to compare with spit-roasted lamb and the variety of Pernese hybrid vegetables and tubers. The two marines who stayed aboard, despite the slightly sarcastic assurance from Kimmer that no enemies could be lurking on Honshu Cliff, were brought heaped platters and non-fermented beverages by Faith and Charity. Within the Hold, the evening was merry and Kimmer, with a glass or two of wine, became expansive as a host. For he had recovered his composure after a long rest and, tactfully, no mention was made of his collapse.

As pre-arranged, Benden, Sergeant Greene, and Vartry met Shensu, his two brothers and the boys, Alun and Pat. Even with nine to tote sacks, it took four trips to top up the *Erica*'s tanks. The boys were short enough to walk upright in the low cave and they brought the sacks out to those who waited to haul them down. The marines were not above showing off their fitness and, using slings, carried eight sacks at a time. Ross Benden decided that four was quite enough and he had no reason to challenge the marines. The Fusaiyuki brothers carried six effortlessly. When the tanks were full, there were still sacks in the cavern.

The next morning, hearing Nev's cheerful morning ablutions, Ross Benden stirred and abruptly stopped. He was uncomfortably stiff and sore from the night's exertions.

'Something wrong, sir?'

'Not a thing,' Benden said. 'Just finish up and let me have a chance, will you?'

Nev took that in good part and shortly was out of the tiny cabin. Moving with extreme caution, and hissing at the pain of abused muscles, Ross Benden managed to get to his feet. Bent-kneed, he hobbled to the hand-basin and opened the small cabinet above, that contained the medical kit. A thorough search revealed nothing for muscular aches. He fumbled for a pain tablet, knocked it to the back of his mouth, and discovered that his neck was sore too. He took a drink of water. He must remember to drain the cistern and fill it with the excellent water of Pern.

A scratch at the door made Benden straighten up, despite the anguish to the long tendons in his legs, but he was damned if he'd show weakness.

'It's I,' and Ni Morgana entered, taking in at a glance his semi-crippled state. 'I thought this likely. Just one trip up and down those racks of a stair and my legs are sore. Faith gave me this salve – wanted me to test it to see if it was something of medical value. It's indigenous. No, lie back down, Ross, I'll slather it on. Supposed to have numbing properties. Hmm, it does,' and she eyed her fingers and the generous dollop she had scooped out of the jar.

Ross was crippled enough to be willing to try anything, noxious or bizarre. He could hardly appear before Kimmer in his present shape.

'Oh, it is numbing. Whee, ooh, ahh, more on the right calf, please,' Benden said, ridiculously relieved by the numbing effect of the salve. The pain seemed to drain out of calves and thighs, leaving them oddly cool but not cold, and certainly free of that damnable soreness.

'I've got plenty for later and Faith says they have buckets of the stuff. Make it fresh every year. Doesn't smell half bad either. Pungent and – piney.'

When she finished doctoring Benden, she washed her hands thoroughly. 'I'd say don't shower today or you'll lose the relief.' Then she turned back to Ross Benden, with a puzzled expression. 'Ross,' she began, settling against the little hand-basin and crossing her arms, 'how much would you say Kimmer weighed?'

'Hmm,' and Benden thought of the man's build and height, 'about seventy-two to seventy-four kilos. Why?'

'I weighed him in at ninety-five kilos. Of course, he was clothed, and the tunic and trousers are rather full and made of sturdy fabric, but I wouldn't have thought he carried that much flesh.'

'Nor would I.'

221

'I didn't judge the women correctly either. They all weighed in a little under and a little over seventy kilos and none of them is either tall or heavy-set.'

Nev mumbled figures under his breath. 'All of 'em, even the kids?'

'No, the three brothers are seventy-three, seventy-two, and seventy-five kilos which is about what I thought they'd be. The girl and the boys are also two or three kilos more than I'd have thought them.'

'With a full tank, we can afford a few extra kilos,' Benden said.

'I was also asked how much they could bring with them,' Saraidh went on, 'and I said we had to calibrate body weights and other factors before we could give them an exact allowance. I trust that wasn't out of line.'

'I'll get Nev to calculate in those weights and let me know how much fuel we'll have in reserve then,' Benden said. 'And what we use as padding and safety harnesses so no-one bounces all over the gig during take-off.'

Folding out the cabin's keyboard, Benden ran some rough figures against the lifting power of the now full tank. 'D'you have a total on their weights?' Ni Morgana gave him the figure. He added them in plus kilos for padding and harnesses and comtemplated the result. 'I'd hate to be considered mean but twenty-three point five kilos each is about all we can allow.'

'That's as much as we're allowed for personal effects on the *Amherst*,' Ni Morgana said. 'Is there room for twenty-three point five kilos in medicinals? I gather this stuff is effective.'

'It certainly is,' Benden said, flexing his knees and feeling no discomfort.

'I'll just get some of this on the marines as well, then,' Ni Morgana said.

'Ha!' was Benden's scoffing reply.

'I don't know about that,' Ni Morgana said with a sly grin. 'But then, you didn't catch sight of Sergeant Greene making for the galley. I think,' and she paused reflectively, 'that I'm doing some empirical tests of this junk and they just got lucky to be chosen as test subjects. Yes, that should save face

222

admirably. We can't give Kimmer any reason to be suspicious, now, can we?' Then she left, chuckling over her subterfuge.

At 0835, when Benden left the galley and proceeded to the Hold, he found Kimmer and the women in the main room, none of them looking too happy.

'We've done the calculations, Kimmer, and we can allow each of you, the children included, twenty-three point five kilos of personal effects. That's what Fleet personnel are generally allowed to bring on voyages and I can't see Captain Fargoe objecting to it.'

'Twenty-three point five kilos is quite generous, Lieutenant,' Kimmer surprised Benden by saying. He turned to them chidingly. 'That's more than we had coming out on the *Yoko*.'

'And,' Benden said, turning to Faith, 'that wouldn't include medicinal products and respective seeds to a similar limit. Lieutenant Ni Morgana is of the opinion that they could well be valuable commodities.'

'For which we'd be reimbursed?' asked Kimmer sharply.

'Of course,' Benden said, keeping his voice even. 'We have to allow for the weight of padding and harnesses to keep you secure during our drop into the primary's gravity well.'

Charity and Hope emitted nervous squeaks.

'Nothing to worry yourselves over, ladies,' Benden said with a reassuring smile. 'We use gravity wells all the time as a quick way to break out of a system.'

'Be damned grateful we're getting off this frigging forsaken mudball,' Kimmer said, angrily rising to his feet. 'Go on, now, sort out what you've got to bring but keep it to the weight limit. Hear me?'

The women removed themselves, with Faith casting one last despairing glance over her shoulder at her father. Benden wondered why he had thought any of them were graceful. They waddled in a most ungainly fashion.

'You've been extremely generous, Lieutenant,' Kimmer said affably, as he settled himself again in the high-backed carved chair that he usually occupied at the table. 'I thought we'd be lucky enough to get off with what we have on our backs.'

'Are you absolutely positive that there are no other

survivors on Pern?' Benden said, favouring a direct attack. 'Others could have carved Holds out of cliffs and remained secure from that airborne menace of yours.'

'Yes, they could have but, for one thing, there aren't any cave systems here on the southern continent. And I'll tell you why I think the rest perished after I lost the last radio contact with those at Drake's Lake and Dorado. In those days I was more confident of rescue and I'd enough power left in my sled to make one more trip back to Bitkim Island where I'd mined some good emeralds.' He paused, leaning forward, elbows on the table and shaking one finger at Benden. 'And black diamonds.'

'*Black* diamonds?' And Benden thought he sounded genuinely amazed.

'Black diamonds, a whole beach full of them. That's what I intend to bring back.'

'Twenty-three point five kilos of them?'

'And a few pieces of turquoise that I also found.'

'Really?'

'When I'd enough of a load of stones, I went into a natural cavern on Bitkim's south-east side. Big enough to anchor ships in if you stepped the mast. And it was there.'

'Pardon?'

'Jim Tillek's ship was there, mast and all, holes and grooves where Thread had scored it time and again.'

'Jim Tillek?'

'The admiral's right hand. And a man who loved that ship. Loved it like other men love women – or Fussy Fusi loved flying,' Kimmer allowed his malice to show briefly, 'but I'm telling you, Jim Tillek wouldn't have left that ship, not to gather dust and algae on her hull if he was alive somewhere on Pern. And that ship had been anchored there three or four years. That's one very good reason why I know no-one was left alive.

'Did you find any sign of human occupation,' Kimmer went on, his voice less intense, his eyes glittering almost mockingly, 'when you spiralled down across the northern hemisphere?'

'No, neither on infra or power-use detection,' Benden had to admit.

Kimmer spread both arms wide then. 'You know there's no-one there, then. No need to waste your reserves of fuel to find 'em. We're the last alive on Pern and, I'll tell you this, it's no planet for mankind.'

'I'm sure the Colonial Authority will want a full report from you when we return to Base, Kimmer. I shall certainly log in my findings.'

'Then do mankind a favour, Lieutenant, and tag this disaster of a world as uninhabitable!'

'That's not for me to say.'

Kimmer snorted and sat back in his chair.

'Now, if you'll excuse me, I must join Lieutenant Ni Morgana on her scientific survey. There are sufficient lift belts, if you'd like to come along.'

'No, thank you, Lieutenant,' and Kimmer flicked his hand in dismissal of such activity. 'I've seen about as much of this planet as I wish.'

Benden was just strapping on his lift belt when Kimmer erupted from the Hold, the whites of his eyes showing in his agitation.

'Lieutenant!' he cried, running towards the small party.

Benden held up a warning hand as one of the marines beside him moved to intercept the man.

'Lieutenant, what power do you use for the belts? What power?' Kimmer cried excitedly as he approached.

'Pack power, of course,' Benden replied.

'Regulation packs?' And, without apology, Kimmer grabbed the lieutenant by the shoulder and swung him round, just as Vartry took hold of the old man's arm.

'As you were!' Ross Benden barked at the marine but with a nod to reassure him, because he understood what Kimmer, in his excitement, did not explain. 'Yes, standard power-packs and we have enough to reactivate that sled of yours, if it's in any reasonable working order.'

'It is, Lieutenant, it is!' Kimmer reassured him, his agitation replaced by immense satisfaction. 'So you'll be able to eyeball the remains of the colony and report honestly to your captain that you followed your orders, Mr Benden,' and

Kimmer stressed the name in a tone just short of malice, 'as assiduously as your noble relative would have done.' Ross grimaced, but his relation to the admiral would have become public sooner or later. 'I thought you looked familiar,' Kimmer added, smugly.

Benden took Ni Morgana aside for a quick conference and she concurred that it was Benden's first obligation to search as far as he was able for survivors. She was quite willing to conduct her own scientific research with Shensu as her guide and two marines as assistants. So she wished the lieutenant good luck and lifted gracefully off the plateau, floating down in the direction of the nearest evidence of Thread, some ten klicks down the valley on the other side of the river.

That matter settled, Kimmer began to pluck at Benden's sleeve in his urgency and hurried him, Nev following, back into the Hold. Maps were still spread out on the table from the previous evening.

'I searched east as far as Landing and Cardiff,' Kimmer said, prodding one map with an arthritic index finger. He dragged it back and down along to the Jordan River. 'Those Stakes were all empty and Thread-ridden though Calusa, Ted Tubberman's old place, wasn't.' Kimmer frowned a moment, then shrugged off that enigma, moving his finger up to the coastline and west. 'Paradise River must have been used as some kind of staging area because there were netted containers in the overgrowth along the shore but the buildings were all boarded up. Malay, too, and Boca,' he stabbed again at those points on the map. 'I went north from Boca to Bitkim but I confess that I didn't stop at Thessaly or Roma where they had well-built stone houses and barns. And I didn't get any further west. The gauge on the power-pack was jiggling too much for me to risk getting stranded.'

'So there could be survivors to the west . . .' Benden pored over the map, feeling a surge of excitement and hope. Then he wondered why Kimmer was willing to take such a risk – that enough survivors would be found for the colony to be left to work out its parochial problems. Maybe the prospect of leaving so much behind, including being the default owner of a planet, was giving Kimmer second thoughts. If fifty years of his life's endeavours was going to be crammed into a 23.5-kilo sack, living out the remainder of his life in the comforts he had achieved might indeed hold more charm for the old man than an uncertain, and possibly, pauper's existence in a linear warren.

'There could indeed be Stakeholders there, but why haven't they attempted any contact?' Kimmer asked defiantly and his eyes quickly concealed a flicker of something else. 'I got the last communication from the west but that could have been for any number of reasons. Now, if you've got a portable unit that we could bring with us, maybe closer to one of the western Stakes, we might rouse someone.'

'Let's see this sled of yours.' Benden didn't mention that they had opened the broadest range of communications on their inbound spiral with not so much as a flicker on any frequency. But Kimmer was right that lack of communication could have been caused by any number of reasons.

Kimmer led them to the locked door which he opened and proceeded down to the next level, a hangar in fact, with wide double doors at one end which opened out on the wide terrace below the Hold entrance plateau. While the sled occupied the centre of the considerable floor space, Kenjo's little atmosphere underwing craft was not quite hidden in the back. Then Benden's attention was all for the sled which was cocooned in the usual durable thin plastic film. This Kimmer energetically punctured.

All four men helped peel the sled free as Kimmer enumerated his exact shut-down precautions. Although the plascanopy was somewhat darkened with age and the tracks of Thread hits, when Benden touched the release button, the door slid back as easily as if it had been opened the day before.

This was a much older model than those now in use, of course, so Benden did a thorough inspection; but the fabric of the sturdy vessel was undamaged. The control panel was one he recognized from text-tapes. When he depressed the power toggle, the gauge above it fluttered and then dropped back to zero. He walked aft to the power locker, flipped up the latches on the power trunk, and lifted the big unit out to examine the leads. Lift belts used much smaller packs, but Benden could see no difficulty in making a multiple connection of smaller units to supply power. Moving forward again, Kimmer stepping out of his way but exuding a palpable excitement, Benden tested the steering yoke which moved easily in his grip.

'We'll just make a link-up and see how she answers to power. Ensign Nev, take Kimo and Jiro and break out twelve belt packs, and the portable comunit. We're going to take a little ride.'

An hour later, once more operational, the old sled drifted under its own power to the narrow lower terrace.

When Benden returned to the *Erica* for rations and a bed-roll, an earnest and anxious Nev accosted him, wanting to join the expedition.

'You don't know what that old man might try, Lieutenant. And I don't trust him.'

'Listen up,' Benden said in a low and forceful tone that stopped Nev's babbling. 'I'm not half as worried about my safety as I am about the *Erica*'s. Kimmer goes with me. I don't trust him either. I'll take Jiro along as well. And Sergeant Greene. Neither of them could get through Greene to me. You'll only have Kimo to worry about and he strikes me as too placid to do anything on his own. Shensu is a proven ally. Present my compliments to Lieutenant Ni Morgana when she returns and relay this order. Either you or the lieutenant are to be on the *Erica* at all times. The marines are to stand proper watches until I return. Have I made that clear?'

'Aye, aye, sir, Lieutenant Benden. Loud and clear, sir.' Nev's teeth were almost chattering with his assurances and his eyes were wide as he dutifully assimilated his orders.

'I'll report in at intervals, so break out hand-units for yourself and Vartry.'

'Aye, aye, sir.'

'We'll be back in two days.' He ordered Greene to collect supplies and carry them to the sled.

'If you will pardon me, Lieutenant,' Kimmer said unctuously as he and Jiro entered the craft, 'I think we can easily reach Karachi Camp today, stopping at Suweto and Yukon on the way. Karachi is a real possibility because, now that Thread is gone, they'd want to activate the mines.'

Surprising himself, Benden gestured with an open hand to the pilot's seat. 'You have the con, Mr Kimmer.' It was as good a way as any to see just how competent the old man had been: if he had actually done what he'd said he'd done. 'After all, you're more familiar with this model sled than I am and you know where we're going.' It would also be easier to keep the old man occupied.

So Benden seated himself behind Kimmer while the sergeant, giving the officer only a mildly reproachful look, took the seat next to Jiro on the starboard side.

The old sled purred along as if delighted by its release from long imprisonment. It answered the yoke with the smoothness of a well-maintained vehicle as Kimmer swung it to port. Kimmer wasn't all bad, Benden thought to himself, and wondered again why the old man had insisted on this search. Was it really to prove to Benden that his folk were the only ones left? Or had Kimmer some ulterior motive? And would Kimmer be surprised if they did find anyone? After overflying the snowy waste of the northern continent and the devastation of the southern lands, Benden could only be surprised that anyone had survived. It was certainly most unlikely that his uncle, who'd be well into his twelfth decade, would still be alive.

They came down from the foothills across the river, obliquely to port of Ni Morgana and her group, and then across a lifeless plain of circles in the dust. There were spots here and there of struggling plant-life but Benden wondered if the wind would scatter the top soil before vegetation could re-establish itself and prevent further erosion. And that was the pattern for the next few hours – broad uneven-edged ribbons, about fifty klicks across of ravaged land – then broader belts of grassland or forest, even thick vegetation neither shrub nor jungle, with the glint of hidden water in rivers and ponds.

The old sled purred along at about 220 klicks per hour. Benden broke out rations and passed them around. Kimmer altered the course and, over the sloping nose of the sled, a large and brilliantly blue lake could be seen. As they neared it and Kimmer obligingly skimmed low, vegetation-crowned mounds indicated the ruins of a considerable settlement.

'Drake's Lake,' and Kimmer gave a sour laugh. 'Damned arrogant fool,' he muttered to himself. 'No signs of anyone, but there may be at Andiyar's mines.'

They overflew more deserted housing and startled a herd of grazing animals who plunged wildly away from the muted sound of the sled.

'Livestock seems to have survived,' Benden remarked. 'Will you turn yours loose?'

'What else?' and Kimmer barked a laugh. 'Though Chio's moaning about her pet fire-dragon having to be left behind.'

'Fire-dragon?' Benden asked in surprise.

'Well, that's what some people thought they looked like,' Kimmer explained diffidently. 'They look like reptiles, lizards to me. It's an indigenous life-form, hatches from eggs, and if you get one then, it attaches itself to you. Useless thing as far as I can see but Chio's fond of it.' He glanced over his shoulder at Benden.

'It wouldn't take up much room,' Jiro said, speaking for the first time. 'It's a bronze male.'

Benden shook his head. 'Humans, yes, creatures no,' he said firmly. The captain was still likely to question his foisting eleven human survivors on her but she'd blow her tubes if he tried to impose an alien pet.

They reached the mine site and landed near the adits. Within was cocooned equipment – ore carts, picks, shovels, all kinds of hand tools, as well as an array of tough plas props for tunnel supports.

'You really had gone back to the lowest level of useful technology, hadn't you?' Benden said, hefting on the picks. 'But if you had stone-cutters, didn't you—'

'When that damned Thread started falling, your uncle called in all power-packs for use in the sleds. That was Benden's priority and we couldn't fight it.'

The living quarters, unlike those at the lake, had been cocooned. Peering in through the thinner patches over windows, Benden could see that furnishings had been left in place.

'See what I mean, Lieutenant. This place is all ready to be started up again. It's nearly two years since Thread stopped falling. If they could, they'd be back here.'

They spent the night there at Karachi, setting up a rough camp. While Kimmer started a fire, 'to keep the tunnel snakes away' he told Benden, the lieutenant made contact with Honshu and spoke to Nev who said the lieutenant was writing up her notes and that nothing of any significance had happened.

Just as Benden was signing off, Jiro came to the sled for a coil of rope and walked off into the forest. He returned not too much later with a fat squat avian which he had roped off a branch and strangled. He identified it as a wherry, as he neatly skinned and spitted it over the fire. During its roasting, the aroma of the meat was tantalizing, arousing a good appetite. It proved to be very tasty.

'Forest wherries are better than coastal ones,' Kimmer said, slicing himself another portion. 'Those have an oily, fishy taste.'

Greene nodded appreciatively as he licked his fingers clean of the juices. Then he excused himself and disappeared into the woods. Just about the time Benden was becoming apprehensive about his long absence, he reappeared.

'Nothing moving anywhere, except things that slither,' he reported to the lieutenant in a low voice. 'I don't think we need to set a watch, Lieutenant, but I always sleep light.'

As Benden saw Kimmer already asleep and Jiro settling down on their side of the fire, he decided a watch would be superfluous tonight. The enemies of this deserted world had retreated into space.

'I sleep light, too, Greene.' And he did, rousing often during the night at slight unaccustomed sounds, Kimmer's intermittent snores or when Jiro added more wood to the fire.

In the morning, Benden contacted Honshu and this time spoke with Ni Morgana who said that her expedition had been entirely successful from the scientific point of view. She would spend the day with the women, cataloguing the medicinal plants and their properties. Benden gave her the day's flight plan and signed off.

They doubled back east and slightly north of the mining site and Drake's Lake, then followed a fairly wide river as it flowed down to the distant sea. And they came upon the stout stone houses and barns that had housed the inhabitants of Thessaly and Roma. They observed herds of beasts, cattle, and sheep in nearby fields but the houses, and barns, had been cleared of all effects. Now just dead leaves and other debris littered the spacious rooms where the shutters had fallen from rusted hinges.

'Lieutenant,' and Greene motioned for him to step a little away from the other two men, 'we haven't seen any of the sleds Kimmer said they used. Nor those three missing shuttles. So, if we find them, wouldn't we find the people?'

'We would, if we could, Sergeant,' Benden said tiredly. 'Kimmer, how long did your sled have power?'

Kimmer's eyes gleamed as he appreciated what Benden did not ask. 'Once I reached Honshu, I didn't use the sled at all, except as a power source for the comunit, for maybe five to six years. Ito got very sick and I went to Landing to see if I could get a medic out here. They'd all left and taken everything with them. I tried some other Stakes, as I told you, but they were deserted too. Ito died and I was too busy with the kids and then Chio's to go off. Then I made one trip to Bitkim and four years later, as I'd no way to recharge the pack, I made that last trip. But,' and he held up his gnarled finger, 'like I told you, just before I lost all contact, I heard part of Benden's message to conserve all power. So they couldn't have had many operational sleds. I think,' and here Kimmer paused to search his memory. His eyes met the lieutenant's. 'I think they didn't have enough power left to go after Thread any more and they were going to have to wait.' He sighed. 'That'd be forty years they'd've had to wait for the end of Thread, Lieutenant, and I don't think they made it.'

'Yes, but where were they?'

Kimmer shrugged. 'Hell, Lieutenant, if I knew that I'd've hiked across the continent to find them once Thread stopped. If I'd had one whisper, I'd've tracked it down.' He swivelled

232

about then, facing west. 'They were someplace in the west from the direction of their signals. Say,' and his face lit up suddenly, 'maybe they went to Ierne Island. That would have been easier to protect than one of these open Stakes.'

So Benden called in the new destination. 'We'll be back by tomorrow evening . . .'

'You'd better be,' Ni Morgana said dryly. 'That window won't wait for anyone.'

There was no question in Benden's mind that the lieutenant would delay taking that window either but he wasn't worried about that. He had to be sure – and it looked as if Kimmer's conscience required him also to be confident that there was no-one of Benden's group still alive.

The run to Ierne Island took most of the rest of that day and was as fruitless as the other. Kimmer suggested one further detour, to the tip of Dorado province, to Seminole and Key Largo Stakes. On the wreckage of a storm-damaged building, they found a com-mast, or sections of it, and evidence of a hurried departure of the inhabitants. In another shed, still partly roofed, the remains of two sleds were discovered, obviously broken up to provide spare parts. The canopies and hulls were well scored and blistered by Thread. Benden appreciated that Kimmer was extraordinarily lucky to have survived at all.

They made their evening camp there with Jiro providing fish which he caught from the remains of a sturdy jetty. The last ten metres, projecting out into the channel, had been snapped off by some tremendous storm, or maybe many. It took a lot of force to break off heavy duty plastic pilings like that.

When Ross Benden checked in with the *Erica*, he roused a sleepy Nev, forgetting that there was a time difference across the southern continent.

'Everything's OK,' Nev said, interrupting himself with a yawn, 'though the lieutenant is sure something's up. She says the women are acting funny.'

'They're about to leave all they've known as well as a very comfortable life,' Benden replied.

'Isn't that. Lieutenant'll tell you when you get back.' Nev

233

didn't seem much concerned but Benden trusted the lieutenant's instincts.

He was wakeful that night, trying to figure out what could have gone wrong. Kimmer was with him. Shensu was eager to leave, too. And with five to guard the *Erica*, which was Benden's main concern, what could go wrong?

He worried about that all the way back to Honshu which was a useless activity. But he'd noticed that those who anticipated problems always seemed able to solve them faster.

When they finally reached Honshu, despite the gathering dusk, Kimmer insisted on manoeuvring the sled into its garage, proving his piloting skills.

'This sled's done more than its designers ever expected, Benden,' Kimmer said sardonically as he reversed it in, 'so humour an old man in rewarding its service the only way he can.'

Benden and Greene left him and Jiro to a ritualistic deservicing. Benden ran up the stairs to the main room. Ni Morgana was there, storing small packages in a case. Benden noticed first that some of the wall hangings were missing and then that the big room appeared to be stripped. Damn it! They only had twenty-three point five kilos each.

'Glad to have you back, Ross,' Ni Morgana said, smiling a welcome. 'We're just about packed up and ready to go.' There was nothing in her manner to suggest anxiety. 'There you are, Charity. If you'll stow that in the galley locker, that's the last.' She consulted her notepad then, reading the last entry as Charity left with the container. 'From your less than jubilant manner, Lieutenant, I gather that your time was wasted.'

'You could gather that, Saraidh,' Benden said, trying not to sound truculent. 'In some places materiel was neatly stored as if the owners intended to return: in others, everything had been left open to the weather, or showed signs of hurried departure. They turned their animals loose and those have multiplied so I'd say that the meek have inherited this planet. You said you'd had more success?'

She reviewed her notepad a moment longer, then flipped it

shut and placed it in a hip pocket. A nod of her head and both officers moved towards the door. Benden was relieved to see one of the marines on duty at the ramp of the *Erica*, having a word with Charity before she entered.

'When I've written up my investigations,' she said with considerable satisfaction, 'there're going to be some red faces. Irrefutably, the Oort cloud supports a life-form which I have observed in its normal immensely sluggish metabolic, activated, and defunct states. Fascinating actually, even if it also has managed to devastate a world and ruin it for further human habitation—' Ni Morgana walked Benden to the far side of the *Erica*, raising her arm as if to point something out to him. 'I don't know what's going on but something is, Ross. I don't believe it's just sorrow for leaving their home that's making the women nervous, jumpy, and accounts for a mass insomnia. The children seem fine and Shensu and Kimo have been most helpful.'

'I thought taking Kimmer and Jiro with me was a sensible precaution.'

'Sensible but Kimmer's quite likely to have given those women orders before he left. I think he did. I just don't know what. We haven't left the *Erica* unattended but each of us who's stood a watch on her has been plagued with headaches. I'll admit to you, Ross, that I fell asleep on watch. I can't have dozed for more than ten or twenty minutes but I was asleep. I can't get Cahill Nev or the other marines to admit that they had similar lapses but Nev had that hangdog expression I've come to know well in erring ensigns. Anyway, after my little snooze, Nev and I searched the ship from prow to the propulsion units and couldn't find anything illegally stowed. Which is what I think's been happening. Oh, we've put aboard everyone's twenty-three point five kilos which were thoroughly searched and weighed before I'd permit them to stow it. Nothing hidden in anyone's bundle.

'And the women . . .' Ni Morgana paused, deep in thought and then shook her head slowly. 'They're exhausted although they swear blind that they're fine, just that this has all happened so fast. Chio released that little dragoney pet of hers and she bursts into tears if you glance sideways at her.'

235

Then she gave a chuckle. 'Nev and I thought to cheer them up and he's a main frame of humorous anecdotes about life in high tech. He's from a colonial family so he's been marvellous at reassuring them. You should have heard the spiel he gave on how they'll be living back on a "civilized" planet and all the advantages of same. They cheer up a bit and then fall into the weeps again.'

Then she turned briskly professional. 'We've got additional safety harnesses for all, by the way, and pallets with a local vegetable sponge that is lightweight but cushioning. I figure that all the women should be strapped into the marines' bunks: the kids and the brothers can use the pallets and temporary harnesses in the wardroom and the marines will take the extra seats in the cabin with us. Tight squeeze but there're only so many places you can put bodies on this gig. Where is Kimmer?' she asked. 'I think one of us ought to keep a close eye on his movements this evening.' Then she looked out to the last of the brilliantly red and orange sunset. 'Too bad. This is such a beautiful planet.'

That night a lavish feast was spread for everyone – except the man on duty on the *Erica*. Kimmer urged the officers and the three marines to drink as much of his fine wines as possible for the tunnel snakes wouldn't appreciate them. When he found the Fleet reluctant to over-indulge, he nagged the girls and the three men to 'eat, drink, and be merry'. Taking his own advice, he passed out before the meal was finished.

'He'll have to be sober by,' and Benden consulted his digital to check, '0900 tomorrow or he'll be nauseous in take-off and I don't want to have to clean that up when we reach free-fall. Good evening and thank you, Chio, for such a magnificent meal,' he added and, after Saraidh had also complimented the women, the *Erica*'s complement left.

Kimmer looked none the worse for the drink the next morning as he and the others reported on time to board the *Erica*. Nev strapped the Pernese in but Benden made a final check himself. The women were all red-eyed and Chio patently so nervous that he wondered if he should get Ni Morgana to give her a mild sedative.

236

At the exact second calculated by Lieutenant Zane, the *Erica* lifted from the plateau, blasting her way skyward, tail rockets blazing.

A fisherman, standing the dogwatch on his trawler off the coast of Fort Hold, saw the fiery trail, vivid against the grey eastern sky, and wondered at it. He following the blazing lance of light until it was no longer visible. He wondered what it was but his more immediate concern was keeping warm and wondering if the cook had made klah by now and could he get a cup.

'The roll rate's too low!' Benden cried over the roar of the engines, exerting all his strength to keep the right attitude. 'She's a slug,' and suddenly Benden realized that the *Erica*'s reluctance could be caused by only one thing. 'We've got too much weight on board. She's too bloody heavy through the yoke,' he said through gritted teeth. He forced his head to look to his right at Nev, strapped in the co-pilot's seat. Ni Morgana was in the next row with Greene beside her while the other marines stoically endured acceleration g-forces in makeshift couches. 'I've got to increase thrust. And that's going to take one helluva lot of fuel.'

Benden made the adjustments, swearing bitterly to himself over the expenditure of so much fuel. His calculations could NOT be wrong. They were also too far gone in their path to abort and, if they did, there was no way to contact the *Amherst* and arrange a new rendezvous. How in hell could she be so heavy?

'Nev, give me some figures on what this is costing us in fuel and the estimated weight we're lugging up.'

'Aye, aye, sir,' Nev said, slowly moving his hand in the g-force to activate the armrest pad.

Benden forced his head to the side so he could see the bright green numbers leap to the small screen.

'Twenty-one minutes five seconds of blast, sir, was what we should have needed,' Nev replied, his voice genuinely strained. 'We're bloody twenty-nine point twenty into flight and still not free! We're – uh – four nine five point five six kilograms overweight! Free fall in ten seconds!'

Ten seconds seemed half a year until they were suddenly weightless. Benden swore as he read the ominous position of the fuel gauge. Still cursing, he adjusted her yaw with a burst of the port jets, swinging her nose towards the sun. He already knew that they hadn't enough fuel to make their scheduled rendezvous with the *Amherst*. And the cruiser would currently be in a communication shadow as it made its parabolic turn about Rukbat.

He called up Rukbat's system on the console monitor. There was no way they could use the second planet as a sling-shot. But, and he pulled at his lower lip, there was a chance they could make it to the first little burnt-out cinder of a planet. They'd come awful close to Rukbat and even closer to the surface of Number One in order to use its gravity well. That would save fuel. But they'd need a different rendezvous point. That is, IF they could get to the same point at the same time, at the same speed and heading in the same direction as the cruiser at some point earlier in her outbound hyperbolic orbit of Rukbat.

'Nev, figure me a slingshot course around the first planet.' There was only the one option left to Benden.

'Aye, aye, sir,' and the ensign's voice was full of relief.

Then in a taut hard voice, he shot out a second order. 'Greene, bring me Kimmer. Tell the others to stay put.'

He flipped open the harness release and let himself drift up out of the pilot's seat, trying to figure out just how Kimmer had managed to sneak 495.56 Kilograms of whatever it was on board his ship. And when? Especially as the man had been under his watchful eye for over three days.

'Lieutenant,' and Nev's voice was apologetic, 'we can't make a slingshot around the first planet: not with the weight on board.'

'Oh, we'll be lighter very soon, Nev,' Benden replied with a malicious grin. 'Four hundred and ninety-five point fifty-six kilograms lighter. Figure a course with that weight loss.'

'What I can't understand,' Ni Morgana said in a flat voice, 'is what they could have smuggled aboard. Or how?'

'What about your headaches, Saraidh?' Benden asked,

seething with anger at Kimmer's duplicity. 'And those cat-naps no-one else's had the guts to report to me.'

'What could they possibly have done in ten or twenty minutes, Ross?' Ni Morgana demanded flatly, her nostrils flaring at his implication of dereliction of duty. 'Nev and I searched for any possibly smuggled goods or tampering.'

Benden said nothing, pointedly, and then scrubbed at his face in frustration. 'Oh, it's no blame to you, Saraidh. Kimmer just outsmarted me, that's all. I thought removing him from Honshu would solve the problem.' He raised his voice. 'Vartry, you, Scag and Helmut will conduct a search of the most unlikely places on this ship; the missile bins, the head, the inner hull, the airlock. Somehow they've over-loaded us and we have got to know with what and dump it!' He turned to Nev. 'Try reaching the *Amherst*. I think it's too soon to make contact but get on the blower anyhow.'

Kimmer overhanded himself into the cabin then, a smile on his face for the fierce expressions on the three marines as they passed him by.

'Kimmer, what did you get on board this ship and where is it? We've got less than an hour to make a course correction and, thanks to you, we've lost too much fuel lifting the bird off Pern.'

'I don't know what you mean, Lieutenant,' was the reply and Kimmer looked him squarely in the eye. 'I was with you for three days. How could I have put something on board this vessel?'

'Stop stalling, man, it's your life you'll lose as well.'

'I'm flattered that you've asked my opinion, Lieutenant, but I'm sure you know better than I what equipment can be jettisoned to lighten her.'

Benden stared him down, wondering at the malevolence in the gaze Kimmer returned. 'You know what weight I'm referring to and it was all put on at Honshu. If I don't know what that was, Kimmer, you'll be the first thing that lightens this gig's load.'

Suddenly they all heard hysterical weeping from the stern and Vartry propelled himself back into the cabin.

'Lieutenant, they started the minute I said we were going to

239

search because the ship was overweight. They know something!'

Benden hand-pushed himself deftly down the short companionway to the marines' quarters, the wailing rising to an eerie ululation that made the hairs on the back of his neck rise.

'Stow it!' Benden roared but Chio's volume only increased. The others were not as loud but just as distraught, plainly terrified and far too hysterical to reply to his demands for an explanation.

Ni Morgana arrived with the medical kit and injected Chio with a sedative which reduced the hysterics but had no effect when Benden questioned her, trying to keep his voice level and reasonable.

'They will not tell you what they have done,' Shensu said, careering into the marines' quarters. Absently rubbing the arm he had bruised, he looked down at Chio. 'She has always been dominated by him and so have the others. If Kimmer can be made,' and Shensu's voice was hard-edged with hatred, 'to give them the necessary orders.'

'I think Kimmer will explain, or take a long step out of a short airlock,' Benden said, pushing past Shensu. There was no time for finesse or bluff with the *Erica* currently on an abortive course for the second planet. They had to make a correction soon. And do it without the excess weight or they'd be beyond rescue. He'd have the truth if he had to space Kimmer and enough of the women to get one of them to tell him what he had to know.

'Lieutenant!' Greene's booming voice was urgent and Benden propelled himself as fast as he could back to the cabin where Greene was searching Kimmer roughly. 'Sir, he's wearing metal. I felt it when I frisked him.' And as the sergeant peeled back the shipsuit, a vest was exposed, a vest made up of panels of gold. 'Shit!'

'Hardly!' Kimmer remarked, smiling smugly.

'Strip him!' Benden ordered and not only was Kimmer wearing a gold vest but a thick belt of gold cast in lozenge shapes. His underpants had pockets filled with thin gold sheets. Greene was nothing if not thorough and even the

240

boots on Kimmer's feet produced smaller gold plates worked into the soles and ankle leather.

'Saraidh!' Benden roared. 'Search those women. Greene, you search the kids, but gently, get me? Shensu, Jiro, Kimo, in here on the double.' Benden took some comfort when the three men proved to be wearing no more than their shipsuits.

Ni Morgana's yell confirmed Benden's guess about the women. All the while Kimmer kept in place his slight, amused smile. It took both Vartry and Saraidh to bring the concealed sheets and gold plates the women had secreted to the cabin.

'I'd estimate that's about ten to fifteen kilos per woman and five per kid,' she said as they looked down at the pile of gold.

Benden shook his head. 'Forty-five kilos is a drop! No where near four hundred ninety-five point fifty-six ks.' He turned on the naked Kimmer who smiled back, all innocence. 'Kimmer, we're running out of time. Now where is the rest of it? Or had you intended becoming an integral part of Rukbat?'

'You don't panic me, Lieutenant Benden,' and Kimmer's eyes glittered with a vengeance that shocked Ross. 'This ship's in no danger. Your cruiser'll rescue you.'

Benden stared at the man in utter amazement. 'The cruiser is behind Rukbat, in com shadow. We can't arrange a different rendezvous. Unless we can lighten this ship, we can't even make a course change for the one chance we have of staying alive!' Benden hauled Kimmer by the arm to the console and showed him the diagram on the screen, and the little blip that was the *Erica*, serenely heading for her original, now non-viable destination. 'We certainly don't have enough fuel to make the arranged rendezvous.' He tapped out the sequence to show the original flight plan. Then, with his finger, Benden indicated the inexorable path the *Erica* was taking. 'Tell us what and where the excess weight is hidden, Kimmer!'

Kimmer contented himself with a wry chuckle and Benden wanted to smash it off his face. But Kimmer was enjoying this too much to give him that satisfaction.

'If that's the way you want to play it, Kimmer. Sergeant, get the stuff and bring it with you,' and Benden hustled the

241

naked barefooted colonist down the companionway to the air-lock and, palming the control for the inner hatch, shoved Kimmer inside, motioned for Greene to throw in the gold, and closed the hatch again.

'I mean it, Kimmer, either tell me what else is on board and where, or you go out the airlock.'

Kimmer turned, a contemptuous expression on his face, and he folded his arms across his chest, a gaunt old man with only defiance to clothe him.

'You've more than enough fuel, Benden. Chio checked the gauge. The *Erica*'s tanks were full. Since you had to have used at least a third of a tank to get here, I'm of the opinion that Shensu knew,' and his eyes travelled to Benden's left where Shensu was standing by the window, 'as I always suspected, where Kenjo had stored his pilferings.' Kimmer drew himself up. 'No, Lieutenant, I will call your bluff.'

'It's no bluff, Kimmer, and if you had any training as a space jockey, you'd've felt how sluggish the gig was. She's heavy, too heavy. We burned too much in the lift-off. The gold on you and the women isn't enough to cause that. Dammit, Kimmer, it's your life, too.'

'I'll have taken a Benden down with me,' the man said in a snarl of hatred and sheer malevolence, his face contorted.

'But Chio, and your daughters, your grandchildren—' Benden began.

'They were none of them worth the effort I put into them,' Kimmer replied arrogantly. 'I have to share my wealth with them but I'm certainly not sharing it with you.'

'Sharing?' Benden stared at him, not quite comprehending the man's words. 'You think I'm blackmailing you? For a share of your wealth?' The disgust in Benden's voice momentarily rattled the man. 'There are many people in MY world, Kimmer, who are not motivated by greed.' He gestured with contemptuous anger at the sheets and lozenges at Kimmer's feet. 'None of that is worth the risk you want us to take. What have you hidden on the *Erica* and where?'

Just then, Ni Morgana beckoned urgently to Benden. He gratefully moved away from the window. His hand hovered briefly over the evac button. Kimmer could stay where he was, just a thin sheet away from space, and contemplate his situation.

'When I was looking for tranks, I came across a vial of scopalamine in the medical chest. It may be an anaesthetic but the right dosage provides the truth so Chio spilled it out. It's platinum and germanium, sheets of it, stuffed wherever they could when they came aboard on legitimate errands,' she said, her voice low enough for Benden's ears only, 'and when they drugged whoever was on the dogwatch. That's why we all had headaches.'

'Platinum? Germanium?' Benden was astounded.

'Kimmer was a mining engineer. He found ores and we've all had to work in them,' Shensu said, pushing over to them. 'I wondered why the workroom smelled of hot metal. He must have had the girls melt the ingots down at night, extruding sheets. No wonder they've looked so worn out. I never thought to check on the metals because they'd be too heavy to bring.'

'Where is it?' Benden demanded, looking up and down the aisle, momentarily bewildered when he thought of all the places sheets of thin metal could be unobtrusively attached within the *Erica*. 'We've got to search the ship! Everywhere! Sergeant, take your marines to the stern. Shensu, you and your brothers start on the lockers.'

'He knew one helluva lot about the interior of gigs,' Nev remarked almost admiringly when the marines found that the missile tubes had been stuffed with metal plaques. These were immediately flushed into space.

'And I watched her, Lieutenant,' Vartry said, aggrieved, when they found that the locker where the medicines had been stowed was also lined with thin slabs of silvery metal. 'I stood here and watched her, heard her tell me she wanted to be sure the medicines were safe, as she slapped sheets top, bottom, and side.'

The lockers in which the 23.5-kilo personal allowances had been stowed also proved to be lined with platinum.

'You know,' Ni Morgana said, bending one of the thin sheets which she had found under Benden's bunk, 'individually these don't weigh much but they damned near coated the gig with 'em. Ingenious.'

243

There were sheets everywhere and still more was found, to be piled at the airlock hatch.

Nev, remembering how he'd entertained Hope and Charity by showing them the cabin, found metal glued to the bottom of the blast couches, lining the inside of the control panel, and thin rolls of metal tacked to the baseboards, looking for all the worlds like innocuous decorations. The viewports had platinum decorated seals. That sent Nev and Scag searching all the ports.

When the pile at the inner airlock door reached the window, abruptly Benden realized the airlock was empty.

'Kimmer? Where's Kimmer?' he cried. 'Who let him out? Where is he?'

But Kimmer was nowhere in the ship. A gesture from Benden had the marines on his heels as they propelled themselves to the galley where the brothers were still searching.

'Which of you depressed the evac button?' Benden demanded, seething with impotent anger.

'Depressed . . .' Shensu's look of astonishment was, Benden felt, genuine. There was no regret, however, on his face or his brothers'.

'I'm not sure I blame you, Shensu, but it constitutes murder. You had opportunities enough while we were searching the ship.'

'We were searching the ship, too,' Shensu said with dignity. 'We were as busy as you, trying to save our lives.'

'Perhaps,' Jiro said softly, 'he committed suicide rather than face the failure of that brain-storm of his.'

'That is a possibility,' Ni Morgana said, composedly but Benden knew she believed that no more than he did. But it was true that, although Kimmer could not have activated the inner hatch of the airlock, the evac button on the outer door was clearly marked. And the mechanism cycled itself shut in two minutes after use.

'This will be investigated more fully when we have time,' Ross Benden promised them fervently, pinning each of the three brothers with his angry glare. 'I won't condone murder!' Though at just that moment, Benden had several he would like to commit.

Returning to the airlock, he found that Nev was busy with a chisel, letting out a hoot of triumph as he peeled off a paper-thin sheet of platinum.

'I'm sure Captain Fargoe wouldn't mind having a platinum plated gig—' His voice trailed off when he caught sight of Benden's expression. He gulped. 'There'd be another twenty kilos right in here.' And he applied himself to the task of removing it.

Benden signalled for two of the marines to assist Nev while he and the others piled the accumulated sheets, pipings, strips and lozenges into the lock.

'Amazing!' Ni Morgana said, shaking her head wearily. 'That ought to make up the rest of the four hundred and ninety-five point five kilos.'

She stepped out of the lock and gestured to Benden who was at the controls. With a feeling of intense relief, he pressed the evac button and saw the metal slide slowly out into space, a glittering cascade left behind the *Erica*. It was still visible as the outer door cycled shut.

'I've half a mind to add their personal allowances,' Benden began, feeling more vicious and vengeful than he thought possible, 'which would give us another hundred kilos leeway.'

'More than that,' said the literal-minded Nev and then gawped at the lieutenant. 'Oh, you mean just the women's stuff.'

'No,' Ni Morgana said on a gusty sigh. 'They've suffered enough from Kimmer. I don't see the point in further retribution.'

'If it hadn't been for the extra fuel, we wouldn't have lifted off the planet,' Nev suddenly remarked.

'If it hadn't been for the extra fuel, I don't think we'd've had this trouble with Kimmer,' Ni Morgana said sardonically.

'He'd've tried something else,' Benden said. 'He'd planned the contingency of rescue a long, long time ago. Those vests and pants weren't whipped up overnight. Not with everything else those women were doing.'

'That's possible,' Ni Morgana said thoughtfully. 'He was a crafty old bugger. All along he counted on our rescuing him. And he'd know we'd have to check bodyweight.'

'D'you suppose he also fooled us,' Nev asked anxiously, 'about there being more survivors somewhere?'

That thought had been like a pain in Benden's guts since Kimmer's duplicity had come to light. And yet – there HAD been no sign of other survivors on the southern continent. Nor had their instruments given them any positive readings as they spiralled across the snowy northern landmass. Then there was Shensu's story and that man had no reason to lie. Benden shook his head wearily and once again regarded the ship's digital. The search had taken a lot longer than he'd realized.

'Look alive,' he said, rising to his feet with as good an appearance of energy as he could muster. 'Nev, try to raise the *Amherst* again.' He knew beforehand that the *Amherst* was unlikely to be receiving. He also knew that he had to alter the course NOW, before they went too far along the aborted trajectory. He didn't have any option. He made his calculations for the appropriate roll to get the *Erica* on the new flight path. He'd worry about contacting the *Amherst* later. He couldn't wait on this correction any longer. A three-second burn at one-g would do it. That wouldn't take up much fuel. And he breathed a silent prayer of thanksgiving. 'Nev, Greene, Vartry, check our passengers. We've got to burn to our new heading in two minutes forty-five seconds.'

He felt better after the burn. The gig was handling easily again. Like the thoroughbred she was, she had eased on to her new heading. And he had done something positive about their perilous situation.

'Now, let's be sure we get every last strip Kimmer added to the *Erica*,' he said, unbuckling his seat restraints. He'd also go through the gig with an eye to what else could be jettisoned. But they'd a long trip ahead of them and precious few comforts for those on board.

'I'll check the women first,' Ni Morgana said, pushing herself off deftly from the back of her couch and grabbing the hand hold to propel herself down the companionway. 'And see about some grub. Breakfast was a long time ago.'

Benden realized how right she was but, under stress, he never noticed hunger pangs. He did now.

246

'Chow's the best idea yet,' he said and managed a reasonably cheerful grin for her.

When she checked the women, she found them still shaken by the emotional prelude and, though they helped her in the galley, they were apathetic. Chio wept silently, ignoring the food Faith tried to get her to eat. She seemed wrapped in so deep a depression that Saraidh reported her condition to Benden.

'She won't last the journey in this condition, Ross,' Saraidh said. 'She's deeply disturbed and I don't think it's losing Kimmer.'

'Isn't it just that she was so dependent on him? You heard what Shensu said.'

'Well, if it is, we ought to sort it out. We can't avoid discussing Kimmer's demise.'

'I know and I don't intend to. His demise,' and he drawled out the euphemism, 'was accidental. I would have preferred to have him alive and standing trial for his attempt to disable the *Erica*,' Benden replied grimly. 'What I want to know is how he got those women to sabotage us. They must have known from our conversations that their extra mass would seriously burden the ship.'

Shensu had floated down the corridor during the last sentence and he gave them a terse nod.

'You must explain to my sisters that the gemstones alone will provide suitably for them,' he said, 'that the stones will not be confiscated by the Fleet to pay for this rescue.'

'What?' Ni Morgana exclaimed. 'Where did they get that notion?' She held up her hand. 'Never mind. I know. Kimmer. What maggots had he got in his brain?'

'The maggot of greed,' Shensu said 'Come, reassure my sisters. They are so tearful. They only co-operated with him on the metal because he said that would be the only wealth left to them.'

'And how did Kimmer plan to remove all that platinum from the *Erica*?' Benden demanded, knowing that his voice was rising in frustration but unable to stifle it. 'The man was deranged.'

'Quite likely,' Shensu said with a shrug. 'For decades he has clung to the hope that his message would be answered. Or else all he had accumulated, the gems, the metals, meant nothing.'

They had reached the marines' quarters and heard Chio's soft weeping.

'Get the kids out of here, Nev,' Benden told the ensign in a low voice, 'and amuse them. Shensu, ask your sisters to join us here and, by whatever you hold sacred, tell them we mean them no harm.'

It took hours to reassure the four women. Benden stuck to his matter of fact, common-sense approach.

'Please believe me,' he said with genuine concern at Chio's almost total collapse, 'that the Fleet has special regulations about castaways or stranded persons. Stranded you were. It would be totally different if the Colonial Authority or Federated Headquarters had organized an official search, then there would have been staggering retrieval costs. But the *Amherst* only happened to be in the area and the system was orange-flagged . . .'

'And because,' Ni Morgana took up the explanation, 'I was doing research on the Oort cloud, Captain Fargoe ordered the gig to investigate. As she will tell you herself when you meet her, it saves you, the surviving colonists, any cost.'

Chio mumbled something.

'Say again?' Ni Morgana asked very gently, smiling reassurance.

'Kimmer said we would be paupers.'

'With black diamonds? The rarest kind of all?' Ni Morgana managed to convey a depth of astonishment that surprised Benden. 'And you've kilos of them among you. And those medicines, Faith,' and the science officer turned to the one sister who appeared to be really listening to what was said, 'especially that numbweed salve of yours. Why the patents on that alone will buy you a penthouse in any Federation city. If that's where you want to live.'

'The salve?' Sheer surprise animated Faith. 'But it's common—'

'On Pern, perhaps, but I've a degree in alien pharmaco-poeia and I've never come across anything as mild and effective as that,' Ni Morgana assured her. 'You did bring seed as well as salve because I don't think that's the sort of medication that can be artificially reproduced and provide the same effect.'

'We had to gather the leaves and boil them for hours,' Hope said wonderingly. 'The stink made it a miserable job but he made us do it each year.'

'And numbweed can make us rich?' Charity doubted what she heard.

'I have no reason to lie to you,' Ni Morgana said with such dignity that the girl flushed.

'But Kimmer is dead,' Chio said, a sob catching in her throat and she turned her head away, her shoulders shaking.

'He is dead of greed,' Kimo said in an implacable voice. 'And we are alive, Chio. We can make new lives for ourselves and do what we want to do now.'

'That would be very nice,' Faith said in a low wistful voice.

'We won't be Kimmer's slaves any more,' Kimo added.

'We would all have died without Kimmer after Mother died,' Chio turned back, mastering her tears, unable to stop defending the man who had dominated her for so long.

'Died because she had too many stillborn babies,' Kimo said. 'You forget that, Chio. You forget that you were pregnant two months after you became a woman. You forget how you cried. I do not.'

Chio stared at her brother, her face a mask of sorrow. Then she turned to Benden and Ni Morgana, her eyes narrow. 'And will you tell this captain of yours about Kimmer's death?'

'Yes, we will naturally have to mention that unfortunate incident in our report,' Benden said

'And who killed him?' She shot the question at them both.

'We don't know who killed him, or if he cycled the lock open himself.'

Chio was startled as if that possibility had not occurred to her until then. She pulled at Kimo's sleeve. 'Is that possible?'

Kimo shrugged. 'He believed his own lies, Chio. Once the metal was found, he would consider himself to be poor. He was at least honourable enough to commit suicide.'

'Yes, honourable,' Chio murmured so softly her words were barely audible. 'I am tired. I wish to sleep.' She turned herself towards the wall.

Kimo gave the two officers a nod of triumph. Faith covered her elder sister and gestured for them to leave.

Over the next several days, passengers and crew settled into an easier relationship. The youngsters would sit for hours in front of the tri-d screen, going through the gig's library of tapes. Saraidh cajoled Chio and the girls into watching some of them as well, as a gentle introduction to the marvels of modern high tech civilization.

'I can't tell whether they're reassured or scared witless,' she reported to Benden, standing his watch at the gig's console. They still had not made contact with the *Amherst* though he had no real cause for worry on that score – yet. 'How many times have you worked those equations, Ross?' she asked, noticing what he had on his pad.

'Often enough to know there're no mathematical errors,' he said with a wry grin. 'We'll only have the one chance.'

'I'm not worried,' she said with a shrug and a smile. 'Off you get. It's my watch.' And she shooed him out of the cabin.

'Lieutenant?' Nev's voice reverberated excitedly down the companionway the next afternoon, 'I've raised the *Amherst*!'

There was a cheer as Ross propelled himself to the cabin.

'Neither loud nor clear, sir, but definitely voice contact,' Nev said with a grin as if he himself were responsible for the deed.

Ross grinned back at him in relief and depressed the talk toggle on his seat arm. 'Ross Benden reporting, sir. We need to make a new rendezvous.'

Fargoe's voice acknowledged him and, though her tone broke up in transmission, he really didn't need to hear every syllable to know what she said.

'Ma'am, we've had to abort our original course. We are currently aiming for a slingshot around the first planet.'

'You want a sunburn, Benden?'

'No, ma'am, but we have only two point three kps of Delta V remaining.'

250

'How did you cut it that fine?'

'Humanitarian reasons required us to rescue the ten remaining survivors of the expedition.'

'Ten?' There was a pause that had nothing to do with interference on the line. 'I shall be very interested in your report, Benden. That is, if your humanitarianism allows you to make it. What is the total of the excess weight you're carrying?'

Nev handed over his pad and Benden read off the figures.

'Hmm, Off-hand I don't think we can match orbits. Can you make it five kps?'

'No, ma'am.'

'Roger. Hold on while we refigure your course and rendezvous point.'

Benden tried not to look towards Nev or at Saraidh who had joined them at the command console. He tried not to look nervous but felt various parts of himself twitching, unusual enough in gravity and damned annoying in free-fall. He clutched the edge of the console as unobtrusively and as hard as possible to keep from twitching out of the chair.

'*Erica*? Captain Fargoe here. What can you jettison?'

'How much is required?' Benden thought of the wealth they had just consigned to space.

'You've got to jettison forty-nine point nought five kilos. You will need to make a ten-g burn for one point three seconds around the first planet, commencing at 91 degrees right ascension. That will put you on course, speed and direction and, we devoutly hope, in time to make a new rendezvous. Good luck, Lieutenant.' Her voice indicated that he'd need it.

He didn't like a ten-g burn, even for one point three seconds. They'd all black out. It'd be rough on the kids. But it'd be a lot rougher to turn into cinders.

'You heard the captain,' he said, turning first to Saraidh and then Nev. 'Let's snap to it.'

'What'll we toss, Lieutenant?' Nev asked.

'Just about everything that isn't bolted down,' Saraidh said, 'and probably some of that. I'll start in the galley.'

In the end they made up the required kilos out of material

which Saraidh knew could be most easily replaced by Stores on the *Amherst* – extra power-packs, oxygen tanks which accounted for a good deal of the necessary weight, the mess-room table, and all but one of the beacon missiles which the gig carried.

'If Captain Fargoe decided you weren't negligent,' Saraidh told Ross, her face expressionless, as they both watched the articles sliding out of the airlock into space, 'you won't have to pay for 'em.'

'What?' Then he saw she was teasing and grinned back at her. 'I've enough I've got to account for, thank you muchly, ma'am, on this expedition without paying for it, too.' He kept trying to explain Kimmer's demise to himself and how he could have prevented it, if he could have.

'Now, now, Ross,' and Saraidh waggled a finger at him. They were alone in the corridor. 'Don't hang Kimmer about your neck. I subscribe completely with the suicide theory. Temporarily of unsound mind due to the failure of his plan. He might just have done it to be awkward, too.'

'I'm not sure Captain Fargoe would buy that one.'

'Ah, but she'd never met Kimmer, and I have,' and Saraidh gave him an encouraging thumbs up.

The moment of truth came two long weary weeks later. The temperature inside the *Erica* began to rise with their proximity to Rukbat's sun, reaching an uncomfortable level. Benden was sweating heavily as he watched the ominous approach of the tiny black cinder of the system's first planet. That poor wight hadn't had a chance to survive. He intended to.

'Burn minus sixty seconds,' he announced over the intercom. He hadn't informed his passengers of the rigours of a slingshot manoeuvre. They'd all black out and, if something went wrong, they'd never know it. Meanwhile, he hadn't had to endure Chio's suspicions or the sorrowful reproaches of the other three women. He'd done slingshot passages before, both actual and in simulation. It was more a matter of timing the burn properly just as the 91-degree right ascension came up on the nav screen. He just hated blacking out for any reason, not being in control for those seconds or minutes.

'Nine, eight, seven,' chanted Nev, his eyes glittering with anticipation. This was his first slingshot. 'Five, four, three, two . . . one!'

Benden pressed the burn button, and the *Erica* lunged forward willingly. As he was slammed deep into the pads of the contour seat, he knew the manoeuvre would be successful and surrendered to the mighty g-forces he had just initiated.

Benden returned to consciousness, the blessed silence of space and the relief of weightlessness. His first glance was for the expended fuel. Point ninety-eight kps left. It should be enough. Provided the course corrections were accurate. He had one last burn to make as they bisected the *Amherst*'s wake and then turned back to her at a sharp vector.

'My compliments, Lieutenant,' Ni Morgana said briskly, unsnapping her harness. 'We seem to be well on our way now. I think the cook has something special for lunch today.'

Benden blinked at her.

She grinned. 'The very same thing we had yesterday for lunch.'

Benden wasn't the only one who groaned. They'd added supplies at Honshu but the fresh foods were long gone and they were down to the emergency rations: nourishing but uninspired. And that's all they had for the next two weeks. When he was back on board the *Amherst*, Ross Benden was going to order up the most lavish celebratory meal in the mess's well-stocked larder. 'When,' and he grinned to himself. That's positive thinking.

When the *Erica*'s sensors picked up the cruiser's unmistakable ion radiation trail, Benden was in the command cabin, teaching Alun and Pat the elements of spatial navigation. The boys were bright and so eager to prepare themselves for their new life that they were a pleasure to instruct.

'Back to your pads, boys. We've got another burn.'

'Like the last one?' Alun asked plaintively.

'No, matey. Not like the last one. Just a touch on the button.'

Reassured, they propelled themselves out of the cabin and

down the companionway, dextrously passing Saraidh and Nev at the door.

'A touch being all the fuel we've got left,' Saraidh murmured, taking her seat. She leaned forward, peering out into the blackness of space around them.

'You won't see anything yet,' Nev remarked.

'I know it,' she replied, shrugging. 'Just looking.'

'It's there, though.'

'And not long gone,' Benden added, 'judging by the strength of the ion count.' He toggled on the intercom. 'Now listen up. A short burn, not like the last, just enough to change our course to match up our final approach to the *Amherst.*' In an aside to Saraidh he added, 'I feel like a damned leisure liner captain.'

'You'd make a grand one,' she replied blandly, 'especially if you have to change your branch of service.'

'My what?' Benden never knew when Lieutenant Ni Morgana's wayward humour would erupt.

'Lighten up, Ross. We're nearly home and dry.'

'Fifteen minutes to course correction.' He nodded to Nev to watch the digitial while he contacted the *Amherst.* '*Erica* to *Amherst.* Do you read me?'

'Loud and clear,' came Captain Fargoe's voice. 'About ready to join us, Lieutenant?'

'That's my aim, Captain.'

'We'll trust it's as accurate as ever. Fire when ready, Gridley.'

'Captain?'

'Roger, over and out.'

Beside him, Saraidh was chuckling. 'Where does she get them?'

'Get what?' asked Nev.

'Are you counting down, Ensign?'

'Yes, sir. Coming down to ten minutes forty seconds.'

Why was it time could be so elastic? Benden wondered as the ten minutes seemed to go on for ever, clicking second by second. At the minute, he flexed both hands, shook his shoulders to release the tension in his neck. At zero, he depressed the burn on the last ninety-eight kps in the tank, yawing to starboard. He felt the surge of the good gig *Erica* as she responded. Then all of a sudden the engines cut out with the exhausted whoosh that meant no more fuel in the tank.

Had the *Erica* completed the course correction? Or had the engines stopped untimely? The margin was so damned slight! And the proof would be the appearance of the comforting bulk of the *Amherst* any time now. *If* the manoeuvre had been completed before the fuel was exhausted.

Like the two officers beside him, Benden instinctively leaned forward, peering out into the endless space in front of them.

'I've got a radar reading, Lieutenant,' Nev said and there was no denying the relief in his voice. 'It can't be anything but the *Amherst*. I think we're going to make it.'

'All we need is to get close enough for them to shoot us a magnetic line,' Benden muttered.

Nev uttered a whoop. 'Thar she be!' And he pointed. Benden had to blink to be sure he actually was seeing the running lights of the *Amherst*. He was close to adding his own kiyi of relief and victory.

Just then the comunit opened to a sardonic voice. 'That's cutting it fine indeed, Lieutenant.' The blank screen cleared to a view of the captain, her head cocked and her right eyebrow quizzically aslant. 'Trying to match your uncle's finesse?'

'Not consciously, ma'am, I assure you, but I'd be pleased to hear the confirmation that our present course and speed are A-OK for docking?'

'Not a puff of fuel left, huh?'

'No, ma'am.'

She looked to her left, then faced the screen squarely again, a little smile playing on her lips. 'You'll make it. And I'll expect to have reports from both you and Lieutenant Ni Morgana as soon as you've docked. You've had time enough on the trip in to write a hundred reports.'

'Captain, I've got the passengers to settle.'

'They'll be settled by medics, Ross. You've done your part getting them here. I want to see those reports.'

And the screen darkened.

'Got yours already, Ross?' Ni Morgana asked with a sly grin as she swivelled her chair around.

'And yours?'

'Oh, it's ready, too. I said that I believed Kimmer suicided.'

Benden nodded, glad of her support. 'It would have had to have been self-destruction, Saraidh. He would have been far more familiar with airlock controls than Shensu or his brothers,' Benden said slowly, considering his words. 'It's really far more likely that he did suicide, given the fact that he had failed to bring along all that metal. Damn fool! He must have known that he was dangerously overloading the ship. He could have murdered us.' That angered Benden.

'Yes, and nearly succeeded. I think he was hoping that his death would have brought suspicion on the brothers as the most likely to wish his demise,' Ni Morgana went on. 'He would have liked jeopardizing their futures. And discrediting another Benden if he could.' When she heard Benden's sharp inhalation, she touched his hand, causing him to look at her. 'You can still be proud of your uncle, Ross. You heard what Shensu said, and how proud he was of the way the admiral marshalled all available defences.'

Benden cocked his head, his expression rueful. 'A fighter to the last . . . and it took a wretched planet to defeat him.'

'Poor planet Pern,' Saraidh said sadly. 'Not its fault but I'm recommending that this system be interdicted. I did some calculations – which I'll verify on the *Amherst* computers – and rechecked the original EEC report. That wasn't the first time the Oort organism fell on the planet. Nor will it be the last. It'll happen every two hundred and fifty years, give or take a decade. Furthermore, we don't want any ship blundering into that Oort cloud and transporting that organism to other systems.'

She gave a shudder at the thought.

'There she is,' Benden said with a sense of relief as the viewport filled with the perceptibly nearing haven of the *Amherst*. 'And, all things considered, a successful rescue run.'